M000032394

PRAISE FOR I AM THE STORM

Author Jean Larch (*Dying to be Free*, Hazelden 2006) wrote the following about *I Am the Storm*:

> "We can all use more (good) entertainment and adventure in our lives; similar to *The Hunger Games* and promising of equal success. Halaas's tales of the future are brilliantly engaging and offers a trilogy to look forward to! A real page turner for readers everywhere!"

Megan Bajorek, contributing blogger for *Love What Matters* shared the following about *I Am the Storm*:

> "The writer takes time to sew in tiny intricacies that give her readers a ton of light bulb moments. A metaphysical mystery with biblical references, set in a post-apocalyptic world, this story is *The DaVinci Code* meets *The Hunger Games* meets something all on its fascinating own. Be ready for adventure."

I AM THE STORM

TRISHA LYNN HALAAS

JUNKYARD DOG

I Am the Storm

Copyright © 2020 by Trisha Lynn Halaas

All rights reserved.

Visit my website: www.trishalynnhalaas.com

Published by Junkyard Dog LLC.

No part of this book may be reproduced in any form or by any electronic or mechanical means, including information storage and retrieval systems, without written permission from the author, except for the use of brief quotations in a book review.

This book is a work of fiction. References to brands, establishments, organizations, or locales are intended only to provide a sense of authenticity and are used fictitiously. Any resemblance to actual persons, living or dead, or actual events is purely coincidental. All characters, incidents, and dialogue are drawn from the author's imagination and are not to be construed as real.

ISBN 978-1-7352036-0-7

eBook ISBN 978-1-7352036-1-4

For Shane

THE REALM

HAND DRAWN BY THE AUTHOR

1

_____

I sprint all the way to the edge of the cliff, one breath from air born, and scream, "Is this real?!" until no words can form and only a garbled growl remains. I stand there in silence. Everything is frozen. The air stands still. I listen. Nothing.

I turn. Defeated. Falling to my knees, sobbing, I don't see or hear the small, white swallow flutter overhead.

Hours later, I lift my eyelids and survey the scene in front of me. It hasn't changed. The blood remains. He's still dead. I'm still alone.

Picking myself up, I amble drunkenly to his body. I kneel down and close his beautiful, once vibrant, honey-green eyes. Eyes that reflected a hidden pond speckled with the golden remnants of a fading sunset. Falling over him, crying, I weep and weep, sobbing for hours more. I can't accept this. It isn't real.

Night creeps on in its obstinate nature. I fall into a deep sleep next to him in the cold alcove. The water smashes onto the rocks below. During my dreamless sleep, that same swallow lands gently on the rock near my head, emanating a nearly imperceptible coo before fluttering away.

_____

AT SUNLIGHT, I wake bearing grave acceptance that he's gone. A black veil cloaks me in darkness yet makes everything clear. The picture has gone black and white. The brilliant and vibrant Technicolor of Oz fades to dull, lifeless slates of grey. Everything is flat. Everything is silent.

I hate silence. I detest it. Yet now, it's more than fitting. It's punishment. Silence has always been louder to me than noise. It makes it impossible to hear them. There aren't even the sounds of nature. It's as if God hit mute. I can't hear anyone inside my mind. The barrier is impenetrable. I've been deserted. I attempt to lift my head from his chest, but I'm completely depleted. Nothing left. Flat-lined. A deep black puddle of despair.

Cerebral movement. Someone new. Someone with strength. I foolishly expect it to be my brother, but I don't recognize this one. I would know my brother. I'm fearful because my connection to him has been physically severed. I can feel it. The light cut out. The line went dead, just like him. This presence doesn't feel deceased.

My unknown company takes over. Picking myself up with steely grace, I move over my brother. I clinically wrap him in the linen sheet I have with me. It's the only thing big enough. I remember the tomb. I realize that's where he should rest; that's the place. I can visit whenever I want. It's meant to be, and I know it.

I hike down to the water through the steep rocks that descend to the beach. It's quite a trek, but I don't notice. Finally stepping on the pink sand, I spot a large piece of driftwood near the shore—just large enough.

Balancing the wood on my back, I climb the way back up. Struggling and slipping on several rocks, I make it back in a trancelike state. I tie him down, securing him so many times he's tethered head to foot. I then attach my weighty sling-back bag with him. Again, I balance the board on my back, this time with an insurmountable weight.

He's a big guy—a really big guy—6'3" and all muscle. I take many tries to stand up. Dangerously teetering for quite a few feet, I fall to my knees, yet again. No matter how hard I try, it's hopeless for me to carry him as far as I need to carry him.

I lay him back down on the ground in silent resolution. *I'm going to do this.* I get up with renewed strength and balance him on my shoulders. Still unsteady, I sigh deeply. One last pull and my mysterious guest returns. Growing more familiar, I begin to trust. I still hear no voices, but the presence is calm and controlled. I let go and sit in the corner of my mind's bleak and cold darkness, letting my visitor carry us along.

SOMEHOW, I make it to the tomb. It appears as I left it.

I set Shane down, plopping next to him in the dirt. My Greek warrior tie-up sandals have worn to nothing during the journey. My feet are ripped and bleeding. I don't even feel it.

I need to open the tomb. A boulder seals the entrance. I have nothing.

I untie my bag from the wood, unzip it, and look inside. Nothing doing, only my silly belongings. Some clothing, *okay—a lot of clothing*, sunglasses, wallet, cigarettes, a kist key, makeup, a barrette, my Slab, shoes, some high heels—all of it useless. With a deep sigh, I sit on the ground. I'm so desperate to get my brother to his final resting place.

I grab one of my silly shoes. The shoes I just 'love' so much. I look at the impractical heel with its 'cool' snake wrapped around it. Its eyes—hammered metal slits—gleam in the sunlight. *Great. I've got a pair of ridiculous stilettos. What am I gonna do? Put on a fashion show? Balance on a runway made of rock. Why did I even pack these?*

Closing my eyes, I cry and shriek holding the shoe. My screams bounce off the rock, desperate and palpable in my ears.

Suddenly, the shoe feels different. I open my eyes suspiciously. The snake has slithered. I look down horrified. I'm actually deathly afraid of them. The snake wraps itself tighter around the heel. The shoe spins, faster and faster, a blur of merging materials. It halts— leaving only a giant hammered nail where was once the heel. I pick up the other shoe.

The same thing happens.

I stand there holding two metal nails. They have grown in size. From the tips of my fingers nearly to my elbow. They are ancient and rusted. Heavy. Dried blood appears in the trail of the snake.

Shaking, I turn toward the entrance, spotting a crude indentation near the top and another near the bottom. The nails pull to the indentations as if by magnet force. I shove them in, first the top and then the bottom.

Nothing happens.

Tired, abandoned, and empty of any presence, I slide to the ground, my back on the rock. I have no tears to give. I look at my brother—my baby brother. I remember tiny glimpses, precious moments from here and there. A collage of images, sounds, and scents.

The baby blanket you came home in, thin and speckled with tiny baby blue footprints, you practicing your antique guitar, opening chords of "Smoke on the Water" on repeat. A whiff of wintergreen Copenhagen long-cut tobacco. Your fishing pole. Your sweaty hockey equipment with remnants of humid locker room. The scent of Ralph Lauren Polo Blue cologne. The safe warmth of your solid chest against my cheek when you had to give me bad news. Your unwelcome laugh after purposely scaring the bejeezus out of me, until I would join in savoring the sound of our giggles. A taste of old-world movie theater popcorn with butter and white cheddar powder. A flash of you falling asleep in that same theater, me following suit to the lull of your deep breathing in leather recliners a bit too comfortable. Your voice singing "Slide" along with the Red Hot Chili Peppers in your red ancient Ford Mustang. Our favorite movie quotes. Our laughs. Your laugh.

I turn my face to Heaven and shout, "I miss you. I miss you so much, Shane. I'm sorry. I'm so sorry. I love you."

I feel the earth quiver, then shake forcefully. The stone begins to recede from my back. The nails begin to thrust into the solid crevices as if driven by a massive invisible power drill. Slowly it creeps, widening its slice of blackness.

I let out a shaky breath and peer inside. It's just as I left it. Empty and cold but the sense of peace lingers. It's welcoming after the harrowing journey.

I go into the cave alone. The chill remains. I sink to the ground to rest for a minute against the cold rock facing the opening. I can see his silhouette from where I sit. I want to cry. I feel the dawn of realization try to break through the resolute black veil that has descended. It's pointless. The veil is sealed. The cold resolve stays. I stand up and go to him. Pulling him inside the tomb, I rest him squarely in the middle.

I walk outside the tomb and stand near the cliff's edge. On the side of the ledge, I see wildflowers growing. Among them, there is a lone tiger lily. I pluck it and bring it back to the cave.

I pull down the fabric that covers him and lay the flower on his chest. I say a prayer to Heaven.

Please hold him and keep him safe for me.

"I didn't try hard enough, God. I'm sorry."

One final tear drips from my eye onto the speckled orange petal gently trailing through the flower and landing on his chest. I kiss his cheek and replace the cloth. Saying one final prayer and apology, I turn to leave.

One last look at my beautiful baby brother, I step out into the sunlight. The nails lie indifferently on the ground near the opening.

During my previous visit to this place the door opened and closed on its own. I'm not sure how to use the nails to do it. I pick one off the ground and then the other. The second my hands clutch both, the gigantic stone rumbles steadily closed. A slow crawl closes the gap.

The nails begin to spin in my fingers but don't take on their previous form. The snakes slither into flexible hammered, metal-like snake straps. They do not look unlike my weathered sandals, much sturdier though. I put them on and begin the long journey 'home'— wherever that is.

What I couldn't see was the rock glowing briefly in its final shove.

2

On my own again, I trudge downhill. Silence remains. My new company—long gone. My line to my brother—still severed. I fear it may be permanent. This must be my punishment. I tried. And failed. I worked so hard to get there in time. I just didn't make it. I should have tried harder. It was out of my control. Yet, the entire situation was my fault.

The silence continues incessantly; I worry it'll be eternal. I've become used to the voices in my head. Jarring at first, they bring me great comfort and strength now. I don't understand it. I have no idea how it works, but suddenly I don't mind arguing with them so much.

Now, this muteness is unsettling. Especially since there is no word from Shane.

I felt it the instant he died. The line had been cut. It had been a line of light and strength. A strong invisible light stretching between us since before birth. If he got hurt, I felt it in my own body, and vice versa. It didn't matter how much distance stretched between us. Now it's gone, and I remain a floating, empty vessel.

AT SOME POINT, I begin to see the start of a small town. It doesn't seem fitted with Artificial Intelligence. I assume it's the Unconnected Shire.

Thank God. Anything to make it harder for *him* to find me. He took my brother away from me; you'd think his job would be done, but I know better. Plus, he and I have unfinished business. For now, it seems the black veil protects me from his radar. That's a blessing; I need to grieve and strategize.

On the left, I spot a tall steeple-shaped bed and breakfast, a perfect place to hole up for a couple days. I need a shower desperately and some food; although, I have absolutely no appetite. Carrying only my bag, I step into the air-conditioned room. A strong scent of fresh lilacs fills my nose, although none are physically present. *A flash of bright green akin to a lush grassy field.*

An older woman, about seventy-five, looks up at me behind wire-rimmed glasses. This confirms Crystal Shire inhabitants dwell in this town, no eye-enhancements. Her thick, most likely once blonde, now white hair topples from the crown of her head in a messy waterfall of curls. She's reading a paper book; I sigh a breath of relief, unquestionably Crystal.

"Hey honey," she says with a tone of concern, setting down her book.

I realize at this point how I must look. Glancing down, I see the remnants of my clothing splattered in blood. My long blonde hair is snarled and tangled around my head resembling a platinum lion's mane, only more unruly. I'm dirty. My skirt and top are ripped in many places. I can feel the layer of dirt and grime smeared on my face. Only my shoes appear untouched. *Whatever that means.*

Crossing my arms over my chest, with my weighty bag slung over my shoulder, I manage, "Hi, yes. I'm wondering if you have any vacancy."

She's already across the room before I finish my sentence.

"Of course, I do, sweetie. Let's get you settled in. Actually, you'll be my first and only guest in some time. I'm Regina. It's nice to meet you…"

"Lyvia," I supply.

She pulls an eggplant purple afghan out of nowhere and slings it around my shoulders. She walks me up the cramped, spiraling staircase.

"I'm putting you in our penthouse suite," she says with a wink. "That's what my husband always called it. It's our biggest room and on the top floor technically, so you know. It has a separate living area and a giant bathtub. I'm sure you'll be comfortable."

7

"Oh, you don't have to do all that. I don't need much..."

"Oh nonsense, it's just me and you here; we should make use of the amenities," she says with a conspiratorial giggle.

With that, she opens the door to an impossibly large lavish, yet cozy, living area. A giant white couch resembling a cloud swells in front of me. Other white pieces scatter around the room. The walls reach so very high, stretching to a cathedral ceiling yielding its original wood. Steeple windows display a sky decorated with bloated white puffs, not unlike the couch.

The walls are fitted to the ceiling with bookshelves. Thousands of ancient paper books balance precariously on aged stubborn shelves. Each is crammed with covers well-worn, yet in great shape. I'm instantly curious about those books. A large mahogany desk takes refuge facing the sole floor-to-ceiling window. One lone book waits patiently on its surface. A door to the right of the desk opens to a large balcony.

An old flat screen TV is fastened to the wall. I even spot a remote control. Welcome to Crystal Shire. To the right, there's a bedroom fitted with a giant bed. Resting on top of it, a down-filled comforter, also a billow of fluff. Two nightstands frame the bed; one holding a rotary dial telephone, the other a brand-new spiral notebook and pen. These items are unfeasibly old and impossible to find. I should know, as a collector of such things. *Seriously, where am I?*

Paintings hang all around the room. Not in any systematic way, more as a patchwork quilt with each frame a different size; some big, most a bit smaller, still many very tiny. They stretch up the massive walls to the ceiling.

There is no theme; some pictures are dark and gory, others whimsical and harmonious. Some beautiful landscapes, others gloomy and sinister forests. There are many portraits. Faces, none of which I recognize, though, a few stares look eerily familiar.

She leads me to the bathroom. A massive claw-foot tub takes center stage. It's updated with a shower head and equipped with a cotton candy pink curtain attached to a track on the sloped ceiling. The silky baby pink material makes me smell baby powder and envision a tiny elephant trinket on a windowsill somewhere.

I shake myself out of it and take a closer examination of the washroom. There are mirrors everywhere. In fact, every wall is a mirror.

There's a built-in vanity area with a small crushed-velvet chair, the color of peonies. Its mirror is fashioned with round bulbous light bulbs. The kind I've only seen in ancient books, pictures of the historical Marilyn Monroe applying makeup in the warm glow. Resting atop the surface I spot a vintage hairbrush with matching hand mirror.

Amenities everywhere—lotions, bubble bath, shampoos, conditioners, concoctions—each fitted with homemade labels in glass bottles that appear to be magical potions. Big fluffy pink towels rolled with great care have been placed in a gorgeous wicker basket. I start to see a trend here. A lush pink bathrobe hangs above the basket pleading for me to don.

I glimpse myself in the multitude of mirrors. Horrifying. I'm not just saying that. I actually startle myself. I look worse than I originally thought. Brown-crusted clay is caked through my rat's nest of hair. Blood splatters my torn clothing, very little of it mine. My face is streaked with ash, yet bearing clean trails where tears have long since dried. I look worse than the day Shane and I took his antique Ford Mustang to the beach, windows and sunroof down. He tackled me out of nowhere. Then we proceeded to have a sand fight. When we got home, we looked as if we had been fighting for our lives in a mud pit. I was combing sand out of my hair for two weeks.

"I'll let you get settled in and cleaned up while I go prepare dinner for us."

"Oh, I couldn't possibly stay in this penthouse, Miss Regina. It's too much for just me. Maybe you have something smaller?" I ask sincerely.

"Call me Regina. Honey, it's not like there is a line out there. This room is yours for as long as you'll have it. You're staying here, and that's the last I'll hear of it," she says sternly, briskly turning away.

"Okay, well, thank you so much. You really don't need to bother yourself with cooking for me. I'm not very hungry, and I don't want to be a burden," I say, still not recovering an appetite.

She's already started down the stairs, calling back, "We've both got to eat, honey, and I know you're famished, even if you don't..." The last four words are barely discernible. I turn back toward the room and step into the living area, closing the door behind me. I'm overwhelmed immediately by number of books; I'll have to ask Regina about those.

I go into the bedroom and set my bag on top of the long dresser. Looking around the room, I notice there's another archaic TV sporting the wall. I spot the remote control. I'm just so curious. I put it on and see a list of television shows, all ancient. I used to watch these shows in my studies. I had them on relentlessly. I loved seeing how culture was once upon a time. Not to mention, I always have a TV or HoloScreen playing in the background. HoloScreens are the modernized version of television you can watch anywhere. Re-watching TV shows and movies is my electronic Xanax. Sure enough, I spot one of my favorites. The same favorite my brother and I shared together. Randomly selecting an episode of *The Office*, I step into the bathroom.

My reflection startles me again. I hear the television show's theme song play from the room. The musical chords fill me with nostalgia as I turn on the water. When the show begins, reminiscence is replaced with harsh reality and cold numbness. I take off my clothes and shoes, zombie-like. While the gigantic tub fills, I examine the potion bottles. Each concoction adorned with a carefully created label. All are identified with one word: 'Conditioner,' 'Soap,' 'Bubbles,' 'Shampoo.' I pour some 'Bubbles' into the rushing water. On the vanity sits a vintage powder puff, the same pink accented throughout the washroom. It looks brand new, though. *Another paradox.*

Finally, the water nears the top and I shut it off. I sink into the scalding bath slowly. It goes right up to my chin. I close my eyes, hold my breath and dip below the surface. I scream and scream then scream some more. The shrieks are muffled through water and bubbles. I come up for air and do it again. And again.

Eventually, I snap out of it. Sitting up, the water rushes down my back. I smooth my hair and wipe my eyes. Detached darkness returns and I sit numb. Finding the shampoo and conditioner, I scrub my hair and detangle it back to its smooth, yet wavy state. I use the bottle labeled 'Soap' and scour away the dried blood and caked dirt.

Her potions smell so good, impossibly good. The soap smells of cinnamon buns accompanied by the scent of a heated cedar sauna. The shampoo smells as gumdrops, yet when they're still in their liquid state before being molded, I imagine. I don't think I've ever smelled that. It isn't a symptom of my Synesthesia, though. This is different. These smells are physically breathable.

Synesthesia is a neurological phenomenon in which stimulation of one sensory or cognitive pathway leads to automatic, involuntary experiences in a second sensory or cognitive pathway. The most basic example of how my brain operates is that I perceive letters and numbers innately with contrasting colors, each different with its own linked color, smell, memory, or other sensory stimuli. I do *actually* see and recognize letters and numbers the same way as everyone else; however, I have an additional perception sense. These conflicting aromas are definitely physically present.

I get out of the tub and dry off in the softest towel I've ever used. I hear the television. It's the episode of *The Office* where Dwight, the "Assistant to the Regional Manager," starts a fire to test the employees' preparedness. He takes a few puffs of a cigarette, tosses it into a small trashcan, and says in earnest: "Today, smoking's gonna save lives."

Michael, the Regional Manager, yells, "We're trapped! Everyone for himself!" The office erupts in panic. Two employees ram the door with a copy machine. Michael throws a projector out the window. By the time Dwight reassures everyone it was a drill, one of the employees has a heart attack.

I laugh thinking of my brother's laugh but can't hear it. When he was here, I could sense him and hear his voice and laugh even when we were apart. Not anymore, now it's just quiet. However, I can't get into the enormity of those implications right now. The grief makes it impossible to accept that I may never hear him again. *All because of my own actions.*

I settle into the plush robe and sit at the vanity. I brush my hair out, shocked at how easily it combs through. There is something to those potions. I brush my teeth with the unwrapped pink toothbrush and labeled bottle of 'Toothpaste,' which tastes exactly of chocolate Andes mints, a long gone treat. Very hard to find.

I take one last glimpse in the mirror. My murky, honey-green eyes are rimmed with black circles and swollen to capacity, yet I still see the eyes of my brother looking back at me. His more green, mine more honey, their shape the same. The sadness and desolation are evident. I shrug off the robe. I see bruises sporadically spackling my body. I look skinny. I know I have to eat, although the thought alone makes me want to purge.

Taking my things, I walk over to my bag and unpack. I figure I'll stay here as long as Regina will allow. I need to regroup and check out those books. Inside the worn sling-back, I pull out my stuff. Surveying the items, I take a quick inventory. Everything's accounted for.

I hold the sandals in my hands vividly recalling their transformation. *What the hell was that? I can't even. Not right now*, I think, shaking my head. *Don't have room to analyze that particular phenomenon.*

I put my hair up in the barrette, one I've had since I was a little girl. It's made of metal, although, somehow, it never damages my hair. It resembles a spiky vine. It can also stretch and shrink to wear as a ring. I always loved it because it could hold the entire thick mane without ever slipping. *Ha. The little things in life*, I think, rolling my eyes.

Dressing in a pair of skinny jeans and a vintage Coca-Cola t-shirt, I'm not overtly concerned. Luckily, I packed clothes fitting for any shire, unsure where I might end up. Eyeing the other clothing, I have no desire to wear any of those uncomfortable ensembles. Gratefully, no one cares what you wear in Crystal.

I step out onto the balcony and light a cigarette. The smoke drifts lazily from its lit tip. I stare aimlessly at the landscape in front of me. This side of the house faces a field edged with woods. Her yard is a giant garden with violets, peonies, chrysanthemums, vines, and lush black roses, tipped with deep maroon—a floral jungle. Statues are hidden strategically around foliage. Trees dot the landscape, growing past the roof.

I take a drag on the cigarette and sigh. *What the hell just happened?* I wonder. I have so many questions; nothing makes sense.

I reenter the living room area, noticing *The Office* wrapping up in the bedroom. The books continue to astonish me. I look at the rows and rows of spines. I have read many of the books in other formats but most I've never heard of, even in my relentless research. Needless to say, my curiosity is skyrocketing.

A soft knock on the door takes me out of me reverie. I quickly turn the TV off and slip on my flip-flops. Like I said, I keep my own trends. I open the door to find a flushed Regina standing there, holding a dishtowel.

"Sweetie, that old oven, how it heats up the whole house. I hope you're not uncomfortable." She wipes a few beads of sweat from her brow, exhaling.

"Oh, not at all," I say. "In fact, I don't know if I have ever been more comfortable in my life."

She gives a sweet satisfied smile and throws the towel over her shoulder. Grabbing my arm, she leads me down the stairs, exclaiming, "All right then, supper's waiting!"

Following her into an ornate dining room, I take in the surroundings. It's gorgeous, very old-world. She has set two places for us with dishes of food intricately placed between. The smell awakens my appetite. I begin to realize I haven't eaten in days.

There's a floral arrangement placed on the table. It's both lavish and delicate. I spot at its center one tiger lily. An invisible stab of pain sears my heart. I recover quickly and take the seat Regina pulls out for me.

"Regina, thank you so much for all of this; you really shouldn't have. I have virtues to pay you," I say graciously.

"Never mind you, buttercup. This is my pleasure. I won't take any payment from you, 'virtues' or otherwise," she spits out the word virtues out as if it were a snake.

Ah, the outlook of Crystal Shire. It's a shire that likes to work-in-kind. Business is not handled monetarily. Services are traded. It really is my favorite shire.

"Okay. Well, if there's anything at all I can do in exchange, please let me know. You really have no idea how grateful I am," I say.

"I think I may have an idea, honey, and I'm more than pleased to have some company," she replies with a knowing look.

My appearance must've said more than words. She begins to spoon heaping helpings onto our plates. Tender beef roast, mashed sweet potatoes, rolls, and crisp green beans. I think I smell something baking, as well. My appetite returns and I devour each bite, slowly, enjoying the decadence.

"Tell me, Lyvia, where've you traveled all the way from?"

Taste of metal, loud rushing sound, flash of red. "Very far away," I reply.

"Hmm. Yes, I would imagine. Don't see many Dark Shire residents walking around these parts."

I freeze fork-to-mouth. How can she possibly know?

"Honey, I've been around these parts for a lot of years. I can spot a Darken miles away."

I technically don't belong to a shire; I wander. However, I grew up in Onyx Shire, the Dark Shire, where my ancestors descend from. We're not very well received in other shires of the Realm.

I can't think of one thing that could've given me away. I wasn't wearing Darken clothing when I came in. In fact, I was dressed in garb more fitting for Turquoise Shire—lightweight and aquamarine. If anything, she should've guessed the water-yielding district. Even though undetectable without enhancements, I refused the color signal when I was eighteen, which would also suggest Crystal.

"I can see it in your eyes, honey. You can never really escape the dark," she says matter-of-factly, rising and walking toward the kitchen. The dishtowel appears back in her hand.

I sit at the table wondering what's in my eyes that could possibly be a tell that my personal energy field is black. That's invisible to the human eye even with enhancements.

She returns carrying the most beautiful overflowing peach pie I've ever seen. The crust rises five inches from the pan. Peach is my favorite; I can't resist it. Her other arm cradles a metal mixing bowl full of sweet vanilla bean ice cream. The delectable aroma takes me to a flash of colors. *So many colors. I taste black pepper. Pepper and pie?* Synesthesia has a mind of its own. My sensory correlations rarely make sense.

"Here, honey, a piece of pie will make everything better. It always does," she says, handing me a bowl of sugary sweetness.

Taking a bite, my curiosity gets the better part of me. "How did you know?" I ask.

"Sugar, I've been around the block more times than I can count. I come from a long line of Darken. In fact, I was myself for many, many years. That was until I came to my senses and realized Crystal was the way to go. It just makes sense here."

I can't argue with that. Crystal Shire does make the most sense. I think people forget that. She gets up and starts clearing the table. I follow suit.

"Oh no, honey, I've got this. You go on up and get some rest. I know you need it," she says with a concerned smile.

"I need to earn my keep…" I say, plates in hand.

With her free hand, she takes the plates I'm holding and balances them the way a career-long waitress would. I can almost see a name tag entitled "Flo" pinned to her shirt.

"Won't have it, Lyvia. You're my guest, and you better get used to it," she replies with a hearty laugh.

As she turns toward the kitchen, I stack the rest of the dinnerware. I can't help myself. I don't like not earning what's given to me. Plus, I have a nagging preponderance I can't ignore.

"Regina," I call toward the kitchen.

"What's up, buttercup?" she calls back sweetly.

"How did you acquire all those paper books in the study upstairs?"

"Oh those," she says, wiping her hands on her apron, the dish-towel now hangs from the strap. "Those were my husband's. He was convinced they were worth more than any artificial intelligence system ever created. He said the words needed to be preserved in their original format. The way they were intended. So I said, as long as you've got a place for them, I'm okay with it. He installed those shelves himself. In fact, he built this entire house." Her last words break a touch. "He passed over five years ago. Not a day goes by I don't miss him."

Understanding more than she could know, I nod solemnly, noting her use of "passed over" as opposed to "passed away."

"I'm sorry."

"I know you are, honey. Thank you. He was a good man, a very good man. Feel free to take a look at any of those old spines, and as I said, you are to stay as long as you'll have me," she replies with deep sincerity.

I stifle a yawn, managing, "In that case, I think I'll follow your advice and head up. Thank you again so very much."

"Nonsense, get up to bed and get comfy cozy. I'll see you for coffee and breakfast in the morning. Night-night, sweetie…"

"Night," I respond, starting up the twisty spiral staircase. I pause, backing down the stairs. Another nagging thought brings me back down.

"Regina, what brought you to Crystal Shire?" I ask.

She turns to face me holding the last of our dirty dishes. "Sweetie, that's a long story. Let's save it for later and get you some sleep," and with that she vanishes into the kitchen.

I shrug, turning toward the mountain of stairs and trudge up. I'm exhausted. Spent. Although, I fear the first night I'm truly alone on this earth will not be one filled with sleep.

3

tepping into the room, I survey the scene. *Those books*. I know I'm not going to reach anything resembling sleep. Scanning the titles, I'm overwhelmed by how many I haven't read in any known format. I've been reading since I was two. I can also recall every memory I've ever had. I've read every book I've laid hands or eyes on, yet so many titles stretch in front of me I've never seen.

There's a novel, *The Witching Hour*. Something about it rings a bell. *Aroma of popcorn. Flash of charcoal grey*. Then I spot a golden cover among the muted spines, titled *Apostles*. I bring it over to the couch and sink into its billowy fluff. I turn the TV on and spot another favorite TV show, *New Girl*. Randomly choosing an episode, I settle in with the book. I recognize the word from the Bible. I haven't seen any Bibles in a very long time. Even then, they're recent translations and paraphrasing. I don't remember a book *Apostles*, only the word. Then again, what was left of the Bible has been long since slimmed.

Opening the cover, I see it has been inscribed. A short word from the author: *Find him*. It's in Latin. First, I skim the pages and realize they're much older than I originally thought. It seems to have been preserved with great care; the pages are beyond ancient. The language is unrecognizable, close to Latin but indecipherable. On the interior back cover, I find another message beneath the cover jacket, which has also been preserved.

"If you go to him," is all I can make out. The writing beneath is smeared and unreadable. *Well, that's cryptic*. I flip through pages.

Nothing seems to relate to finding anybody. Then again, it's a language I can't translate but for a few words. *Ha.*

I close the book and survey the shelves once more. I find a very large book with ornate designs on it. This one I recognize. It's so heavy, I can barely manage to get it off the shelf. In fact, the books on either side begin to fall down as I stretch reaching. Still, I'm able to wiggle out the massive book and shove the others back in their place.

The Complete History of Technology, a book I'm well-versed in. I've researched it for years, especially the last two. I fall into a dreamless sleep with the book straddled in my lap. I wake up some time later, stiff and sore all over. I manage to put the book on the mahogany desk and barely make it to the bed.

I SPEND the next two days at the mercy of Regina. Intermittent between fitful dreamless sleep, I listen to old television shows and skim book-after-book.

On day three, I wake with systematic determination. Time to strategize and regroup. I need to locate a station and fuse in. I doubt I'll see where he is, but I need to check. I need a game plan. According to Regina, the only station close by is near the library, a place you won't find in any other shires. *Sounds good to me, maybe I'll check that out while I'm out there.*

"You go through town. You'll see a small road, looks more like a path, dear, on the right. It's unmarked. Turn down there and follow the windy road. You'll end up at the library. The station is located directly behind it. Here's some cucumber water and snacks for the trip," she says, handing me a small paisley bag. I hoist it over my shoulder along with my sling-back satchel and head out.

"Thank you so much, Regina. I'll see you tonight," I say over my shoulder.

"Sure thing, hon. I'm making lasagna and homemade garlic bread for dinner; dessert's a surprise. Bring your appetite, I've made too much," she laughs heartily, waving me away.

Turning down the road, I start into town. Not many people are around, which is not surprising, given it is the most rural shire. I fit in fairly well. Another pair of jeans, this time donned with a Led

Zeppelin t-shirt. I've pulled my hair to the side with my favorite hair clip. I love being in Crystal. I can wear all my vintage, historic clothing and nobody pays attention. There aren't any rules for these residents.

I spot a woman about fifty, wearing a housedress straight out of the 1960s. A man is walking around dressed in denim jean overalls. I also spot a teenage girl sporting bellbottom jeans and a top straight from the 1970s, complete with fringe. It's a stroll through ancient decades of fashion.

I see another woman, probably twenty-five or so, definitely around Shane's age. Her straight sandy hair is painted generously with highlights from the sun. It's long, well past her shoulders to the middle of her back. She's wearing a short blue lace Bohemian jumper over her thin figure. Worn slouched ankle boots complete the outfit. She has three dogs on leashes. She walks up the path to what I assume is her house, a small cottage hidden in foliage away from the main road.

There are two little boys circling their momma like sharks, while she organizes her belongings. I spot suckers in her right hand. *Blood in the water.* I see two guys walk out of a restaurant on the right. They're boisterous and laughing. One of them is doing an impression I don't recognize. The other is laughing so hard he can barely catch his breath. It makes me miss my brother deeply.

I continue through the hilly town. I spot an apothecary on the left. There's a woman my age outside sweeping the porch. Her long, thick blonde hair curls around her face, resembling a golden Clydesdale's mane. She looks up at me and waves. At first, I stand frozen but then remember where I am. I give a little half-wave and smile, continuing on my journey. She goes back to sweeping.

The people become more scarce and the buildings sparser. The road fades from pavement to dirt. The trees thicken. Lush greenery surrounds me. The trees meet above my head creating a tunnel built from nature. The sounds of wildlife encompass me. It's welcoming given the eerie silence I experienced when on 'mute.' I hear water bubbling somewhere, a babbling brook. The air chills under the canopy's shadow. I can smell dewy grass, but then I taste hot sauce, not sure what that's about.

I follow the hilly dirt road for what seems a very long time. I don't know for sure though, I haven't turned on my Slab. I'm waiting to do it when I'm not at Regina's house, just in case. Thinking I may have passed the street, I start to turn around. There's no way. I've been watching carefully.

I hear a voice. I stop and listen. Nothing, still radio silence. I decide to continue up the path awhile. Over the hill, I spot it. A very small clearing on the right side of the woods. If you weren't looking for it, you'd never see it.

I start down the narrow pathway. It's not an easy trek. It's bumpy and rocky with twists and turns. There's even the tiniest, most rickety 'bridge'—I use that term loosely—I've ever seen. That's Crystal Shire for you, not always up to date with modernization and safety protocols, evidently. The bridge hangs from ropes so frayed I can't believe it's still suspended. I look for any other way to cross. Nope.

"Okay. I could maybe use some help here…" I plead to the voices. "Come back, guys. How about the new one that helped me carry Shane? Anyone?" Nada.

Why. Why am I about to cross a bridge hung by dental floss? Looks as though someone put it together in the 1500s. It might as well be string-roped soup cans.

Well, okay. It's not as if I haven't been through worse. Let's do this. I rub my hands together as if the gesture will somehow magically transport me to the other side.

It doesn't.

Okay. I step onto the first board. The bridge swings dramatically.

"Wow. I'm not that heavy, asshole," I tell the bridge. I realize I'm talking to a bridge.

With each careful step the bridge swings dauntingly. I have to step and cling. Wait for the swinging to stop. Step and cling. I get a good momentum going and think I'm going to make it.

Suddenly, the bridge dips and I hear a snap. I start shaking and attempt to steady myself. Below I see the babbling brook I heard. It's wide and appears deep. I don't know what to do. I figure if I lie down, my body weight will balance better. Then I can scoot the rest of the way, which is not close.

I start to scoot, my bags snug under my arm. I only have about fifteen feet to go. Inch-by-inch, I crawl. Nearing the end, I hear another snap. The left side has come undone. I'm now dangling from a floss bridge. I slip off the bridge holding on by my fingers. I wobble back and forth. Dangling from one thin frayed rope, I briefly glimpse a whir of memories. Accompanying smells of powdered donuts and a sharp twinge of burning rubber on hot concrete, then hot sauce again. *I have a mission. I can't die yet. He has to pay.*

I inch closer and closer to gaining purchase when the rope frays even more, and I jerk toward the water. I'm just inches from the edge of land.

I decide I'm close enough to swing and grab the ledge. Getting a momentum going I sway upwards. One hand grabs the slat of wood that appears firmly attached to the ground, then the other. Believing I'm out of danger, I begin to pull up. The nails holding the wooden slat pull with it. *Who designed this thing?*

The water continues churning below, beckoning me into its dark mystery. I become mesmerized by its deep blue intensity. I'm tired. I want to be done. I just want to see my brother again.

Fine. You want me? Take me.

I let one hand go. The wood slips sharply. I hang from the edge of this tiny plank. I imagine a small ship in a bottle akin to the ones they used to construct. The plank, a minuscule board off the side of the miniature vessel. A tiny platinum haired doll dangles precariously over frozen polymer waves.

I sway one-handed, my bags stretching my shoulder from its socket. My fingers continue to slip. I'm fine with this. I can see Shane. But the mission…

Well, God decides all that.

One-by-one my fingers release. I let go. I start to free-fall, closing my eyes.

4

I jerk. Hard. I look up.

A giant hand has grabbed ahold of my arm. He pulls me up as if I'm that miniature doll and tosses me to his side. He hasn't broken a sweat, nor is he out of breath. He's the size of Captain America, maybe a little bit broader. Not as big as Shane, who was larger, the size of Thor. Darker complexion too, olive-skinned, with deep brown eyes resembling fountain Coca-Cola. Light caramel foam lines the inner irises, melting into outer rims of the cola's dark syrup.

He's wearing jeans, sporadically ripped and torn from use, held up by a thick, worn leather belt. The buckle is large but simple; one silver and gold wrapped prong fits through thick, tan aged leather. His t-shirt is well worn and vintage. It's green, most likely once clover now faded to mint. He has work boots on. They're scuffed, slouchy, and loosely tied.

My shirt is disheveled, and my hair has blown into a nice swirl on top of my head, not unlike a soft serve vanilla ice cream cone. I adjust my top and smooth my hair back into the barrette. I lean back on my elbows with a deep exhale. I'm more than a little indignant. I thought I was about to see Shane. Now, not only do I not get to see him, I have to continue this mission. *Ugh.*

"You okay?" he asks sincerely.

"I'm fine, unfortunately," I mutter the last word.

He runs his fingers through his thick, dark shoulder-length hair. It's slightly wavy, as if having been previously pulled-up.

"I just saw this white, fuzzy ball bouncing off the edge of the bridge and had to see what it was."

"What was it?" I ask.

"Your hair," he says with a hearty laugh—an almost familiar laugh. I think of the boys in town, then of my brother. I still can't hear his.

"Well, thank you," I say, realizing how rude I've been. *Okay, you didn't get to see Shane. You've got work to do for him,* I reaffirm myself.

"No sweat," he says. "So what on earth brings you out here?"

"I'm Lyvia," I respond, holding out my hand not wanting to answer that question.

"Dagan," he replies, shaking it. His hand makes mine look tiny. In fact, I bet he makes most people look tiny.

"You know you kind of look familiar," he says with consternation.

"I get that a lot." I turn away, praying he won't recognize me. "I'm trying to find a Fuse Station near the library."

"That bridge is a goner," he points back to the dental-floss-constructed viaduct behind us. "They're supposed to replace it, but it doesn't get much traffic. Plus, if you go up the main road about twenty more miles, you can cross there."

Regina never mentioned this. I'm sure it's because she hasn't been out here in many years.

"Well, they might want to now," I reply, watching its fragile strings battle the strong wind.

"Sure, we'll see," he says, rolling his eyes. "Crystal Shire does things in their own time."

This is true.

"So, you're lookin' to fuse in. Which shire?" I catch him quickly glance at my forearm.

"Yeah, I'm nomadic," I say, self-consciously rubbing said spot. The signals are imperceptible to the human eye. You need a signal-reveal to see what shire someone belongs to. Even though I don't have the mark, it makes me uncomfortable.

"Me too, but you had to start somewhere," he implores leadingly.

I'm annoyed by his inquisitiveness. Darkens don't get the best rap.

"I'd rather not say."

"Okay. Don't get your panties in a bunch."

"Ew, I hate that word."

"What word? Bunch?"

"No, the other one."

"Oh, panties, why?"

"It's just dirty to me or something," I reply, while scrunching my face.

"My grandpa used to say that all the time." He's laughing so deeply now; I can't help but do the same.

"That just makes it worse somehow," I say, sitting up. "You think you can show me where this place is?"

"Sure, what kind of gentlemen would I be if I didn't?"

I hate asking for help. I could be drowning with nothing but a splinter of wood while a ship floats by equipped with an entire rescue crew, and I'd say, 'Oh, no thank you. I'm good. I got this.' It's actually ridiculous.

He offers his hand. I stubbornly refuse it. I don't want to appear helpless, besides I'm just standing up. I push up forgetting the weight of my bags and promptly land on my ass, a puff of dust.

"Wow," he says, eyes widening, shaking his head. He grabs my arm before I have a chance to argue. He lifts me off the ground as if I'm a rag doll and sets me on my feet.

"This way," he calls over his shoulder, already trekking through the woods.

I follow him while noticing fauna's song. The leaves rustle and crickets chirp as the sound of water distances itself. The path twists and turns. It's narrow and rocky. The thicket grows even darker. It feels like night is descending; although, it's only three o'clock in the afternoon.

"How far is this place?" I ask.

"We've still got a little ways to go."

"Are you hungry?"

"I'm always hungry," he laughs again. *That laugh.*

"Well, I've got some nourishment," I say.

We find a tiny clearing off the path. A few large rocks are inexplicably placed to the side; we each take one. His resembles a stool, mine —an oversized granite chair. Inside Regina's bag, I pull out two glass bottles of cucumber water and cream cheese and olive sandwiches. *Two of everything… Curious.* There's also some potato salad. She even included peanut butter cookies that have chocolate-covered peanut butter candies smushed in the middle.

"Wow. I haven't had a cream cheese and green olive sandwich since I went to Boblo Island. It was a renovated amusement park when I was little. That was a long time ago," he says wistfully. "I was probably just five-years-old at the time." He takes a colossal bite out of the sandwich.

I try to remember the last time I've had a cream cheese and green olive sandwich. I think I was three. *Whiff of fresh cut grass. A far away whistle. Flash of silver.*

"It's been awhile for me too."

"So, Lyv, tell me about yourself," he says matter-of-factly.

I freeze. My brother called me Lyv.

"Well, Dag," I reply, taking his lead. He chuckles. "I was born. I grew up. Now, I'm in a forest with a strange man eating 'Boblo' sandwiches, hoping I don't get murdered." *Well, it wouldn't be the worst thing.*

"I don't wanna murder you, Lyvia. I just want to take you to my secret lair and play dress-up." His stare is unnerving.

I stop chewing, trying to remember what I can use as weapons. I guess the shoes, given they turn into nails again. Of course, this is happening. As if my history with men would presume any differently. I shouldn't be surprised. Wouldn't be the first time something just as horrifying happened to me.

His stare is broken, and he laughs and laughs. He cracks himself up. I can't help myself. I join in.

"Your turn," I say, when the giggles subside.

"Nope, your answer was unsatisfactory, Miss Lyvia. We can try again in the next round," doing his best old-timey game show host. "You do not get the prize."

"The prize being... your life story? I think I'll survive."

"Harsh. Okay... Here it goes... I was born. I grew up. Now I'm stuck in a forest with an obstinate Maltese."

"Okay. Now, that was harsh," I say, with a deep chuckle.

"I actually come from a long line of Granites, but I love to study and write. After my grandma died, my grandpa became unconnected. I went to live with him for many reasons," he says, but doesn't commit to the rest of the thought. "Anyway, I found it a much better fit. More subjects to research in Crystal. Don't get me wrong, I'll always have the greatest respect for Granite Shire, but it wasn't for me."

I'm not going to pry, but I'd like to know those "reasons."

"I can definitely relate," I tell him, offering no more.

"I know you can," he responds with a very knowing look—too knowing.

Now, I'm uncomfortable. I shift on my rock and offer him a cookie. He eats it in one bite. Then, I give him the rest of mine.

"So, how much farther do we have?" I ask.

"Probably about another hour with our current pace," he replies sardonically, already back on the trail.

We make the rest of the journey in relative silence. I wonder what I'll see when I fuse in. I wonder where I'll find him. After what seems like forever, the trail begins to widen. A massive building that looks completely out of place stands at the edge of the forest. It appears the forest picks back up right behind the library.

"The station's back this way."

He takes me on another windy path that circles the building. I see at the very back hidden in a patch of trees: The Fuse Station. It resembles an ancient gas station that's been remodeled to modern-day. There are only four terminals. As we walk past them, I see they are unoccupied.

Recognizing I require privacy, he says, "I'm gonna be in the library. You can get me there when you're done. I'll take you back to town."

"You don't have to do that. I think I can manage," I reply.

"Oh, like you did on the bridge?" he calls over his shoulder. "I'll see you in a bit."

5

Facing the entrance, I walk up to the fourth terminal. The AI senses me immediately creating an invisible barrier to make the terminal appear empty, unless you tried to walk up to it. I pull out my Slab, open it, and set it on the ground. It lights up to create my welcome hologram.

"Hello, Lyvia, it's been a while," the voice I programmed speaks. A disappointed parent.

"I know, Persephone. It's been a rough week."

"Well, hopefully, I can help," she replies with a little more enthusiasm.

"Yeah, hopefully," I mutter.

"Am I connected unlinked?" I ask, knowing the answer.

"Always, you're *always* unseen, Lyvia," she says. I almost detect a note of annoyance, a technological eye roll. I did program her to have a personality, but come on.

"Show me where I am."

The hologram shifts to an aerial view of the library with full color and resolution. It's so real; it feels as if you can actually touch it.

"Pan out." She shows me the town further away. Then, she spans even further to encompass the entire Crystal Shire.

"Show me where Shane is." She takes me to the tomb. It looks good, undisturbed. I see a white bird near the opening; I'm good with that.

"Show me the route from the tomb to Regina's."

It's a long journey. I'm shocked I was able to make it. Now that I'm squared away with priorities, I ask the big question.

"Where is he?"

The hologram spins furiously. I know why. He's nearly impossible to track. *Fucking Gold Shire*.

Luckily, Persephone is different. I created her with some help. She's completely detached and isolated from the Realm's Framework which is supplied from Gold—molecular-atomized-artificial-intelligence. The Gold Shire is responsible for energy, including power, communication, and technology with the exceptions of Crystal—which is solar powered, and Onyx—which runs on lunar energy. The remainder of the shires rely solely on Framework for power. Framework uses energy in space, from molecules and atoms to the tiniest neutrons. It harnesses the energy to power the network. This system governs every shire residents' personal energy field through its spacial artificial intelligence as well. Persephone surpasses all of this, though.

"More difficulty than usual, Lyvia," Persephone updates with a note of strain.

"We gotta find him, Seph," I say. The spinning gets faster with spiraling images of geography—trees, roads, fields, water, more water, buildings, until it's just a whir of color. The image freezes; I recognize it instantly, the alcove.

"Last known location," Persephone finishes.

"We know this already, Seph," I respond, looking away from the site, still a bloody scene.

"Show me the shires." She shifts to view the entire landscape. Color-coded rays of light depict the different regions. There are a total of seven shires making up the Realm. Each one is responsible for its resources and specialties. Gold Shire, the Light Shire, also goes by Golden. It controls energy, power, and technology using its Framework. Turquoise Shire encompasses marine study as well as atmospheric research, also known as Shire H2O. Emerald Shire is responsible for land, vegetation, and produce. Onyx Shire, also known as the Dark Shire, studies the universe, the great beyond, and the spiritual world. Ruby Shire, also known as Fauna, is accountable for animal life and studies. Granite Shire, often called Mortal, carries human studies. It encompasses both medical and physical needs of the human body. This is where hospitals, medical schools, and such are located. Crystal Shire, commonly called the Unconnected Shire, encompasses the human mind. Its subjects of expertise include science, theology, history, mathematics, philosophy—all academic subjects. Crystal's specialty is knowledge of everything related to humanity.

Since the Great Rain, land on Earth shrunk immensely. The only terrain not covered by the ocean has been reduced to one sizable island. The landscape is a slightly vertical oval. The outer rim of the Realm is composed of Turquoise Shire, a ring of blue light encompasses the expanse on Persephone's map. The period of Great Rain affected the Earth's atmosphere and weather. Extreme climate changes occur despite shrunken terrain. This outer area is always summer. In fact, the entire realm's climate is relatively warmer than it was historically. No snow. The most outer limit's weather and scenery resemble what was once Hawaii.

The next circle inside the terrain, a double ray of green and red light, is composed of both Emerald and Ruby, land and animal. Their terrain includes grassy farmland, jungle, and even forest. Vegetation covers everything. It's hot and humid in some areas, cool and dry in others. The red light becomes concentrated going north depicting a more urban setting, Downtown Ruby.

Further up, the next ring of light is grey. Here is the heart of the city, Granite Shire. The buildings gleam in the aerial view. Every shire's buildings are constructed from its specialty materials. Slate granite dominates the Mortal Shire; polished stonework marbles its structures.

Located at the very north of the Realm, I spot concentrated yellow light—Gold Shire. Gold Shire's gold-plated buildings dazzle and shine from Persephone's aerial plot. It marks the very top of the Realm.

Circling Gold Shire is a thick black ray. *My old stomping grounds.* Onyx Shire depends on lunar energy, which it harnesses to keep the Shire dark 24/7. Walking into Onyx, night descends. Stars and universe surround you. It's similar to walking into a real-life observatory.

Downward, Crystal Shire is the furthest point from Gold to the south, stretching around the mouth of the Realm's river utilizing only solar power.

"Show me Crystal again, Seph," I say, and she's doing it before I get the third word out. She swiftly brings the aerial view of Crystal to span across her holographic screen. Its white light glows.

"Zoom in."

She does so, and I begin to see the buildings reflect prisms from their crystalline forms. The area is vastly expansive. Here and there, you see concentrated buildings but unoccupied land predominates. There's no rhyme or reason with the design of the landscape. The main river of the Earth's now shrunken landscape flows from the ocean into Crystal. Eventually, it forks into four smaller rivers, but resting at its mouth is the Cush of Crystal.

The Cush is the area where the ocean meets the river. It's the oldest site in the Realm. There are waterfalls and forests, cliffs, ancient caves, and prehistoric landmarks that span the area where the water's flow connects. It's also the location of The Rock, in all of its primordial mystery. It's a very mystical place, yet extremely dangerous. Crystal Shire is not a popular location; most people never set foot there for their entire lives.

"Pinpoint Shane." She shifts and another white light beams from his tomb. He is located near the Cush. I thought so from my initial visit.

"I'll keep searching, Lyvia, but he's made it impossible."

"Okay, sounds good. Show me the Dark Shire Vortex. I gotta get out there to contact Shane."

A vortex is a place where energy is directly entering Earth, while at the same time, projecting from it. It's where communication overlaps for all three dimensions. This means that a vortex allows people to communicate to Heaven, Earth, and Hell while in its location. Energy vortexes have to be protected with spiritual armor. An open passage is extremely dangerous. Vortexes are unheard of these days, besides Dark Shire Vortex, which is operated by Darken. The vortex has been protected and guarded against any communication to or from Hell. It only allows messages from Heaven in the form of phone calls.

Someone mans the archaic phone booth at all times. Messages are then forwarded to appropriate location and passed on. The story goes that the first Darken family found the Dark Shire Vortex and built its communication system, including the barrier to Hell. The vortex is one of the oldest sites in the history of mankind still in existence. It's the only one left.

Persephone pans the landscape. The screen turns black and fills with stars. Home. She hovers over a spot and begins to zoom in. The giant, ancient red phone booth is gone. I stare at the screen in horror.

"What happened, Seph?" I whisper.

"I would imagine the same thing that happened to Shane," she says.

"Him," I spit the word out. "How am I gonna talk to my brother?" I ask, pacing the small space.

"I'm sure we'll figure out something," she says.

"I like your positivity, Seph, but what the hell? I can't believe it's gone, the one and only line to Shane in the afterlife. Damn it."

"I know," she says.

Silently pacing the terminal, I speak, "We have to find him." I resolutely come to a stop in front of the Slab.

"Already on it."

"All right. You know I have to keep you unconnected while I'm in Crystal, but keep working and I'll get out here as soon as possible to check in," I reply.

"You got it, boss," she says, and promptly shuts down.

I pick up the Slab, close it, and put it in my bag. *That was massively depressing, not to mention, traumatic.* I see flashes of the bloody alcove. Then the empty space where the phone booth—the Dark Shire Vortex —once stood, I get a chill. The one form of spiritual communication is severed. I just want to go back to Regina's and collapse on the white billow of fluff.

Sighing, I turn to the library. The building seems to reach the sky. It's modernized but retains its original charm. Made of giant concrete blocks, it looks similar to an archaic castle, complete with a narrow moat. The roof transforms into crystal towers on the corners. I love everything about it.

I walk up and open the round wooden door by unhooking its heavy chain. Walking in, it smells musty, library type of musty. I breathe in the ancient paper book scent deeply. It's one of my favorite aromas. The corridor is empty. There are two old cigar chairs tilted toward each other on the right. A framed signal-latch hangs above the chairs. The archaic bronze shackles make me shudder. Below, a small table sits between the two chairs holding three hardcovers. I'm curious to see what they are but hear a loud bang from another room. It sounds as if someone dropped something heavy.

I pass the corridor and walk into the main room. Reminding me of Regina's study, the bookshelves scan the entire library ceiling to floor. There are doorways and rooms, each one I see is covered with books, empty of people. No sounds other than the bang I heard a moment ago. I travel toward the boom through a tunnel-shaped hallway and emerge into a smaller room. This one is loaded with books as well. I spot Dagan. He's sitting at an antique desk made of thick oak in a matching chair. He has a very large book propped in front of him, the source of the bang, I presume.

"Hey," I say. He shoots up startled, startling me as well. I'm known to be very quiet and often forget someone might not have heard me coming.

"Oh, hey," he says, gathering his composure. "Didn't hear ya."

"What have you got there?" I ask, eyeing the monstrosity. It's the same one I wrestled off the shelf last night.

"It's *The Complete History of Technology*. The author put together every single piece of information he could find all the way from its inception to today. Pretty interesting stuff," his last three words are laced with sarcasm.

"Why are you reading it?" I ask curiously. I'm gravely familiar with the book.

"Well, for the sake of knowledge, I guess. I don't really know, yet. Someone once told me it would be imperative that I learn the ins and outs of technological history. I figured it couldn't hurt. I like to be efficient in all subjects, all shires."

Mr. Dagan, I'm not satisfied with that response, I think.

"Me too," I reply. "Career student and writer. I love my research." *The understatement of the century.*

He begins to put the book back. It looks tiny in his hands. I wonder how he even dropped it.

"When I went to pull it down, it slipped off the shelf with a mind of its own," he answers my unspoken question.

Before I can even muse as to how he knew, he replies, "I assume the source of the sound gave away my location. Looks as though I'm not combat ready," he says with a laugh.

Thinking about locations, I feel urgency to pinpoint one particular person.

"So, do you guys ever get any Lighters out here?" I ask, oh-so-casually scanning book titles.

"Nope, not really, not since Levi has gone off the Frame. So, probably about a week? I don't know. I don't really keep up with all that stuff."

Levi. A butcher knife sears through the heart-shaped spongy, pink tissue in my chest. *Him. Of course, you don't keep up with that stuff. Too busy flipping through ancient books.* Mean. I scold myself. *You were doing the same thing a week ago.*

"But, before that? Did a lot of them pass through?" I ask.

He takes a minute before responding. He seems to do that. He's very careful with his word choice. I can't tell if that's because he's such a thinker, or because he is hiding something. My suspicions lean toward the latter; although, it's probably a combination of both.

"There were a few for a while, rented a couple houses. Seemed to be going permanent. You know, we get members from a lot of shires out here, so I didn't think much of it. Thought they were lookin' to unconnect, like most do. They came out here a lot, to use the Fuse mostly. Only saw one or two actually use the library. I kept my eye on them; I don't trust them. Any of them," he says seriously.

Probably better you don't.

"So, did they leave immediately after he disappeared?" I ask.

"What's with the interest? Used to be a Lighter?" he asks, one eyebrow up.

"No, never. I just wondered is all," I say, surreptitiously scanning the great wall of books.

"Okay," he replies, clearly not believing one word I just said. "Well, they stayed I'd say another day, then headed out. It did seem like they were in a hurry, but I figured they had to find their 'leader,'" he says the last word dripping with pure condescension. "If you're not a Lighter, then what's the interest?"

"It's a long story." I start putting some of the other books he laid out away.

In Crystal, everyone does for him or herself. Stores, pharmacy, local restaurants, etc. Each one is managed and run by the owner, all help and services are made in trade. This means the library is run the exact same way. Each patron is free to use but must clean up after himself when finished. It's an honor system, I guess. I never understood how businesses could operate in such a fashion. Yet, as I grew older, I realized it's the only way to efficiently run a society, as long as everyone is on board and does his or her part. If you are unconnected, you understand that, or you're welcome to leave. In such case, the citizens hold a vote. That rarely happens. People pretty much stick to their shire codes, regardless of which one.

"Well, I'd like to hear it."

"Well, I'd prefer to share it another time," I say, reaching up to put the last book away.

"Okay. You wanna head back?"

"Sure, thanks for everything." I want to say more but for some reason, I don't.

He walks me out around the castle the way we came. There's a fluttering that gets way too close and way too loud. Flapping wings descend upon my head. I shriek, flailing my arms in a frantic panic and sprint down the trail looking as if I just escaped the clutches of a ghastly face-painted clown. Not a fan of clowns. I manage to escape the bird's wrath and try to compose myself. My hair is frazzled and clothes askew.

"Birds freak me out," I let out, breathing heavily, hands on my knees.

"Wow," he says with huge wide eyes. "It didn't even touch you. You were about 'this far' from extreme danger," he says, stretching his bulky arms wide. He starts laughing, hard. One more "wow," and he catches up with me.

"Avian flu?" he asks.

"No," I answer, laughing. "I'm not concerned about an ancient pandemic. More so, their little bones, and hard little beaks…" My face scrunches up. "I don't know, the fact that they can fly—just seems unnatural. As long as they keep their distance, we're good." I sneak a paranoid glance upward.

"I think you're safe," he says as he climbs ahead of me.

"Isn't there something that freaks you out, some animal?"

"Squirrels."

"What? A squirrel? And you're giving me a hard time?"

"They're just so fast and unpredictable. And their little bones, come to think of it."

"Oh, you're just screwing with me," I say, stubbornly laughing.

"I wouldn't dare," he replies melodramatically. "The truth being— I don't know. I can't pinpoint it. But they have a mischievousness and inhuman speed that doesn't sit right. I don't trust 'em."

I nod solemnly, while rapidly adding squirrels to my list of things that freak me out. We head into the thicket, the trail narrows as we progress.

"Okay, Lyv, you gotta give me something," he breaks the silence after a few minutes. Another sting at his use of Lyv. I decide I really do have to give him something. He did save my life and all.

"Okay, but then you have to," I reply.

"Deal," he says.

"Well, I grew up Darken. Long line. Very mysterious," I tell him earnestly. *I don't even know half the secrets hidden in my family line.*

"Okay. I had a feeling. You just have the aura. No mark, though. Which means, you decided to unconnect at eighteen?" he asks.

"Nope. You know the rules," I say, wondering how he knows I'm markless.

"Okay. Well, I come from a long line of Granites," he starts.

"Wrong answer, contestant," I cut in. "I already know that. You have one more spin, would you like to buy a vowel?" I try my best at game show host. Really, I'm Vanna White from *Wheel of Fortune*, complete with arm presentation.

"Okay, Vanna," he says with a chuckle. I'm impressed he picks up on such an obscure reference.

"Let's see. I'm a pretty boring guy. I like to work around town here and there. For whatever I need and more. I try to help, give back. I like to box, hit the gym whenever I can," he finishes.

"You're up." He swiftly picks up a rock and tosses it into the woods. The gesture makes me taste cinnamon. *Smell bonfire. Hear a flag flapping in the wind.*

"I pretty much wander. I don't like to stay in one place too long. So, I figured I should be nomadic. I mostly research and study every-thing. I feel like there is so much knowledge out there that's very important in times like these."

"You're right about that. I went down to," he freezes before he can finish. "Did you hear that?"

Of course, I heard it, sharp and clear. A twig snap. Too heavy to be an animal. Also, too much silence following. *What in the actual hell is going on in these woods?*

6

Dagan grabs my arm and takes me into the clearing where the rocks sit, our lunch site. We crouch behind them. My form is easily concealed, his a bit more difficult. Luckily, two large boulders seem to do the trick.

It's impossible for Levi to know where I am. Even if he were to locate the Fuse Station, it would never work. Persephone is virtually untraceable. I test her frequently. The only reason I waited to connect in the Fuse was out of pure paranoia. Even if he could somehow high jinx my Slab, she would tell me immediately and we would run. Still, I don't want to risk trouble for Regina.

Knowing that Seph is completely safe, this is unnerving. I think again to weaponry. All I have on me are the shoes. I don't have the slightest inkling how they work or even what they are. They opened a tomb. How would I use them as a weapon? Toss them at the assailant? I do happen to be trained in hand-to-hand combat. It's something I took interest in for a while and continue to train. Still, if they have any type of rayguns, we're done for.

There's a rustling in the leaves. *Taste vinegar. Smell stagnant polluted water.* I wonder if Dagan has any weaponry. As much as I hate to admit it, I do find his presence a bit calming. *He's a big guy*, I tell myself.

"I thought I heard something east of me," a male voice says.

I sneak a peek around the boulder and see a form. He's probably using audio Framework channels. Slabs can perform that kind of magic.

"Slab?" I mouth to Dagan questioningly.

He shrugs behind the rock.

"Dude. He's not gonna be out here. I mean, come on. I don't know why you guys left me here anyway. You know he'll come back when he decides to come back. We don't even know where he's hiding."

"You have to follow orders, Squid."

I can hear the other voice as clear as day. Because of my condition, my senses are heightened. I can pick up Framework channel frequencies. For others, only the receiver can detect the voice on the opposite end. It's as if the voice comes straight to the receiver's mind, bypassing auditory hearing. This happens through the use of a Slab. With my amplified hearing, I can pick up the other voice without technological help.

"It's a waste of time."

I've got to get this guy. He might have information, but how am I going to do this with Dagan here? He knows nothing. He probably plans to hide and let the guy go. *Damned unconnected, peace-loving hippies.*

And there's the added obstacle—*I must get him to help. I can't do this alone. I'm weaponless, besides the nails, which are shoes at the moment. I really need to figure out how they work. Should I throw them at the guy? Even if they transform into nails, maybe they'll just change back to heels on impact. Hand-to-hand combat in stilettos. Followed by what? Kidnapping him and... Taking him where? A nearby squirrel's den?* I shudder at the thought.

But then, Dagan darts behind his rock toward the voice. He's extremely quick for his size. He shoots effortlessly through the trees. He's to the guy fifty feet away in a matter of seconds. He knocks him out with a giant fist. Then, looks over at me peeking from behind the rock.

"Should we take him to my place or question him here?" he asks, so casually I would think he just inquired if I prefer cream in my coffee. I snap into mission-mode.

"Where's your place?"

"This way," he slings the guy over his brawny shoulder. The guy also resembles a rag doll even though he's two of me. He turns into the woods following an unseen trail. I struggle to keep up, again, surprised by his speed. The sharp twists and turns add difficulty, though I stay steadfast in his wake. The blow keeps the Lighter out, and we trek deeper and deeper into the woods.

A clearing begins. I spot a large castle-shaped cottage made of the same concrete as the library. We go inside. It's impossibly larger inside than out, not unlike Regina's. This guy is full of surprises. He carries his accessory as he would a beach towel over his shoulder. The man's arms dangle as wet noodles might. I follow closely behind. We pass through a corridor into a den, then a study.

There's a living room at the end of the hallway. I can only catch tiny glimpses of each space's layout. I pass leather chairs, a coffee table, a massive grey flannel couch, and a huge fireplace. Thick dark wood spreads everywhere from the ebony-stained hardwood floors to where it climbs the walls, ending about three-quarters of the way up in sharp diagonal angles. It disappears into a ceiling made out of crystal. The living room also sports a massive fireplace, but that's all I can make out before Dagan opens a tall door on the left.

The door reveals a twisty staircase descending through wood-plated concrete walls. As I scurry behind him, I have a sudden thought regarding my safety. I quickly push it aside, however. *What's the worst that can happen? Death? Fine.* Call me reckless. Call me stupid. *I'm going to avenge my brother and die doing so if need be.*

After a trek so low, I figure we passed sea level a long time ago, he lands with a heavy thud on a shiny black landing. No dust, just flawless, smooth black floor spans ahead of us leading into a tunnel. As he walks, the floor lights the path ahead. We walk for about ten minutes when the tunnel splits into two pathways and dead ends at a door straight ahead.

He balances the Lighter on his shoulder and pulls out his wallet from his back pocket. He thumbs through until he finds a kist key. When he goes to replace the billfold, a round token-shaped object falls out. It has some sort of engraving on it. I swoop down and scoop it up. Dense and hard, not metal though. He reaches and swipes it before I even get a glimpse. Still, I recognize it. I have a similar one residing in my wallet. This is confusing. *I thought mine was one-of-a-kind.*

He uses the kist key to open the door, and I realize he has some kind of neural network down here. Once open, he ascends more twisty steps, effortlessly swinging his bag of potatoes as we climb. We reach a platform. A black wall swishes open to reveal a finished basement. 'Lair' would be a bit more appropriate.

I survey the terrain. I say terrain because it's a massive space. I spot doors sporadically placed around the circumference of this main room. One stands open. Behind it, I see more stairs leading downward. *What the hell?* The colossal area resembles an underground tower. It's reminiscent of a castle's tower, although the walls are lined with very dark wood also breaking into crystal near the top similar to upstairs. Its sharp angles slice into the original stonework. *Cool.*

There's no chill down here. It smells of bonfire—not a fireplace but an actual autumn evening bonfire. The floor is made of black onyx. Its smooth glass surface isn't unlike black ice. There are modernized fixtures here and there. Most I recognize. Some I don't.

I also spot quite a few ancient items. Among them—exercise equipment complete with vintage barbells sits on the floor, comic books in impossibly pristine condition, record albums, and hardback books line the shelves. Old framed posters fit the walls, along with sports jerseys and hats. The theme here is old-world American sports, such as baseball, football, and hockey. These sports are still played today, although these United States' teams remain pre-Great Rain. I recognize a couple of them, including Shane's favorites. *Curious.* The room spans around the platform from which we emerged. It's circular and appears to be split into thirds. One section contains a table, eight chairs, and a kitchen area, all of which are composed of black onyx.

The next third is raised and reachable by steps; it holds a massive over-sized plush coal black sectional couch, adjourning loveseat, gigantic oversized chair with accompanying ottoman, and six enormous movie-style recliners, all shiny black leather. An old-world movie screen completes the area. The furniture is huge. I'm talking gargantuan. *I'm Alice in Wonderland, and I've just gone down the rabbit hole.*

This section can only be described as a man cave. More sports memorabilia lines the walls, including signed jerseys. A blue and silver football jersey shakes loose a memory. *The taste of savory Velveeta chili cheese sauce fills my mouth. I feel heavy cold snowflakes land on my head. I look upward to feel the wet cold drops on my face.* I shake off the invisible snow and rush to catch up.

The way my memory works is basically video-graphic on steroids. I guess the best term would be experiential. An 'experiential memory,' a phrase I coined myself. I see, hear, and feel everything in the memory as if I'm essentially re-experiencing it. My senses absorb phantom former happenings, which can be extremely useful. Some-times, however, it can be wholly unhelpful. If I allow my thoughts to drift, I can be taken into any of my memories. At times, I suddenly find myself reliving some rather inconvenient past times. It's all a side effect of the Synesthesia.

We head to the last third. It's the highest level. This one's even more interesting, mostly due to the bare walls. The only occupying furniture consists of a thick and heavy old wooden desk and three chairs. One chair sits on one side and the other two face it. It's an exact replica of an old-world police interrogation room. The table is even stained with coffee mug rings. There's a rotary telephone on its surface.

Then, I see it. The same bronze signal-latch that is currently hanging in the library. Anyone can get a signal-reveal, which is a device used to reveal a person's mark. The apparatus exposes the invisible color tattooed on a person's arm, which dictates the shire to which he or she belongs. But only shire leaders have signal-latches, and last I checked, Crystal doesn't have a leader. *Very peculiar.*

He flops the Lighter in the single chair. Then he walks over to the bare wall. He waves his kist key and the wall reveals a triage of weaponry. He takes out some glowing strings and looks at our pris-oner. He puts them back. Instead, he places the man's right forearm into the signal-latch with clinical speed. It's bronze and resembles ancient-world shackles. I stand there watching him.

"What the hell." I say. A declaration, not a question.

"What?" he asks innocently, as he cinches the latch. His eyebrows raise, and I see him as a small boy creating a fort in the living room with every roll of toilet paper in the house. A strip of the fragile tissue wrapped around his head, a miniature ninja.

"Where are we? And more importantly, who are you?" I demand hands on hips, almost stomping my foot. Almost.

"I'm Dagan," he says, drawing out the sentence. "And we are in my basement."

I roll my eyes.

"Oh, Dagan, is it?" I ask sarcastically. "Just for your information, this is not a 'basement.' This is a villain's evil lair. Except for the man cave and kitchen. Not sure if villains have kitchens. Well, they probably do. They have to eat, right?"

I'm rambling, which means I'm nervous. I have reason to be. We just kidnapped a guy and brought him to a secret underground cave. Oh, yeah, a cave equipped with torture devices. *I'm stoked.*

"Okay. But, if I give more background, you do too."

"Fine. Why did you decide this would be our best course of action back there?" I ask.

"Way I see it, Lyv, these Lighters are up to something bad. Ever since their new 'leader' started up with his big ideas… Ideas that are dangerous. I know you're smart enough to know that. Otherwise…" He trails off not completing the thought. He starts another—"Otherwise, you wouldn't have gone along for the ride, willingly, I might add. What's your beef with the Lights?" His trailing off prompts inquiry on my part. He had something else to say about me just then. I decide to let that linger for now. I try to figure out how much truth to give him. Knowing that he has yet to give me the whole enchilada, I go with—

"I have a history with Lighters, and you're right. They're up to no good." *Levi is up to no good*, I add mentally.

"Keeping it mysterious," he eyes me slyly.

"As are you," I reply.

"What do you mean? Ask away," he says.

"Well, you have a signal-latch, for starters. Not only are there only seven in existence, Crystal Shire's is supposed to be preserved in the library, as it appears to be hanging there at this very moment."

"Oh, you noticed that," he laughs. The guy's still out cold. I wouldn't want to get punched by Dagan.

"It was preserved in the library. Actually, it still is. Well, an exact replica, anyway."

"Okay," I say, drawing out the word. "We'll come back to that. He had a Slab. How was it operational in Crystal?"

Before he can answer, we hear a moan. The Lighter starts to come to.

"Come on, we've got work to do." He walks over to the man.

The man is younger. I would say about twenty-eight. He is muscular built, large, but not quite as large as Dagan. I can't think of anyone besides my brother, whose Titan form surpasses Dagan in size and height. They are two colossal guys. The Lighter has ocean blue eyes and short dusky brown hair. There is a solid bump forming where he was struck.

"What the? Where the? Son of a—" he sputters as he looks around the dank interior, eyes landing on his two abductors. "Who are you?"

"Never mind that," Dagan says, trying to sound all business. He whips a chair out at the other side of the table and straddles it backwards. He pushes out the other one, never breaking eye contact with our Lighter. I stand unmoving. I haven't seen him in business-mode. It's quite entertaining.

I walk over slowly, deciding to take his lead. I slide into the chair, arms crossed, doing my best female detective pose. We do need information.

"You've got intel, we require, Mr. uh," I look at him, inquisitively. He offers nothing.

"Please don't make us use the latch," I add, ominously leaning forward. I steeple my hands under my chin, but not quite, as my elbow slips off the ledge, and I have to make a quick recovery.

The Lighter looks at us as if he must be dreaming.

"Okay. You don't need to use the latch," he says, shaking his head. "My name is Xane. I came out here with a bunch of us to check things out."

"What kind of things?" Dagan asks, leaning further back in his chair. His mammoth muscular form looks absurd but his size threatening enough.

"You were using a Slab," I interject.

"Yeah, so?"

"They're inoperable in Crystal. All Framework is. You have to use the Fuse Station."

"Oh, yeah, he gave special ones to the Inner-circle and Middle-circle," he says. "You guys got any water? Aspirin?"

"I'm sorry, but that's not how this works, Xane," I say, knowing full well I have absolutely no clue how 'this' works, but I'm eager for information, "Answer some questions, then we talk requests." I lean back in the chair, elbow perched on the armrest, one hand 'thought-fully' poised under my chin. He studies me incredulously.

"You know, you look really familiar," he says, seeming this-close to placing me. The *Price Is Right* wheel slows in its final stretch. Ding. Ding. Ding... *Ding...*

"I get that a lot," I reply, braving a look at Dagan. He looks at me thoughtfully.

"I can promise you both, we've never met before today. I just have a familiar face. Now, answer some questions, or so help me God, I will latch your ass." I pound my fist in accompaniment.

"Okay, okay." He leans back, eyes wide. "Obviously, you know I'm a Light. So, you can probably gather that I was looking for our 'leader,'" he says the last word with almost as much disdain as Dagan and I. "Nobody's seen him since the Great Reveal was scheduled to happen."

The Great Reveal, I mentally sneer. *The single moment that ruined my life forever.*

"See, Xane, this much we already know. Should I just latch in?" Dagan starts toward the bronze shackle.

"No, no, no. Please don't," he pulls back pleadingly.

Getting latched is incredibly painful. Depending on your strength, one session can put you on your ass for weeks. It's very draining, but it does give the wearer's entire history from birth. Not that we need all that. We only need the last five years if this guy doesn't cooperate. Even then, it'll be excruciating. Since Crystal Shire inhabitants are markless, their latch works a little differently. All seven signal-latches can read signals, except for markless Crystals. The Crystal signal-latch is the only one that can read an unconnected resident. Each latch is composed of its shire's material—gold, turquoise, emerald, onyx, ruby, granite, and bronze for Crystal. I'm still curious as to how Dagan procured the bronze one.

"When was the last time you saw him, Xane? Physically," I ask in my sweetest good-cop voice.

"The evening before the reveal, he had a gathering to give one of his speeches. Also, he wanted to make sure everyone knew what their role was."

"And exactly what was your role, Xane?" Dagan asks, sitting forward in the chair.

"I just reached Middle-circle status, exactly a week before. There's no one that knows the entirety of his great 'manifesto.' We all have our roles, but nobody is aware of anyone else's."

"Well, what is your role?" Dagan exclaims, pounding a giant fist on the table.

Okay. He needs to take it down a notch. His Mitch Rapp-level interrogation technique is going a bit too far. Mitch Rapp was a book turned movie character in the 2000s. He was a terrorist driven patriot who was recruited for the CIA. His idea of interrogation was cutting off a pinkie finger before even asking the first question. No patience, no tolerance, and pretty badass; however, it's not as if our 'prisoner' is making information extraction all that difficult.

Xane slouches in his chair, the exclamation having no effect. "You guys, I've been one foot out of Gold for weeks now. I was just about to take off on those assholes. I do what I want!" he exclaims, throwing his head and free arm upward. "In fact, the moment I was about to unconnect, I got pulled up in rank, meaning more responsibilities. So, curiosity, you know. It took over, as it loves to do," he leans forward.

"One time when I was little I was on vacation with my family. When I got back, my friends had come up with this 'genius' plan, as they described it. They wouldn't tell me what we were up to, only what part I needed to play," Xane continues.

Dagan sighs deeply, rolling his eyes. He leans back and glances down at a non-existent watch on his wrist. "This better be good," he says, lifting his eyes from his invisible timepiece.

"Okay, okay. So, I'm told that all I have to do is get this kid, Winston, to the culvert that connects the freshwater lake to the river by my old house. Easy enough. Plus, with curiosity pushing the agenda, I was in. We used to swim down there. The water rushes through the metal tunnel creating a giant wake. We would tie up rope and battle the roaring current," he demonstrates the scene with his hands.

Suddenly, I taste cherry Kool-Aid. *A flash of slate coral-fossilized Petoskey stones, pebbles coated with patterns that resemble rays of sun.*

Sounds of buzzing insects fill my ears. A stifling heat encompasses me making it hard to breathe. It feels like waking up in a tent as the rising sun cooks its inhabitants.

I snap myself back to the present, taking a breath of the lair's cool air. Xane looks into an imaginary distance, probably envisioning that long-ago summer day—his boyhood memories on replay. Dagan's not amused. *Shocking.*

"Listen up, buddy. I'm wicked tired, and Miss Lyvia here has just about had it," he says, pointing his right thumb at me.

I look at Dagan dubiously. The guy's been in our 'interrogation chamber' for a total of twenty minutes. I'm starting to get the sense that Dagan's an impatient guy, which is just fine with me. If I can handle Shane's unrelenting restlessness, severe instant gratification tendencies, and zero impulse control, I can handle a little impatience.

Suddenly, thick creamy Calder eggnog sprinkled with nutmeg coats my tongue. Shiny red and green wrapped boxes adorned with bows of all sizes overflow beneath a lush twinkling tree. The snapping pops of a crackling fireplace fill the air. A small dark figure sits on the very edge of a couch in the tree's glow, well before sunrise. His silhouette holds a gift in his lap, shaking with excitement and eagerness. He'll probably open it the second he gets a witness.

"Okay, so, you and your friends..." Dagan starts again, sighing. He rests his elbows on his thighs and shakes his head gravely as he looks down. The dramatic display reminds me why we are in this current situation. Christmas memories swiftly move to the background.

"Xane, we hate this just as much as you do. I know ya could really use some cold water and a couple of aspirin. We'll be real happy to getchya some. Just gotta ask a couple more questions, dontcha know," I say, trying for good cop but sound exactly like Marge Gunderson in *Fargo*, complete with Minnesotan accent. I was going for something a little more Beatrix Kiddo in *Kill Bill*, a badass good cop version.

So, that just happened. They both look at me perplexed, unsure how to respond to that particular presentation. I don't blame them.

Dagan breaks his incredulous stare and shakes his head again. Between he and I, we are the female-male version of *21 Jump Street*. Oh, you know, just the usual—Schmidt and Jenko trying to shake some info from our captured 'perp.' We might as well unknowingly eat a few drugged Rice Krispy treats before we infiltrate a frat house.

"So, it was a very warm day, even for summer," Xane continues.

Dagan starts to say something but stops instantly the moment our eyes meet.

"I get Winston to the culvert. Only my friend, Riley, stands waiting. He tells Winston that the culvert is actually a portal to another dimension. He says if he goes through the tunnel he will be transported to an invisible plane. It's so hot and humid—all I want to do is rope surf the current. Plus, I have no idea what the guys are up to with this whole story. I had never gone down the culvert to the lake; although, I knew it was no 'portal.'

Riley's story is so convincing, Winston decides to try it. Riley takes him down to the tiny pool framing the tunnel. He pulls a giant, thick rope I've never seen out of the water. He tells Winston to hold the rope and follow it to the end of the 'portal' where transportation takes place. Keep in mind, the current is strong—stronger than strong—it could wipe you right off your feet. It could probably rip a few layers of your skin off. It could…"

"We get it," Dagan cuts him off. "Move on."

Xane gets serious. "So, this Winston kid gets the rope. He disappears into the tunnel. It's not a short tunnel. It's pretty long. I don't know how far, technically. Probably a thirty-minute trek through the current, granted it's not high tide, which this 'genius' idea hadn't taken into account.

After about ten minutes, we hear an echoing scream and the current pressure rises. Riley won't go in. He's too scared. I'm known to be a bit reckless, even back then, so I take ahold of the rope and climb up. The water is rushing to my knees, whereas it began at Winston's ankles. The water pressure is like quicksand. I can barely gain headway, but somehow, I do. I yell—'Winston!' and again —'Winston!' but hear nothing.

I walk for five minutes, the water is rising steadily but not that fast. I continue yelling, starting to get worried. I make the ten-minute, halfway mark and see a shadowy figure hunched to the side of the tunnel a few feet in front of me. Winston is pressed against the curve of the tunnel, taking deep breaths. He locked himself in the metal grooves of the tunnel, although the current continues to battle furiously.

He squints, eyes flooding with relief when he recognizes me. 'I let go of the rope when the tide started rising,' he says, through heavy exhales. I tell him to grab the rope from me and we'll finish the rest of the way together, having absolutely no clue what awaits us. Knowing my crazy friends, it's not gonna be good."

Dagan groans and rubs his eyes with growing frustration. "Dude, this got a point?"

"Just let him finish," I interject, enjoying the vividly painted picture, wishing for popcorn. Dagan gives me a sharp look. I wait a beat before meeting his eyes. My look shuts him down, instantly. He sits back with an indignant stare. I look at Xane to go on.

"Okay. We've got about a quarter of the way left, five minutes or so. But the water is near our waist, almost tripling our time. We move at a snail's pace. We are both getting tired. At this point, the water is nearly to our chests. It's getting to the point where we have to try to swim along the rope to keep us tethered. I can see the opening. Sunlight is streaming in. It's getting bigger. Winston is doing great at keeping up, as the water is nearing the top. Our heads are only a foot below the metal ceiling. When we finally emerge, there is no one there, none of my friends. I look around the wide lake and see nothing but trees. We swim over to the bank and climb out breathless.

'Where are we?' Winston looks around in awe. I just stare at him.

'Winston. We're in the lake. The one that funnels through the tunnel.' That kid, I tell ya," Xane shakes his head. "So, I'm looking around for my friends wondering what the hell they had in mind with this 'portal' stuff. Just then, Winston and I hear yelling. Spotting movement in the woods, we sprint toward something red among the trees. I see Georgie's red shirt and Taylor too. I'm pissed. These assholes don't tell me anything and then I get sucked into the culvert to find Winston? I'm about to crack some skulls, so to speak, I mean they're my boys and all, but still. However, the closer we get to the scene, worry replaces anger. First, we see flailing limbs accompanied by crying and screaming.

They've been lifted off the ground and hover, becoming frozen in the air. Unseen pressure squeezes the life out of them. I stop Winston with my hand and survey the scene. Both boys are suspended fifteen feet off the ground. Pure agony etched on their faces."

"A Framework trap," I interject.

"Yup," Xane answers. "I didn't know what to do. I knew that if I stepped into the crosshairs, I would be right up there with them. I also knew they wouldn't last more than seven minutes once the invisible pressurized chamber reached capacity."

"What'd ya do?" I ask eagerly, sitting forward, really craving some buttery popcorn. Dagan gives me a look that says, 'If you don't settle down, I'll make sure you never taste salty buttery popcorn ever again.'

"What I did was this. I located the snare midway the length of a giant oak tree. It was shaded from the sun, and you know how natural sunlight interferes with those."

It's true. Direct natural sunlight is pretty much the only weakness of Framework traps. It has to be placed in a 24/7 shaded or covered area, or it won't operate.

"Minutes have been ticking by this whole time. I reckon they got prolly two left, at most. I climb that oak faster than anything in my life. The snare is soldered to the trunk, however, looks like a long time ago. I have a kist key on me. I use it to pry the snare loose, knowing the key itself would do little good with my age limit. I wrap my arm around the tree as far as it will go placing the snare in direct sunlight. I hold my breath. Drops of sweat cover my body, which had dried from heat."

"Okay, Shakespeare, let's speed this up," Dagan says impatiently, clearly not enjoying 'story time' as much as me.

"Who's Shakespeare?" Xane asks, slouching again.

Dagan rolls his eyes. I get it. Most shires barely concentrate on historical culture. Pretty much just Crystal, actually.

"He's an ancient writer," I say. "So, did it work?"

Xane looks pleased to continue with his story of suspense. He smiles his mysterious smile.

"Of course, it did. Probably took twenty seconds of pure sunlight and whoomph—Georgie and Taylor flop to the ground, desperately clutching for air. I fall from the tree, triumphantly holding the snare," he says, patriotically lifting an invisible trap with his free arm to an unseen sky.

"Okay," Dagan says, deeply exhaling. "And how does any of that relate to our questions?"

"Well, had I known the plan, I wouldn't have gone along with it. I wouldn't have gotten Winston into such a predicament. I woulda talked those idiots out of the whole she-bang. So—way I see it, this guy with his great 'manifesto,' is probably pulling some ass-backwards plan that is not going to work and will probably result in things a lot worse than a Framework trap."

7

Dagan gestures for me to follow him through a motion-censored sliding door behind the wall of weapons. Inside, I find us behind the neural network wall acting as a two-way mirror. I feel like Larry Bosch, another long-forgotten author of a detective series. Bosch was a Vietnam War vet, tunnel rat. He was a great investigator, short-tempered, not unlike Mr. Rapp over here. He braces himself on the ledge.

"I think he's telling us the truth," Dagan says, eyeing the guy.

"But, are you a hundred percent sure?"

"Nope," he says, putting his hands in his pockets, shaking his head. Still staring at the back of Xane's.

Looking at Dagan's solemn profile, I feel a spark of light flicker in the now empty pit that is my soul. It feels like the glimmer of a new spiritual link, the call of the Dark Shire. It's only a dim flickering right now, not the strong beam of unseen light that connected me to Shane. It's more a lambent glow of hope. Whatever his real 'reasons' are, I know that Dagan and I ultimately want the same thing—to finish Levi.

"Well, I may be able to help with that. And you don't need the latch."

"What do you mean?"

"I have Synesthesia," I start.

"Okay," he says. "I'm familiar with it." Not surprising, he's familiar with every subject it seems.

"But what does that have to do with getting intel without the latch?" he asks.

"I don't know if it will work. But with my condition, I have telepathy. It's something I've had to develop, and I get lots of help from my spirit guide." I hate explaining this. This is why Darkens don't get the best rap. Believers and nonbelievers. "I actually have a lot of spirits visit me, mostly deceased family and friends, but I haven't heard any since…" I trail off, shaking my head.

"Since when?"

I ignore the question.

"I can hear most voices clearly, but at times it's loud and crowded. I can't make any promises, but it's worth the try. It's gonna be painful for him," I say.

"How painful?" he asks.

"Headache would be the closest description. One that makes you think death is the only medicine. But, it's over before ya know it," I say the last sentence brightly, brushing my hands together as if 'all in a good days' work.'

He looks at me strangely.

"I'll just follow your lead."

"I like your thinking," I reply confidently. I walk over to Xane. He sits up straight looking at me a little bewildered as I stride purposely toward him.

"This may hurt a little," I say dramatically placing my hands on each side of his face, hoping the added drama might up my chances of success. I close my eyes and push his temples together. I pause.

Nothing.

I say it again followed by low humming of the *Rocky* theme.

Nothing.

I take a few steps back and start from the top.

"This may hurt a little," I say as if it was 'take one,' hands rising to his temples, I throw my head back, squint my eyes tightly.

Nada.

I do a twirl and spin and throw my hands up to his face, yet again, "This may hurt a little," this time said in a booming voice emitting deep from my chest.

Still nothing.

I drop to the floor and crawl toward him as if I've been stranded in the desert searching for water. I climb up his chair and exclaim, "This may hurt a little," I close my eyes, convinced this spectacle has got to get some attention.

Naught.

I turn to perform my next take—

"Stop," Dagan stares with wide eyes. "Stop. Whatever is happening, Miss Monroe." Shakes his head. "Method acting. I like your commitment to the role. But—uh—I don't think it's working right now."

My hair has become tangled during my performance. I pull it out of my clip to refasten. Xane stares at me from his chair.

"What. The. Hell. Was. That." A statement.

"It was an act of desperation," I say stretching out the barrette. *God, I could really use my friends back. I miss them all. I miss you, Shane*—I almost say the last four words out loud but catch myself. *The scent of leather fills my nose accompanied by a freshly lit cigarette. Sound of horse hooves on a dirt path. Shaky whirring images of scenery from a crazily horse-driven cart.*

Suddenly, the hair tie grows in my hand. The spiky vine expands retaining its round shape. Dried blood-spattered thorns pierce through a band of ancient metal. It grows to the size of a crown. A crown made of thorns. *Nearly identical to Jesus' Crown of Thorns. Maybe, those are the nails that crucified Jesus too…*

My hands shake violently at this transformation. *First the shoes, now this?* It's very, very heavy and sturdy.

"Lyvia… You've just unveiled the Crown of Thorns," a voice says in wonderment.

From my bag.

8

"Seph, you're supposed to be turned off." I carry the crown to my bag and shuffle around blindly with one hand, feeling for my Slab.

"I know, Lyvia, but the neural network down here has an extra barrier against the Framework. A somewhat spiritual barrier..." She trails off cryptically, as I pull her out.

"What's that about?" I look at Dagan.

"Hello, Dagan," Persephone transforms herself into a realistic hologram. She's life-size and opaque. You'd think she was 100% real if you didn't try to touch her. Today, she is dressed in green. Usually favoring neon colors, she's got on skinny jeans, a vintage t-shirt, and tennis shoes, all varying shades of glowing lime. Her dark straight hair is pulled up in a no-nonsense ponytail. She's thin and has a sprightly nature. She walks up next to him, pulling herself up to sit on the edge of the table. He looks on.

"We're going to need to get to know each other," she says, seeming to already know more about him than himself. Most Slab technological holograms have nothing on Persephone or most Dark Shire Slabs. Lunar technology allows for much better technological advances. Still, I have yet to see one as good as her. That's how I like it. Clearly, Dagan has never seen one so lifelike.

"What the hell? Is that your Slab?"

"Nope. That's Persephone."

"Hi, Dagan. I'd shake your hand if I could," she says smiling. "Wow. You've got a nice place here." She pops off the table and takes a look around.

"I can see you still love your old-school football," she muses, as she surveys the man cave. *Wow. Persephone is better than I thought. I'll be drilling her when we get a minute alone.*

"Seph, let's stay task-at-hand. What is this?" I ask, holding the crown.

"That, my Lyvia, is the Crown of Thorns. Worn by Jesus Christ, Himself," she replies, examining the intricate headwear I hold awkwardly.

"What does it do? Who is it from? How does it work? Why do I have it? Is this really from Jesus' head?" I spit out questions faster than I think them.

"Well, it goes with the nails, you know," she points to my shoes.

"What nails?" Dagan asks.

I ignore the question. "Seph. Why didn't you tell me any of this earlier at the station?" I ask, annoyed that my program knows more than me. A lot more, apparently.

"I wasn't positive it was completely secure, but here... Well, there's an impenetrable barrier. Nothing could get through," she says, eyeing Dagan suspiciously.

"Um, hi. Hey, guys. Would someone mind telling me what is happening right now?" A forgotten Xane interjects from his interrogation seat.

"Minute, Xane," I say, with a hand to silence him.

"Seriously guys, I can't—"

"Minute," I tell Xane again, this time dragging the word out slowly and loudly the way my aunt always did when we were kids and driving her crazy.

"What does it do, Perseph?"

"It gets you your telepathy back," she replies, lounging on the man cave couch. Bored. "Dagan, what's with the different teams up here?" She rolls on her back, pointing at the walls.

Dagan looks on aghast, and a little bit violated.

"It's really none of your—Persephone, is it?"

"Yup."

"None of your biz."

"Okay," she replies, brightly popping off the couch and rejoining us in the interrogation room.

"It gets them back, Seph?" I say, hopefully holding the crown tightly.

"Yup," she says, twirling her hair again.

"I just put it on?" I ask, still examining the weighty headwear.

"Yup, you just pop it on like this," she drags the last word out while she demonstrates by manufacturing her own glowing lime tiara, "and viola, the voices are back." She says this with the drama and flair of the Cheshire Cat. I think she's chewing bubble gum now. I roll my eyes.

"Okay," I turn back to Xane, putting the crown on my head. "This is probably gonna hurt a little." Once on my head, the crown feels weightless. Thorns push into my head, though not unpleasant. More like pressure point therapy.

"So, what now?"

"You don't hear anything?" Persephone asks from where she now lounges, a movie-theater recliner.

"Nope, Seph, just radio silence."

"Hmm," she says, now on the couch stomach-down, face cradled in hands looking upward thoughtfully. Her feet sway behind her head.

"Well, is there some password I need?"

"Nope. From what I know, your specific Onyx bloodline preordains access to the divine properties of certain holy relics instantaneously. No handbook required."

"What's with the lighthouse, Dagan?" She's in the man cave again, still looking at the wall of artifacts. There's a lighthouse near the top. I hadn't noticed it before. I wonder why it has piqued her interest.

It's a miniature replica of a white lighthouse at the end of a naturally made pier of rock. It juts into deep blue water, which I've seen in parts of the old northern United States and Canada. It was the deep, cold abyss of the rough and mean Atlantic Ocean, back when there was more than one ocean. I look away from the water that seems to be magically churning below the lighthouse.

"Seph, seriously. Task-at-hand," I look over to Dagan. "Sorry, she gets distracted easily and likes to be nosy."

"Nosy, like in how I found the alcove for you?" She asks now standing next to me, arms crossed, popping her bubblegum. I roll my eyes again. She knows better than to share that information with strangers.

"What alcove?" Dagan asks.

"Some old ancient one I was studying," I spew the lie out quickly. "Persephone. Please tell me how this thing works," I say, pointing to my new headpiece.

"Well," she's in the kitchen now sitting on the table, hugging her knees. She's got a Blow Pop in her mouth. I know it's cherry flavored, her favorite. She takes it out with an audible pop.

"The wearer has to be from the first Darken family's ancestry. Which you are," she says, pointing at me with her sucker. "Supposedly, it recognizes your bloodline and poof—you've got your friends back." When she says 'poof' she splays her hands open and hologram-created pixie dust explodes from her fingertips.

"Well, that's clearly not what's happening here, Seph," I say, exasperated.

"All right. Let me think." She's back in the interrogation room with us. "Xane, is it?" she asks, sitting on the edge of the table meeting his eyes.

"Uh, yes," he replies with trepidation.

"There's something familiar about you, Xane," she drawls, appearing to search his soul. "I can't pinpoint it, but I will." With this, she mounts off the table and joins Dagan and I on the other side.

"Well, guys," she says conspiratorially, making us three a tiny circle. She's got her back to our 'prisoner.' She's whispering loudly. Xane is three feet away.

"I think he knows more than he lets on," she deduces.

"Thanks for the conclusive observation," I say, frustration growing. "We already know this." I look at Dagan for some back-up. His facial expression is clearly painted with, 'You brought her to the party. She's all yours.'

"Seph, can you and I talk a moment, privately?" I ask her, hoping if I get her undivided attention, we can make some progress. Yet, I'm also quite aware I never really have her undivided attention.

"Sure thing, boss."

She's already waiting for me in the man cave. I walk over, not possessing her magical hologram powers. Once in the area, I motion her over to the loveseat at the back of the room. We are out of the eyesight of the boys. Remember, this is a huge area down here. I climb up the massive chair, pull my knees up under my chin, and hug my legs.

"Can they hear us, Seph?"

"Nope," she says, popping up next to me, also hugging her knees. "The acoustics in this area make it impossible. He designed it that way, but I'm not sure why. Hmm. I'll find out, Lyvia."

"Okay, Seph, but not right now," I say sighing, although, I do really want her to get to the bottom of the entire Dagan mystery. *One thing at a time.*

"The crown..." She trails off while looking up at an imaginary sky.

"Yes, the crown," I say, pointing at my head in an attempt to bring her back to the present.

"Okay, Lyvia," she says, snapping to and staring into my eyes. "It is in fact the crown Jesus wore. It is a spiritual object. This means that it can cross all planes in its material form yet retaining its spiritual properties."

"What." An assertion. "All three of them?"

"Yup. Heaven, Earth, and Hell," she replies, looking at Dagan's walls. "What do you think is up with the—"

"Focus." I cut her off.

"Okay. The three planes. Only someone who can cross over the three planes can use the object. So, Jesus, for example, because He is God. God passed down certain objects to specifically chosen families during ancient times. The initial Darken family bloodline just so happens to be one," she says this while trying on hats in an imaginary mirror. She settles on a lime green winter hat complete with earflaps. Doesn't even faze me. I'm used to her hologram shenanigans.

"Does that mean I can cross over the three planes?"

"Kind of, yes," she replies. "The chosen ones can, anyway."

"I'm chosen?" I ask. Not sure I possess the traits that God would choose me for.

"Your ancestors were given the relic. Only the chosen ones in your bloodline can use it on all three planes."

"So, my family has had this since the beginning… And it has spiritual powers. What about the shoes, Seph?" I ask, pointing to my feet.

"Oh yes, the shoes." She's got the hat off now, her no-nonsense ponytail back. She lies stomach down, feet swaying behind her head again, her face propped up with one hand as she thoughtfully examines the shoes.

"Well, you probably already figured out that they are two of the Nails of the Cross, the ones used to pierce Jesus' hands."

"So, there's a third?"

"Yes, but it's elsewhere…" she trails off. Another mystery I can't explore right now.

"How does it all work? I mean, the shoes just did it on their own. What can they do? Just open tombs?"

"Oh no," she says, now trying on different footwear. Clover green ballet flats don her feet. "They do a lot more than that." Now she's got lime green, almost neon yellow socks on, with glowing green Birkenstocks.

"Like what?" I ask.

"Well, they can…" A voice in the other room cuts her off.

"Lyvia, anytime now. We gotta question the perp," Dagan bellows. It's so muffled I can barely hear it, but I still heard it. I look at Seph.

"This loveseat is inaudible. Protected by an invisible sound barrier. You can hear them, but not the other way around."

"Okay, Seph. He's right. We gotta get back. We can talk about all the rest of this stuff later. How does this thing work?" I say, again pointing to the crown.

"Lyvia, it's supposed to just work," she replies, clearly perplexed.

"Oh God, I could really use your help right now," I say, reaching up to the sky-high ceiling, a plea to the heavens. "And I really miss you, Shane," I add quietly.

Hanging my head, I turn toward the man cave entryway. Suddenly, I feel a prick on my head, not painful, but unpleasant.

"What the…" I put my hand up to the crown. The thorns begin to push into my skull; not piercing the skin but feeling as if they might. The pricks become more intense. I start to think I'm bleeding. I get a decapitating headache and fall to my knees.

"You got it, Lyvia," Persephone exclaims, hopping and clapping.

I don't hear or see her though. I have both hands on my head. I feel warm sticky wetness. I squint my eyes open and see red crimson on my fingertips. The pain is blinding. I feel as if my head might explode. I start to take the crown off, anything to stop the pain, but then it subsides as quick as it came.

"Whoa," I say, standing up. The blood is gone.

"You hear em, yet, Lyvia?" Persephone asks, inquisitively searching my face.

"No," I answer, frustrated I may have gone through excruciating pain for nothing.

"Not yet," she replies knowingly.

"Guys," Dagan's voice.

"Coming," I say, my voice becoming audible as I cross to the interrogation room.

Xane and Dagan sit across from each other. Xane looks bored. Dagan looks borderline homicidal.

"You get it to work? This guy is driving me nuts," he says.

"Who? Me?" Xane asks innocently. "I'd say you just heard a pretty interesting story—free of charge, I might add."

"Oh, story time!" Persephone exclaims, taking my unoccupied seat across from Xane. She steeples her hands under her face expectantly.

"Well, so this one time, my buddies and I decide to go out to the lake. Good ole' Georgie has to go to the bathroom, which was more like one of those old-ass outhouses, and there's this bee in there, it goes right up his shorts and he runs—"

"Dude. I really don't wanna hear this story again," Dagan says, leaning back in his chair, looking bored. Persephone and I whip our heads around to venomously stare at our rude interjector. Then, we return our gaze to Xane.

"Did he get stung?" an enraptured Persephone asks from her seat.

"Well, he came running out with his shorts around his ankles and a look of panic on his face," Xane shakes his head, laughing. "He didn't get stung. But, he did miss the toilet because of the whole thing and sprinted to the lake, jumping in to wash the piss off." Xane laughs as if that was the funniest story he's ever told.

Persephone joins in. "So, you guys are just standing there

watching the scene play out—an invisible terror." She is cracking up. Dagan and I are not amused.

"It was even worse the first time," Dagan states, deadpan.

I stand there plotting my next action. I can't hear anybody, but that doesn't mean much. I've got to try. I figure if I add my theatrical flair, it may help this time. Fingers crossed.

From the top...

"This may..."

"Hurt a little," Xane and Dagan finish simultaneously, complete with eye rolls.

It doesn't affect my performance.

"...hurt a little."

I thrust my hands to his head and push his temples together. Nothing.

I sigh leaving my hands in place. I look up and silently pray for something to happen. Nothing. About to give up, I start to remove my hands.

"OW!" Xane wails.

A rushing light fills my senses. I see only white. A loud whooshing blocks out all sound. A stream of pictures replaces the light. I know what this is. The telepathy has returned.

I see Georgie sprinting to the lake as if he's on fire. The water is glittering in the sunlight. I'm looking through Xane's eyes. He's laughing. The next image he's younger, sitting on the couch watching *The Ten Commandments*. He's mad. I think he's in a time-out. His mother sits next to him, enjoying the film.

Now, he's older than he was at the lake. I recognize the setting—Gold Shire Coliseum. He looks down at his right arm. He's being marked with the Golden signal. He's nervous and apprehensive but follows through and gets marked.

A little older, but not much, he sits on a bed. It's a bunk room, where the younger Lighters have to start their resource training. He's reading a book on the Framework. He's bored out of his mind. It's torture. He's wishing he transferred shires. Ruby or Mortal, he thinks wistfully. But then, around the same age, he's sitting across from a beautiful girl... Through his eyes, she's lit from behind angelically. He's nervous. So is she.

Now some time later, but again not much, I see from Xane's eyes —him. It's Levi. Front and center, he's putting on his show back in Gold Coliseum. I see only Lighters at this performance. He's got his guitar and is playing something I haven't heard before. And, I've heard a lot of his stuff. I mentally shake my head at my previous stupidity.

"Okay, everybody. Now that we're all together, I need to go over some things," he says, putting his guitar away.

Levi is wearing his typical 'uniform.' He's a rock star. Slim jeans, white t-shirt, bowler-style tennis shoes, and a fitted leather jacket completes the ensemble. He's six feet tall and well-built. He's got medium-length, wavy hair tucked behind his ears, and a well-groomed beard. With his thick brown hair and ice blue eyes, he resembles classic actor Travis Fimmel. Gorgeous rocker. I mentally roll my eyes. *This guy.*

"I know you're all excited…" he trails off, going to sit on his stool, center stage. He perches on the stool; one leg carelessly rests on its lowest rung. One elbow carelessly rests on a thigh. He's so at ease. It's his element.

The crowd is sitting restless and eager. I can see girls about to swoon. I want to gag and tell them he's really not all that.

Xane is different though. Despite the Lighter girl he met, he's still uneasy in his new home. He has trepidation and worry. I need to know where this is coming from. Either he's just smart and knows some of what I know, or he knows more than me. Hopefully, the scene will continue to enlighten. I'm getting mentally drained from my new device.

Levi surveys the audience. He looks up at the ceiling. He loves drama and loves teasing even more. He revels in his moments of silent suspense.

"Those of you Inner-circle, you know your role. I assume you all know it by now, Inner, Middle, and Outer. Inside and out. If not, please find your counselors to get all the information. You know how big this is. It's our Great Reveal," he says the last two words spreading his hands outwardly as a magician about to perform the most impossible trick known to man. Which, knowing Levi, might actually be.

The crowd awes at his hand gesture. Again, I want to puke.

"I expect all of you have your directions memorized. This is incredibly important." He stands up and looks into the crowd. He spots him.

"Xane."

Xane jolts back in his seat. He did not expect to get called out. I'm wondering why the hell he did. What does he know? With my telepathy, I can't read exact thoughts, unless it's in real time. When I recede into memories, I take on the receiver's senses and emotions, not necessarily thoughts or previous knowledge. In addition to being inside Xane's head, I can also occupy space outside of him within the memories, similar to an invisible hologram. I'm sitting in the empty seat next to him. Levi looks at the seat, and I swear his eyes meet mine. *Impossible.* Memories cannot be changed. I'm invisible. He should have absolutely no clue that I'm present. I get a chill.

His eyes shift to Xane, "Did you finish the book?"

"Uh, yeah," he replies. I can feel guilt at his deception.

"Oh, Xane. Xane, Xane," Levi drawls out. "Tsk, tsk, tsk, dude. Ya can't fool me."

Xane is in disbelief. And a little scared.

"So, what I'm gonna do is promote you to Middle-circle status. Then Willow will be able to help you out," he says with a wink.

Xane looks at Willow across the room. It's the girl from the earlier memory. She's still lit from behind. Willow smiles shyly.

"Okay everybody," Levi calls with a handclap. "We've got one week. Seven days to make it great." He walks over to his guitar, picks it up so naturally you'd think he was born with one in hand. A few opening licks and I'm transported to the present.

The crown releases its pressure. I open my eyes to find Xane passed out. That happens sometimes. It was a mental roller coaster for him.

"Whoa," Dagan says, stunned. "Is he gonna be okay?"

I don't respond right away. I'm trying to distill my new information. The crown shrinks back down to a barrette. I secure it in my hair.

"Oh, him?" I point to Xane. "He'll be fine. Some water and an aspirin when he comes to. He's gotta man up."

"What'd ya see?" Persephone asks excitedly.

"Enough to know Xane's got some questions to answer when he's finished with his beauty sleep."

"That's good and all, but how will it help us?" Dagan asks.

"Yeah, how will it?" Persephone chimes in antsy, next to Dagan.

I look at my audience. All two members eagerly waiting for me to give the big answer. *Jeez, I've got nothin'.*

"I didn't get much, but Xane is more important than we thought. Levi personally singled him out of the crowd and asked if he read 'the book.' Which initially, I assumed was the book of Framework, but now I'm not so sure."

"You saw Levi?" Persephone asks, concerned. She's more than a little aware of my history with him.

"Yes, he was putting on one of his 'shows,'" I say, rolling my eyes.

"Did he do that thing?" she asks.

"No, not this time. Or, at least not while I was there," I answer. He and I had a secret signal when he was entertaining the masses. He'd find me in the crowd, cock an eyebrow, twirl, point finger guns at me and wink—very Michael Scott. He knew how much I loved *The Office*. Now, I cannot believe the nerve. *Yuck.*

Dagan sits passively observing our exchange. Smart.

"What did he talk about?"

"Well, time-wise, it was a week before the Great Reveal. He was hyping everybody up. Played some new songs at the opening and closing."

Persephone looks to the ceiling and fakes a yawn.

"I know," I reply exasperated. "He was telling everyone they should have their roles memorized by now. I don't think Xane even had one yet. In fact, I'm starting to suspect the Rookie Lighters had very, very little knowledge of his plan. So, he promotes Xane to Middle-circle, telling him he can work with someone on that level to get ready."

I don't mention Willow. Seems too personal. Especially knowing that Levi uses people for his gain relentlessly and drops them just as quickly when they're no longer of use.

"And?" Dagan asks, reminding us of his presence.

"And, that's it," I say, a little defeated.

"No," he's says positively. "Now we've got some specific questions. Ya done good."

Kid. I finish the sentence in my head. It was a quote from *The Office* that my brother said to me all the time. Sharp pang. This one is very sharp.

"Kid," Persephone finishes out loud. "Ya done good, kid." She is standing in front of me with wide earnest eyes.

"Thank you. Both of you," I say, turning to Dagan.

"Ow," a voice garbles.

9

Xane lifts his head and blinks his eyes open repeatedly.

"That sucked," he says, looking at me violated, as if I just walked in on him naked.

I don't know what it feels like for the other person. I haven't had it done to me. However, from my point-of-view, it feels like I'm visiting the corner of your mind. I walk into your head and you know I'm there, but you can't do anything about it because your reminiscences can't be changed. It gets worse, because the receiver knows what's going to happen, whether they like it or not. It's his own memory and cannot be altered. As far as I know. Levi's stare flashes through my mind.

"Well, ya know Georgie now," Xane laughs. I picture him trying to run with shorts around his ankles. I laugh.

"Xane, what was the book?" I ask eagerly.

"*The Complete History of Technology*," he replies.

I look at Dagan pointedly. He bows his head. And I think—smirks. *I can't even.*

"What was your job?" I ask.

"I had to memorize literature," he replies.

"*History of Technology*?" I ask.

"No, something way different."

I realize how easily he is now answering questions. I know it's because of Willow. "It was a book about Heaven," he says. "And not like Darkens' Heaven. It was talking about a *new* Heaven."

Darkens study all Theology. Some have been given the gift to communicate with the Spirit World. My entire family has the gift. It can run in bloodlines; although, there are members of other shires who also have it.

"A *new* Heaven?" I ask.

"Yeah, the thing is, apparently, Levi found a new way to speak to the Spirit World, but it's different. With the upgraded Framework system, you get to physically go there."

"Who was given the literature?" Dagan asks.

"Gold Shire was first. That's all I know. But not everyone—only those selected 'at this time.' It seemed as if it was supposed to be given out strategically. I don't know if we all got the same thing. And that's it, that's all I got, nothing about anyone else's role. Not even..." He trails off, undoubtedly thinking of Willow.

"So why are you out here, Xane?" Dagan asks.

"Good question," Persephone pipes in.

"Yeah," I add, deciding to gang-up on him.

"Hey, guys, we're on the same team, I promise you that. I was gonna transfer out a long time ago but didn't. I wouldn't mind leaving now, actually. If all the circumstances were to fit together."

I know what he means. He can't leave if Willow doesn't. "Okay, Xane, maybe we can work together," I say slowly.

"I came out here immediately after the Great Reveal was supposed to happen. I was told to check the entire area for any sign of Levi. They think he's hiding out in Crystal. I'm not so sure, myself. The guy's a magician; one second he's there, then—poof," he says, flicking his fingers out. "He's gone. But gone, gone, you know? With the new Framework, we should be able to locate him instantly. The thing is, he designed it. So, he could easily avoid detection."

"Okay, Xane, but people can't just disappear. I don't care who you are," Dagan says. "Maybe when the world was bigger before the second Rain, but with today's advancements, and the decreased size of land, there's just no way. Even in Crystal. I think we should keep looking for him." He directs the last part at me.

"Xane, is there any information you may have to give us a jump-start?" I ask.

"The only information I have is the literature," he says.

"Do you have it with you?" Persephone asks.

"Yeah, I do," he says and pulls out a small gold rolled-up book from his left pocket. I'm surprised it's a paper book. Then again, to avoid technological detection, it's the best idea.

"We were supposed to memorize the information, then destroy the book. I haven't memorized it yet," he says, looking downward, handing it over. Dagan takes it and starts flipping through quickly.

"Are they going to be looking for you?" Persephone asks, appearing on the table, legs dangling over the side. I notice she's back in her lime green tennis shoes.

"Good question, Seph," I say, with my eyes on Dagan. He's back to the beginning of the book reading more carefully.

"Probably. Yeah. Most likely," Xane says, leaning back in the chair, looking bored again.

"What's the plan?" I ask Dagan. "We can't have them coming out here. Who knows what could happen? They'll want to question us."

"Did you read the whole thing?" Dagan asks Xane, ignoring me.

"Well, most of it," Xane replies, looking at the ceiling.

"What does it say?" I ask Dagan.

"I need to read it over more carefully," he replies. This comment does not surprise me. He seems to be someone very thorough with absorbing and dissecting new information before coming to comprehensive conclusions.

He continues—

"...but it seems like his book is incomplete. It doesn't include the entirety of the plan. Actually, not even close. It's extremely vague, lots of propaganda."

"Xane, when were you supposed to check in?" I ask.

"I don't know. What time is it?" he asks.

Rain. The sound of rain suddenly fills the entire basement. I think it's a symptom, but everyone's faces suggest otherwise. It's so real, I actually put my hand out to see if I can feel it.

"We've got company," Dagan said. "But that's the first alarm. Means they're just about twenty-five miles from the outskirts of the forest."

"Okay, but I'm sure they have vehicles," I say nervously.

Main transportation in the Realm is provided by the SkyChariot, a giant futuristic train that runs the length of, and around the entire Realm. Otherwise, people have personal vehicles, both ancient and novel. Ancient ones are not only restored but equipped with modernization. Still, there are a lot of collectors that have been able to keep even the most archaic vehicles in factory condition. Each shire's preferred mode of transportation depends on their resources and specialties. For example, Shire Turquoise uses boats and many other modes of aquatic transport, as well as Sandies, which resemble old-world sand buggies. Plus, they've got air travel, such as jets and planes. Emerald favors trucks and updated tractors, called Crawlers.

"Yeah, they've got Goldsters. Every Inner-circle has one," Xane replies, still looking bored. I stare at him incredulously. How is he so calm right now?

Goldsters resemble hotrods. Even I have to admit they're pretty badass. The closest thing to compare would be the archaic 1977 Ford Thunderbird Coupe T-Top. They're more sophisticated because they're fitted with Framework. However, shape and style—identical.

"Shit. That means they could be here in twenty minutes."

"They still gotta get through the woods and my other preventative measures. So, we need to get Xane back without them seeing us. And we need to do it before they hit the forest, or we will have a real problem on our hands," Dagan says.

I can only imagine as to what he means by that. "Other preventative measures"—looking around his lair, I don't want to know what they are.

"Ugh," Xane sighs in his chair. "I really don't want to go back."

"Yes, you do, Xane," I say, meeting his eyes, an unspoken reminder.

"Yeah, yeah, I know," he replies.

"So, he goes back and gets more intel. They're gonna be watching for him because he just fell off the face of the earth. And, they're gonna be looking for where he was last pinpointed. How are you gonna get him back to his people? How will he get Willow and escape?" Persephone asks. *Wow. She knows about Willow. What else does she know about these guys? I gotta get her alone.*

"They're not my people," Xane mutters. I ignore him.

"Do you have any suggestions, Seph? Or should we just keep asking the obvious?"

"Well, my suggestion is… Me," she says, swinging off the table.

"How so?" Dagan asks.

"Well, I infiltrate Gold Shire," she says, pacing back-and-forth, thoughtfully.

"What? Seph, you know the Slab has to be in the shire, and more importantly—within twenty feet the Coliseum to get you in there."

"Well, I never said I had all the details," she says, examining the interrogation rotary phone.

"Is this operational?" she asks.

"Well, it's—" Dagan starts.

"Persephone." I interject in my sternest voice.

"Okay. Well, you're gonna have to figure that part out. But if you get me in there, I can get so much intel," she says, twirling her ponytail. "And figure out the best strategy to get Xane and Willow out."

"Who's Willow?" Dagan asks.

"Not important right now," I say. "Do you know how tight security is in Gold right now? Even if we can get close enough, we could get captured."

"Use the Holy Nails," Persephone answers, now lying on the couch with her arms crooked behind her head.

"How?" I ask.

"They protect you from the Framework," she replies. "Give one to Dagan and you guys will be set."

"We'll need to be able to communicate totally free of Frame. Completely off grid."

"I might be able to help with that," Dagan says.

I raise my eyebrows.

"Just because I don't have Holy Relics doesn't mean I don't have a few tricks up my sleeves." He walks to a wooden door on the other side of the massive space.

I quickly fall in behind. He swipes his kist key and the door rolls open slowly. Inside is a closet, actually more of an infinite hallway. Although narrow, the walls stretch very high and there is no visible end. Shelves line the walls floor-to-ceiling. Resting on their surfaces— ancient artifacts. I spot a Sega Genesis video game console and controllers. *Geographic shapes. Cubes drifting down. Electronic chords fill my ears with a progressively rushed melody. Please be a line. Please be a line. I need one horizontally. Desperately.* I beat *Tetris* on that game console once, my claim to fame. I had unearthed a functioning system. With a little tweaking, I had it back and running in no time.

VHS tapes and DVDs, a Discman, a boom box, CDs and cassettes —Red Hot Chili Peppers, Eminem, Justin Bieber's *Purpose*, Kid Rock's entire collection, even the one featuring "Chicken in A Pen," a favorite of mine and Shane's. *Curiouser by the minute.* 4 Non Blondes, Led Zeppelin, Blind Melon, lots of rap. Many others.

A myriad of vintage toys litters some shelves. A Talkboy from *Home Alone*. A Stretch Armstrong doll; his rubbery limbs beckon for me to pull. Beanie Babies slouch on top of each other. A Teddy Rupskin sits patiently waiting for someone to press 'record.' A View-Master is propped up on a stack of circular film-strips. I wonder what's on them.

Stacked board games: Clue, Candyland, Sorry. A Skip-it and a Bop-it lean against each other, old comrades posing after a win. I see a Mattel Magic Nursery My Bundle Baby doll, *unopened*. I had one as a kid. I don't know where my parents found it. They always surprised us on Christmas with impossible-to-find gifts. Supersoaker squirt guns, a collection of Street Shark figurines still in plastic, and Razor Scooter hangs upside down on a shelf. It takes everything in my power not to rip open that Bundle Baby doll to find out if it's a girl or boy, or twins. *Please be twins.*

Large, very old cameras pose on dust-free shelves, both film and flash. Old photo books are arranged in neat stacks. In fact, everything is neat. As far as the eye can see, all the items are organized perfectly. *Do I sense a little OCD? Not that I can talk.* Antique typewriters. One has an aged piece of paper loaded in the type bar. There's one line. It's too small for me to see. I don't snoop but curiosity nags, a toddler ceaselessly tugging my hair. I ignore the chubby baby fingers and continue my scan.

Neat rows of vinyl records and a player. Floppy disks and very archaic computers, then some newer models and laptops. Newspapers, antiquated paper currency, and coins too. I spot musical instruments; a drum set and acoustic guitar. I spot clothes where the closet curves from sight. Way too far down to really look, but there is a shelf lined with hats above the clothing-draped hangers. *Me thinks someone might be a hoarder...*

Dagan walks in about fifty feet and scans the shelves. He finds what he's looking for, reaches up, grabs the items, and walks toward me. We head out and the door closes behind us. In his hands, he carries two very old walkie-talkies. They're small. The size of very outmoded cellphones—the Nokia kind with the snake game on it. I was good at that one too.

"Those work?" I ask, as he turns them on and hands me one.

"Breaker, breaker one-nine, over and out." His voice crackles from my speaker.

"That's a ten-four, breaker, Roger that copy. Out and over," my voice speaks from his device.

"I don't think that's the proper usage of prowords," Persephone comments.

"I'm new at this," I reply, laughing.

"Okay, okay. We can go over the details for this part, once we get Xane back to the forest," Dagan says, unlatching Xane's right arm.

"He's right," I say.

"Ugh. I don't wanna go back," Xane says, rubbing his arm.

"Xane. Yes, you do. We're going to do some recon," I say with a wink to Seph. *See, I can use prowords correctly.* "You need to go back and keep doing exactly what you've been doing. You cannot act suspicious in the least. We still have a lot to figure out about Levi. Just play your role. We'll contact you when we get the back-half figured out."

"What time is it?" I ask Persephone.

"It is 8:23p.m." she says, back in the room.

I need to message Regina and let her know I'm okay. I feel badly for missing dinner. "Seph, can you send Regina a note? Let her know I don't know when I'll be back."

"Already did," she replies brightly. "I didn't want to be rude."

Regina's cheery voice plays out from the Slab. "Take your time honey. I figured ya might have an adventure out in those crazy woods. Take care, sweetie, and I'll see you when I see you."

"Thanks, Seph," I say, looking around the room. "We ready?"

Persephone vanishes in a poof of glittery smoke. I stick my walkie and Slab in my bag. Dagan's fits in his back pocket.

He takes us through the tunnels and back up to the main floor. It's dark, both outside and in. The floor lights up, but other than that, utter blackness. I'm disappointed I can't get another look at the layout.

Once outside, the trek through the woods is quiet and uneventful. The crickets' chirp drowns out all other noise.

"That's the clearing up there," Dagan says, pointing to a break in foliage.

We quickly stage Xane's performance and go over his lines. We have about five minutes before the Lighters will get to him. We find a massive tree trunk about ten feet away from where Xane lies. It's big enough to hide both of us, comfortably.

We wait in silence until we hear voices. Xane continues to feign sleep on the ground.

10

"I think the signal was last seen here," a voice says. It's a guy. Young, probably Xane's age.

"I see him. Xane—hey—hey, Xane, you all right, bud?" a second voice says. This one is also male, also young.

"Huh?" Xane asks, sounding—in fact—very dazed. I roll my eyes.

"Xane, what happened?" the first voice asks.

"I-I-I-I don't know," he says confused. "I was walking on the path and I tripped." I can see a light shine over the path. The spotlight lands on the large branch we placed front and center.

"You've got a nasty black eye," the second voice says.

I sneak a look at Dagan. He smirks.

"I think I fell face first."

"Oh, man, there's blood on the branch," the first voice says, shining a light over.

I rub my cloth-covered hand where I cut it. Not deep of course, there wasn't much blood with the actual wound.

"Jeez," Xane's voice says, 'surprised.'

"Well, we left the Goldster out at the library. So, we have a little bit of a hike, but we can get ya back to the Coliseum and get one of the on-call Grey Docs to look atcha." The professions of the Mortal Shire include all medical fields. Those performing medical duties are often called Grey Docs.

"Okay," Xane says, standing up. "Man, I feel like I was punched by The Pazmanian Devil." He's referring to a one Vinny Pazienza, a classic boxer from back in the day. This is not a line we rehearsed. I sneak a look at Dagan. He shrugs.

"Hey, did you guys find him?" Xane asks, intelligently changing the subject.

"No, man, nothing. Nobody got any word from anybody 'bout it," the first voice replies. We see the three walk up the path. Bouncing spotlights dot the trees.

"What now?" I whisper to Dagan.

"Hey, Miss 'My-Accessories-Turn-Into-Holy-Relics'—you tell me!" he exclaims.

"Well, Vinny," I say, arching an eyebrow. "We gotta get to the Coliseum. The train will take too long."

He stands up and starts walking. I rush to catch up.

"I've got a Camocar not far from here," he says nonchalantly. A Camocar is a vehicle designed to act as a chameleon. It's made of glass and works as a two-way mirror, although transparent, not reflective. The inhabitants are concealed completely. There are not many in existence. In fact, I thought they were all gone a long time ago. *Who is this guy?*

I follow in the moonlight. It's bright enough to see fairly clearly. We come to a tiny clearing that appears empty. 'Ironman' pulls out his kist key and the vehicle turns opaque. It's shiny black now and resembles an old-world Porsche.

"Wow. Tony Stark, you are just full of surprises," I say.

He looks at me sardonically. "Really. You're the one traipsing around with her very own female Jarvis," he says.

"Touché."

The vehicle is so small I can see that it will easily make its way through the trees. He opens the door for me, and I step into another location that is much bigger than it appears on the outside. *It must be a Crystal thing.*

He maneuvers around the trees with ease—his direction rote. We emerge from the forest twenty miles from the path I took. We turn onto a concrete bridge over the same brook which nearly claimed my life by way of dental floss. Yes, a *concrete* bridge.

"Okay, so what's the plan?" I ask.

"Well, we each take a nail, right?" Dagan says.

"Yep," Persephone's muffled voice replies.

I pull gold, strappy shoes from my bag to switch out of my current warrior sandals. I slip on the new heels and tie their gold ribbons into bows behind my ankles.

Holding the sandals in my hands, I ask, "Are they going to transform into nails?"

"Not sure," she says. "But it doesn't matter what form they're in."

"Okay. So, we have to get through the gates... I can't go in the front."

"How come?" he asks.

"I just can't."

"Okay."

"Can you?"

"No."

"How come?"

"I just can't," he says seriously.

Okay. More mystery. I won't pry, because there is no way in hell I'm divulging why I can't go in there. "So, the hard way," I say, speculatively.

"The hard way," he echoes.

We still have a while left in the drive. Crystal and Gold are on opposite ends of the vertical and slightly ovular Realm. Gold on the north end, Crystal on the south. It's a couple hours' drive even in a Camocar. I rifle around in my bag for suitable attire. I feel a familiar loose flowy dress, very pale champagne gold. It's short and resembles a slip. I find my nude trench coat as well, same length. This bag is bottomless. *I'm Mary Poppins with a sling-back, as opposed to a carpet-bag. Who knew?*

I remember the hidden entrance to the Coliseum. One I frequented back in the day. It's an underground tunnel—usually manned though. I can probably stall whoever's on duty long enough to get Seph in there for a quick scan. I pull a chin-length angular crimson wig out of my bag.

"You sure this is your first time?" Dagan asks with a sideway look.

"Yes, this is just for my day-job," I say, adjusting the red bob in the mirror. I hate this one.

"I like the blonde better," Dagan muses, watching the road.

"My thoughts exactly," I reply, donning nonprescription cat-eye rimmed glasses, reminiscent of Miss Monroe in *Some Like It Hot*. I walk into the back of the car. Yes, walk. It's massive inside. I press a button and a screen appears between Dagan and I.

"This mean you got us a plan?" he asks.

"A dash of a plan," I say, flicking my fingers over an imaginary culinary dish.

"Would you like to share it with the team?"

"Of course," I answer, changing out of my Crystal wear and into that of Gold.

"I know a secret entrance. I'm going to go up there and distract whoever's on duty. While I stall whoever is there, Persephone can do a quick scan," I tell him, moving to the front of the vehicle.

"What do you need from me?"

"I need you to get Seph up there."

"I can't get near there, Lyvia," he says.

"Don't worry, I'll have them occupied. You'll run up the tunnel and get twenty feet from the building. She does her thing. Silently, I might add."

"Copy that," Seph's voice, garbled by fabric.

"Then you get back to the car and wait for me. Twenty minutes, no more. Longer than twenty, you leave. Trust me on that."

"I'm not gonna just leave you. It'd be such a waste after saving your life and all."

"I won't die. Trust me. I'll be able to handle it. Just leave after twenty."

"Okay," he reluctantly agrees.

"When I get the guard away from the entrance, I'm going to signal you," I pull out the walkie and hit a button. His walkie beeps once. Short. Quiet.

"Then I get twenty feet from the building and open your Slab."

"Yep. Just flip her open and Seph can do the rest," I reply, applying red lipstick. It's not easy. The Camocar does not boast the smoothest ride. Still, if I'm going to Gold, I need my armor.

The roads through Emerald and Ruby are curvy and disjointed. Rugged terrain marks the area. Vegetation and hills require loopy paved pathways.

"Welp, hopefully your dash of a plan pans out."

"Hopefully."

We transcend into downtown Ruby. This is where the landscape morphs into city. Ruby's sky-high garnet-encrusted buildings stretch to the clouds. The streets are paved in varying shades of deep red stones, same as the buildings. What isn't gemstone is black marble. There's no traffic. It's late, but the city is alive as usual.

Teenagers loiter beneath a streetlamp on a corner, looking for customers. Probably peddling blulix, short for blue elixir, a modern drug. It affects everyone differently: enhances humans, tweaks brain activity to amplify your greatest abilities, turns you into a genius, artist, star athlete—nearly superhuman. The side effects are nasty, though. I've seen it firsthand.

A bench homes a body for the night, a breathing pile of dirty mismatched clothes. Ruby Tower stretches in front of us. As we pass by the massive structure, I can't help but think of Dorothy's red slippers.

Soon rubies start to get replaced by various shades of stonework— Granite. Granite is urban, same as downtown Ruby, although, everything is constructed with rock. What isn't built from granite is glass. All the stonework in the city is sculpted. It's one gigantic mural. Pictures swirl on the sides of buildings and flow into statues. The rock is sanded and smoothed. They gleam in the night's glow.

We continue north and my stomping grounds descend. Since it's already night, there is no visual cue to alert: "You are now entering the Lunar Shire." I don't need that though. I know this place. It's in my bones. The road is paved in shiny black onyx. The sky is filled with stars; they loom so close you think you can catch one. It's more rural here, as is Crystal, just flatter. We pass by lake after lake. The rivers flow through the land and create tranquil pools making the Lunar Shire a woodsy paradise.

We roll the windows down and humidity envelops the car. The hot sticky air tastes of home. It's delicious. *Scent of bonfire. Resonance of gentle lapping waves. Popping fireworks in the distance. Taste gooey chocolatey marshmallow with a crunch.*

"Okay. We need codenames," Dagan breaks the silence.

"Why? It's only me and you. I think we can recognize each other's voices, and it's a secure line," I say, tasting the sticky night air. Sweet.

Cherry ChapStick. I rub imaginary balm across my lips, nearly tasting its saccharine fruity flavor.

"Listen, listen. It'll be cool. Umm... I'll be Stark."

"Ah, so you liked that Ironman reference, Tony? Okay, Stark it is."

His laugh is contagious.

"Okay, okay," I say, giggles subsiding. "I'm Harley."

"As in, the motorcycles? Those were cool."

"No. As in Harley Quinn."

"The Joker's girlfriend?"

"Yep."

Moment of silence.

"She's pretty nuts."

I laugh, saying, "I'm known to be a little nuts."

The trees begin to thin, causing my stomach to clench. We pass the tree line. The natural border between Heaven and Hell. Lush green grass is covered in flowers. The slightly hilly terrain gradually turns from onyx to gold brick. Gold Shire is both rural and urban, like Ruby. The Coliseum is located in the downtown area. Gold is where you go for shows, celebrity sightings, gambling, shopping, you name it. It's the Las Vegas and Hollywood of present. It's all about the Gold. The buildings condense and the giant Coliseum comes into sight. I start to get nervous.

"Okay, so I'm going to go in and..."

"Distract..."

"Right, distract. I'm going to go in and distract. You're going to sneak up with Seph." I rub my hands on my bare thighs.

"Hey, we don't have to do this," Dagan says with a tone of worry.

"No, no, it's fine. We do. I just don't know which one I'm dealing with."

"Which one what? Or who?"

"Who. It's a who. Who I'll be dealing with."

"Levi?"

"No, he's still hiding."

"Who?"

"Don't worry about it. I told you no matter what, I'll be fine. You just need to leave after—"

"Twenty minutes." He cuts me off.

"Yeah," I say, with a deep exhale.

I direct him around the curvy hidden passageway. It twists around the building then dips below ground level. About forty feet he turns the car back around and parks.

"You got this?" he asks. Concerned.

"Yeah, I got this," I sigh, stepping onto the gold-pebbled walkway. It's not just gold in the city. It's lined with canary diamonds and other yellow gemstones—only the best, though.

"I'll push this when I'm in," I say, touching the walkie-talkie I have snug in my bra underneath my arm. Flattened warrior sandal snug on the other side. I really hope I don't have to take my coat off. I hand Dagan my other shoe.

"Perfect," Dagan replies, patting his pocket where my right shoe now rests.

"Okay, see ya in twenty," I say, spinning on my toes and strolling down the yellow brick road.

THE STRUCTURE IS MASSIVE. Also made of gold. It's tall and shaped as an amphitheater. *Of course.* When I reach the spot where the tunnel dips below ground, I lose sight of the architecture. The tunnel gets dark. I know the turns by heart. I see a glow around the last corner. I stop and take a breath. *Please don't be Gustav. Please don't be Gustav.*

I round the corner. Chad. Huge breath of relief. I can handle Chad with my eyes shut. My heels echo their click-clack around the bend; it opens into a huge gold lobby. Extravagant.

Chad is slouched in a large gilded couch. He looks up from his Slab. Long dirty blonde curly hair. Twenty-five. Cute. Untrustworthy but for the most part harmless. *Please just be him.*

"Hey Chad," I call with a wave, click-clacking my way over.

"Lyvia, is that you?" he asks, standing up.

"That it is," I say with a little spin—gotta grease the wheels. "How are you doing, Chadry?"

"Not too bad, Lyvia. Not too bad," he drawls. "You lookin' for Levi? He's not here."

"Really? That sucks," I reply, clearing my throat. "I need a drink."

"You want me to get ya somethin', Lyvia? Here, stay right here and I'll get you a Tab? Or Earl Grey?"

"Let me come with you. I wanna see what's stocked."

"Where's your bag? I gotta check it for Persephone. You know this," he says.

"Didn't bring it for that very reason, Chadry."

"Okay. Lemme check your pockets."

I splay my arms wide and he pats them quickly, just as tired of the antic. As I hoped. The others would be a lot more thorough, an uncomfortable amount. Defiling.

Inside we find the eatery. Baked goods, sandwiches, eggs, midnight bacon—anything you want. There's a staff on duty 24/7. I take a seat at the bar. It loops around the center of the room. The kitchen resides in its middle. I order a fresh squeezed orange juice in a martini glass. It's ice cold. Garnished with a twist. Chad orders a beer. I press the button pinned to my side.

"You can drink on the job now?" I say, glancing at the clock. I need to stall for fifteen minutes.

"We can do pretty much whatever we want soon," he replies with his lips around the beer bottle. "Just getting a taste of what's to come." Takes a slug.

"And what's to come, Chad?" I ask, taking a sip of ripe liquefied oranges. Succulent.

"Levi was looking for you. Night of the reveal..." He trails off, preoccupied. I follow his glance. His Slab displays a picture of the front entrance. The lane branches out to the tunnel. My chest clenches in fear.

A golden vehicle the size and shape of a Bentley passes the front and continues toward the tunnel. The shot changes and follows the car into the shaft. It enters eventless. Sigh of relief.

"Kkkssshshhh," sizzles from my side.

I bolt out the door before Chad has a chance to react. I sprint the pathway only pausing briefly in a dark crevice to remove my shoes. They swing by straps in my hand. I run the rest of the way up. My bare feet leave a trail of echoing slaps. When I reach ground level where the tunnel opens up, I see no movement.

Suddenly, I hear boots thud the ground. More than one set descends. Leisurely pace. I scan the area in front of me. Still nothing. On instinct, I dart left at the fork taking a narrow golden sidewalk to the surrounding road. Two voices emerge from the tunnel.

"So, you just let her go?" Sam.

Chad and Sam, couldn't have asked for a better duo.

I slip behind the glittery marble wall. It's about five feet tall and surrounds the Coliseum. The Lighters reach my fork and turn right. *Phew.*

I peek over the wall and see nothing has changed. *If he abandoned me here... So, help me, God...* Then I hear the almost imperceptible sound of rubber rolling on pavement.

I hitch the wall and sprint to the sound. An invisible door opens, and I slip in next to Dagan closing the door as quietly as possible. Unnecessary. The Lighters are nowhere to be found.

"What happened?" I ask, settling into my seat.

"I was just about close enough and pulled Seph out, but then a Goldster rounded the corner. Two guys. They were driving right up at me. I dove for cover and that's when the button depressed."

"Did you get any information?"

"No," he replies, dejected. "Couldn't get close enough."

"Well, that's okay." The tree line to Onyx creeps closer. "We still have Xane in the lion's den. We can do some of our own research, then check back in with him when we get something."

"How will we check in? That didn't go very smoothly."

"Lesson learned. Honestly, we can tackle that when it gets closer. We need to hit some books."

The ride is quiet for the most part. Each of us processing the last few hours—exploring our own personal labyrinths.

"Ya think we'll find anything at ye ole' Palace of Books?" I ask, breaking the silence.

"Sure, but I don't even know where to start," he says. I find that hard to believe for someone who practically lives there, but I let it go.

"Well, *History of Technology* seems as good as any." I sneak a look at his profile for a reaction.

"Yeah, that's what Xane said he had to read, right?" he asks, eyes never leaving the road.

"Yeah, the same one you dropped today..." I say leadingly.

"I'm not sure why I pulled that one out to be honest," he replies thoughtfully. "It just kind of happened." He offers no further explanation. I decide to let that go, too. I figure if I'm not divulging my secrets, why should he?

The drive back seems much quicker. Onyx flies by, a blur of nightscape. We pass through Granite, then Ruby, and finally Emerald. It's still night when we reach Regina's.

"Tomorrow morning, nine o'clock?" he asks as I climb out the car.

"Sounds good. See ya then," I reply, shutting the door.

He drives off. I assume. It's silent, and I couldn't see the vehicle once I closed the door.

11

I walk up the stony pathway to Regina's. Solar lamps create a trail of stars that illuminate the path. Flowers adorn the walk. I see dew glitter in the moonlight on delicate petals of silk. The canopy of trees touches to create a tunnel of vegetation. I can only catch glimpses of the stars through tiny openings. I spot Orion.

Coming in the front door, the renovated farmhouse creaks. I plan on going right up to bed. I'm exhausted. Ahead on the steps, I see a note:

Dear Lyvia,

I set aside a plate of lasagna and bread in the oven. I'm sure it will still be warm. There's parmesan cheese in the fridge, along with drinks. Tiramisu with homemade whipped cream too. You just come and go as you please, dear. There will always be food available in the kitchen. I'll see ya when I see ya.

Love,

Regina

I look toward the kitchen. My stomach growls. *Fine.* Walking through the dining room, I head into the completely white-tiled kitchen. Where there isn't tile, there is wood. All different types and shades. Dark stains and light stains of wooden grain pierce through the porcelain white tiles blanketing every surface. Some of the tiles have designs. Most do, in fact. Tiny ornate details you wouldn't notice unless you decided to take a closer look. Some are in the shapes of animals, some landscapes, and tiny flowers. A tiny gleam of light reveals the stencil so quickly you are unsure it's even there.

The countertops look to be flattened Arctic glaciers back when they still existed. I'm mesmerized. I spot the wood oven. It's huge. It resembles an old-school pizzeria oven. It's surrounded with aged red brick.

I open the metal handle on the circular latch and see a gigantic plate of food in a wrought iron skillet. The skillet is heaping with a huge cube of lasagna and a chunk of garlic bread that smells amazing. Using an oven mitt in the shape of a cupcake, I pull it out.

In the fridge, I find a can of Tab. *What? How?* Tab is my favorite beverage. It's a 1970s Coca-Cola product that was actually the first diet pop, or soft drink. It tastes the most like Coca-Cola for a diet beverage. But I digress. I always ordered my supply from an obscure soft drink company that had the recipes for the various brands. I could always tell the difference. I grab a can, suspiciously, and head to the dining room. There's a place set.

I settle in, pop the top of the Tab, and take a deep pull. Wow. This is the real thing. More mysteries. The lasagna is heavenly. It doesn't need parmesan cheese. The sauce is homemade and creamy. The bread is crusty and also homespun. I finish rather quickly and leave room for tiramisu. I must have my dessert.

After finishing the creamy sweet gooey goodness of her decadent dish, I clean up and head upstairs to bed. Walking into the room, I set down my bag. Going back-and-forth in my mind, I finally pull out my Slab.

"Hey Seph," I say, waking her up. "Are we secure enough?"

A second of silence.

"Yes, Lyvia, we are. I checked. All of Crystal is still good, but I know that we are doubly secured at Regina's."

"Why is that?" I ask, changing into a nightshirt, one of Shane's. It's oversized and sports the 'Beast' from the old movie *Sandlot*.

"She comes from a long line of Darken. You already know that. She's got this whole house armored up. We good. Ay," she says with both thumbs up, `a la Fonzie from *Happy Days*.

"Okay, Fonz," I reply, letting my hair down and sitting at the vanity. "What else do you know about her?"

"Well, everything's really obscure, Lyvia. The channels are set up to block all angles, all worlds," she says, examining the outer wall.

"Heaven, Hell, life." I look into my reflection solemnly. My eyes. Tired. Sad. Shane's eyes blink back. Determined. Strong.

"Yeah, so she's got communication barriers for all three, which means though…"

"She's got capabilities for all three. Which means…"

"It's a vortex," we both say at the same time, eyes meeting in awe.

"Ahh, okay. So, her house is a vortex." I pace the room. "I knew it was old. It must've been built here because of the spot. But there's only one vortex left in existence."

"Or so we thought," Seph adds, joining my pace.

"Interesting, Seph… Interesting." I slather 'Lotion' all over my skin. It smells of Christmas shortbread, savory and buttery, accompanied by the scent of fresh pine needles. Impossibly fresh. It's amazing. Then, I brush my teeth.

"Well, it's safe to say this is our home base," Persephone says, lying down in the tub.

"Yes," I reply, spitting out the last of my toothpaste.

"And that means we can really get down to business." She looks over the side of the tub.

"The rotary telephones…" I trail off, abandoning the vanity. I walk over and sink into the side of the bed. I look at the red historic phone hanging above the nightstand. I touch its round dial warily.

"You think I can talk to Shane?" I ask Persephone, hopeful.

She sits next to me cross-legged on the bed.

"I think you can't get your hopes up," she replies seriously. "This vortex isn't supposed to exist, and there is a ton of spiritual armor. Hell is definitely closed off. I'm just not even sure you can get connected to Heaven. It's worth a try, though."

I stare at the phone as if suddenly it might blow up.

"Okay, Seph, here goes nothing," I announce, picking up the receiver.

I put it to my ear. Nothing. Not even a dial tone.

"Is there a trick?" I ask.

"Did you try pound or one for line-out?"

"No, Seph, you know the one in Dark Shire doesn't do that. Do I have to with this one?"

"I don't know," she shrugs. I look at her.

"What? This doesn't exist. I don't have knowledge of novel discoveries," she examines the phone.

I turn to pound. Nothing. I rotate the dial to one. Silence.

"Try your favorite number," Seph says thoughtfully. "Both of yours."

"But it's not long enough to be a phone number."

"And this isn't an archaic phone. It's a spirit phone. Just try," she replies.

I put in eight and then six. Zilch.

"I said, both of yours." Scolding tone now.

I place my finger in the plastic finger holder and turn the dial to eight then six then four then one.

Suddenly, the phone lights up `a la Zoltar in *Big*, the fortune telling machine.

"Connecting," says an angelic voice through the receiver.

A soft click. Tiny whir. Then I hear it. His laugh. My heart soars out of my chest. I thrust the receiver into my ear willing it to go straight to my brain. I never thought I'd hear that sound again.

"Is it you?" I ask weakly, tears streaming down my face.

"Of course, it's me," he laughs again.

I'm half-laughing, half-ugly crying. It's not pretty.

"So, you met aunt Regina, huh?" Shane asks, clearly preoccupied —his usual setting.

"Aunt Regina? Shane, we will have to come back to that. What's going on? Can you come back? If so, how? How do we do this?"

"That little bitch took my hammer," Shane says over the whispery line.

"Who? Levi? What hammer?"

"Yeah, him. Lyv, I had him. I closed his portal."

"Yeah, what's with his portal? It's a man-made vortex, right? Straight to Hell, not 'New Heaven' as advertised, do I have that correct?" I ask, twirling the phone cord between my fingers.

"You are correct, Lyvia, and the prize…" He sounds like a game show host.

"Your death. Because I figured it out too late," I reply downcast.

"No. And stop that, Lyv. None of this is you. God came to me. He gave me a hammer."

"Was it like super old?" I ask.

He laughs. "Yep, Lyv. 'Bout as old as those nails."

"Did it…um, control the weather?" *Please. Oh, please let it be his.*

"No, it's not Thor's, Lyv. He wishes." Eye roll, I assume. "It can do a lot more than his. It's the first hammer ever created. By the way— Thor was real. But he wasn't a 'god' or 'demi-god'—the mythology is inaccurate and a bit… exaggerated. You know how those things go."

I rest my forehead in my free hand.

"He couldn't fly, his hair wasn't actually that long and…"

"Stop," I say, putting my palm out to an imaginary Shane lounging on the chaise at the foot of the bed. It's large, modern, and cushy. I envision his arms bent behind his head, legs draped over the velvety edge of the loveseat-like boudoir bench.

"Do not ruin this for me. It's Thor, bro. Thor, the God of Thunder." *Thunder, feel the thunder, lightning and the thunder.*

"You know you're gonna look it up anyway," he replies. I roll my eyes.

"Oh, you just know everything… What does your hammer do?"

"I don't know what it's capable of yet, but I know it's the Holy Relic of all Relics. The first tool and eventually weapon ever created…"

"It's the one that was used to…" I realize.

"Yup… with…"

"The nails."

"And he says I have to close this portal because it goes straight to Hell—run by Lucifer himself, Levi," he spits out the name. "So, I go there and close the portal. Yay, easy, right? Nope, definitely not. Because as it turns out, my body has to be reunited with the hammer to come back to Earth."

"And, Levi has it."

"Yep, 'bout sums it up, Lyv."

"Where is he?"

"That's the problem."

"Hell." We both say in unison.

"How can I get there?" I ask.

"Lyv," he starts in a warning tone.

"No, Shane. No. This time, I'm helping. You tried it your way last time."

"There's another vortex besides this one in Crystal."

"Really?"

"You've been there twice."

"What? Seriously?" My eyes light up in recognition.

"Yes, it's barrier-free. You can even see and feel my spirit form there. It's all kinds of weird, really. This whole thing is... Remember when we would sing in the car?"

"Of course, I do. What does that have to do with anything?"

"Nothing, that was fun though," he says.

"It really was, especially when I didn't know the words."

"Which is all the time," he teases. "But the best was just listening to your made-up verses. Somehow just better."

We both start singing "Rock Star" by Nickelback, butchering the words. We laugh uncontrollably.

"Okay, you need to get to the tomb. I can help you out as much as possible with going to Hell and back, but it's not as easy as just standing in the tomb. You need to do some research at the library and Aunt Regina's. I don't know all the specifics. You will need your nails, that's for sure. Ask Seph for guidance. Tell her I love her, and I think she's hilarious."

"Heard that, Boss," Persephone says with a salute toward the phone. "Both back 'atcha."

"Okay, so research vortexes and crossing planes. What about Hell, Shane? What's that like?"

"I saw it briefly before I got here, Lyv," he says ominously.

"Oh my gosh, I don't even want to know."

"No, but you have to. It's a scary place. Your worst nightmare 24/7. Literally—your worst fucking nightmare," he speaks the last four words slowly with deliberation.

He continues, "It's kind of like Heaven in the sense of transcendental planes, but whereas Heaven is an infinitely better realm of endless possibilities, Hell is identical to Earth, just much worse. You're aware of your past, present, and future, yet as you re-live your life's events, minus the good parts, you can't change anything.

Levi personally selects every good memory and removes it. You're aware of that too. It's as if you experience an open lobotomy with no anesthesia. You have no power. Helpless. All you can do is sit back and undergo it all over again.

Each harrowing loss. Minute of humiliation. Fight. Nasty word. Drunken escapade. Bad decision. Death. Wound. Surgery. Relapse. Disappointment from others. Disappointment in yourself. Hurt. Heartbreak. Each soul-crushing shock. Stab of pain. Every 'worst moment of your life' on repeat, at his amusement.

Every letdown. Bullying, victim and culprit. Hurtful notion. Terrifying second of true fear. Every person you ever hurt. Anxious moment. One-way love. Suicidal thought. Every single, horrible repressed and forgotten memory back to life to revisit. Each self-deprecating minute. Abandoned moment. Powerless second. Missed opportunity. Traumatic experience. All of them. Lost, empty. Utterly and completely alone.

It's black and white unless he adds color to the gore. Sometimes he changes things in certain ones, makes them worse. Slower, scarier. You don't expect it. And you still have no control. He feeds off sin. All the bad decisions you made because of his influence; you have to relive."

"It's his fun house, Lyvia. There were creepy clowns on repeat. Clowns, Lyv," his voice sounds severely traumatized.

"Oh shit," I respond lugubriously, putting my hand to my forehead.

"Um, yeah I know you feel the same way about them. Try to prepare. It's bad. Imagine the worst. It'll be worse than that, but it gives you a starting point," he says with a shaky breath.

"How long were you down there?"

"Not sure. Time doesn't make sense there."

"How did you get out?"

"During one exceptionally terrifying clown-day… He switches shit up, Lyvie," he says this nickname with especially reserved tenderness. "There just aren't words. It's endless. Then, during one particularly horrifying experience, I felt a hand grab my arm. I was nine-years-old in clown-hell, then I was thrown sideways for an impossibly long time until I tumbled onto a field on the Spirit Plane back to my actual age."

"What's that like?"

"Weird. See-through. Hard to explain," he sounds distant.

"Did you find Mom and Dad?" I ask.

"No, not yet. It's different than you'd expect."

"Like how?"

"There's really no destination. No one-place stop. No 'Heaven' plastered on a giant sign made out of sun-rays. A giant free-for-all. Nope. I guess there are levels. I'm not really sure where I am. It's a lot like Earth, although more beautiful and flawless. Even though things are solid, they're semi-transparent, if that makes sense. I think the higher up you advance, the clearer things get. Right now, I'm in a fog, a blur. Grainy, almost. Still, I can see you. You can't see me. See, from your point-of-view, you are surrounded by so much fog, you can't see anything from the Spirit World. You can't see me even when we're right next to each other."

"Which is when?" I ask.

"All the time," he says through a smile. Then he laughs. I soak it in with greed, start to share a smile. *Taste of copper. Flash of white feathers. Silky speckled orange flower petal between my fingertips.*

"Even right after…"

"No. Not then," he cuts me off.

"That's when you were in…" I say with dawning realization.

"Hell," he finishes.

"Well, we both were."

"You speak the truth, sis," he responds.

"I'm gonna need weapons, Shane."

"So far, you have three. Your hair-tie and shoes. You're gonna need more. Aunt Regina's got some background on that."

"You talked to her?" I ask, a little betrayed.

"No, jeez. Relax," he says. "She's got other sources up here. I just need to know what's going on."

"Of course, you do," I reply, laughing.

"Okay, I can't talk much longer. I have lines open on Levi, and I need to check on them. I can't have him doing anything unexpected, such as coming back up from Hell anytime soon."

"When can you talk next?"

"Not sure, Lyv. I'm super busy up here with keeping an eye on Levi. I gotta figure out his next move. You know he's got a backup plan," he replies. "Oh, yeah, and you'll need my skates."

I know he's talking about his hockey skates. He skated professionally when he was Leader of the Dark Shire.

"Why? What will those do? It's not as if I can wear them," I respond.

"No, you won't need to wear them. I just need you to bring them to the tomb."

"You can skate up there?"

"Sort of. I can't explain it, really. Just bring 'em," he says.

"Okay. I love you, Shane. I miss you," I say, not wanting to hang up. Ever.

"I love you, more, sis," he says. "This much…"

I picture his huge arms stretching out high above my head. Arms that were once attached to a roly-poly toddler. *A wisp of blonde curls. Taste of smooth puréed banana baby food. Flash of a baby pacifier attached to tiny denim overalls.*

"Remember, I'm right 'dere' with you, Lyv," he says 'dere' the way he said 'there' when he was tiny.

"Okay, love you, Nane," I say.

"Love you, Lyvie," he replies, his voice growing fainter.

A whir. A tiny click.

"You are now disconnected," that same angelic voice from earlier speaks.

As I hang up the phone, Persephone and I stare at each other, our eyes widened to capacity.

12

"Whoa," I murmur, pacing the room.

"You have a lot to do," Persephone takes the words right out of my mouth.

"Ya think?" I ask sarcastically. "Sorry, it's just... That was a lot." My pace has quickened—a beeline around the entire suite, bathroom included. Persephone lies on the fluffy couch. I think she's looking at a magazine.

"Are you kidding me, Seph? A magazine at a time like this?"

"What? It's a good issue. It's *Retro-Photo*. You know the one with ancient photography? Well, there's this ancient site, prehistoric, and I think if the photographer had just waited another twenty-seven minutes, the light would have really been perfect." She has one eye closed and holds the book out, turning her head.

I stare at her incredulously.

"It's just the sky would have been a little darker, so the blues would have really stood out, and the light from the sun—"

"Per-se-pho-ne," I say, standing next to her, hands on hips. "Stop. We can save that for another day. We need to strategize."

"Fine," she rolls her eyes and evaporates the magazine. *This is what I get for creating a Slab with a personality.*

"So, first things first," I say, ending there.

"Seph, I don't know which first things are first. Oh my gosh, I can't do this. Who do I think I am? I think I can just march down to

Hell…" I've picked up my beeline path. "And what? Ask Levi nicely if he could please give me my brother's ancient hammer back? Oh yes, I'm sure, he'll just hand it right over. 'Oh, hey, Lyvia, great to see you. Oh—this? This old hammer? Sure, it's all yours. It's not as if it destroyed my huge plan of tricking the remainder of the human race to voluntarily come to my playground. How do you like it by the way? The clowns treating you all right? The Devil's playground, Seph —the Devil, himself!" I stop, hands-on-knees. I'm breathing heavily, feeling a panic attack coming on.

"I need a cigarette," I say, grabbing the pack and ancient Detroit Red Wings Zippo from my bag.

"Reel it in, Lyv," she sounds like Shane. I walk out to the balcony. Persephone perches herself on the rail.

"Okay," I say, blowing out smoke. "Okay. Step One."

"Step One. Talk to Regina in the morning. We need more clarity on what she knows," she replies. "We need to get as much as we can."

"Yeah, yeah, then what?"

"Then she tells us what to do next."

"Okay. Well, I have to meet Dagan at the library. What time you think we can wake her up?"

"I'm sure she'll already be up whenever we are."

Okay. We'll have to catch a ride in Crystal out to the library. Shouldn't be too hard. I put the cigarette out in the tiny ashtray that sits on a wrought iron table adorned with two matching chairs. I return to the bedroom.

"So, wake me up at 5 o'clock in the morning." I envelop myself in the downy goodness of the bed, knowing full well I'm not really alone anymore.

"Sounds good, boss. Goodnight," and with that Persephone vanishes in a puff of glittery smoke.

As I stare up at the ceiling, I notice it's made of porcelain tiles reminiscent of the kitchen. Etched in these ones are stars, constellations, and galaxies that glitter in the moon's glow.

"Levi." The word slashes my lips. A knife through plump soft flesh. *Him.*

Guitar chords. Soft downy gold-plated couch. Creamy crème brûlée coats my tongue. The first chords of "What Is and What Should Never Be" by Led

Zeppelin, a band from the 1970s, fill my ears. One of my guilty-pleasure songs. The memory comes into focus.

Worn, fitted jeans. White t-shirt. Two bare feet balanced on the champagne glass coffee table. Guitar in lap. He's sitting across from me in the penthouse of Gold Coliseum. At this time, Levi is the Leader of Gold.

And I am his girlfriend.

We had met years earlier, never fully committing. He had so much charm, endless amounts of charisma and coolness. The guy's a rock star, for Heaven's sake. I'm not just saying that. He performs concerts. He's loved by nearly everyone of every age. He's also a genius. We used to talk about it. He told me he had Synesthesia too. Or so I believed. His real condition: The Devil Incarnate.

"It just explains everything," I sigh out loud, looking for the Big Dipper on the ceiling.

He just *knew* stuff, stuff that was impossible to know. I figured he could read minds, the way I can, but he was *really* good at it. Moreover, he was really good at *changing* minds. Something I've had no success with. He didn't always have success either, though. Those cases were very rare. And, he didn't take failure lightly.

I was writing an article for *Dark Times*, our shire's news cycle. It's my main source of income that's not family money. I was asked to interview him. I wanted nothing to do with it. His on-screen boyish charm and good looks irked me. He was entitled, too suave, and too public. I preferred being an under-the-radar journalist. I even wrote under a pseudonym and wore wigs and disguises to interviews. Okay, that was more for fun. *But—ugh, he was cute and intriguing. It was my job.*

"Hook. Line. And Sinker." I roll my eyes and squeeze them shut.

His intelligence; that was the clincher. He had it all, though. Humor, intellect, attentiveness, magnetism, captivation, understanding, and, oh yeah, he's hot as hell. *Literally. Ew. Pun.* Over coffee, he became so relatable. Suddenly, I wanted to be in his club. And he wanted me there. I didn't make it easy for him. There was always something I didn't trust. Couldn't put my finger on it.

"He wore me down though," I exhale loudly as I roll over to face the window.

Flashing lights. Golden brick walkway. Taste of lipstick. Itchy stockings.

Gold Shire attire. Ick. For four years, we had a back-and-forth. One of us not wanting to commit for various reasons. Then, last year, it seemed all the pieces fit. I gave in. I got swept up in his lifestyle.

"*Our* lifestyle," I spit out.

The parties, wigs and disguises 24/7 to stay under-the-radar, the lavish dinners, the intellectual talk, his limitless resources—it was all helping me write my book at the time. I had grown bored of *Dark Times* and wanted my next great feat. I figured a book would be just the ticket.

I was so wrapped up in my 'world' that I failed to see who was staring me right in the face—Lucifer, the Devil, himself.

Levi was appointed the leader of Gold Shire by birthright; the same way Shane became the leader of Onyx. When Levi was young, his genius was glaringly apparent. He restructured Gold Shire's entire Framework, opening all kinds of communication possibilities. His 'Slabs' are owned by anyone who has enough virtues. His device made every personal computer, phone, camera, etc. obsolete.

I created Persephone with spiritual help, because there was still something I didn't trust about the guy. I needed a clean Slab. She doesn't look anything similar to his, either. His mass-produced devices are shaped as a scroll. When rolled out, they're the size of your hand. They're made out of thin flexible glass and etched in gold.

Persephone is made out of archaic moonstone, although surprisingly lightweight and flexible. She is shaped as a notebook. If you didn't know better, you would think she's a historical paper notebook, similar to the one I keep on me at all times.

On top of his technological genius, his talent as an artist was unparalleled. In fact, he was a triple threat—musician, actor, and singer. Everyone loved him.

"How did I miss it?" I whisper to the universe outside my window.

I'm smarter than the average bear. I should have seen this, especially while I was researching my book. The subject to be explored was the history of Gold Shire, the shire that prizes extravagance above all else. I was comparing its system with that of Crystal's, a shire that places God above all else. I got more involved with Crystal; that was the problem. Because of my bias, I focused primarily on the Unconnected Shire. The Gold parties, concerts, dinners; once mesmerizing, grew into irritating obligations. I escaped into my book.

Shining Ruby buildings, vegetation-covered Emerald domains, concrete city limits—I started to travel and check out the other shires. Research.

"Yup, research," I roll my eyes and flip onto my back. The tile galaxies seem to twinkle. I spot the North Star.

Levi told me vaguely about his plans concerning the Great Reveal. He always had a competitive streak when it came to Dark Shire. Needless to say, Shane and he were cordial, but that's it.

He wanted Dark Shire's vortex. Impossible. It is a natural passageway that was created at the beginning of time. I knew there was absolutely no way he could create and upgrade his own. I figured it would be similar to his failed Framework Spirit Receivers, which were personal phones that should have been able to reach the Spirit World.

Yeah, not a chance. That was a colossal failure. According to Levi, the only reason they worked in testing but not to market was because some unseen spiritual barrier had been put up. He suspected Dark Shire. Now, I suspect God.

"I knew those things wouldn't work," I say, flopping my arms outside the down comforter.

The Slabs did, however. Massive success. I figured he had moved on from his obsession to connect to the Spirit World. Stick with what he knows, what he created—the Framework. He never had any business dealing with the Spirit World. That's Onyx territory.

While I was traveling, he became just as distant. That was fine with me. I was reconsidering the relationship. I should have realized how dangerous he was, especially when I heard the Great Reveal was official. I just thought it would be another Spirit Receiver sitch.

"Stupid." I throw my hands above my head.

He wanted me at the Great Reveal. Of course, he did. He needed his arm candy. A place I had never been comfortable. I liked disguises when it was sporadic for the paper. It became exhausting day-to-day. I was finishing up research in Turquoise and decided this would be the last Gold event I would ever attend. It was time for this to be over. I finished up with the Turquoise Leader the morning of the Great Reveal eve.

I took the SkyChariot, which ended up being an adventure in itself. Levi asked me to meet at the alcove that evening at 8 o'clock. Sunset. He wanted to show me what was in store. I hadn't heard much from Shane at that point. He had his hockey season going, along with preparing for football, then baseball, not to mention his responsibilities as Dark Leader. He was always a busy guy. We sent a few messages here and there, but I hadn't seen him since before I started my travels.

When the chariot hit Emerald, a farmer got on. He was loading his animals into a cart. One cow was being particularly stubborn. I was watching the minutes tick by. I'm late to everything. Perpetually. It even annoys me. I wanted to make it on time to prove that I could be on schedule for once.

Another stop, a bunch of Granite teenagers got on. Laughing, dancing, and playing with their Slabs, they put on a show. Until, one of them cracked her head on a hand pole during one wild dance move. The train made an emergency stop in Granite. Then, the system went down. Framework was imperfect. The train got delayed often. I was going to be late.

I jumped off and found a vehicle rental shop in the city. I rented an old Ninja crotch rocket. I looked ridiculous. There was no time to change. I had to wear my Turquoise attire. A short, feathered grey skirt with tiny built-in shorts, thank God. An aquamarine lightweight corset-style top, and my original Greek warrior sandals completed the outfit. It would have to work. Luckily, Shane had a Ninja and taught me how to ride it. It was my only chance to get there in time. Persephone supplied the directions.

At 7:58p.m, I climbed the rocket up the last hill. As I breached the crest, I saw a familiar 6'3" form standing with his back to me. It was Shane.

Suddenly, he flew backwards landing in a heap on the ground. I saw Levi standing there, something large in his hand. I looked at Shane on the ground, completely unmoving. By the time I looked back up, Levi was gone.

Running over to Shane, I saw the blood. He had been battered up pretty badly. A lot of blood. No heartbeat. I tried CPR desperately, knowing it was for naught. I could tell he had fought hard. A large stab wound was most likely the cause of death. The battery alone wouldn't have done it, but I wasn't about to get an autopsy.

"Levi." The word slithers from my lips. A snake slinking its scaly body across the room.

He will pay.

I pull the powder pink silky sleep mask I find in the nightstand's drawer over my eyes and finally drift into an uneventful sleep.

13

"I'm going to start whispering extremely quietly, and gradually raise my voice until you WAKE UP—" Persephone shouts the last two words.

"Ugh, okay. Okay. I'm awake." I sit up and lift the corner of the sleep mask off one eyeball.

Squishy tie-dyed stress ball. Matching t-shirt and ripped denim skinny jeans. Persephone is sitting on the edge of the bed dangling her legs. Deep colors spray her fitted cotton t-shirt. The jeans are worn and adorned with tie-dyed tennis shoes. Her hair is pulled back in her signature ponytail.

"It's gonna be a long day, Seph," I say, swinging my legs over the side of the bed.

"Yup," she replies, now fingering a tie-dyed Rubik's Cube.

"How does that work?" I ask, toothbrush in mouth.

"It's all about the patterns," she replies in deep consternation.

I look in the mirror. My hair is standing up straight from my head. I look as though I have 1980s 'mall bangs.' I sleep completely face-down on my stomach, so I'm rewarded with this look every morning. I finish brushing my teeth and work on the mane. Regina's products make it an easy task. I throw on some make-up, a flowy 1970s hippie top and jean shorts. My snake warrior sandals complete the ensemble. I walk down to the fore' and hear Regina in the kitchen.

"Morning, Lyvia. Did you sleep well? I've got eggs, pancakes, bacon. Have a seat, dear."

"Sounds good," I say, sitting down. "I slept very well, thank you."

She's singing quietly. I think it's "Winnie-the-Pooh." My mother always sang that to me when I was little. She comes into the room and sets the dishes on the table.

"Help yourself." She disappears into the kitchen and returns with coffee and fresh-squeezed orange juice.

"Wow. This looks excellent, Regina," I reply, pouring a large mug of coffee. I'm not a morning person.

"So, you've figured it out," she says, spooning eggs onto our plates.

"Figured what out?" I ask, piling pancakes onto mine. I lather them with butter and pure maple syrup. I take a bite of the fluffy goodness. It melts in my mouth. I think I detect fresh-squeezed orange juice in the batter. The maple syrup tastes as if it came straight from the tree. Sweet, syrupy goodness—pure and simple.

"What do you think?" Regina replies sarcastically, fixing herself some pancakes.

"Oh," I say, fork paused at mouth. "I was just so curious about the phones and then Persephone…"

"I know," Regina laughs heartily. "Persephone and I go way back now. Don't we, Seph?"

I flip open the Slab on the table. Persephone appears in a chair, popping bubblegum. "Hi, Miss Regina," she says, blowing a bubble.

"Well, good morning, Seph. I love your top," Regina replies.

"Oh, this old thing," she replies, pulling her shirt away from her body. "It's one of my favorites."

"It suits you," Regina says, turning her head to the side.

"Thank you," Seph responds shyly. "I told her about the spiritual armor on the house, then we put two and two together."

"Well, you are some very smart girls. I knew you'd figure out the puzzle when you got the pieces."

"I apologize for intruding, Regina. I should have asked permission…"

"Nonsense," she cuts me off. "You don't need permission to do anything in this house. We go way back, Lyvia."

"Or so I've heard," I say suspiciously. She laughs.

"I guess word does get around no matter which transcendental plane you're on."

"So, we're related?" I ask.

"Yes, my dear. We are. You are my great-grand-niece, mother's side. We thought it best for you to figure it out on your own."

"Who's we?"

"You know, I've known about you and your brother all your lives," she says, ignoring my question and taking a sip of coffee.

"How come we never heard of you?"

"When I switched over to Crystal, I just lost touch. You know how life is. I got used to my simple existence and going into Onyx is quite the opposite of simple. Your mother sent pictures and videos, detailed letters. She loved you both so much. So proud."

"I know," I say, missing her intently.

"Then—after she and your father, well, vanished, it's not like you and your brother try to keep low profiles or anything." She laughs. "The Dark Leader and his professional sports, and you—with your gorgeous rock star... You did good with the disguises, Lyv." She winks at me over the lip of her coffee cup as she takes another sip. "But, I've been watching you. Long before Quinn Harley."

I decided to flip-flop the comic villain's names for my pseudonym.

"Ugh," I roll my eyes at my foolishness.

"Honey, it's not like this tiny world's filled with available men. And he is cute," she laughs again.

"Yeah, he is cute," Persephone adds, twirling her hair.

"Yeah, and he's also the Devil."

"There's no way you could have known that," Regina replies.

I take a bite of syrupy pancake. Regina adjusts the napkin on her lap.

"There's no way any of us could have known that. Just like you, we were all completely deceived. He's the Devil, you know. He's got power. He's the reason for our second Great Rain. It was because of human sin, God brought rain the first time with Noah. It was because of free will and the choice for goodness, he stopped it. This is our last chance. So, of course, Lucifer would attempt to thwart us and bring back the rain. Finish off the world. Finally take everyone left down to his play place. Truly achieve Hell on Earth," she says.

Our Great Rain happened slowly. A more modernized version of the ark, well, seven of them this time. It was a hundred years until it finally stopped, creating one island that is now the Realm. It's the only land on the globe that hadn't been touched during that time.

"He must've been pissed God stopped it again."

"I'm sure he was," Regina replies.

"I just never thought he would take human form."

"No one did. Except God, probably," she says, taking a last sip to drain her mug.

"Well, now what?"

"Well, now you find Levi and get the hammer back. That's now what," she says swiftly, getting up and clearing dishes. *She knows about the hammer. Sheesh. What else is this woman aware of?*

"Yes, I know about the hammer… And the nails," she says from the kitchen. "Honey, I live in a vortex." *Yeah, that explains it.*

"What do you know about this hammer?" I ask.

"Well, it's a primordial Holy Relic from Jesus' time. In fact, it was the hammer used with those nails… On Jesus," she answers, coming back and clearing more dishes. "The Darken lineage can be traced all the way back to the Bible, as you know." This is true. We learn it in shire training. Schooling becomes strongly based around each shire's responsibilities. Dark Shire, being the spiritual sector, is familiar with theological history.

"The relics have been passed down through our family for years. The hammer, however, was not on the earthly plane. That was in Heaven. I still don't know how your brother got his hands on it, or how he knew what Levi was up to," she says, returning to the room and smoothing the tablecloth before settling into her chair.

I'm trying to remember where I got the shoes. *Glittery wrapping paper. White shimmering flakes float around in a snow globe. Santa sits at a desk in the crystal sphere, sleepy golden retriever puppies litter his ankles. Smell of cinnamon and pine needles. Sweet crepe suzettes with creamy strawberry filling melts in my mouth. Christmas morning. I see Mom smiling expectantly over the corner of the open gift on my lap. A pair of stilettos line the box. A snake wrapped around each heel. Hammered metal slit eyes glint in the tree's glow.*

"Well, that's certainly the question of the day, isn't it, ladies?" Persephone asks the room. She's sitting cross-legged on the table wiling away on her Rubik's cube again.

"It certainly is," Regina says, absently brushing invisible crumbs off the tablecloth.

"Well, can I get any info at the library? We're heading out there today."

"Certainly. Did you meet Dagan, by the way?" she asks, oh-so-casually disappearing into the kitchen.

"Yes, we did. He's funny," Persephone says now empty-handed, her attention completely focused on the current topic. "And cute..." She leans forward, head perched on steepled hands.

The guy reminds me of my brother. We're Hansel and Gretel following the trail of breadcrumbs, though I hope for a different ending.

"What's up with him? I could only get a partial read on the guy. Images and things from here and there but I couldn't break into his energy field for a full work-up," Persephone continues.

"He's a quiet one. I actually don't know that much about him, and I've been here a long time. I know he was born Granite and came out here to live with his grandpa when he was young. When his grandfather died, he became Crystal's Leader."

"But Crystal doesn't have a leader," I interject.

"That's because Crystal's is unspoken. He's not a leader in the sense of a king, the way it is with the other shires. He is chosen by the people and by the Lord."

"What do you mean?" I ask intently.

"The Rock in the Cush," she replies. "It's another vortex. All vortexes were designed during creation. They are all the oldest sites on Earth since day one: 'Let there be light,'" she snaps her fingers. The light blinks in unison. I swear it.

"So, these spots where energy is projected and absorbed create channels to the other planes. The Spirit World and our world overlap. The different energies converge. The Rock consists of the oldest rocks and gemstones in the universe. They have been here from—" she snaps her fingers, and the light blinks again. I swear. "Day one."

"God, himself, appears at The Rock?" I ask.

"No, it's the Holy Spirit. He's invisible and only the Crystal Leader can hear His voice."

"So then how do you know it's God?" Persephone asks, sitting cross-legged in a chair at the table.

"Well, that's where faith steps in, my dear," she replies. "That's why only a few choose to be unconnected. We all have faith in God, The Rock, and the chosen leader. We haven't been wrong since the beginning, so, it works for us."

"Okay, so that explains the signal-latch." I remember the bronze shackles.

"Yes, ma'am," she says. "Now remember, these vortexes, especially un-armored, also pass over to Hell. And Hell, that's a different beast. There's no preparing for it, honey. I've seen it. Near-death experience. Saw the Spirit World too. Hell... It wasn't good." She shudders. "He never showed himself to me; otherwise, I would have never allowed Levi as far as he got up here." She looks into an imaginary scene of pure horror. "You just have to be strong, Lyv and have faith."

She places her slender hand on my shoulder and looks intently at me. Her smile-lined blue eyes bore into mine. "Spiders," she mutters nervously rubbing her hands together. "My God, the spiders..."

I fidget in my chair. *Clowns and spiders. Two of my biggest fears. In addition to every other horrible event one gets to relive in Hell. I hate this guy.*

"So, how can Dagan help?" Persephone asks, a little too excitedly. I wish she had her Rubik's cube.

"I don't need help," I say indignantly. "I mean maybe he'll share some of his knowledge of—I don't know—a Crystal Leader who can hear God? And then I'll be on my way. I've got a mission."

"The snakes," Regina whispers with another shudder. "Honey, you're gonna need all the help you can get."

14

W ith my overweight bag and accompanying lunch sack strung over my shoulder, I head up into town to hitch a ride. There are people milling about who look familiar from yesterday. Someone hit slow-motion. Everything moves at a leisurely pace in Crystal. Prism buildings gleam in the sun. Interwoven wood and concrete make the buildings appear both ancient and modern, which is accurate. The town is paved in archaic rock found and collected around the land as it got swallowed up by the storm. It's a patchwork pebbled walkway featuring every color of salvaged gemstone.

The mother and her two baby hammerheads from yesterday sit near the playground. This time the baby sharks are eyeing a baseball. I wave. She waves back. I realize she looks familiar and then I place her; her name is Mercedes. She's the Leader of Granite. There isn't a gender preference for shire leadership. I've met her at several events with Levi. She's preoccupied with her boys and I have to lot to do, so I settle with a wave.

Two old men exit a diner. One is holding a yellowed ancient newspaper. It's astonishing at first glimpse. *How is it in such pristine condition?* A teenage girl with honey blonde hair walks by holding a paper book to her face. I love Crystal. I watch her expertly multi-task and try to catch the cover. I can't. She narrowly misses a man hustling in the opposite direction by less than an inch, his long black wool coat brushes her page. *Mirror, mirror on the wall.* I'm looking at myself a billion years ago.

The young woman with the dogs from yesterday passes on the other side of the road. She's got more this time. Mostly pit-bull mixes of one sort or the other. One looks purebred Staffordshire Terrier, fawn and white colored. One favors German Shepherd in her mix, her large pink ears stick straight up like Yoda. She's a pretty, brindle colored pup with a pink collar. Another mix, this one favoring Labrador dons a blue collar. His adorable puppy dog eyes glance back toward Mom periodically to make sure she's still there. A short Jack Russell flits about nervously in the group. She skitters underneath the taller breeds. A small fluffy Shih Tzu stubbornly brings up the rear with the air of a princess.

Today, the woman is wearing jean shorts and a cropped white t-shirt with brown leather strappy sandals. Her hair is pulled up in a messy bun, long pieces float around her face in the breeze. The dogs are taking her for a walk. There's something about her that seems familiar, but I still can't place it. Distant déjà vu. *I need to introduce myself when I'm back in town. There's something about her.*

I start to look around for possible rides. Nothing. I waited too long to ask. I thought I would still have options as I neared the town limits, but not today. I get close to the dispensary and see a pile of loose golden honey curls in a crystalline window. *I gotta meet her.*

As I walk up to the door, I see the bouncing curls. I knock. She opens the door revealing a tiny boy attached to her leg, a little girl peeking from behind her, then a somewhat older girl appears on the other side of the doorway.

"Who are you?" asks the little boy from below.

"I'm Lyvia," I say, stooping to his eye line. "And, who are you?"

"I'm Axel," he replies with a big smile, bright blue eyes shining behind thick-rimmed glasses. His blonde hair is ruffled. He's wearing a blue t-shirt that seems to be rebelliously placed on backwards and inside out.

"I'm Reese," says the oldest, holding out her hand. I take it. It's slender yet strong. Her hair is thick akin to her mother's, although the color of very faded red bricks. She's got the same inquisitive big blue eyes as her brother. She holds a pen and spiral notebook, similar to mine. She checks her watch. She's wearing a Hermione costume from *Harry Potter*. Boy, the fashion treasures in this place.

"I'm Anika." A muffled voice projects from behind her mother's long dress. She has her thumb in her mouth. She says her name like Monica minus the M.

"Well, hi, Anika." I stoop back down.

"Hi," she responds, bravery growing. She emerges from the billowy fabric of the dress, a tiny hand outstretched. Her wide, root beer-rimmed, honey-hazel eyes bore into mine. Her milk chocolate curls balance precariously on her head, which is adorned with a crystal tiara, slightly askew. She's wearing a gold Disney princess Belle dress, tiny high-heels and a clutch. Oh, and elbow-length gloves.

"Okay, guys. Jeez. Hi, I'm Scarlett. It's nice to meet you. Come on in," she shakes my hand and disappears into the house. Her baby ducklings flounder in her wake.

She's wearing a long dress. It seems almost reminiscent of *Gone with The Wind*, although, modernized, thinner fabric, not as bulky. No window curtain with rod in this one. Elegant, classy. I feel so underdressed until I remember you wear whatever you want out here. Her updo frames her eyes, caramel root beer matching Anika's. She has impeccably placed red lipstick on. She's so fancy. I'm already mentally rifling my wardrobe for anything similar to this dress. Nothing. *Gotta get on that.*

I follow her through the store, which is filled with potion bottles, not unlike Regina's. A lengthy passageway takes us through the store down into her home. Along the way, I hear muffled barking.

"Oh, that's Vanellope, our dog," she says over her shoulder casually.

"Can we get her, Mom? Please, please Mom?" Axel pleads.

"Nope. Not now," Scarlett replies.

"Please, please, Mom. Please."

"No."

"But—I wuv you, Mom." I sense crocodile tears behind that one.

"I 'wuv' you too, baby. Next time." Axel runs ahead, Vanellope already forgotten.

"Bought ya some time," Scarlett whispers to me over her shoulder. "Um. She's… she's ahh… kind of hard to describe. You'll get the privilege someday, I'm sure."

We arrive in a kitchen. It's large. The inside of the entire space is larger than possible. I'm starting to get used to it. Her kitchen consists of ivory and dark, thick wood. The floor is hardwood too; although, it alternates lighter and darker stains.

Reese and Anika take seats at the counter. Reese is poised on her stool, notebook open and ready. Glitter pen in hand, she reminds me of myself at that age. Anika, on the other hand, huffs and puffs her way up the stool, reaches the top and lands in a golden swell of fabric. She sits forward, head dramatically falling into the crooks of her elbows.

Oh. Wait. Yep. That was more my style. A combo of the two—heavy on the Anika. Scarlett stands at the counter cutting an apple. Axel hangs on to her leg, eyeing me suspiciously.

"So, what brings you out here?" Scarlett asks.

"I'm heading out to the library. I walked up there yesterday. Nearly died on the bridge, if you can call it that," I respond.

"Oh yeah, nobody uses that anymore."

"It's a goner at this point."

"Mom, Mom, Mom. Can I have ah apple? Can I have ah apple? Can I have ah apple?" A chorus echo from Axel.

"Sure, Ax, here," Scarlett leans down and hands him a few slices.

"Did you meet Dagan?" she asks, as she puts things away. "He's out there often."

"Actually, yes, I did. Very nice, he helped me find the place."

"Yes, he's nice. Don't ya think so, Ani-bug?" she asks, a wink toward the tiara-bejeweled head. Anika slumps back in the chair with a harrumph.

"Mom. Now I'm embarrassed," she declares, throwing her arms down.

"She's got a little crush," Scarlett mouths the word 'crush.'

"Mom, she just likes him cause of his accent," Reese adds, rolling her eyes and writing feverishly in her notepad. I wonder what it says.

I did detect a Granite accent there. I think of Shane and how much Dagan reminds me of him. He's a long-lost brother to me, one with a mysterious background. He's a cryptic Ferris Bueller running around Crystal doing as he pleases, while his sister teeters with annoyance.

Besides as much as I abhor Levi, I hate to admit—I'm deeply heartbroken. He made me care about him. He got me to love him.

Even near the end, there was attachment. And, he ended up being Lucifer, himself. So, no thank you very much. I prefer complete independence. Still, Anika's 'crush' is adorable.

"Well, if anyone can help you around the library, it's him," Scarlett says, as she washes her hands.

"I'm meeting him there at nine o'clock this morning. I was actually wondering if…"

"Oh sure, Lyvia. We can give you a ride. Right guys?"

"Right," Axel says, taking some cautious steps toward me.

"Right," Reece echoes, distracted in her notebook.

A deep sigh. "Right." Anika exhales through her teeth, clearly not over her embarrassment.

"Let's see, what time is it, Ree?"

"7:43a.m." she replies, inspecting her moonstone wristwatch.

"Very precise, that one," Scarlett says, leaning over the counter. "You want some tea? We have time."

"Sure," I reply.

She bustles around the kitchen. "You like Earl Grey?"

"My favorite, actually." I spot movement near my feet. Then, a tiny tapping on my snake strap.

"Ooh Mom, it's a snake," Axel says, inspecting the strap with his finger. His head is turned nearly upside down as he follows its head to its tail. He's fully engrossed.

"Wow. Those are too cute. Where'd you get 'em?" Scarlett asks, taking a look. She pulls the hem of her dress up. "I got these last year. I need some new sandals." Black stiletto boots go above the knee. Matte coal leather features an intricate design etched around the shoe. It's a mystical forest. Trees, vegetation, a small pool, an outline of a unicorn and a werewolf all wrap through the etching in the leather.

"Whoa," I say entranced.

"I know," she exclaims. "I found them out in Mortal last year at a market. I couldn't believe they were my size." The design continues into the heels, although the trailing flowers slowly gain color. They're bright and vibrant in the tapered stiletto style heels. *I have to find another pair. Okay, task-at-hand. I feel like Persephone.*

"How long have you been out here?" I ask.

She tends to the steaming teal tea kettle. "Hmm let's see. My husband and I brought the kids out here a year ago. We wanted to try out Crystal. We were Darkens before."

"Me too," I say, pouring cream and sugar into my tea.

"I thought there might be somethin' bout ya," she replies, dipping her tea bag in her fragile teacup.

"I just love your tea set." I inspect the intricate floral patterns that don the ancient porcelain.

"So do I," Anika exclaims excitedly. "Mom, can I have some?"

"Sure, honey," Scarlett replies, filling a tiny cup half-way. She dunks the tea bag in twice before she removes it. "Don't want it too strong," she whispers conspiratorially to me. She hands Anika the teacup and turns back.

"Hey, Reesy—can you please take Anika and Axel and get them ready for the road?"

"Sure." Reese grabs Axel's hand. Anika takes one last sip of her tea and trudges behind the other two. Her tiny heels click-clack on hardwood floor.

"My husband passed over last year. Shortly after we moved here," Scarlett says, her tone lowered.

"I'm so sorry," I reply. I know she too is navigating the unspoken waters. The deep, dark pool of black. If you have ever lost anyone close to you—you're in the pool, aimlessly drifting in its clammy black water. There are the people in the pool, and then those outside the pool, the ones lounging on beach towel-lined chairs. But—they'll be in the pool someday, too. The minute someone you love is taken away is the minute you're thrown into the inky black lagoon. *The pool of grief.*

"Thank you. It doesn't get any easier," she says, taking a sip of her tea.

"My brother died five days ago, and I don't see it ever getting better. Only worse," I respond, trusting her implicitly for some reason and simultaneously wanting to tell her everything that's ever happened to me while watching historic romantic comedies. Maybe after a day of shoe shopping.

"I'm so sorry," she says, hugging me.

"Thank you. Maybe they've met up there." My eyes travel to the ceiling and I take a sip of tea.

"I bet they did," she replies knowingly.

"We were gonna meet up with my brother in town this afternoon for lunch. We can pick him up and bring him with us, then get lunch after. If that's okay with you?" She takes my empty teacup and hers to the sink.

"Of course," I reply. "I'm the one asking for the favor. I'm at your mercy."

"Sounds good." She wipes her hands on a dishtowel and calls up the stairs, "Hey you guys..." A quote from the movie, *The Goonies*. "We gotta hit the road. Reesy, everyone ready?"

"Just about, Mom," a voice squeaks from above. There's shuffling at the top of the staircase.

"Stop. I don't want to wear that," a tiny boy voice.

"Too bad, Axel, just put it on," Reese says.

Finally, tiny footsteps begin to fall.

"Wait." Anika declares, freezing on the third stair from the top. Only visible are her ruby-sequined Dorothy replica, Mary Jane shoes. "I need my bracelet."

Walking into the foyer, Scarlett takes out a large over-the-shoulder bag. It's exactly the same as mine—same worn leather, same ornate design, same splashes of color. I wonder if hers too, has the powers of *Mary Poppins*. I imagine so as the heft to pull it out seems a little exaggerated for the size of the purse. I wonder where she got hers.

More scuffling upstairs. Hushed hurried voices.

"Let's go, guys," Scarlett calls, half-way out the door. She's got on movie star sunglasses, `a la Audrey Hepburn.

TEN MINUTES LATER, we pile into her shiny black modernized Range Rover. It's huge. A family could live in this thing. A tiny hand with impeccably painted pink nails appears between the front seats. A moonstone heart dangles from a rainbow of gemstones. The heart changes color in the sunlight—baby pink, white, cottonwood blue, silver.

"I want you to have this," Anika says, peeking over the seat.

"Wow, Anika. That's gorgeous, but I can't take your bracelet. It's yours," I reply gratefully.

"Nope. I want you to have it." She grabs my arm and expertly fastens the bracelet in place. She examines it intently. Squinting her eyes, she whispers, "I knew it."

"You knew what?" I ask.

"I knew you were a secret werewolf, just like me. I can tell because the stones reveal true werewolves when they put them on. It's all about the sparkle. They get more sparkly-er on us," she murmurs the last sentence, a tiny hand cupped over my ear.

"I'm honored, Anika. Just honored. Thank you," I reply as I inspect the beautiful piece.

"Okay. Buckle in, everyone." Scarlett looks at me with the last word.

I whip my seatbelt on as quickly as the kids.

15

We drive back into town and pull in front of a storefront. A big, muscular guy is walking out. He's about 6' tall, short hair the color of cocoa powder and eyes the color of caramel-rimmed root beer, almost the same as Scarlett's. He's wearing jeans and a Detroit Tigers t-shirt. I know this because I unearthed a similar one years ago. I have a fascination with ancient Detroit because of my heritage. I like these two.

He comes over to the passenger side. "Hi, I'm Connor," he says, shaking my hand. His hand encases mine.

"Nice to meet you," I reply.

"Hey guys," he waves over my shoulder.

"Uncle Connor, Uncle Connor, Uncle Connor—" Axel calls from the rear.

"Hey buddy," he says, climbing in the back with the kids. We start down the road.

"How are ya guys?"

"Fine. Mom tried to fix that light bulb in the kitchen," Reese says casually while writing in her notebook. From Scarlett's expression, I'm getting that was a loaded contribution to the conversation.

"Tell me not the florescent one…" he says cautiously.

"Yep, that one," Reese replies.

"Hey—it wasn't that bad," Scarlett says, pushing the car's speed past its limits while swerving around corners.

"It was like Cw-istmas, Maa-weee Cw-istmas, Mommy," Axel calls out from the back.

"It was not like Christmas," she mutters under her breath. Out loud—"Maa-wee Christmas, Axel."

"How was it like Christmas?" Connor asks.

"The snow," Anika exclaims. "It all came floating down."

"Snow?" Connor's face is perplexed.

"Well, she tried to turn the bulb like you do a regular light bulb. And poof—snowflakes made of glass," Reese says, still writing. "I told her to let me find the instruction manual." She rolls her eyes.

"Well, thanks for the recap, Reese," Scarlett says. "I'll have you know; the body count was zero. And, nobody was injured."

"There shouldn't be any talk of a body count!" Connor bellows. His face is pricelessly incredulous. "Just let me know and I will do it."

"Okay. Okay. It looked easy," she says, swerving around a tree. The road narrows as the thicket grows.

"I tried to change my chandelier once," I recall. Dark Shire uses ancient forms of electricity as well. Another *Back to the Future III* setting: 2020, except it's always nighttime. "I wanted a simpler design. The one that was up was gold and intricate, gaudy. I figured you just unscrew it, unplug it—just like an outlet and put the new one in. So, I unscrew it just to find guts of wires, different colors and widths. There is no outlet. There is no plug."

"Did you turn the power off first?" Connor asks.

"Yep. I hit the switch," I reply.

"Like the light switch?"

"Yeah, I flipped the light switch off."

"But not the circuit breaker?"

"No. Just the switch."

He shakes his head slowly and solemnly. "God had his eye on you that day." His eyes are wide.

"I guess He did," I reply, having had absolutely no clue I was involved in something dangerous enough for that reaction.

The car hits a bump and swerves to the right, but Scarlett regains control instantly.

"So, where are you from?" Connor asks me.

"Dark Shire, I'm unconnected though."

"Like us," he nods. "How you likin' Crystal?"

"Oh, I love Crystal. Always have. I think I might eventually move out here. I'm pretty nomadic."

"I get that." He looks out the window.

Suddenly, the library looms in front of us.

"Can we come, Mommy? Can we come? Please," Anika asks.

"Sure, but what's the rule?"

"Put everything back exactly where we found it," all three reply in unison.

"And girls…" Scarlett starts.

"Watch your brother," the ladies chorus. They race in front of us.

Connor opens the giant door. We follow the kids into the main anteroom. I start my search for Dagan assuming he's beaten me here. I'm about seventeen minutes late. *Not too shabby for this girl.*

He is nowhere to be found, and we look *everywhere*. I'm lucky to have Scarlett, Connor, and the kids. They know all the secret nooks and crannies. There are a lot of them in this old castle.

"Well, we should check his house," Scarlett says, exiting a room. We move to the foyer.

"Come on guys," she calls. The girls come running from opposite directions. "Where's your brother?"

They look at each other, then behind themselves as if he was right there a second ago.

"Come on," she says, disappearing into a tunnel. "Connor— mission: Axel; last seen… Girls, where did you last see him?"

"I'm in the right wing." Connor's shout is muffled by the billions of pages occupying the space. "No sign of him here. Moving toward you."

"Okay," she shouts back. The tunnel forks.

"Girls, you each take a tunnel. Yell when you find him." She and I continue forward to the largest room and split ways. Shelves reach the gigantic ceiling. It's a rat maze navigating through these narrow passageways.

"Axel," we take turns yelling. I round a corner and see the tiniest bit of blonde fluff sticking out from a mountain of books. Coming into full view, I spot two knobby knees hidden in the pages.

"Hey you." I kneel down next to the breathing paper fort. A giggle erupts from the pile and a head pokes out between covers.

"Hi, Lyvia," he says with a huge smile.

"Hi, Axel. Lemme help you out there," I grab his hand and lift him to his feet. The books scatter around.

"I got him," I call out to Scarlett. "Aisle: Two-Six-Nine-One."

"On my way," she calls back.

Putting the books back quickly and messily, I scoop him up and meet her at the end of the aisle. The girls join us. Anika has a folded paper crown on her head. It's very well crafted. Gold edges the paper.

"Anika, I told you no book destruction," Scarlett chides as we make our way outside.

"Mom, it was already loose," she shrugs.

"Okay. It looks pretty." Scarlett unlocks the Range Rover. "Let's try his house."

She navigates the forest as well as Dagan. Ten minutes later, we pull up to the clearing in the forest. His 'cottage' appears in the midst of trees. We pile out of the car and spread out SWAT team style. That's if the SWAT team consisted of five puppies making beelines with no particular destination in mind. There are doors all around the perimeter.

Scarlett and the kids take the left way around. Connor and I take the right. All the doors are sealed shut. Connor and I are about half-way the length of the house when we hear a vehicle far away but getting closer. We run the way we came, bumping into our cohorts at the front of the house.

"Rear entryway," Scarlett says, breathing heavily.

"Around back," Connor replies, taking a peek.

She nods. "We should hide. We don't have time to get to the car."

We spot a grotto out in the woods. Scarlett swoops up Axel, Connor swoops up Anika, and we sprint to the cavern. From our vantage point, we see a Goldster pull up. It's Inner-circle. I know this because it's not the rookie Thunderbird style. This one is Bentley-styled. I also know this because I have spent a lot of time in that particular vehicle.

The doors open and four men jump out: one very large, two slightly smaller, and the fourth, 6' tall and muscular. They go straight into SWAT team mode, looking a helluva lot more professional than we just did. They've got rayguns—Framework weapons. The beams can slice through nearly anything. They're shaped as old-world guns. The rays can be programmed to create a small jolt similar to a stun gun, or slice straight through matter, X-ray vision-style. I recognize those four forms—all too much.

We cower in the grotto. Scarlett holds Axel whose face is buried in her neck. Anika's is buried in Connor's. Reese's head peeks below mine in the opening. The four guys disperse around the house checking all the doors. When that's finished, they begin to survey the landscape.

"Should we check the woods?" a gruff voice asks. *Bryce.*

"Ugh. Guys, really? He's not gonna be easy to find, and he knows these woods better than the animals that live here." Another voice. *Chad.*

"Why would he hide in the woods?"

"So we don't find him, Sam." Chad again. "If he knows the woods better than anyone, no one can find him there. Jeez. Do I have to spell out everything for you?"

"Shut up, all of you. We will check the outer perimeter. You two go west. Bryce and I go east. I want coverage of at least a hundred yards into the woods. Then we can go. Now, move." *Damien.*

My skin crawls in the clammy cave. The cave that's only about fifty yards into the forest. Maybe they're not smart enough for geo-accuracy. *Who am I kidding?* They all have special Slabs. They'll be over here in a matter of minutes.

Suddenly, the copper head that was hovering beneath mine vanishes. I look out the cave to see two skinny legs running through the clearing. In her path—Anika's paper crown. I look behind her to see Bryce and Damien about fifty feet east looking in the opposite direction.

I stand there frozen watching as she reaches the crown. Scarlett notices her absence and sprints to the entrance. Connor stops her with a hand. Reese picks up the crown and begins to sprint toward us. She is about fifteen feet away when a sudden invisible jolt takes her down, the crown floating softly to the ground.

Two thick sets of boots march up next to her unmoving—but clearly still breathing—body. I see one crush Anika's perfectly folded crown into spongy soil. Connor is holding a silently frantic Scarlett back with one thick arm. Anika and Axel silently clutch their respective necks.

"What do we have here?" Bryce, the biggest—and creepiest one—says, walking in a slow circle around Reese's still form.

Damien stoops down and lifts the hair from Reese's face.

"I'll kill him with own my bare hands," Scarlett whispers full of unbridled rage.

"She's young, Bryce. Don't be gross," Damien says. "Go get the other guys."

"Let me just," he stoops down.

Scarlett's entire body shakes with fury from the darkness of the cave.

"Bryce. If you don't get away from her and get those guys, I swear to you..." He doesn't need to finish his warning sentence. Bryce is already making his way to the others. Damien's the one in charge here. As usual.

Once again unarmed, I look to the other two adults. Nobody expected this.

Suddenly, Connor pulls an object from his waistband.

"Is that an ax?" Scarlett asks incredulously.

"A tomahawk," he replies with a shrug. "For protection."

I sit on the floor of the cave and un-tie my sandals.

"What are you doing?" Connor whispers urgently. "Wardrobe change?"

"Hopefully, not just a wardrobe change," I whisper. "I have a history with that guy." The shoes dangle from my hand. "Stay here and try not to kill anyone with that thing. If anyone gets too close, just knock them out." I take a deep breath and emerge into the sunlight. Squinting my eyes until they adjust, I walk barefoot to Reese's form, tip-toeing over branches.

"Look who it is," I say to Damien who's squatting down searching his Slab. He looks up at me. Recognition dawns.

"Lyvia," he drawls, breaking into a smile and standing up.

"Damien," I reply, not returning it.

"Long time no see," he says. "She with you?"

"Yeah, she is. So, I'm gonna need to take her and leave. Now."

"Oh, well, Lyvia, you know I can't do that," he counters. "Levi's been looking for you." He circles around Reese slowly.

"Well, isn't that convenient. I just so happen to be looking for him too," I reply, standing still. The cold damp earth melds to my bare feet.

"I could take ya," he offers.

"No thanks, Damien. I'll find him myself."

"I'd say suit yourself, but he pretty much told me to bring you to him by any means necessary, so you and your little friend here are coming with us."

Footsteps. Muffled conversation. *The gang's almost back.* I jerk my hand as if doing so might transform the shoes. No such luck.

"You got company, Dame?" Sam calls as they near us. "Who's the blonde?"

Bryce, Sam, and Chad join our little posse.

"Lyvia? You went blonde," Bryce says, stepping up to me. He reaches out to touch my hair. I jerk back violently.

"Okay, jeez. It sure is pretty." The last sentence is drawn out... A serial killer before he takes a snip of it home for under his pillow.

"I don't like to be touched. You know this, Bryce," I sneer.

"Oh yeah, I do think I remember that. But, we could really have fun, Lyvia." He's huge. Bigger than Shane. Wide as a bulldozer. He has blonde hair and a round face, rosy cheeks. He's a massive Gustav in Willy Wonka, albeit on blue elixir. I wish I could watch him drown to death in a chocolate river.

"Bryce, get away from her. Both of them," Damien says, before Gustav can gravitate toward Reese. "Sam and Chad tie her up," he points to Reesy's petite body.

They get out glowing Framework zip-ties, reminiscent of Dagan's, and begin to tie Reese's ankles and wrists. I wiggle the shoes back and forth in my hand, willing them to transform.

"Now, for you, Lyv, we can do this the easy way or the hard way," Damien drawls, moseying over to me.

"Don't call me that," I warn. He has sandy brown hair that curls up around his ears and the nape of his neck. If you take away who he works for and what he does for a living—he's hot—movie star hot. The boy next door—Chris Pine-esque—piercing blue eyes, gorgeous smile. Pure evil.

"I think it's safe to say we're doing this the hard way," I say, whipping my weighty shoes at his face. I make contact—a sick, crunching sound. I follow up with a jab to the throat. He falls back but recovers quickly. I expertly duck his swing and kick out his legs from beneath him.

The shoes, still shoes, continue to dangle from my left hand. I give him space to get up, scared he'll swipe me if I get too close.

"You need us, boss?" Sam asks, almost finished with the zip ties.

"Just say the word," Gustav appears behind Damien, salivating. A vicious, snarling dog eagerly awaiting his master's command.

"No. I got her," Damien replies, wiping blood from his mouth.

"Do you?" I ask, twirling the shoes menacingly.

"Yeah. I do."

I swing the shoes at him again, this time the other direction. He senses my decision quickly and seizes the sandals. He rips the straps from my hand and tosses them into the woods. I see them land near the crushed paper crown about ten feet away. I duck around him ninja-style and sweep out his legs. He anticipates my next kick and grabs my leg taking me down with him. Using both legs, I kick him in the mid-section. It doesn't faze him. We're both on our feet quickly.

I go for another throat jab, but he anticipates this as well, grabbing my arm and clocking me in the head. Heavily. I lie on the ground dazed. I blink into focus. A blurry Damien is moving toward me. Behind him, the picture clears and I see the other boys attempting to move Reese.

Please, God. I could use a little help here.

Damien gets closer. He grabs me by the shirt and lifts me up. My midriff is bared. This really annoys me. I'm getting seriously pissed off. I never liked these guys.

"Come on. I know you've missed me," he says. He grabs a giant handful of my hair and jerks it. Hard.

"We could've had some fun times. But, you play—So. Hard. To. Get." The last four words are punctuated with yanks. I think he takes some scalp with it. Now I'm really pissed. Don't fuck with my hair. The only one who touches these locks, besides me, is my mother.

That's it. I go for a kick to the groin. He dodges it and grabs me by the neck up against the tree.

"You know, I've always loved you, Lyvia," he speaks this in a low tone against my ear.

"What about Levi?" I ask. "I'm sure he wouldn't like that too much."

"Levi's busy."

"With what?"

"Big plans, Lyvia. Big plans."

"I still don't think he would like this. Any of this."

"That's where you're wrong, Lyvia. He says we'll be able to do whatever we want."

"When?"

"When we get there."

"Where?"

"'New Heaven,' of course, Lyv," he says with a wink. "Now, I think you and I are going to be very happy." He traces a line up my bare leg.

"I said, don't call me that," I spit, reaching up to stick my thumbs in his eye sockets. He breaks my hold swiftly and clocks me in the head a second time.

Black. Gritty soil is in my mouth muddied with blood. Cool spongy ground presses against my cheek. The picture is worse this time. Focus—impossible. I see a shadowy Damien rubbing his eyes before stooping down to grab my shoulders again. He pins me up against the tree.

"Come on, Lyv, your face is too pretty for all this," he says, touching it gingerly where he just smashed it a second time. The other hand pins my neck against the rough bark. I try to snap to full consciousness. His hand travels again to my thigh.

Help. Someone. Anyone. Please.

His finger continues its upward path along my leg. It's now past the hem of my cutoff shorts. I squeeze my eyes shut waiting for this to be over.

All of it.

16

Suddenly, there's a hushed whipping sound to my left. Squinting, I see a silver blur on the ground. It's spinning. Then, a swish.

Two gigantic spikes take refuge in my hands. My head clears instantly. I knock Damien out in one fell swoosh. The gigantic nail makes an audible thud against his head, but I can tell he's not gravely injured. Bryce comes running at me, raygun at the ready. I mentally urge the other nail. *Movement in palm.* Shaky at first, it shoots out knocking Gustav on his wide ass, returning to my palm in seconds. I do the same to Sam.

Chad, however, has taken cover in the thicket. I search the area. The trees are thick and vary in shape and size. I spot movement to my left. Suddenly a nail, with a mind of its own, shoots out, darts around trees, and disappears in a swoosh. I hear a faint thud and look around.

The nail lazily makes its way back to my palm, swirling around tree trunks. It's an inner tube floating down a twisty lazy river. Settling into my grasp, I clutch them both. They transform back to sandals. I put them on and motion for Connor and Scarlett to join me. They set their respective children on the ground. We run over to Reese and Connor cuts the zip ties with his tomahawk. She's starting to come to.

The four guys lie motionless around us. I think they'll be out for a while, but we have to get moving. Reese, a little dazed, stands up, rubbing her head. Axel hugs her legs. Connor looks around assessing the situation. I can't spot Anika.

"Where's Anika?" I ask. We all spin around in our spots but see nothing.

"Anika," Scarlett says in a fierce whisper.

Suddenly, I spot her tiny form squatting down next to her destroyed crown. "Mom, they ruined it," she says quietly. Dejected.

"It's okay, honey, we can make another one. Now, come on, let's go," Scarlett whispers, waving her over.

She trudges to us holding the damp, crushed paper. We scoop them up and head to the car. Reese still rubs her head; although, with further examination, we see that she is fine.

"What the hell was that about?" Connor asks, once we are all buckled in and backing out of the forest.

"Oh yeah, I used to know those guys," I reply.

"We've gathered that. What the heck was with those giant spikes?"

"Oh yeah, those. That's a new development for me. Don't even know where to begin…"

"Sheesh," he says, looking at the whir of scenery out the window.

"My thoughts exactly," I add, watching the world fly by.

WE MAKE it to the house. Scarlett prepares a snack for the kids as if this was a daily occurrence. Nothing fazes this girl. Once the kids are settled with their cheese, crackers, and various cut vegetables, the adults reconvene in the kitchen.

"Lighters, right?" Connor asks.

"Yep, Inner-circle," I reply.

"You know, you look kind of familiar," he says, as if noticing for the first time.

"Yeah, I get that a lot." *My most over-used phrase.*

"No, there's something else," he says thoughtfully. *The Price Is Right* wheel is back in action. Its final descent. Ding. Ding. Ding. Ding… *DING*—

"I've seen you on *Realmcast.*" *Realmcast* is the Realm's modern-day entertainment source. Like all Framework, it's virtual reality.

"With the Gold guy, what's his name? Levee? Guy thinks he's a mixture of Steve Jobs and Elvis. More like Lex Luther and Meatloaf," he says.

Scarlett and I just stare at him.

"Okay, okay, a tiny bit better looking than Meatloaf," he acquiesces. He studies me for a second.

"You dyed your hair. It really suits you," he says sincerely. He has sarcastic humor topped with boyish charm. I can definitely tell they are siblings.

"Actually, those were wigs. I like to stay under the radar," I reply sheepishly.

"It's Levi," Scarlett corrects. "I recognized you this morning. I prefer the blonde."

"Thanks, me too," I say. "How come you didn't say anything?"

"Oh, I don't pry. I figured you'd talk about it if and when you were ready."

"Thanks. I appreciate that," I say sincerely. "I really loathe talking about the absolute worst mistake of my life."

"Don't we all," Scarlett replies, pulling out sweet tea and crumpets. Yes. Crumpets. Connor devours three quickly.

"Okay. Time to regroup. Lyvia, what exactly did those guys want?" Scarlett asks.

"I really don't know. Obviously, they wanted to take me to Levi. I don't know if they know where he is though, because I don't know how they think they can get there."

"Where?" Connor asks with his mouth full.

"Hell," I reply, casually. His eyes shoot wide open. He nearly chokes on his crumpet.

"How do you know that?" he asks, regaining his composure.

"I have my sources," I say, thinking of Shane.

"Why is he in Hell?"

"Because he's the Devil," I answer, taking a bite of buttery crumpet. It melts in my mouth.

"What?" Connor and Scarlett ask, simultaneously.

"Yes, the Lucifer, in all his glory," I reply, rolling my eyes.

"I knew the guy was bad, but come on, the Devil?" Connor asks.

"Yes, the Devil. His Great Reveal was supposed to be a vortex like Dark's, but his not only communicates with Hell, it works like a portal. Transportation, but it only goes one-way. Down. His 'New Heaven' is actually Hell. And, he is the King."

"That's horrifying," Connor says, taking a gulp of his tea.

"Well, I'm helping," Scarlett says, throwing a dishtowel on the counter.

"No, you're not," Connor says.

"Oh yes, I am," Scarlett replies. "You do *not* mess with my cubs."

We all look into the adjoining dining room. Reese is eating her snack simultaneously reading a thick book. I think it's Edgar Allen Poe. Wow, she's a smart one. I spot Axel eating his snack under the table, a toy bulldozer rolling up and down the table legs. In the other hand, squished cheese and crushed crackers are held tightly.

"I just need a spa day," Anika says. "A cushy robe and slippers. I need to get pampered." I follow the voice with my eyes landing on Anika in her chair. She's leaning back with a cucumber slice covering each eye.

"Like mother, like daughter," Connor says, observing the display.

She and I laugh.

"So, what's next?" Scarlett asks.

"I don't really know. We have no clue where Dagan is, but those guys were looking for him. I was just a bonus find. I still need to research at the library. I'm sure those guys woke up by now. I don't think they would stay there. I imagine they'll need to report to their leader, however they do that."

"Well, I'm coming with you," Scarlett says. "Connor, can you watch the kids?"

"Um, no," he replies. "That's not what we are gonna do. Obviously, this girl has secret weapons, but I think either just she and I go, or we take the kids to Mom's and all go together."

"Mom's it is, then. I'll send a note and tell her you're on your way to drop them off. Hey guys, get ready. Uncle Connor is taking you to grandma's."

"Okay Mom," the three answer in unison. Anika pops a cucumber in her mouth. Reese leads the way. Anika follows. Axel falls in behind, a trail of cracker crumbs in his wake.

"Okay, Mom wrote back: 'Sounds good.' So you're good to go. Hurry up, guys. Bus is leaving," Scarlett calls up the stairs.

Scuffling at the top of the stairs. Small feet begin to scurry down the steps. The kids come running into the foyer, but they lose Anika along the way.

"Anika, let's go," Scarlett hollers from the doorway.

"Coming," she responds. She appears holding her crushed crown. The flimsy paper is completely unfolded and nearly dry.

"Hey Anika, can I see your crown paper?" I ask.

"Sure," she says. "You can have it."

I take the paper from her and realize it's a hastily hand-written note:

Lyv,

I waited as long as I could, but got word some not-so-good people... lookin' for me. Whatever you... NOT... my house... not safe... to Cush... by the... statue... don't... find me... look for you... Perseph... Directio... See you...

Daga...

The words are nearly indecipherable. The ink is smeared all over the crumpled damp sheet.

"Where was this, Anika?"

"It was sitting on this gigantic book," she says. "In one of the smaller rooms." Most likely *The Complete History of Technology* in the room he 'dropped' the book in.

"I'm gonna hold on to this. That okay with you?"

"It's my pleasure," she motions me to her. I stoop down. She puts her tiny hand against my ear again. "Secret werewolves have to stick together. I made it for you. I just had to try it out first," she whispers between a sweet smile.

"All right, let's go guys," Connor says, keys dangling in hand.

"Okay, Uncle Connor." Axel begins to march out; Anika follows behind.

"Following the leader, the leader, the leader, following the leader... wherever he may go," they sing from *Peter Pan* marching in their little line of two.

Reesy motions me over to her. She takes my hand and places a tiny object in it. "This will help keep you safe *and* brave. Don't look until I'm gone, okay?" She looks at me earnestly.

"I promise," I whisper. She closes my hand with small slender fingers tipped with frosty blue nail polish.

"Thank you, Reesy," I say. She jumps in the Range Rover and they head off. In my hand lies a miniature Shopkins figurine. It's shaped as a sleeping bag, the cover is folded down—yellow with pink hearts. Two painted eyes are closed and adorned with curly eyelashes. A tiny mouth is stretched wide in a yawn. Two tiny stub arms stick out on each side.

I tuck my new companion in my pocket and follow Scarlett to a lamp on the long hall table. The end of which opens into the foyer. I hadn't noticed before, but there's a tall platform stiletto chaise lounge across from the table. It's black and modern with a red sole. The lamp is shaped as a lipstick bottle. Black with a slanted red tipped lampshade. We gain nothing with the extra light. The ink is too runny.

"I gotta go back to the library," I say, looking up.

"You think it'll be safe?" she asks.

"As safe as anywhere," I reply. "I need information on vortexes and crossing transcendental planes. Really, I need the oldest books that are in there."

"Well, I know right where those are. Here, put out your hand." She squirts 'Lotion' on my hand. It smells of freshly baked confetti cupcakes with homemade buttercream frosting. *Silky ribbon laced ballet-pink, pointy stilettos. Loud music. Flashing lights. Scent of black licorice.*

"Do you smoke?" she asks, snapping me out of my reverie.

"I do, in fact," I reply.

"Let's have one really quick. We have time," Scarlett says, walking outside. On her porch, we settle into vintage iron chairs equipped with black-and-white polka-dot cushions, very comfortable. We both light our cigarettes.

"Those shoes are pretty awesome," she says, looking at my sandals. "They saved our lives." She exhales.

"I know. The problem is I don't know how they work. They have a mind of their own, otherwise I wouldn't have let this happen." I point to my bruised face. While it's still tender, it's healing very quickly. No pain. *Suspicious.*

"Well, they saved us. Thank you," she says.

"Anytime," I laugh.

"So... You and Levi..." She trails off... "What was that like?" She taps her cigarette against the glass ashtray.

"What?"

"Sleeping with the Devil..."

"Ugh," I roll my eyes. "Stupid. That's what it was. Blind and stupid."

"Well, we all make mistakes."

"This is true," I reply, stubbing out the butt.

Connor pulls up in the Range Rover. We meet him at the car and get in. "Where to, ladies?" he asks.

"Back to the library," Scarlett responds.

"Really? Is it safe?"

"Doesn't matter. I've got to go there. And if I know anything about those Inner-circles, it's that they're already back in Gold Shire by now."

"Sounds good. Let's hit it," he replies.

17

When we reach the library, it's beginning to get dark. Scarlett takes us to the antiquated books section. It's walled-off. She pulls out an ancient-looking skeleton key.

"All Crystal Shire residents eighteen and up get a key," she explains. We go through the door into a narrow tunnel and emerge into a circular room. The books are stacked with such care. Flat, not upright. They're very old, primordial. The smell of old hardcovers fills the room. The whole castle, really, but this room especially emits the scent of aged paper. Still, the books' condition is nearly immaculate. This is spiritual preservation at work.

"Okay, vortexes and transcendental planes."

Expertly navigating the room, Scarlett points out where to look. She obviously spends a lot of time here. "I work here in-kind sometimes," she answers my unspoken thought.

We split up and scan the shelves. Scarlett looks for vortexes and Connor looks for transcendental planes. I look for a Bible. I know there has to be a copy here. I'm hoping it's an old one. Finally, I spot it. It's the oldest book in the room. It even has its own shelf. The cover is preserved and written in Latin. I scoop it up, carefully.

"I've got something," Connor says from across the room. He carries a thick book. Leather bound with thin pages. "Just says *Vortex*. Super old, like all of 'em, but this one is really aged."

"Looks good," I say, inspecting the fragile spine.

"*Transcendental Planes*," Scarlett exclaims, emerging with an equally archaic book, similar cover.

"Perfect. It's a place to start. Thank you, guys." With that, we lock up the room and head back to Regina's. I've got some studying to do.

"THANK YOU SO MUCH, GUYS," I say through the open car window.

"Well, just keep me posted," Scarlett replies. "I need to help in any way I can."

"Me too," Connor adds.

"Will do. I'll send notes with updates." I wave them off and head straight to the kitchen. I grab a Honeycrisp apple and some cucumber water and climb the stairs. I don't have much of an appetite, but I need to eat.

In the room, I change for bed. Donning one of Shane's old oversized t-shirts, it's blue and features his hockey team—*The Wolves*. I brush my teeth and wash my face. Then, I walk over to the coffee table where the books lie. I pick up *Vortex* and settle into the downy fluff. I tuck my feet beneath me.

"Hey Lyv," Persephone speaks with a tone of seriousness. She appears on the loveseat cross-legged. She's in a cotton-candy-pink t-shirt and flamingo colored fitted jeans. Tennis shoe-d feet peek beneath her bent legs. Splashes of color spray the white canvas shoes. A hardcover balances between her knees.

"What's up?"

"I did some digging and found some pertinent intel on Dagan," she says, looking up to meet my eyes. "Really pertinent…"

"Okay, lay it on me," I reply.

"It's kind of huge, Lyv. You might want to hug a pillow." I set the book to the side and grab the nearest one.

"The day your parents went to the Cush," she starts.

I'm gravely familiar with the trip. My dad, quite the gambler, had won a sizable bet. Problem was, the man he bet against wasn't good for the money. Instead of cash, he offered a vehicle. Not just any vehicle. Shaped like the Batmobile, this novel automobile could fly at light speed, enter other dimensions, and time travel.

"Winner, winner, chicken dinner!" Pops exclaimed when he

received the keys to his new toy. He decided to take my mom to one of the most legendary places in the Realm. A place no man had gone before.

In the Cush there's an archaic statue placed above a waterfall. The sculpture is carved out of ivory and shaped as a giant tree. A nude woman and man are featured beneath the limbs. An apple hangs from the branch between them. A massive snake wraps itself around the tree trunk. Also, around the tree are animals, plants, flowers, and even a unicorn in the mix. *The Garden of Eden.*

No one knows how it was constructed. It couldn't be reached without Pop's new toy. According to legend, the statue isn't just a statue; it's a Holy Relic. That means—holy properties. Allegedly, the sculpture infuses infinite wisdom, pre-original sin, to those within its immediate vicinity. The waterfall is treacherous. There have been many failed attempts to reach it.

"They climbed into the new car. It absorbed its wheels and lifted off the ground."

I clutch the pillow tightly already knowing the ending. She touches my shoulder. I can almost feel heat coming off her phantom extremity.

"Shane and his friend were going to take it for a spin when your parents returned," she continues.

"What friend?"

"His best friend, Dagan."

I stare at her wide-eyed. Tossing the pillow to the side, I walk to the bed slowly. I sit down. "Wait. So, Dagan and Shane are friends…"

"Yup," Persephone replies, playing with an imaginary plastic phone. The archaic 1990s Dream Phone board game to be exact.

"I was talking to myself, Seph."

"He's not wearing a hat," a younger male voice cries from her bulky hot pink cellular device.

"It's not Dan," she mumbles, flipping through cards sporting pictures of the guys in the game. 1990s mushroom haircuts don many of the heads. You call their phone numbers to see which one 'likes you.'

"How long?" I ask, flopping on my back.

"Ever since Shane was appointed leader. They hit it off at one of the boxing matches between Crystal and Onyx." *Wow. How did I not know this?*

"He's not at the beach." The male voice recording plays through the phone's speaker. Lower this time, borderline creepy. "Hmm… Not George. Darn. He's cute," Persephone says, putting his card to the side.

"Seph, does Dagan know what happened to Shane?" I ask louder.

"He knows that Shane is missing and it's not good," she says, dialing. A chorus of electronic beeps followed by a low brrr-ring.

"What?" I shoot up. "How? Why didn't he tell me?"

"I know who it is, but I'm not telling…." The voice taunts from the pink earpiece.

"Seph," I shout, staring daggers.

"What?" She looks up from her cards. "Oh. Let's see. Dagan plays his cards close to the vest. He probably wanted to see what you know."

"But why wouldn't Shane tell me about him? Best friends and all."

A low brrr-ring…"You're right. I *really* like you," the voice exclaims. "Yes," Persephone drawls out, arms up. "It's Steve. You know he's the cutest." She flips through the cards.

"Yeah, with his hoodie and slightly messy mushroom cut… A little dangerous…" I reply. "No. Seph, focus."

"Okay, okay," she swipes the game pieces away and they disappear into thin air. "People get busy. You had your hands full. He would've probably introduced you at some point."

"He didn't."

"Nope."

"So, at the waterfall…"

"When your parents went up to the statue, the tide shifted unexpectedly and the car vanished. Never came back. Shane and Dagan waited there for two days."

"I had no idea Dagan was there."

"He left before you showed up."

We never heard from our parents again. I like to think they found their way to another dimension, maybe the Spirit Plane.

"How do you know this, Seph?"

"I have my sources," she winks and poofs into a puff of hot pink glitter. I try to process this. *Shane and Dagan.*

"I bet he's looking for Shane," I infer aloud. "That's why he's in the Cush. Oh my gosh, Seph, the statue—" I call jumping up. "The note, that's where he is."

"Let's try Shane," I exclaim. "He's got info."

I rush over to the bed and pick up the phone. Persephone perches on the nightstand. I turn the dial eight, six, four, one and wait. Nothing. I try again and still get silence. One last time and I hear the whir and soft click. The phone shakes in my hand as I press the earpiece to my head.

"I'm sorry, but the spirit you are trying to reach is temporarily unavailable." Click. I stand there with the phone in my hand.

"Unavailable? What does that mean?"

"He told you he was busy, Lyv," Persephone says, adjusting her hair in an imaginary mirror.

"Okay, but we need to get to the Cush," I reply, rifling through my bag. I pull out some fitted jeans and a long-sleeved t-shirt. Light grey and very thin. I top it with one of Shane's hoodies. A black football one adorned with *Eaglets*, his amateur team when he was in training.

"Do you know how to get there?" I ask.

"There should be a map in the *Vortex* book that you got from the library," she says. I really want to know where she gets her intel. Maybe one day when I'm not trying to destroy the Devil, himself, I can drill her. I find a large intricate map in the book. It appears 3D and full-color. In fact, where there is water it looks as though it's flowing. Light sheens on different marked spots. I see The Rock. Its ancient location flashes when I shift the book. I see one silver particularly large waterfall glittering brighter than any other. There is a sparkling white figure near the top. The statue.

"There it is, Seph," I say, pointing. She looks over my shoulder.

"Yep, that's it," she confirms brightly.

"Can you mimic the map?" I ask. A mimic is the same as taking an old-school picture. The only difference is she captures the entire book in 3D. Then she can read it as though she's got the real thing. Very helpful.

"Already did," she says, finishing her scan.

I pull my hair back up in a messy bun using the shrunken crown. I look at my sandals. The trek is very long through a wooded mystical forest. You have to travel the length of the forest trail to get to the falls and cliffs. It goes upward gradually along the mountainous region finally opening to the mouth of the waterfall. Our destination. The strappy sandals just won't do. Neither will stilettos.

I search through all my things. I've got three other pairs to choose from, but they're all wrong. Flip flops, dressy wedge ankle boots, and over-the-knee-black stilettos, similar to Scarlett's with the corset tie back, but no design. *Her boots are so cute*, I think. *Oh, wait, I feel one more pair.*

I unearth a pair of red-bottomed Christian Louboutin shoes, which remind me of my snake heels. They are also stilettos, although open-toed and covered with sparkly gold vines that wrap around the foot. Various bronze and chocolate diamonds adorn gold flowers along intricate straps. The vines go up past the ankles where they break into gold tulle that puffs out into mini tutus. Part of my Gold Shire attire. I guarantee they have no magical powers, especially considering who surprised me with them.

"These won't do," I say to Persephone. She's inspecting the gold footwear.

"You won't last a half-mile," she says. "The sandals worked very well on your last trek."

"That's true, but it's cold and muddy in the Cush."

"They're Holy Relics. Just wear 'em," she replies. I pick them up and carry them to the couch. After I get them fastened, I walk over to my bag and pack.

"You sure we're unseen in Crystal?" I ask Seph as I pick up the Slab.

"Yep, 100%. I have my sources," she says again with a wink.

"Okay, let's hit the road."

"Should we bring Scarlett and Connor with us?" she asks.

"No, it's late, and she's got kids. I'm sure he has a family himself. It's dangerous, and they'll be a distraction. Besides, I'm doing…"

"This alone," she finishes.

"You got that right," I say, closing the Slab. Persephone's holo-gram gets sucked into the notebook.

Downstairs, I find the same paisley bag from before filled with food and drinks. No note this time. I know from the map where to pick up the trail. I have to go through town again. The path is on the left, just past the trail that leads to the floss bridge.

18

I t's just before midnight when I leave. The town is eerily dark. Silent. Creepy. I keep along the street and hear a shuffling down an alleyway between two crystalline buildings. In the shadowy passageway, I spot a gigantic form step toward the opening. *Bryce.*

"I thought you boys would be home by now," I announce into the darkness.

"Nope, Lyvia," he replies, stepping into the moon's grey glow. "Levi sent message we should hang out a bit longer."

"Where's your group leader?" I ask, trying my best to sound steady.

"Oh. Damien," he rolls his eyes. "He had us split up. Wasn't sure where you'd be."

"So, you're the lucky one then," I reply, standing firmly on my spot.

"Oh, I'd say I'm the luckiest," he drawls, licking his bulbous lips. They shine in the moon's glow. Two overlapping, bloated pig intestines.

"I'm not so sure about that." *Stay strong, Lyvia.*

"Come on, Lyvia." He steps closer. "You're a little old for my taste, but I've wanted a piece since the first day Levi paraded you around. I liked you best as a redhead."

Ew. Red is my worst color. Doesn't fit my complexion. I switched it up often. That one was specially reserved for diverting attention. *Of course, this creep would like it best.*

"Yeah, you looked like a schoolgirl. Pippi Longstocking with glasses." He steps even closer. We're about eight feet away from each other.

"You are disgusting," I hiss, deciding whether I should try to run. *Where are his friends?*

"Lyvia, you know I gotta take you with me." He licks his ballooned lips again. "But I'm thinking we can have some fun first."

"I don't," I respond. He steps closer. Five feet. I toss my bags to the side.

"You know how much fun it's gonna be in 'New Heaven?' Lyvia, you will love it there. We can do anything we want." Three feet.

"As great as that sounds, Bryce, it's not for me."

"I think it is." A step closer and he reaches for my hair. "We can make you red again." I jerk away from his Italian sausage fingers tipped with dirty nails.

"Oh, Lyvia, you know I like a fighter. Maybe you can bring your spikes out again. Whatever those were. I like it rough, you know…"

He reaches to grab me, but I adeptly duck his massive arms. He loses his balance momentarily, and I gain some space. I don't know when his pals are going to make an appearance. I figure I can outrun him, until I spot the raygun tucked in his snug waistband. *Shit.*

"I like this game, Lyvia, but you should know—I always win." He raises a bushy blonde eyebrow. It resembles a fat maize caterpillar attached to his forehead.

We circle each other slowly. I try to figure out how I can get these shoes off and will them to transform. *Why did they not come with instructions?*

"Come on, Bryce. We both know that isn't true. Levi's your boss. Oh, and Damien, right? Wow. You get two big bosses ordering you around. Definitely sounds like winning to me."

"You don't know what you're talking about. You're just eye candy." He takes a giant step toward me. I dodge out of reach. He lunges again, a huge fist misses me by inches. I figure I can keep using his size against him. A few more swings and misses, and Gustav is breathing heavily. *Not enough cardio,* I think to myself.

"Come on, Bryce. Can't you do better than that? You look like Chunk from *The Goonies,* but on blue elixir, I'll give you that," I provoke, breathing moderately.

"Who's that?" he asks, standing upright.

"Don't worry about it," I reply, taking a step back. I can tell he's going for another swing. I duck and kick him in the groin, hard. It doesn't affect him. My money is he's on elixir. The 'lix' has him immune to pain right now. My blunder gives him the upper hand. He slams me against the brick wall. Five giant sausages cover my throat. *Not this again.*

"Now we can have playtime," he whispers against my ear. His breath covers my nose, spoiled beef stew with remnants of bourbon. I want to puke. My feet dangle helplessly. Looks as though the shoes might be sitting this one out.

"Hey, Bryce, what've you got?" A voice sounds from the darkness. *Chad.*

"Damn it," Bryce mutters against my ear. Hot sticky breath cloaks the side of my face. "I guess I'll just wait for another time."

"Yeah, I got her," he calls loudly to Chad.

"Sweet, I'll tell Damien." Chad appears in the moonlight. He's wiry and strong, young. Curly dirty blonde hair adorns his head.

"Put me down," I sneer through gritted teeth.

"Not yet, sweetie. I remember what happened last time."

"Put her down. Now." *Damien. Welcome to your circus. Reign in your damn monkeys already.* Bryce drops me to the ground unceremoniously. I rub my neck where his bulging fingers were clutched.

"You okay?" Damien asks with a touch of tenderness.

"Been better," I manage.

"Look, Lyvia, it'll be easier if you just come with us. So, let's just try that," Damien implores, about two feet away from me. "Okay? What do ya say?"

"I say, that I have somewhere I need to be and it's not with you."

"I think you're not gonna make it to that waterfall," he replies, now two feet in front of me. "And, I need to search you this time. None of us can figure out where those metal spikes came from."

"Where do you propose we go?" I ask, shifting gently from foot-to-foot. Nothing happens.

"Can't tell ya that, Lyvia," he replies, looking me up and down. "What's with the side shuffle?"

"Damien, could you and I possibly talk somewhere without an audience?" I ignore his question with a glance at his troupe.

"Not a good idea, boss," Gustav growls, placing a thick pink hand on his raygun.

"Bryce." The name hangs in the air; a slowly swaying Salem witch. "I decide what ideas are good. Never you. *Never. You.* Do you understand?"

"But—last time, you know, she had those things and you know—" he stutters. His pink face flushes so red it looks akin to excessively applied Santa Claus rouge.

"Damien, I just want to talk to you. Figure out what's really going on here," I interject, equally wanting to lessen the crowd and find out how in the world Damien knows I'm heading to the waterfall.

"Yeah, okay," he says, eyes finally meeting mine. "Guys, get Sam and wait in the Goldster. I'll be fine."

"Got it," Chad says, spinning away. "Come on, Bryce." Bryce stares a beat before turning around.

"Later, Chunk," I give a small wave. I can't help myself. He pauses a second but continues on. *Good choice.*

"Let's take a walk," Damien leads, taking my arm. I actually don't mind the gesture. Damien and I have somewhat of a history together, not romantic per se, but history nonetheless. I'm still peeved from earlier, although my wound has fully healed. *Interesting.*

We walk along the path toward the forest. Solar streetlights dazzle the pebbled gemstone walkway with large pointy stars. We find a bench in a clearing near the beginning of the forest. Through the trees you can see the rushing brook. Moonlight dances across the water—a very fast quickstep on its aquamarine surface.

"Where's Levi?" I ask, sitting down. The bench is large and shaped as a horseshoe. He sits across from me.

"I can't tell you that," he answers, taking out a cigarette. He hands me one and lights it. "But why do I think you already know the answer to that query?" he mutters, mouth wrapped around the cig he's lighting.

"Because I do."

"Thought so," he says, elbows now resting on his thighs.

"I need to go there, but I need to do it on my terms," I say.

"Lyvia, that's fine. I don't have orders to bring you in anymore."

"Why?"

139

"Not sure. Levi doesn't even tell *me* everything. All he said was to keep a look out for you and report back."

"And how do you do that? Report back?"

"Guess 'report back' isn't accurate. He comes to me. Just like he always has. I wait. He comes on his time."

"What? He said to keep an eye out, but just let me go on my merry way? Then why'd you just try to get me to come with you just now?"

"Oh Lyvia, you know I can't make everything easy on ya. Gotta have a little fun."

"Gustav back there didn't seem to understand that."

"Chunk doesn't understand a lot of things," he laughs. "I don't have to tell you that. *The Goonies*. That's a good one, by the way."

"Thanks," I laugh. "But, still, he didn't seem to get that."

"Yeah, Levi told me what was up right before I got to you."

"How do I even know you're telling the truth?"

"Because, Lyvia, games aside, I think you know how I really feel about you." He flicks his cigarette and takes a drag.

"Well, what was with that display earlier today?" I ask, taking a drag of my own.

"Come on, Lyvia," he replies, exhaling smoke. "I know you feel the same way. I'd rather you come to that conclusion on your own." Damien was my only friend for a long time. Levi's number two; he was with me whenever his boss was busy. And as one could imagine, his boss was busy a lot.

"Damien," I start. "I can't even fathom the implications of this information. Levi."

"Yeah, yeah. I know. Levi." He puts his cigarette out and tosses it in a small trashcan at the end of the bench.

"I really can't entertain anything like that. You must realize," I say, doing the same. I always knew how Damien felt. I think it would insult him to act like I don't know. I also think it's best to keep your enemies close. Also, I had thought him a close friend once upon a time.

"Fine," he responds. "But you do know, I have to do whatever Levi says. This time, he wants you to keep going. So, I let it happen. However, I don't know what the future says."

"How do you know where I'm headed?"

"Levi."

"That's it? He didn't say more?"

"Of course not."

"It's Levi," we speak in unison.

"Lyvia," he says, standing up. "Don't think this makes me a good guy. I have plans too." His voice fades with his disappearing form.

I wait a beat before continuing my journey.

19

The thicket at night appears unlike its daytime counterpart. It's grown eerie in the absence of sunlight. I pull out my kist key. A kist key is a neural network device. Usually associated with Framework, they can also be unconnected, such as Dagan's. It's a multi-use device. It acts as a modernized technological Swiss army knife. You name the tool, it has it.

I clip it to my hoodie and an orb of light illuminates the path. The sound of crickets and cicadas fill my ears. The air is damp and chilled with nighttime. I walk past the path to the floss bridge. The trees thicken and vines hang among their branches. Their limbs twist into skinny, spooky fingers that claw at the starlit sky. I find the clearing on the left—the path that leads to the mountain and eventually, the Cush. The soil gets thicker and spongy. Branches and dead foliage clog the walkway.

Suddenly, my sandals swish around my feet. The silver blurs so fast—two beams of grey light swirling around each foot. They stop. They've transformed again. This time—hammered metal, slouchy boots. The laces are loose, and the sides flap open. They're heavy duty, featuring bootlaces that gleam in the moon's glow, long snakes tied in droopy bows.

"Where were you guys when Gustav was choking me to death?" I scold, looking down at them. No response. I forgive them for the momentary lapse in action, I have to admit the footwear has been incredibly valuable, thus far. I continue up the twisty, hilly path. I spot movement to my right and freeze. I swipe my hand up to silently turn off the kist key. I listen. *Nothing*. A pause. Then, more movement.

I see the hind legs of a giant white animal about ten feet away from me between trees and foliage. It resembles a wild horse—a huge, free Clydesdale. I quietly move closer to the white beast hoping not to scare it. It turns its body to the side and slowly lifts its head. I'm about five feet away. Upon first glance, the profile confirms a horse. However, as moonlight illuminates the animal, I see at the top of its head one massive, spiral ivory horn. *A unicorn.*

Wh—at? I say to myself drawing the word out, slowly and high-pitched quoting James Franco's in *This Is the End.* Wow. They're not supposed to be real. *What's happening in Crystal?* I walk up to it, gently. In the moonlight, I see it's a she.

"Hey girl," I coo, edging closer. She huffs and puffs horse-like.

"Hey," I say again, slowly reaching out to touch her. She lets me and I pet her coat, softly. She turns to me and nuzzles her giant nose in my neck. I nearly topple over as her large head snuggles against me. I reach to touch the horn. It's massive and covered with short, yet thick, velvety fur. It's as hard as bone.

A twig snaps behind me. The animal spooks and expertly gallops away around trees. Its vast form is as graceful as a swan. She's a disappearing flash of shimmering light. I turn back to the path and see a shadowy figure just on the other side. I creep down and crouch behind a tree trunk. Two legs, this time human, walk the moonlit trail.

"Hey, Lyvia." An all-too-familiar voice speaks evenly.

Levi. I shudder involuntarily. No wonder his merry band let Dorothy go on her way. *Sparkling champagne bubbles pop on my tongue. A scent of crisp, woodsy cologne. Sunset over a lake. White sand between my toes. A strong breeze blows my hair around and guitar chords fill the air.* Wait. The music is real. I roll my eyes and sigh into the darkness.

"Hey Levi," I respond, standing up from my hiding spot.

"Long time no see," he says, perched on a rock near the path—he holds his guitar, fiddles with its strings.

"Not long enough," I reply, stepping into the tiny clearing.

Black shirt, long sleeves, pulled up to his elbows. Worn, fitted jeans. A tattoo peeks out from the scrunched material on his muscular right arm. His hair is mussed expertly. He smiles his half-smile, mischievously. I used to love that smile.

"Oh, Lyvs, you don't mean that," he purrs, using his special nickname for me. Something I also used to love.

"You don't get to call me that anymore, Lucifer," I spit out his true name.

He plays the opening chords of "You Don't Know How It Feels" by Tom Petty. "Yeah, that's my given name," he stretches out the note. "But I don't go by that anymore."

"Oh, really?"

"Yeah, I needed something fresh." He starts playing "Highway to Hell" by ACDC. *This guy.*

"Well, I don't know, Levi," I say. "I always preferred the classics."

"That you did, Lyvs. That you did," he drawls, strumming his guitar.

"You know what I want," I say.

"Ahh yes, that old piece of junk." His fingers move deftly up and down the instrument. A series of plucks create a melodious sound that fills my senses.

"Yeah, the hammer," I reply, hands on hips.

"Well, Lyvs, you find yourself in quite a predicament here." He rubs his head, musses his hair. This only adds to his cuteness factor, a move unconsciously developed over time that still makes me weak in the knees. *Almost.*

"Why is that, Leevs?" I ask, since apparently we're using nicknames.

"Way I see it, Lyvs," he starts playing "The Siamese Cat Song" from *Lady and the Tramp*. "As the flame burns Lumière's candle wick, you need to beat Cogsworth's tick-tick-tick."

"Oh, you talk in riddles now? Ladies and gentlemen, we have in our midst, the one the only... Alice's very own... Cheshire Cat," I splay one hand outward, presenting the 'star of the show.'

"Lyvs, if we're gonna talk riddles, I prefer the Joker, or hey, maybe the actual Riddler. Not sure, but you know the cat is just too PG for me."

"Okay, Levi. What are you getting at with your *Beauty and the Beast* puzzle?"

"I knew you'd guess it. You always did love that movie."

"The original—better clarify that."

"Of course, the original, Lyvs. I know you."

"No, you really don't. I need that hammer, Levi," I say, impatience mounting by the second.

"You are welcome to come with me and get it. Problem is, I left it at my place. You haven't seen the new digs yet, Lyvs. I think you'll like 'em."

"Okay, so you're saying I come with you right now to Hell, and you hand it over. And then I leave? Just like that? I'm not buying it, Leev. What do you get out of it?"

"Oh, Lyvia. What makes you presume I want anything? Besides you, of course. But, I'd never want you against your will. I've been around for quite some time, you know? And you, my Lyvia... Well, there's just no one like you. Never has been. There's something special He did when He created you. I don't know what it is, but I do know I love it." An internal cringe at his use of 'my Lyvia.'

"Let's just say, I go with you," I begin. "What's up with the riddle?"

"Ahh, yes, the riddle," he drawls. Fingers again up and down the instrument—an ominous tune this time. "I think you have a new friend somewhere? Do I have that correct?" *Dagan.*

"What's going on? Is he in danger?"

"Come on, Lyvia. You know all about that waterfall, don't you?" Now he plays heavy, gloomy tones.

Heat rises to my face in a fury. "Yeah, I do, Levi. It's dangerous enough by itself. What have you done?"

"He'll be fine, Lyvs," he says. "Granted you get there in time... Tick-tick-tick..."

"Oh, for fuck's sake, Levi. So I go with you, or sprint to the waterfall and *hope* I make it in time?"

"Hammer or Dagan... Hammer or Dagan," he says, motioning his hands like an antique balance scale.

I know this guy. Well, as much as anyone can know the Devil. What I can tell you is this: there's not a snowball's chance the guy is going to let me leave Hell with that hammer. I need help and more weaponry—if it exists. I need a plan before I enter his play place. When I do, it will be on *my* terms. Plus, I like Dagan. He's a good guy, and apparently, a friend of Shane's. Moreover, he's looking for Shane. Which means, we team back up. *If* I can get to him in time.

"You know something I really love about you, Lyvs? I can't get into your mind. Not even a little bit. I have to admit—I've tried, but nope. Something about you. Your mind is a locked abyss... One that even I'm not privy to."

"Well, thank God for that," I reply.

"Well, you can thank Him all you want," he says, looking upward. "But I'm not in much of a mood to thank the guy that banished me to Earth with your kind. You are the only one, Lyvs. The only human in"—finger quotes—"'His image' who mystifies me. I still love you, baby."

"I didn't know the Devil was capable of love," I respond.

"Hey," he plays the chords to "Stairway to Heaven" by Led Zeppelin. "I used to be an angel, you know. Just like Mikey, Gabe, and the rest of the gang. I was high up too."

"Or so I've read," I reply. "How much time do I have?"

He plays the *Jaws* theme. *Duhhhh-na, Duhhh-na. Duhh-na. Duh-na. Duh-na.* "Just enough... If you hurry..." His strumming blends into the opening of the *Rocky* theme song, "Eye of the Tiger," before he vanishes into thin air.

Wow. Never seen him do that before. I don't even want to know the extent of his power beyond this new disappearing act. I assume he doesn't need a vortex to get to Hell.

I stick that information in my back pocket.

For now.

20

I pull out my Slab and pop it open. Persephone emerges.

"Wow. That was intense," she says, walking around the site. She's looking at the rock he was sitting on. She's dressed in head-to-foot black—leggings and an oversized sweatshirt, finishing off the look with black converse tennis shoes. She likes to dress for the occasion at times.

"I'll say. Okay. Seph, we don't have time to analyze that. How far is Dagan? How long will it take?"

She pulls out the book she has scanned. "You've got about twenty miles left to the statue."

"Can you connect to Crystal's grid? See what we can see?" Crystal's grid is similar to the Framework but runs on solar energy. Framework Slabs generally can't connect, and I'm unaware if Persephone can override the spiritual barriers in the shire's district.

"Lemme see," she says, thoughtfully perched on Levi's rock. "I have a much better connection at Regina's, but I'm picking up a grid-iron that will give me a cloudy image."

"Okay." She pulls up a 3D map just as she did in the Fuse. This one is grainy, reminiscent of a picture taken without enough light.

"Show me the trail." She isolates the path. Twenty miles of twisty darkness.

"Show me the statue." She pulls up an aerial shot of the waterfall.

"Zoom in." Near the top of the falls, I see a blurry light grey fixture.

"Zoom in again." The statue grows in size. I can somewhat make out the giant structure. It's still a very gritty image.

"I don't see him."

"Me neither," Persephone replies, now standing next to me.

"Are we too late? That asshole. Didn't even give me enough time to try," I say, pacing the small clearing.

"Wait, I see him," Persephone says excitedly.

"Where?" I ask, hustling back to her.

"See," she points. "Right there."

In the sandy image, I spot movement near the bottom of the sculpture. His form looks small. He is sitting at the foot of the piece. Shivering. I can't make out any features beyond that.

"First of all, how did he get up there? Second of all, what's the rush? As long as he stays there, we can get to him in time."

"The waterfall has high-tide just like the ocean. When your mom and dad went up, the tide shifted unexpectedly."

"So, you're telling me the tide is shifting again."

"Yes," she replies.

"How much time?"

"Three hours."

"I can't hike twenty miles in three hours. What a sick joke, Levi," I say, perching on a rock. Not his.

"What are we gonna do?" Persephone asks, shutting down her map.

"Well, I was hoping the 'Slab that knows all' might have a suggestion…"

"I got nothing," she says with a shrug. "But we should at least get moving."

"Yeah, yeah, I know, Seph," I say, standing. "I just don't see how we can do it, but we have to try."

I close the Slab notebook and begin the trek. My pace is pretty fast. The flat terrain allows for a run but nowhere near the pace of our ticking Cogsworth. I'm sweating and out of breath. I have to break for water. I pull out the Slab.

"How far have we gone?"

"Five miles," Persephone answers, crossed-legged on the forest floor.

"What? That felt like ten," I reply, taking a huge gulp of water. "Time?"

"You have two and a half hours left."

"We're never gonna make it," I say, wiping my brow and putting the water away. "Too bad these shoes don't turn into instruments for flight." I inspect the boots. The matte metal sheens indifferently in the night glow.

"How am I gonna do this? If I lose Dagan too… I just met the guy. And Shane liked him. Let's go. We have to try." I put my Slab away and get moving again. The path begins to narrow, and the trek becomes steeper, my pace—slower.

"How far, Seph?" I ask, stopping again for water.

"Ten miles to go. One hour left," her voice says from my bag.

"Damn it," I say, putting the water back. "I shoulda just went to Hell. Who knows? Might be better than this. I really don't want Dagan to die—not because I couldn't get there in time. Again." I hang my head in defeat, but I stand anyway.

A scuffling in the brush. A soft neigh. A turn to see my new friend eating some foliage.

Maybe…

I walk gently over to her. She lets me pet her and nuzzles my ear, nearly pushing me to the ground again. I touch her horn. It's so cool.

"You think you could take me up to the mountain, girl?" I ask softly.

Another soft neigh and she lowers her massive head.

Okay. I haven't ridden a horse since I was sixteen. That was a horse with a saddle. This is a gigantic 'horse of different color.' The *Wizard of Oz* quote pops in my head. I think of Dagan and his boyish smile. His laugh. The fact that he and Shane are best friends.

"Here goes nothing."

I try to swing my leg over the unicorn's vast midsection. 'Try' being the operative word here. I slip off and fall heavily to the ground. Up in seconds, I give it another try. I swing my leg a little higher and harder but slip off, yet again.

"Okay, girl, I'm gonna get up there," I say, brushing my hands together and revving up.

Yes. I'm revving up. A running start.

"Bear with me!" This time I rush up to her and take a huge hop. My leg makes it over her hindquarters but starts to slip.

"No, come on," I breathe, sliding down her side.

She lowers her front, and I gain traction. I use her mane to steady myself. She lifts her head back in an 'all buckled up?' gesture. I wish she was equipped with seatbelts.

"Okay, let's go," I say, bracing myself for the ride. Can unicorns fly? I don't see wings on this one, but who knows? I have shoes that turn into Holy Relics. I'm beginning to think anything is possible.

She gallops gracefully and majestically along the path's hard turns. Then she takes a detour into the woods.

"Seph, do you know what's going on?" I ask, gripping the mane for dear life.

"She's just taking a shortcut," Seph's muffled voice answers.

"Um, like a treacherous one?"

"Well, let's just say the ride's going to get bumpier."

"Great," I reply through shattering teeth.

Sure enough, Persephone is accurate. The woodsy hills get steeper and steeper. The trees and brush get thicker. My ride darts around obstacles as a minnow shifts around rocks in a stream.

The forest thins and a giant rock wall looms ahead. It's larger than Mount Rushmore and darkened with night. We emerge onto a path leading up the mountain. This one is rockier. I have my kist key's light on, although the unicorn seems to glow. She almost floats above the uneven terrain. The suspicion of concealed wings interrupts my thoughts.

The trail continues to climb steeper by the minute. The sound of rushing water builds. It overwhelms my senses. *Cold water. Jagged rocks below the current. Rapid falls and teetering rafts. Looming clay covered cliffs. The scent of sunscreen. Large white floppy sunhat. Gold aviator sunglasses.*

In the present, we finally emerge onto a flat landing. The waterfall pours ahead. It's very wide and getting wider by the second.

All I can make out is a tiny muscular arm dangling over the side of the cliff. The precipice is jagged and goes straight upward. He's incredibly high. I can see the colossal statue stretch straight to the sky behind him. It's magnificent, seems to glow with light other than that supplied from the moon. Looking at the path from which we emerged, the unicorn has taken a shortcut over terrain that is humanly impossible to navigate.

The water continues to rush. I realize, yet again, I'm gravely unprepared. Not sure how I expected this to go, but clothing and makeup won't help, again.

"Use the nails," Persephone beckons from the bag.

I take off the boots. I'll try anything.

"Nails—" I yell and shake them. Does nothing.

"Please, Shane, I don't want to lose your friend. He knows you. I just met him. I want to know him. And, really, I could use his help to get you back," I whisper skyward.

I see the lifeless arm. The water relentlessly pours down. The boots and I are now sopping wet. I drop to my knees.

"Are you serious, Levi? This is not a game, you asshole," I scream to anyone listening.

I stand up holding the boots and walk toward the unicorn, hanging my head. Just then, the shoes spin becoming the glorious Holy Nails they are. I walk back over to the cliff and jab one into the rock.

An invisible force lodges the point into the stone. The same happens with the other. Steadily, the nails make the climb. It's not easy. The spikes jab and pull with shaky and severe jerks, as you would expect of giant primordial nails being driven into rock. Not a smooth ride. My hands hang on for dear life. Wet and slippery, I manage a secure grasp of the crude metal with each jab as if there is unseen help. The water maintains its sideways path toward me.

I continue the climb. About ten feet from my destination, the water begins to graze me. The added force, though slight, increases difficulty. Five feet away, it's steadily streaming down my back.

I barely see the last three feet, but I finally make it to the ledge. I climb over by swinging my legs to step on the steady, rock driven nails. My hands are shaky and arthritic. I move to the clearing out of the water. There is a slight echo in the nook. The landing is directly underneath the statue. Beautiful white ivory spans above my head, the foot of the statue.

I spot Dagan's body dangling precariously over the ledge. The shifting water picks up momentum. He's one wisp of wind away from going over. I start my way toward him.

"Dagan," I yell. It's useless. The water is too loud.

It's slippery and dark. As I move closer, I see he has been severely beaten. His shirt is torn to shreds. The water continues to build around me. The torrential downpour encompasses my senses. Suddenly, I hear nothing but white noise. Closer to the ledge, the backsplash of water builds.

I see nothing but a watery dark figure in front of me. I get down on my belly and scoot toward him. I notice an old thick scar running around his ribcage. I reach for his hand. The water has caused him to slip. I manage to grab his palm, but his downward momentum picks up and his body slides easily off the ledge. His strong muscular fingers slip through my grip.

I push to the landing's edge, still flat on my belly. I see his black figure disappear into the endless depths below. He vanishes into the treacherous cliffs, jagged rocks, and relentless rushing falls below.

I scoot back as far as I can under the massive structure. *Had Dagan been conscious, perhaps he could have been farther back in here*, I think, huddled against the stony wall.

Shivering and shaking, I assess my situation. The water is rushing so violently now, it could take an arm off. I can't see anything. It starts to engulf me in the crevice. Water is rushing around my ankles and rising.

I'm trapped in a liquid coffin.

The water continues to rise. It's to my knees now.

Suddenly, I feel two smooth and very heavy metal points slide into my hands. I can't climb down with them. Impossible.

But then, they spin. Maybe they have other powers...

Sandals. They transform back into Greek warrior sandals. *Are you kidding me.*

I put them on in the knee-high water, not sure what else to do, besides mentally prepare to see Shane again. Disappointed in myself for not getting here in time. For not stopping Levi.

I think about jumping.

I've lost everyone. I'm done. I just can't do this anymore.

I take a few steps to the ledge. The water is violently falling in front of me. I hear only white noise. I breathe in and take another step.

The sound changes, a break in the noise. A majestic white light shimmers through the current. A giant white downy feather wing parts the cascading sea.

The unicorn, which I must now name, enters the crevice. She bends and scoops me up. My bags are still fastened to her neck. Of course, she chooses this moment to reveal her wings. It's a sick, cosmic joke.

Charley, as I have named my new friend, soars through the sky. I hold on to her mane for dear life. She flies straight down the falls. I look to find Dagan. Fruitless. The waterfall is too colossal. Its enormous power just swallowed him up, Captain Ahab sucked into his watery grave.

She soars past the falls over the trees to level out. Winds begin to calm as her giant wings span out not unlike a swan's. I lie my tired head against her neck as she floats over dark whirring scenery.

21

Charley sets me down in front of Regina's. I gather my bags. A quick nuzzle and she vanishes into the sky as if she'd never been there in the first place. In the kitchen, I empty Regina's soaked paisley bag. The inside is as dry as a bone. I put the indestructible food containers, which are mysteriously still cold, in the fridge and go straight up to my room. I have no appetite. I haven't processed the last few hours yet. In fact, I still haven't processed the last few days.

What just happened?

I fill the bathtub and strip down. As if I haven't had enough water for the rest of my life. This pool is scalding hot though. I sink below the surface but don't scream this time. I don't have it in me.

I lie against the cool porcelain of the tub. Comatose. Numb. I stare into space for a very long time. My head is still silent. I haven't heard anything of that nature since I used the crown.

A sharp anesthetic scent fills my nose. I feel phantom thin cloth of a patient's gown between my fingers. Pain sears through my upper right arm. I subconsciously rub said spot. The scar is softer now but grooved. Thicker at the top, it runs from my upper shoulder down the length of my outer bicep about seven inches. The Grey doc said it would be a pencil-thin line. It's more of a wide felt-tip marker, the kind used for old-world presentations. I shudder at the memory.

Meanwhile, the water has turned cold. I drag myself out of the chilly tub, dry off, and slip on the robe. I turn on the TV and choose my favorite movie, *Almost Famous*. Between the scalding bath and thick robe, I start to overheat. I go to my bag and pull out a silky, lace-edged, sea-foam green set of pajamas, a camisole, shorts, and a paisley kimono. I change out of the pink robe and place it back on its hook.

Back in the room, I sit on the floor with my back against the bed and hug my knees. I rest my head in my arms. Death seems to follow me around. It's as though Levi's real desire is to make sure I'm utterly alone. Then he can finally make me his 'queen.'

How can I possibly go up against the Devil? I'm only one person. Maybe I should just go with him. I'm so sick of this fight. He took away my person. My person. Mine.

Now, this? He's going to win. He is. I didn't even stand a chance up there. I barely made it to see the ending. Again. Plus, this time, I had Holy Relics. Made no difference. I'm done.

"Why don't you try to call Shane?" Persephone asks from my sling-back bag.

"I'm the reason Dagan died, Seph." My voice is muffled in the crook of my arm. "Levi. He did that because of me. I don't want anyone else to get hurt."

"Well, everyone will get hurt if you go with Levi."

"What do you mean?"

"He wants Hell on Earth, Lyv…"

I walk over to my bag and pull her out along with my wallet. She appears perched on the couch. She's wearing pajamas, a matching set featuring polka dots. They're topped off with fuzzy pink slippers and a complementing sleep mask that holds her hair back from her face. She's holding a notebook and a glitter pen. Her hair is down and straight. In the wallet, I find what I'm looking for and sit across from her in my flowing kimono. I tuck my feet underneath me.

"Right…"

"That means everyone on Earth will be in Hell for eternity. There will be no more Heaven for them. The angels and spirits on the Spirit Plane will be safe—in a sense. They won't be in Hell. But… They'll have to watch their loved ones in torment for eternity. They will be powerless to help them."

"Right now, they can help. Somewhat," I say, rubbing the engraved bone token in my hand. A fish is carved on each side of the coin. Shane gave it to me a while back. It features St. Jude the Apostle, Patron Saint of desperate cases and lost causes. Shane's deeply involved in community outreach and support, hope. Always hope. I didn't see the engraving on Dagan's, but I have a feeling he received it from the same person. Blue elixir runs rampant these days. The drug steals too many lives. The coin is a token for those in recovery, each is personalized by shape and material, but Dagan's felt identical to mine.

"Yes, right now spirits can help loved ones get to Heaven. Meet them on the Spirit Plane."

"Okay, right. Let's try Shane," I say, standing up and walking over to the phone.

Persephone writes in her notebook. I dial our numbers but get the same unavailable message as before. I hang up the phone and the tiny action alone depletes me completely.

Unable to regulate my body temperature, I find I'm cold again. I replace the kimono with one of Shane's hoodies. This one is well-worn, blue, and adorned with the Easton Hockey logo. Slipping under the puffy covers, I settle in for some sleep. It comes fast and heavy.

"HEY, LYVS." A familiar voice jars me awake.

Startled, I shoot up dramatically and rub my eyes. I squint to see a recognizable silhouette leaning in the doorway to the living area. An object rests against the frame—a guitar-shaped object.

"What are you doing here? Haven't you done enough?" I say, flopping back down on the pillow. I have no fight to give. I cover my eyes with one arm. "Seriously, Levi. Why are you here? You know I'm not going with you. You know that's not the ending."

"Right now. Not the ending, right now," he drawls, walking over to the bed. "It can always change, Lyvs."

I'm sleepy. My defenses are gone. I'm taken to a humid sticky summer evening. *Silky fabric between my toes. Warmth on my cheek from the crook of his neck. Soft evening glow. Synchronized breathing. The whir of a fan. Cascading flowers line the balcony outside ajar French doors.*

He steps up to me and brushes his fingertips down my arm. The gesture is so familiar, I forget my current situation. Suddenly, I'm sucked back to that summer evening in his penthouse.

"Lyvs…" he purrs, a finger trailing my scar.

"Leevs," I murmur sleepily through closed eyes.

"Tell me about this… battle scar."

"Not much of a story," I nestle closer.

"Tell me. I like stories."

"I fell. Broke my arm. Had surgery. The end."

"Lyvs, I know you're a better storyteller than that," he whispers against my hair.

"Okay, fine. I had a seizure because of the Synesthesia. Apparently, when my brain short-circuited, or whatever happens, I landed on my rotator cuff and shattered it. Not much of a story like I said."

"Well, what were you doing when it happened?"

"Why don't you tell me about this," I change the subject, outlining the tattoo that adorns his left arm.

"I wanted a tattoo. I got one."

"Oh, Leev, I know you're a much better storyteller than that. What is it?"

"It's a dragon, Lyvs."

"With seven heads…" I say, outlining each one. It wraps around his entire arm. The heads are intricate and meld into one another. Different sizes and shapes designed by someone on an acid trip.

Back in the present, Levi sits on the edge of the bed next to me. I roll away from him. He traces my arm again. I move over and give him room to get in. He shifts in next to me and we take the same pose from that summer evening. In the crook of his neck, my voice vibrates.

"Why are you doing this, Leev?"

"I want you, Lyvs."

"Then why would you kill people I love?"

"Oh, Lyvs, you know they're in a much better place than this now."

"So what, you did them a favor?"

"Yes, Lyvs, I did."

"Okay, if you felt righteous enough to save them from Hell, why would you want me there?"

"Because, Lyvs. It won't be Hell for me and you. It'll be perfect."

I SHOOT up in bed patting the area around myself. Nothing. I'm alone. I'm sweating and breathing heavily. It's still dark out. I go to the bathroom and splash my face with cold water. I brace myself against the sink and look in the mirror. My eyes are red-rimmed and sleepy. Water is dripping down my chin.

I spot movement behind me in the mirror.

"Seph..." I call, whipping around.

I spot my Slab closed on the couch.

It was just a dream. I check the bed again. I walk to the door and open it slowly. Taking a peek, I see nothing on the shadowy landing. I turn back to the room, satisfied it was only a dream. I walk over to the bed and see something gleam just under its end. I squat down and slide it out.

A golden guitar pick.

22

In the morning, I wake to so much light and heat, I feel as if I'm on the surface of the sun. I walk over to the window and spot an old-world light switch. Although when I flip it, the window turns completely black and fills with stars. Dark Shire's are similar, but they fill with sunlight. I sink back into the bed.

Levi.

I'm going to need more weapons. If the guy can persuade me into talking to him that easily in my dreams—if it was a dream—I'm going to need artillery.

I keep the blinds open but turn on a lamp. I work better at night. I go into the library and scan the books. I need to start from the top. I climb the rolling staircase ladder to the highest row of books. It takes a while before I find what I'm looking for. I recognize the spine snug at the very end of the third row down.

It's aged and leather bound in faded shades of aqua. The blues brush the leather akin to ocean waves. It almost appears to be moving. Reminds me of the water beneath Dagan's lighthouse. The title floats down the spine in gleaming silver. The outside jacket is adorned with one word etched in the same silver: *Leviathan*. The inside cover reads *Leviathan: An Angel of Light*.

The term came back to me from my theological studies. "Leviathan" in the Bible refers to a sea monster whose goal was to destroy God's creatures by eating them. It also threatened the upheaval of the waters of Chaos. I read this book when I was researching the Great Rain. Leviathan is also used in the Bible as an image of Satan. *Levi.* Clever.

It's believed the reason for the Great Rain is because man continued to sin after Jesus was crucified. In fact, it got steadily and then rapidly worse. Humanity imploded on itself. Natural disasters became regular occurrences. Humans were poisoning themselves to death with drugs every second. Violence was a natural everyday circumstance. Self-inflicted deaths, murder, sickness, rape, lavishness, selfishness—these became common-day routine for everyone. Ordinary and expected. A world of complete desensitization. That's when Noah's rain made a comeback resulting in reduced landmass. Still now, evil perseveres. *Wash. Rinse. Repeat.*

I figure if Levi caused the Great Rain, then he is in fact, the *Leviathan.* His plan was to take over Earth by means of water. He continued to fuel human sin and gain numbers in Hell. Pushed his Father until he received a reaction. He figured if you're going to banish me down here with these creatures, then I'm going to control them in my own little playground.

"But we have free will," I say aloud.

Exactly. That's why he has to get humans to choose sin on their own accord. He just dresses it up. Makes a vortex straight to Hell, no further sins necessary. No need to wait for the rain this time. *Free trip! Now! One-way. All-inclusive.*

I take the book out to the balcony for a cigarette. I grab my aviator sunglasses. The light is blinding. I flip through pages. I find one entitled *Job 41:33.* I recognize the name from the Bible.

It's an archaic copy, thicker than the one I had. The pages resemble a pirate's olden treasure map, crinkled and tea-stained, yet preserved to the best shape possible. It closes with a flap around the front tied with a leather string.

'On Earth there is not his like, a creature without fear.'

Hmm. Does sound about right. Levi is one confident guy. Going up against God, Himself. No fear. That does narrow down weaknesses. I flip a couple pages.

Psalm 104: 25-26:

'Here is the sea, great and wide, which teems with creatures innumerable, living things both small and great. There go the ships, and Leviathan, which you formed to play in it.'

Beneath the excerpt, I gleam the following:

Leviathan were created at the same time as the other animals on the sixth day, after humans. They were sea-dwelling creatures. They lived in the ocean, while humans thrived in the Garden of Eden eating only vegetation. They died out after the first flood, Noah's. There is speculation that crocodiles originate from Leviathan. Most animal-life has also gone extinct these days due to the limited climate and resources, yet crocodiles are still around.

The ocean remains the biggest mystery known to man. We, to this day, still know more about the universe than we do about what is at the bottom of the ocean. All we know is that since the first flood, we have not seen any of these creatures. However, we've never gone that deep, especially when the water began to rise. It became impossible to study.

On a personal note: the depths of the ocean scare me far more than that of the universe. I go back into the living room and settle into the couch. I flip through more ancient pages.

Isaiah 14:12-14:

'How you are fallen from Heaven, O Day Star, son of Dawn! How you are cut down to the ground, you who laid the nations low! You said in your heart, 'I will ascend to Heaven; above the stars of God I will set my throne on high; I will sit on the mount of assembly in the far reaches of the north; I will ascend above the heights of the clouds; I will make myself like the Most High.'

"That sounds familiar."

"What does it say?" Persephone sounds through her closed cover.

I walk over and open it up. She sits facing me on the opposite loveseat. She's wearing tight fitting jeans with a White Stripes band t-shirt and red and white striped socks. She has a glowing crimson string in her fingers and is making a cat's cradle.

I read it again, this time out loud.

"Well, Lucifer means 'angel bearing light,'" Persephone deduces. "He was God's closest archangel. Michael was next in line."

"So, what does that have to do with the Leviathan?" I ask.

"Not sure. Keep reading."

"*Daniel 10:6:*

'His body was like beryl, his face like the appearance of lightning, his eyes like flaming torches, his arms and legs like the gleam of burnished bronze, and the sound of his words like the sound of a multitude.'"

"Sounds like a dragon," Persephone says, making a witch's broom with her string. She wiggles the brush head with her fingers.

"Sure does," I respond, reading further.

"*Psalm 18:8:*

'Smoke went up from his nostrils, and devouring fire from his mouth; glowing coals flamed forth from him.'"

"So, definitely part dragon," Persephone confirms.

"*Isaiah 27:1-13:*

'In that day the Lord with his hard and great and strong sword will punish Leviathan the fleeing serpent, Leviathan the twisting serpent, and he will slay the dragon that is in the sea,'" I continue.

"Part serpent, part dragon. Great."

On the next page is a detailed sketch of the beast. It has the body of a snake with large skeletal wings resembling that of a bat or dragon. There are fin-like spikes underneath its chin. The head resembles a gigantic snake with huge sharp teeth. According to the drawing, the wings function as fins. I have a sneaking suspicion they're capable of flight, too. Or used to be.

"Seph, it's horrifying," I say, holding up the book for her.

She looks up from the glowing string teacup steepled in her fingers. "What the hell?" she exclaims, collapsing her teacup and coming over to join me on the couch.

"I know," I reply, studying the detail. The body seems to be made from some sort of rock. The drawing is raised and bumpy, very rough feeling. I can't tell how the texture was achieved on paper. I also notice that it appears to have arms that collapse into the body. The arms appear human, except with long skinny fingers. The legs, too, except resembling more of a spider. Its snake eyes have red centers. They gleam in the room's light. At the back of the open throat, I see a ball of fire waiting to erupt. It also has a snake's tongue.

"Ew," I deduce. "That's what he really looks like?"

"No, that's what the lower order fallen angels look like," Persephone replies. "Turn to page twenty-five."

On page twenty-five, I find the following passage:

"*Revelation 13:1:*

'And I saw a beast rising out of the sea, with ten horns and seven heads, with ten diadems on its horns and blasphemous names on its heads.'"

"What." A beat. "His tattoo…"

I trace the new picture. Same rock-like texture. Same everything besides bonus heads. Seven truly terrifying large heads splay out from its massive serpent body. They're not snake-like. In fact, they all look human. Or at least mostly human, part beast. Haunting. The picture makes them look as though they're moving, floating around each other similar to a hologram.

"Well, he didn't always look like that, you know," Persephone says, back to her glowing string.

"Once upon a time, he was an archangel."

"Yes, and they don't look like humans either. Unless they choose to. They're beautiful, though, not ugly like those beasts."

Toward the end of the book I see a page featuring a giant staff. Moses's. The staff is featured alone—parting two walls of sea. It's very tall and wooden. Crooked.

Defeat of the serpent must be committed in his own dwelling, the place called Hell. To get there, one must utilize the Holy Staff to part the waters of the vortex in order to travel to the depths of Hell.

I need that staff.

"There's a picture of Moses's staff," I say.

"Ahh yes, also known as the 'Rod of Moses.'"

"Where can I find it, Seph? It doesn't give a map," I say, scanning pages.

"Let's see," Persephone replies, producing a book out of thin air, a Bible. "Moses had a staff in his hand while God spoke to him at the burning bush. He told him, 'And thou shalt take this rod in thine hand, wherewith thou shalt do signs.'"

"Like part the Red Sea," I nod.

"Yes, and the battle at Rephidim."

"So, I need the staff to unlock the vortex in the tomb to get to Hell."

"Yes, it seems when Lucifer was banished to Hell on Earth, it was not technically on Earth. Earth is a mixture of Heaven and Hell. Just look around you. There's so much good, not just evil," Persephone explains.

I touch the moonstone heart hanging from my bracelet. I picture the tiny sleeping bag figurine in my pocket. Axel's chubby little fingers wrapped around his bulldozer. Then, my mind wanders to death and destruction, violence, rape, and tiny bottles of blue elixir.

"You see, the plane crosses over in the same way as the Spirit World," she continues.

"And that's why Lucifer can cross over from Hell to Earth."

"Yes, Hell is actually located inside the Earth," she reads from another book.

"What book is that?"

"The Dead Sea Scrolls," she replies.

"You know Hebrew, Aramaic, and Greek?" Stupid question. She's fluent in all languages, current and dead.

"Stupid question." She rolls her eyes, answering my unspoken thought.

"So I have to go through the sea to get to the center of Earth, which is Hell's physical location. I have to find another primordial Holy Relic to do so. Oh, easy peasy."

"Yeah," she replies, thoughtfully flipping through her pages.

"I don't even know where to start," I say, rubbing my tired eyes. It's still daytime. I'm exhausted.

"Here's an endnote," she responds, inspecting the bottom of the page. "It roughly translates to: 'God shall judge through sin and death. He will send those deserving to Hell. Otherwise, an instrument needeth be used to part the waters of the downward path.'"

"Where is this instrument?"

She flips through pages. "Okay. Moses's staff was left in the care of his ancestors. Which happen to be near the sea."

"Turquoise."

"Yes, Turquoise Shire has a direct link to him."

"Looks like we're going to Turquoise," I deduce.

"Looks that way. Maybe you'll see Brooks..."

I flush involuntarily. "Maybe. Haven't even thought of it." I shrug, walking over to my bag.

"Hmm. Yeah, I'll bet," Persephone replies preoccupied.

Hands in bag, I look over at her. She's holding a Barbie and a Ken doll. They look eerily familiar. One has long white-blonde hair, the other medium-length, shaggy dirty blonde. *You have got to be kidding me.*

"Seph, that's ancient history."

"Not sure about that," she says, changing their clothes. Summer attire.

My blind search is futile. This bag has no bottom. I dump its contents on the bed. An incredibly sizable jumble mounds the covers. I start rifling through clothing.

"It's been so long, Brooks. Too long." Persephone speaks for Barbie. She's got a dream house now. Her hologram turquoise and wooden Barbie-sized mansion is situated along a recognizable powdery beach. I roll my eyes.

"I know, Lyv. I've missed you so," she says in a deep voice. She pulls Ken's arm out and links it with Barbie's. "Let's go out to the beach like we used to."

I ignore this display.

"Oh yes, I would just love that, Brooks. Remember the one time we went down to the water… It was a beautiful sunset, shimmering on pristine waves. There was a slight breeze. You touched my cheek, then slid wind-blown strands of hair behind my ear, and we—"

"Enough, Seph. I get it," I say, now laying out possible outfits. "Like I said that's ancient history. Probably won't even see him. I gotta go right to the leader."

"Then why, pray tell, are you laying out possible outfits? Your hottest possible outfits…" She mumbles the last sentence under her breath.

"I'm just trying to find something suitable for the terrain," I reply, finally selecting an ensemble and taking it into the bathroom.

"Isn't that your favorite skirt?" Persephone asks from the floor. She's belly-down with her miniature Brooks and Lyvia walking along the hologram beach.

I ignore her question and turn on the walk-in shower. The heated water sprays down on my head and from the sides as I wash up. Once I get out, I put on some makeup. Not too much, mind you. Well, maybe a little more than usual. Gold dusted, smoky eyes topped with a glossy nude lip.

I spot a towel with a tiny embroidered word on it. *Hair.* I wrap my hair in it. It becomes warm on my head. Within seconds it slips off on its own accord. My hair is completely dry and styled, loose and wavy. It looks as if I just used an iron.

I dress in, yes, my favorite skirt. It's short and lightweight, flares out slightly. The fabric layers in flaps. Slits cut open in the front on each thigh. Always kind of reminded me of Wonder Woman's. I have it in a variety of colors and textures. It's my signature piece. This one's aquamarine but sheens as fish scales in the light. I pair it with an equally lightweight strapless white top, sweetheart neckline and a corset back with matching aquamarine ribbon, tied in a bow. With a spritz of 'Perfume' that smells like butter cookies and a touch of pumpkin spice, I reenter the living room.

"Wow," Persephone says, looking up from her dream house. Mini Lyv and Brooks are now entangled in each other's arms on the beach. *Good Lord.*

"What? It's Turquoise attire," I reply, packing my bag. I debate leaving some things here, but I don't know when or if I'll be back. Looks as though the hefty monstrosity will be continuing the journey as is.

"It most certainly is," she says. Mini Brooks is running his fingers through mini Lyv's hair.

"Okay Seph, put it away. We need a game plan," I tell her, strapping on my warrior sandals. I check to make sure I still have my necklace on. It features a small platinum cross and a rectangular tag, a gift from my brother. The tag reads, "I love you, love Shane," in his handwriting. He sent it to me when we were away from each other last year.

Persephone waves her hands over her mini 'Brooks and Lyvia: Lovers on the Beach' doll set, and it vanishes from sight.

"If we leave now, what time will we get there?"

"If we leave right now, no stopping for chitchat, we can get there by six o'clock tonight."

"Okay. That would be good. I think Noelani will be finishing up her meeting by then. We can grab some food in the city on the way." I flash to the necklace I have never seen Lani without. I put Seph in my bag and head down the steps.

"Regina," I call, but get no answer. That works out. I can get on my way.

Outside, I make my path through Regina's jungle garden. The myriad of colors creates a stained-glass effect. The petals almost paint a picture. I can't tell what it is though. I spot Regina's paisley bag hanging from a clothesline.

23

As I walk into town toward the start of the SkyChariot, I spot movement from my left. A large pit bull comes bounding at me. She jumps up and I grab her front paws.

"Hey, girl," I say, noticing her gender. I set her down. She waggles her tail and paces in front of me back-and-forth.

"Chloe—" I hear a woman's voice calling from a cottage tucked in the foliage. She appears at the mouth of the trees obscuring her home. She's wearing a short 1970s style dress with billowy sleeves. Slouched boots. Her hair is tied up in a messy bun.

"Hi," she calls as she walks over. "I was tying up the others when she shot off."

"Oh, it's no problem. I love dogs," I respond, laughing and squatting to pet Chloe. As she nears me, I can't help but catch that familiar feeling again. I feel as if I know her but from a different life or something.

"I'm Claire," she says, holding out her hand.

"Lyvia," I reply, shaking it. "Nice to meet you. You've got a lot of dogs."

"Yeah, my boyfriend and I adopted them," she replies, joining me with Chloe.

"That's awesome. He must really love dogs too."

"Yeah," she responds noncommittally. I sense something there. Sadness.

"Were you born here?" I ask, changing the subject.

"No, I was born in Ruby," she answers. No surprise there, with the animals and all. "Switched about three months ago, before—"

She gets cut off when Chloe freezes. The hair on her back spikes straight up. She seems to have spotted a small animal. A squirrel to be exact. *Ugh.* Claire grabs her collar at the speed of light sensing the bait as quick as the pit bull.

"It was nice to meet you, Lyvia. I gotta get her back. See you around," she waves with her free hand.

"Sounds good. Bye, Claire," I call out, continuing my path. It's a little bit of a trek to the SkyChariot stop right outside of Crystal. It's beautiful out. The town looks livelier than I've seen it since I've gotten here.

Two guys are unloading bags of cement. It looks as though they're repaving an area. I spot three girls slightly younger camped around the fountain on the other side of the walkway. Two are sitting on the stone ledge. The third is sitting on the ground. Her eyes are shaded with large sunglasses and her head rests on the fountain's granite lip. Her finger lazily traces circles on the gemstone-pebbled road. The other two giggle at a magazine between them sneaking surreptitious glances at the boys.

A couple strolls by in the opposite direction holding hands. She looks up at him and nuzzles her head against his shoulder. *Yuck.* I want to rip their hands apart and yell, "It's not real!" because I, for one, know it never is.

Coming outside a clothing store, I spot a familiar golden mane. "Scarlett," I call with a wave. She's got heaping shopping bags in each hand. A bored Axel follows behind. Tiny fingers clutch a bag. A sticky red licorice rope is clasped in the others.

"Lyvia," she calls back, heading over. "How's it going? Any news? Dagan?"

I don't have the heart to tell her about Dagan right now. I just can't do it. "No word," I answer, stooping down to Axel. "Hey buddy, remember me?"

"Yes. Hi, Via." Via. That's a new one. I like it.

"You want some? You want some? You want some?" He holds out his gooey red candy. His eyes are magnified by the thick black frames of his tiny eyeglasses. It may be the cutest site I've ever seen.

"Mm that looks good, Ax, but it's all you." I tousle his hair and stand up.

"Nothing, huh?" Scarlett ponders, the bags pulling heavily at her arms. "That's weird, but not entirely. He disappears sometimes. I'm not sure where he goes. I think it's mostly research. He must be hiding out still. Have you learned anything about Levi and all that?"

The truth is I want to fill her in on everything, but I don't have time. I must get to Turquoise. "No, not really. I'm headed out to Turquoise. I gotta meet with the leader up there for some information that will help, hopefully."

"Okay, well, if you need anything, let me know," she says, giving me a half-hug with her full arms.

"Bye, Via," Axel calls. He swings around a giant shopping bag and hugs my legs.

"Bye Axel," I squat down for a proper squeeze.

"Okay, I'll see ya later, guys," I say, standing back up. "I'll keep you posted, Scar."

"Please do," she says, already hustling away. Her arms look they won't make it much farther. I'd wage all the virtues I have to my name that she'll make it home without having to stop and readjust once. *Superwoman.*

Onward I go.

Smack. Smack. Smack. Slapping against sidewalk. I steer around children playing double-Dutch with jump ropes. Each rope glitters in the sun before taking turns to clap the walkway.

A tall guy brushes past me on the detour. He's wearing a baseball hat, sunglasses, t-shirt and jeans.

A memory forms. *Slap. Slap. Slap. Black inky waves gently spank smooth damp sand, a gentle hand lashing velvety flesh. Moonlight. A strong wind caresses exposed skin with hot humid kisses. Phantom suntan lotion and fresh clean aftershave fill my nose. Flash of black. Thick gooey copper coats my tongue.*

I do a quick double take. I always have to be aware of my surroundings. Because of my need to stay under-the-radar, I keep on my toes, especially now. I flip back casually and take a quick scan. The guy gets lost in the crowd almost instantly. Of course, 'livelier' today.

I catch him cross to the right and head into a bar. I decide to take a speedy backtrack. *Something about him.* I should don a disguise. When you see a guy enter a bar alone—or with people—you can expect him to linger. I spot a bathhouse two doors down.

Bathhouses in Crystal are reminiscent of the time when men swam in tight prison-striped onesies that went down to their calves, and women wore swim dresses with petticoats. The hems were shortened. But still.

These bathhouses, though, serve as the town's rest areas, not just changing rooms. They're much more than a pit stop. Lounge Cache's feature hotel luxury and amenities. Each contain separate men's and women's parlors with every convenience and service one might need —free of charge.

I walk into this one and go straight for the ladies' wing. Just follow the pink. The cotton candy hallway opens into a cavernous room with walls of mirrors. My eyes are immediately drawn to the large aquamarine pool in the center. The sea green water looks like a Turquoise surf, just smaller. The floor has the texture of damp spongy sand, although it's not.

At its center, stands an extravagant statue of a woman. She's in a mystical, magical forest. Long, straight, straggly hair frame her openly defiant face. She's wearing swaths of torn cloth tied around her breasts and hips. As I move around the statue, it melds into another woman.

This one is slightly older. She lies upon a chaise lounge. It's shaped as a stiletto heel reminiscent of Scarlett's. This one is very old-world. 1950s with a shorter, still narrow, heel. This elongates the elegant piece. The woman is draped along the chair with the back of one hand over her forehead. She dons a long satin gown with neck-laces, bracelets, and a headpiece. A large wispy feather sticks out from the diamond and pearl beaded headband worn over long flowing locks. Her other hand grasps bunched fabric. Below the hem of the hiked satin slip, two bare feet point out naturally.

Continuing around the oceanic pool, I find one more woman etched in stone. Unlike the others, this is not mystic or romantic. It's dark. Vines twist around her. Jagged branches bound her as though she's a kidnapped victim. However, she seems to be the one controlling the rope. Her arms are splayed upward from her sides as if she's raising the dead. Her face is breathtakingly beautiful. Equally terrifying. Her facial expression is entrancing and powerful, and... Something else. Nearly imperceptible but lying beneath her hypnotizing grin—*malevolence*. Her eyes follow me. The irises appear to be made of chrysocolla.

Sexy would be another word. Her body type is that of nude models in the 1500s. Curvy in all the right places. Her ample bosom peeks above twined thorny creepers. It seems as though the vines branch out from her very essence. Her expression says: "I already know all your weaknesses. And... I plan on abusing each and every one, until I get what I want."

A fleeting memory flashes through my mind. *Thirteen-years-old. Middle-year training. Skylar Safrin, prototype of 'mean girl.' Evil bitch. Snide remarks and humiliation, yet, I'd do anything to feel part of her clique. Approval, acceptance, all of it—fake.*

A never-ending vanity runs along each side of the fountain. Bubble light bulbs frame the reflective glass. Potion bottles, robes, plush towels, and pink powder puffs line the mile-long counter. I eye the delicious spread ahead of me as though it's a decadent Thanksgiving meal. Perfumes with simple labels: 'Lavender-Laced Honey Ice Cream,' 'Pumpkin-Pied Butter Cookie,' 'Peachy-Cobbler Shortbread.' Lipstick bottles swirl around a crystalline display: 'Nectar,' 'Violets,' 'Black Cherry.' Lotions and creams: 'Baby Face,' 'Plumpy Lips,' 'Cashmere Body.'

Oh, no I can't stay for supper. Gotta stalk a stranger on my way to kill Satan. Also—might have a creeper lurking behind me. Just thought I'd take a quick peek at all these goodies for the sake of additional torture. A child's stubby fingers splayed out on glass. Sharks swim in slow circles one transparent slice between true danger. *But I want to play...*

Silk robes and slippers fit snug in a basket. There are changing room suites, tiny hotel rooms minus the beds and other furniture. Each features a love seat, vanity, shower, more amenities, and a separate vanity for hair. This is filled with products as well. I go in and rifle through my bag. Near the bottom, I unearth a wig. It's a brunette shoulder-length, asymmetrical cut. I pull out a pair of cat-eye sunglasses. My aviators are too telling. I top off the disguise with a nude trench coat.

On the way out, I spritz myself with 'Peachy-Cobbler Shortbread' and a smear of 'Cherry Bomb' lip stain. A bite of stuffing and mashed potatoes out the door. A fleeting look at the 'Cashmere Body' cream.

I really wanted some turkey.

24

I head back to the bar in my new guise. It's very rustic. The kind of establishment that's been in place so long, it doesn't exist to you anymore. Just a blur between buildings you frequent. One day, you take a longer look thinking—*Has that always been there?* Then —*Oh my gosh, it hasn't changed.*

I spot my follower in the last booth. His back is to me and he's looking down at a beer bottle, twirling it lazily in his hands. I see dirty blonde hair curling up around the rim of his hat. The suntan lotion and clean aftershave was real. I slide across from him before he looks up from his hands.

"'And you can tell *Rolling Stone* magazine that my last words were... 'I'm on drugs!'" I say conspiratorially across the table.

"'Russell, I think we should work on those last words,'" he replies, without glancing from his sweaty bottle. It's my favorite line from the movie *Almost Famous*.

"Hey, Vee," he says, finally lifting his sea-churning aquamarine eyes to meet mine.

"Hi, Brooks," I reply, squeezing the webbing between my thumb and forefinger.

"What can I getcha?" The bartender calls over. He's young, probably 25. Cute. Goofy grin.

"I'll have a…"

"Dirty martini—filthy—with three olives," Brooks finishes for me.

"Okay. What gives? Why are you here?"

"Well, I—" He's interrupted by the bartender who sets a large martini glass in front of me. A red stirrer stabs three gigantic olives. I take a sip. It's salty and perfect.

"Vee, you look really great," he says, looking into my eyes. "Although, this hair was never my favorite." He laughs as he reaches over and tugs a lock of the wig. The playful gesture flushes my cheeks. I pick up the stirrer and slide an olive into my mouth. As I chew, I take a sip of my drink.

"You too," I say, putting my glass down. I cradle my chin in one hand, abashed. Nervous habit. "What are you doing here?"

"Lookin' for you, of course," he chuckles. *Dimples.*

"Well, you found me," I say, shrugging my shoulders.

"Yes, I did. Well, actually, you found me."

"Oh, so you're telling me you didn't see me just now?"

"Well, I did think that short blonde head looked familiar." He takes a swig of his beer.

"I'm not short," I say stubbornly. *Five-seven is respectable.* "I thought I smelled sunscreen and aftershave."

"I need to brush up on my tailing tactics. Too close to the target," he responds, twirling his bottle again.

"Target?"

"Okay, okay. Subject." He leans back and laughs. His surfer physique casually slouches in the booth. The definition of *cool.*

"Whose orders?"

He laughs mischievously this time. *Rough sea waves. Rickety boat. A lashing storm pelting skin.*

"No orders, Vee. Lani was worried. I was too. We never heard from you after you left that day."

My heart clenches at the mention of 'that day.'

"I know," I say. "A lot happened that night."

"I figured. Just glad to see you're okay," he replies tenderly.

"I've been better, but for the most part I'm whole."

"Where were you headed?"

"Actually, out your way. Can you believe that?"

"Can't get enough of the beach, huh, Vee?"

"You know it. So, you wanna accompany me?"

"Thought you'd never ask," he says, taking out his Slab. He goes up to the bartender and pays our tab with virtues. I slip off the wig, glasses, and trench coat and stuff them in my bag. I finger comb my natural hair. *That's better.*

"Ready, Veevee?" he asks when he's finished.

Veevee. Ten-years-old. Sand buckets and shovels. A compact Brooks finishes an intricate sandcastle. More like a sculpture of a medieval palace. He breaks into a slapdash grin before sprinting off to the surf.

"All set." I down the rest of my martini and stuff the remaining olives in my mouth. Not very ladylike, but I'm not one to waste two glorious, vodka-soaked green olives in an empty glass. I grab my purse and follow him out the door. We start to make our way up the cobbled gemstone path. The crowd has thinned a bit during our afternoon drink.

"How's Shane, Vee? I haven't seen him on *Realmcast* since before I last saw you. You know he's on there all the time."

"Oh yeah, I think he's taking a break for a little while," I respond vaguely. I've known this guy for a very long time, but I don't want to say the words out loud. I'm going to get my brother back.

"Is he here? In Crystal?"

Technically, yes. But I go with—

"Not sure. Last time I checked, he was lying low in Dark." Not quite the truth, but the day before the Great Reveal, that was his last known location.

"At your parents?"

"Yeah." Shane lives in our parent's house. He could have moved into Onyx Hall when he became leader, but he wanted to stay home. I understood completely. Plus, it's not just a house, it's a mansion.

"No one's seen him for a few days now. For the most part, everyone thinks he's at one of his solo training missions. Getting ready for the upcoming season. Drills. Conditioning." The last word floats down provocatively as he steals a sideway glance.

"Conditioning?" I ask. We both laugh, hard. I recall a television show we watched when we were younger. A guy on it was describing what his football team was doing back home. He had to explain to another participant what conditioning was.

"Oh, you know, runnin' around the track," we say in unison wistfully.

Brooks pulls me into a shady alley between two beaming crystal apartment buildings. We walk over to the wall. I lean up against it.

"What?" I ask innocently.

"What about Levi?" Three words loaded with sleeping grenades. "Everyone's looking for him."

"He's in Hell."

"Figured. Levi the Leviathan."

"When and how did you figure it out?"

"Lani, she had a vision. Levi's natural state."

"Oh no," I say, imagining the gruesome scene.

"Why are you really going to Turq, Veevee?" He props himself against the wall with one tanned arm above my head.

"I don't know if I can tell you, Brooks," I say, looping a finger in his jeans belt loop.

"Listen, Lyv. I wanna help. Lani does too."

"I need the staff, Brooks." I look up into his eyes; their intensity strikes me. Each iris forms an ocean swell about to plunge into the perfect wave. If only I had time for a swim.

"What for, Lyv." Statement.

"I gotta go see him, Brooks. On his turf."

"I'm going with you."

"No, you're not. No one is."

"Who do you think you are, Vee?" he asks, pacing the alleyway.

"I know what I'm doing."

"You remember when we were kids and you found that map?"

"Not sure I know what you refer to…"

"Yeah, it was a treasure map. X marks the spot," he says as he stops under a balcony. He jumps up. His fingers brush the awning. He lands and jumps again, but this time he latches onto the lowest rung of a fire escape ladder and swings back and forth. "Anyway, you decided we should find the treasure. So, into the woods we go…"

"I knew what I was doing then too." I harrumph, crossing my arms over my chest.

"We got chased by a bear, Vee. An adult black bear."

"Okay. I've got reinforcements this time." Not quite a lie—I've got Persephone and Holy Relics.

"Seph's a program, Vee," he sighs, lackadaisically meandering back.

"Not just her. Trust me, Brooks. This is between the two of us."

"Vee, you know I listen to you, so don't come yelling at me when a bear starts chasing you," he responds, hands up innocently.

"I won't. Just help me get the staff," I say, heading out into the sunlight. He follows.

WE REACH the SkyChariot stop right beyond the town limits. We take the stairs up to the platform. It's very high off the ground. The train resembles the 'people mover' that used to reside in Detroit. Not too busy today, we score two recliner seats near the back. The chariot soars through the air above trees. As we see the world whiz by, a question springs forth.

"So, Brooks, how did you find me?"

He rolls his eyes. "Well, no sign of you in Lunar. This was the next logical stop."

"True. Did you go there?"

"No, just checked in with your sources." I do have a lot of sources in my hometown. The train continues to rocket through the sky, a moving brush of scenery.

"So, Lyvia, what happened that night? Haven't heard or spoke to you since."

That night. When I boarded the train in Turquoise, I would have never guessed the turn out. "I went out to the reveal. I saw Levi, but he disappeared."

"That's it, Vee?"

"That's it."

"So you need the staff to get to Hell for a conversation?"

"Kind of. I need to talk to him and that's where he is."

"Okay. I'll leave it at that."

The train swishes to a stop in Emerald. Fields of wheat, beans, and other crops span this particular stop. Other stops in Emerald are akin to stepping into a tropical rainforest. The imagery turns from green to red as we enter Ruby. We swish to a stop downtown. I follow Brooks down the stairs to the paved walkway. The buildings are dense. Sharp ruby and black marble skyscrapers stab the sky. The concentration of architecture resembles old-world New York City.

I already know where he's headed. Pizza. Ruby has the best pizza. Still, I prefer Onyx's square deep-dish style. Ruby's giant, floppy slices are second best. He orders two slices with virtues and we stand at a high-top table. The pizza cheese is hot and gooey, greasy. I blot mine off with napkins. Brooks folds his in half and takes a huge bite. When I finish blotting, I do the same.

"It's been a really long time since I had one of these," I say around a mouthful.

"Same here," he replies, taking a drink of his pop.

Red-checkered tablecloth. Flickering candle glow. Scent of burning wood.

"You think Lani will just give it to me? The staff? She's worn it around her neck since birth. Literally."

"I do," he replies solemnly. "After what she saw."

"I saw a picture," I offer.

"No, Vee. I don't think that's quite the same. What she saw—life-like? Horrifying."

"I can only imagine," I say, taking a swig of my drink.

"Me too." He takes a bite of his pizza. Cheese stretches from his mouth.

"Hopefully, he won't be in that form."

"Vee, I really don't think you should go alone," he says, putting a hand on my arm.

"I guess maybe you could come with me up to that point," I say, meeting his eyes. I can't always rebuke help.

"Okay. Good," he responds with a huge bite of pizza.

"So, we need the staff and Shane's hockey skates," I say. *Hell Trip Checklist.*

He looks at me questioningly.

"Honestly, I have no idea," I say with a shrug.

"Doesn't Shane have them?"

"No, they're at the house."

"I don't follow. Why would you need his skates for a trip to Hell?"

"Well, you know I have my sources. I was told to bring them. Come on, it can't hurt, Brooks," I say, nudging his arm.

"Whatever you say, Vee." He crumbles his napkins up and tosses them over his shoulder absentmindedly. There's a trashcan behind him. He makes it. I walk over and stuff mine into the bin the boring way. We head back to the chariot. We've got a little while left. There are two unoccupied recliners facing each other again, and we snatch them up.

"What else is happening in Turq?" I ask, settling comfortably into the plush seat. I stretch out my legs.

"Well, Cory's the same as always," he replies, leaning back and doing the same.

"Is he still spinning donuts in his Jeep-Sandie?" He located an ancient Jeep Wrangler and modernized it to operate as a Sandie.

"What do you think?"

"I think if snow still existed, he'd have to get a winterized version."

"True," he replies, distractedly watching granite swirl below in shades of grey.

"How's Lennon?"

"Len?" he says, tracing circles on the glass. "She's good."

"Brooks. What gives?"

"What?" he asks, still running a finger on the transparent surface.

"Something's up. You're not much of a talker, but you can do better than this," I scold.

"What do you want me to say, Lyv? I'm just confused is all. After what happened with us, then these new developments... Levi being the Devil," he trails off, blowing fog on the glass and making a baby footprint with the side of his fist.

"I know. I'm sorry," I reply honestly. "That night was crazy, and I'm not going to say I regret it. Because I don't think I do. I do, however, believe in my heart of hearts, that I can't be with anyone right now, and there's no foretelling how long that will be."

"I can respect that," he says, finishing up his baby toes with thumbprints.

"That's it? No resentment? No anger?"

"You know it doesn't change anything with us, Lyv. That kiss... It just happened. But we've known each other so long, our friendship trumps all that. Promise. It was just a kiss." He stretches his arms above his head with a yawn.

Was it, though? Conflicted.

"So we get the staff, and then what?"

"Then we go to Onyx, get the skates, and head back down to Crystal," I answer.

"Doesn't sound too bad," he says.

"Yeah, well, that all depends on one person."

I glance down and notice my fingers tracing an invisible fish. The same one that resides on a token in my wallet.

25

Passing over Granite, we briefly stop again in Emerald. The doors open and humidity saturates the train. Vines dangle right outside the entrance, too humid for me. Finally stopping in Turquoise, we disembark. Aquamarine stones pave the walkway until it turns into sand. The hills of white powder resemble snow. We walk down to the shoreline. Scattered turquoise-encrusted wooden homes begin to concentrate along the way. The sturdy wooden structures are whittled to appear as waves on driftwood.

The pathway transforms to wooden stairs. We descend toward the oceanic rhythm. Turquoise Villa rises into view. It sits alone at the edge of the sea. A large wide structure spreads along the oceanfront, also wooden and turquoise. It's heavier on turquoise, though, and donned with a substantial dose of aquamarine gemstones.

Lush coconut. Dry crusted sand. Five-years-old. Infamous stairs known as 'Ye Ole' Wooden Peak.' We had to take breaks every ten steps. It takes a while to reach the Villa.

"You still got that fishhook?" I ask. I wasn't sure where it came from, but it popped up when we were young and never left his side. One time he nearly died because of the thing.

"What? This thing?" He produces a palm-sized ancient fishhook.

"Where'd you get that? Really?" I ask suspiciously.

"Ahh, just found it one day when we were little." He twirls it around his fingers expertly as if he was born with it in hand.

We reach the gates, which are open at the moment.

"You think she's in?" I ask.

"Yeah, she's in," he says as we reach the surmounting wooden doors. He holds it open for me. The structure is very tall. The ceiling is steepled and alternates wood and glass. The side facing the sea is entirely glass. The ocean roars beyond the pane, a churning depth of mystery. We walk into the main room. It's a large lobby. Crushed velvet in various shades of blue cover the furniture. Brooks meanders to the wall and hits a switch.

"Hey guys. I'll be down in a second." A voice fills the room clear as day. Framework intelization. She can probably see us from her Slab.

"Sounds good, Lani," Brooks says, lifting his finger from the button. He settles in for the wait on a giant, overstuffed sea-green chair and takes off his hat.

I step up to the window. The sky is overcast today. On the steps it was sunny. Now grey, menacing clouds block the sun. The water looks black in the clouds' shadow. I can't help but think what's down there.

"Hey guys," Lani says. She musses Brooks' hair as she brushes past.

"Lyv, it's good to see you." She envelops me in a hug.

"Good to see you too," I reply. The scent of sunscreen and orange blossom wafts off her tanned shoulder.

"You guys hungry?"

"We got pizza on the way," Brooks says, inspecting his hat. Bored.

"You got anything sweet?" I ask.

"You know it," she replies, and we follow her to the kitchen.

Down the hall we make our way to the east wing. The kitchen is massive. An aquamarine mosaic adorns the walls and floor. Everything else is chrome. Noelani walks to the fridge and pulls out a dish. Then she goes to the pantry and returns with two more. Taking off the lids I see rice pudding, homemade peach pie, and a giant chocolate cake.

"Mm," I say, analyzing each choice. *Pros. Cons. I love them all. Chocolate sounds good. But... Nope, I have to have the pie. Wait a minute. I haven't had rice pudding in too long. But the chocolate... No, the peachy goodness for sure, it's my favorite... mmm creamy pudding...*

"Just pick one," Brooks says, draped over a stool.

"Mind your business," I reply with a flick of my hand. "Okay. I'll have... Peach pie with ice cream if you have it, please."

She prepares a chunk at lightning speed with her electronic Heatwave, it uses molecular atomization to heat food; the closest comparison would be a combination of a microwave and wood burning oven. No more radiation or smoke and works quicker than its predecessors. The heaping slice gets a scoop of home-churned vanilla bean ice cream before arriving to its final destination. She gives me a spoon, and I dig in.

"So, I hear you need the staff," she says, pulling out a stool. Her long, thick auburn hair frames her face. She wraps a curl around her ear. She's wearing her trademark floor-length maxi-dress. She's got one in every color of the rainbow and prints too. Some are strapless, some one-shoulder, and still others have sleeves. Today, she's wearing a billowy deep blue, stormy print with spaghetti straps and slip-on leather, strappy sandals. Her only jewelry consists of a wooden snake dangling from a leather cord around her neck. Her eyes, the color of caramelized crème brûlée, bore into mine imploringly.

"It seems that way." I shrug. I take a bite of gooey, warm pie balanced with the slight chill of ice cream.

"Lyv, I don't need to tell you how dangerous this is. But, I have to tell you that seeing the seven-headed dragon, Leviathan, whatever the hell he is—in person—is what nightmares are made of."

"I know. I'm trying to mentally prepare myself."

"There's no mentally preparing for that," she replies with a shudder.

"Yeah, well, Levi has always been a creature of mystery. No clue it was this bad and scary."

"Yeah, I mean, he's a real piece of work," Brooks interjects. "But, damn." He leans back and laces his fingers behind his head. "He's turned the volume up to eleven."

"I'll say," Lani replies, searching an imaginary distance. She fiddles with her wooden snake.

"So this staff..." I lead.

"Yes. The staff." She takes my bowl and spoon to the sink and begins washing them.

"If you don't already know, it has been passed down since Moses parted the Red Sea. My line has had it in possession since then. When

I was predetermined to become the appointed leader, it was placed in my care at birth." She dries the dishes and puts them away.

"What exactly does it do?"

"Well, part the Red Sea for starters," she laughs, drying her hands on a small towel.

"We've gathered that," Brooks says with a yawn.

"Okay. Okay. He also used it at the battle of Rephidim. But, first and foremost, God gave him the staff at the burning bush as a tangible vow."

"What do you mean?" I ask, resting my chin in my hand.

"Moses needed to know it was God at play, so God gave him a physical item for proof. Not just for Moses, though. Humanity has a tendency to discount things, especially novel or unpopular beliefs. The tasks that He was assigning Moses were not easy. It would be an instrument of assurance for the Egyptians, a sign of trust and faith."

"Tell her the other part," Brooks says, leaning forward. Suddenly attentive.

She leans over the counter on her elbows. "Well, all these generations later, it has been passed down with an accompanying scroll. A warning, really."

"Really? A warning?"

"Yes, the message reads: 'Upon resurgence of the seven-faced dragon, the Rod of Moses shall prove essential in the serpent's defeat.'"

"Wow," I respond, digesting this information. Yet, equally perturbed my Relics didn't come with instructions. Then again, I'm just grateful to have them.

"And the vision…" Brooks hedges.

"Right. The vision." She closes her eyes for a second. When they pop back open, she looks distressed.

"That bad?" I ask.

"Worse."

"Well, give me something," I say when she pauses again.

"Well, it was weird. I was sleeping, so it felt like a dream at first. The initial couple minutes I was talking to someone familiar, but I don't know who it was or what we talked about. Sorry, that part's not helpful," she says, brushing some crumbs off the counter. "I just remember a feeling before going into the second half. Fear. Whatever was talked about, I knew something bad was coming."

"Do you have any idea who was warning you?" I ask.

"Not one bit."

"Okay, whoever it was just vanished?"

"No, I was the one who vanished. I was sitting in the common room on one of the chaise lounges. Whoever was talking to me was indistinguishable, surrounded by fog. I can't even remember a voice at all. Only forewarned impending doom.

Then suddenly, I was standing someplace I've never been, a mountain somewhere. A cliff, really. Near water but not Turquoise. Almost seemed old-world, but not."

The tomb appears in my mind. I begin to get an inkling of who she had a conversation with.

Noelani continues, "I'm standing on this cliff with the water right below me. The overhang curves over the waves to impede my view. I start to walk toward the ledge when I see movement just below the lip.

Levi's face slowly breeches the crest. Massive head. His expression is stretched in a grin of pure evil. I'm horrified. I stumble backward until my back meets rock. There's what feels like boulder behind me, but I can't turn around to look.

'Oh, Lani, tsk, tsk, tsk,' Levi says, shaking his head. 'What am I gonna do with you?'

'I have an idea… A yummy one.' A separate voice.

A second giant head materializes to the left of Levi. Its human face is stretched grotesquely and misshapen with a giant, leering grin. A clown, kind of like the Joker—Jack Nicholson's version. Fat and sweaty. He keeps popping out at me like a Jack in the Box toy, even humming the weasel tune. He zooms within inches from my face. His breath is utterly disgusting.

'So sorry, Gulch.' A hiss. 'But thisss one'sss mine.'

Another head reveals itself over the ledge. Looks human, but off. Then I nail it. Snake-like with slick hair and slit eyes. A long forked-tongue lashes out at me. It snaps at my ankles. Leers at me like a prized possession to be fawned over. Then I hear an unsettling grinding noise before a giant, vulture-human face floats above me. His long pointy beak grates back and forth, a sickening gnashing.

'No, she's all mine. Only me. And I say we go to her place for real and take them all…'

'I don't even know why we're talking to her. There's no point. She's gonna die anyway. Let's just go home.'

This one resembles a blob fish, gooey and puffy. Round bulbous nose and cheeks, beady little eyes, and huge puffy lips set in a frown. It's as if God mashed some putty around and made sure it was as depressing as possible before it dried.

'Shut up, Sadler,' a seething voice sneers. 'Why are we here?' The ugliest hairless cat's head I have ever seen comes forward. Naked, wrinkled skin set in an expression of simmering rage. Its evil, pissed off cat-eyes churn with fury.

'I say you let me take her for a spin. I'd love to try this one on for size. So pretty…' The next one ascends so slowly; it really ups the creep-out factor, as if that's necessary. It's octopus-like. Eight tentacles frame the face and its massive forehead. Round bubble eyes set back into folds of skin. He floats right up to my face and stays there.

'Everyone knows the pecking order, you idiots,' an evil whisper. 'And I'm first in line.'

I don't know what the one meant by 'trying me on,' because Levi tells them all to shut up. By this point, he is clear of the cliff and hovering above my head. He has a long snake body. Human-like arms and legs, albeit long and spindly with giant bat wings. The heads are attached to long dragon necks. He's a flying serpent with seven heads, two wings and two arms and legs."

"Holy shit," I say wide-eyed. "What did he say?"

"So, he lands on the open rock in front of me. He's huge. Each head was about my size, so you can imagine. They all keep floating up to me. Intrigued, hungry, and awaiting their master's consent. Levi tells them to back off, and they drift away. His face comes within two feet of me. He tells me not to give you the staff. Says if I do, bad things will happen."

"What bad things?"

"Oh, you know, condemned to Hell for eternity."

"What? Then I'll find a different way."

"No, Lyv, you don't." She takes off her wooden snake necklace and hands it to me. "I can take care of myself. Heaven and Hell are between me and God. Not Levi, no matter what the asshole says."

"So, this is it?" I ask, examining the wooden pendant. "How does it work?"

"Besides the cryptic scroll, there aren't instructions. It's up to God, I guess. How it works, when it works. Regardless, it works. You just have to figure it out."

Boy, does that sound familiar. "Okay. Dark Shire next," I announce, inspecting the piece. Another Holy Relic to add to the collection.

"Brooks, are you going with her?" she asks.

"I don't think you should, Brooks. I really think you should stay here. I'll be fine. Trust me, Levi does not want to kill me."

"Just take you to Hell for eternity," he replies, inspecting his hat again.

"I can handle Levi. I can't put you in unnecessary danger."

"So you're going, Brooks," Lani says, brushing her hands together in an 'okay, that's settled' kind of way.

"Ugh." I roll my eyes. "I swear if anything happens to you, I'll be pissed."

"You'll get over it," he says, hopping off his stool and meandering to the doorway where we say our goodbyes with hugs and prayers to keep safe.

"Do you wanna catch the train back, or do you want me to drive?"

I think about it. The train is fast but has stops along the way. Plus, his vehicle isn't exactly street legal. We'll get there in no time. "How about you drive?"

"I figured," he replies as he lopes around the villa.

The garage is at the east side of the establishment. We pop in a Sandie Roadster made for both beach and land. It's a cross between a sand buggy and Jeep. We head up north. It's dusk. The vehicle moves about as fast as the Camocar. Should only take about an hour to get there.

"I'm not looking forward to this," I say, watching the scenery darken.

"How come?"

"It's just been awhile."

I choose not to divulge the real reasons.

26

Dusk abruptly turns to black as the tree line descends. Anxiety mounts. This isn't just a drive-through like last time. I have to go to the house. I haven't been there in quite a bit. I usually meet Shane in other shires because we travel so much. I have a hard time going back there.

I'm impressed Brooks remembers the turns after so many years. Soon, we pull up to the vast homestead. A cobbled Petoskey stone walkway twists between trees and vegetation toward the massive structure. The house is constructed with aged brick and log. It's a Victorian-style mansion.

Beyond the structure lies an extensive backyard. Actually, garden. Flowers bloom year-round. A maze is sewn through the blossoms. This walkway is made of black onyx. It gleams in the lunar supplied lighting. Past it there is a small wooded area, where a path through the trees opens to a very large lake with snow-like sand also found in Turquoise.

We round the bend into my backyard when I hear it. The first chords of "I'll Be," a song by Edwin McCain. It's our song—Levi and mine. This time—a different take. Same soft notes with a malicious twist. The chords strangle me. The melody is an impatient phantom serial killer who's been hiding out for an uncomfortably long time.

I motion for Brooks to stay back but follow. I continue around the bend.

"Levi, that's low even for you. And you're, you know, the one and only 'Lucifer.'" Punctuating the last word with air quotes, I come to stand in my parent's giant backyard. There's a massive porch that runs out into another made of wood and onyx but mostly stonework. Petoskey cobblestone walls pave the ways. The garden's spiral maze of flowers and vines swirls around the center —a giant marble archway. Statues adorn the pergola as well as benches.

He's leaning against a sleek, plush black lounger, guitar in hand. He starts strumming the chords for "Always Remember Us This Way" from *A Star Is Born*, 2018. Another one of 'our' songs. Given we have a few, these are heavy hitters.

He goes back to "I'll Be" and sings a few lines.

I stand arms crossed. Not amused. "You're not supposed to be here. In fact, you're supposed to be in Hell. I'm meeting you there. Remember..." I say slowly, wide-eyed with a measured nod.

"Oh, I remember, Lyvs, lookin' forward to it," he replies with an upbeat strum.

"Ugh."

"You'll like it."

"K. Anyway, why are you here?"

"Well, thing is Lyvs, I need to make sure you don't get something that's in that establishment right there," he says, using his golden guitar pick to point at my parent's grand manor.

"Levi, just leave," I state, hands on hips. "You know you can't go in there. Now I actually know *why* you can't go in there. So get out of here." When we were together, Levi always had an excuse not to enter the house; now I gather, it's because the abode is blessed.

"Maybe I can't go in, but I can get someone else to..."

"Hey Brooks, come on out," he speaks to the darkness.

Brooks immediately does. I've seen this show before. It's bad. Now that I know he's the Devil Incarnate, I'm terrified for Brooks, who currently stands awaiting Levi's next command.

"Brooks, can you do me a huge favor?" Soft high picks on strings. "It's not that bad, I promise. Somewhere in that house there's a pair of hockey skates. I'm gonna need those. Ya think you could do me a solid?"

"No problem, man," Brooks says, thumbs tucked in pockets. "You got a starting point?"

"Lyvs?" Levi says, looking at me, eyebrows raised. "Upstairs? Downstairs?"

I start to answer him honestly. Words compelled by truth. Powerless. "They're in the—"

That's when the thorned crown does her thing. My hair tie stretches to a jagged wreath atop my head.

"Wow. Haven't seen that in what? About 3,000 years," Levi says, still cradling his guitar. The music has ceased.

"Didn't bode too well for the last guy who wore it." He strums Doobie Brothers, "Jesus Is Just All Right with Me."

"Neither did those." He nods to my feet without looking up.

"Brooks, go wait for me over there," I say, pointing to a bench. "I'll be done here shortly."

He starts to turn.

"Brooks, don't move," Levi says, playing Queen's "Don't Stop Me Now."

He freezes.

From this, I conclude the crown makes me imperceptible to Levi mentally but unable to protect Brooks.

"Go into the house, find the skates, and bring them to me," he commands, adjusting his finger placement. His tone has altered. Cold. Calculated.

Showtime.

Brooks tries to open the door. It's locked.

"Can't get in," he says, mussing his hair.

"Lyvs, all you," Levi replies, splaying an arm toward the door.

"Oh, man. Sorry, Levi. I don't open my house to the Devil."

"Lyvs, I would suggest you rethink that logic."

"Leevs, I would suggest you leave the premises. Now."

"Why do you insist on the hard way every time?" He sighs deeply.

A tortured scream breaks our eye contact. Brooks grabs his head as he falls to his knees in agony.

"I'd say this wasn't fun for me, but the truth works sometimes," Levi states, flicking his hand.

Brooks rolls into the fetal position clawing at his eyes.

"I won't kill him, Lyvs. Not yet, anyway," he says, making a fist. Brooks removes his hands from his eyes and clutches his stomach.

Blood oozes from gashes where Levi has ripped his skin. Now he pounds his mid-section with incredible force.

"I can keep going," Levi says, raising his arm.

"No. Stop."

"You gotta open that door," he replies, twisting his fist in the air. Brooks' screams intensify. I didn't think that was possible. I analyze my particulars. The nails. That's all I got. *Come on, guys.*

"I said, stop," I proclaim, holding my hand up. "I'll do it."

The screams stop. Brooks lies still, panting heavily. I walk over to him mid-way to my destination. I stoop down.

"No..." Levi enunciates slowly, chastising a child. He lifts his hand—

"Okay. Okay," I acquiesce, rising. I climb the steps to the large glass door. A lunar panel is fitted to the left of the entry. Made of moonstone, it's Onyx's version of Framework technology.

"Go ahead," Levi drawls, his patronizing tone fills me with hatred. I lift my hand to the screen.

"Hello Lyvia," a familiar male voice speaks. "Please look into the panel for facial recognition." I hesitate. There's shuffling behind me. I turn to see Brooks standing. He rubs his eyes. Blood smears across his cheeks.

"You know I'm not a patient man," Levi says, inspecting his guitar pick. Brooks moans and grabs his stomach.

"Yeah, okay, fine. Stop," I call, standing in front of the panel. The moaning diminishes.

"Now scanning," the male voice says. A light radiates from the screen.

"Lyvia, it's been too long."

"I know, Stone. Way too long," I murmur to the comforting presence of our home's intelization system.

"Lyvs," Levi drones edgily.

"Everything all right, Lyvia?" Stone asks.

"Yes, everything is fine, Stone. Please open the door."

"Of course." The door slides open.

"Bout time," Levi spits. "Get on with it, Brooks."

Brooks walks slowly into the house. He gives me a wary glance along the way. Behind us, Levi starts playing *Landscape* by Florence and the Machine. *My* song. I can't stand to hear it from him. One stab after another.

"You can't just use people to do your bidding," I remark, making my way back over to Levi.

"Uh, who says, Lyvs? I've been doing it for quite some time now. It's kind of my thang," he drawls, playing chords from one of his originals, "I'll Make You Act." The irony of the song's title is not lost on me.

"Well, I'm pretty sure God says."

"Oh, Him?" He rolls his eyes. "He doesn't seem to mind that much. I mean, He doesn't make it easy, but you guys sure do. I'll win. I've been toiling away down there, making progress. I'll get what I want."

"You don't get to be God, Levi. There's only one, and He's got a monopoly."

"It's time for Him to take a back seat. Let someone else run things for a while. Show 'Him' how it's really done."

Then, the shoes spin. Awkward, heavy nails take refuge in my hands.

"Oh, playtime's over, Lyvs?" He crosses his arms with a pout. "I hate business."

"Well, this should be quick," I respond, urging a spike forward. It shoots from my hand straight at the target. I wait for the sickening crunch. Instead, Levi raises a palm and the nail halts midair before landing unceremoniously on the ground. I try the other. Same outcome.

They rapidly return to my palms. A few more rounds of that before I change direction and clip his arm. Clip maybe an understatement. The metal has burned a chunk of his limb away. Not just a chunk, half his bicep muscle. Sizzling flesh curls away from the wound. *Ew.*

We get diverted by a noise in the house before resuming stance. I whip the nails out in a distracting manner and clip his other arm. The first hole has begun to repair itself. The skin stretches together lit by fire. He looks down at the second injury. Annoyed.

"Fuck. Okay, Lyvs, you wanna play rough? Let's go."

He walks toward me and I hear a voice inside my head.

'Vee, I found the skates and am heading out. I can't stop myself.'

Okay. Just come out and be prepared for back up.

I urge a nail toward Levi's advancing body, but it stays in place—vibrating wildly.

"I think I've seen enough of those." He swipes his hand through the air and the nails fall to the ground. Clink. Clink.

"Levi, you're not going to win," I say, pleading a nail. It shakes on the ground and starts to float, but an invisible force shoves me up against the stone wall. The nail clatters back to the ground.

Brooks appears through the glass door holding a pair of men's black-and-white hockey skates.

"Set them on that bench," Levi says, not wavering his gaze from me.

Brooks sets them on the bench and sticks his hands in his pockets. Takes a seat. Leans back. Nothing fazes this guy.

"Lyvs, when will you just give up this silliness? Get off the ride. It's not taking you anywhere. My road, though, my ride, has endless possibilities." He steps closer. Less than six inches now.

"You're making me do this, Lyvs. All of this," he says, stretching an arm wide. "All you have to say is yes and—"

He doesn't finish his sentence. His face flashes for an instant. Horrifying and zombie-like, yet unearthly. Haunted. Ripped, torn flesh. Terrifying black-filled eyes. *Evil Incarnate.* Then—back to Levi in a spilt second. To the point where I'm not even sure I saw it. But I did. I can't unsee that.

He sags forward and flops on the ground. Brooks stands behind him with a golden harpoon. Levi's fallen form lies still for a second. We gain space around him, not sure what he's capable of.

Then—a guitar pluck behind me.

I spin around. Levi lounges on the black chaise again. Looking back, there is no sign his body has ever fallen.

"You know better than that, baby," he says, playing "Baby, Hold on To Me" by Eddie Money.

Brooks picks up his harpoon. Leans against it.

"Dude, I got nothin' against you, but I know that Vee really needs those skates. So, let's just call a truce."

Levi laughs. "Wish I could say the same, man." He plays "What Goes Around Comes Around" by Justin Timberlake. "But, uh, yeah, you kissed my girl."

With that, he vanishes from the chair. Brooks and I stare at each other. His face freezes. He lets out a cough and falls face forward.

Levi stands behind him. I follow a giant blade down to a silver, two-handed ancient sword. Between us a Brooks-shaped form rises from his body. A figure of flaming orange circuitry hovers above him. Suddenly, the spirit shoots vertically toward the heavens. His body lies unmoving on the ground.

"Ugh. Lyvs, I hate getting this dirty." He wipes the bloody steel on Brooks' t-shirt. The crimson spreads a gruesome inkblot.

The nails find my hands. They shoot out. Gigantic bullets. He bats them away with his weapon. They clatter and return. Clatter and return. We go through the same routine a few more times.

Then—I duck and swipe very low. The nail clips his calf.

"Damn it, Lyvia. I've seriously had it." He lunges forward. The blade swishes above my head. I shoot a nail to clip his other calf and roll away. Closer to the skates.

"Hey Boss," a disembodied voice says from around the corner. *Damien.* The kiss witness and Levi's source.

"Yeah, Damien, I'm gonna need you to get those skates, over there." He points with his blade. "And take them to the car."

"Sure thing. Hey, Lyvia," he says, walking obediently toward the skates.

From a crouching position I swing a nail toward Levi's face. He stops it midair. At the same time, I urge the second at Damien. It knocks him out with a thunk. He collapses on the ground.

Levi and I square off in my childhood backyard. I spot my giant playhouse to the east. A mini replica of the home complete with identical carpeting. I always loved that thing. It even has a matching tower in the middle that descends to its counterpart's matching glass steeple. A spiral staircase leads to the highest point, a round circular bedroom. It's a huge playhouse house full of a mishmash of furniture. I kept the furniture different in the playhouse, changed it often. I never liked getting used to 'same.'

A green turtle-shaped sandbox lid. Upside-down, leaning side-to-side. Invisible waves take us home. A tiny house awaits. A small blonde head races me to the door. We already know who will win. No matter what I 'try.'

"You got the rest of your posse?" I speculate, returning to the present.

"Nope."

"So, how ya gonna get the skates?" I ask, twirling a spike.

"I guess we're at a crossroads," he replies, flipping his blade.

"Well, I'm not carrying them for you, and I'm not leaving without them."

"See that's the thing, Lyvs. My only recourse is to make sure you stay knocked out until after Damien comes to and we're on our way." He licks his lips and advances slowly.

"I like that thing better when it's a guitar," I reply, forcing both spikes at him. They miss and return. Miss and return.

"This is getting old, Levi. You kill Shane, then Dagan, and now, Brooks? I'm sick of it." I take off the crown and whip it toward his head. A ray of light resembling an oracle spreads forth. It slices through one of his hands and regains purchase on my head. The hand vanishes from the ground and regenerates with fire back to clutching his sword.

"Lyvs." He holds the sword unthreateningly in front of him. "I didn't kill Dagan. He's just stuck in time."

"What the hell does that mean?" I stand up, breathing heavily.

"Much to learn you have, young one," he replies, casually balancing the sword point on the ground.

"Stop the shtick, Yoda. What are you talking about?"

"There's more than just communication vortexes, Lyvia. There's what's called a 'Time Ring.' Loops. Fall into one of those, you can get stuck there forever. Just loop after loop after loop. Now, it sounds like Hell. And, sure, it's similar. But my place is so much more fun." The sword has transformed to a guitar. A sexy track beats from the instrument. He slides into a Michael Jackson 'moonwalk' as he sings the hook from, "Yeah!" by Usher.

I never saw a flaming form rise from Dagan's watery grave.

"How do I get him out?" I ask, twirling the nails in my hands.

"You don't," he laughs, while fiddling his strings. "You know, whenever it transforms, I have to re-tune. So annoying." He rolls his eyes.

I glance at the skates. *If I could just get to them... And what? Throw them around my neck and run? I won't get far.*

He starts playing some eerie, ominous chords.

Suddenly, he is right beside me. He brushes hair off my neck.

"I'm sick of the games, Lyvs," he drawls—now appearing directly in front of me.

I drive the spikes into his shoulders. They burn through flesh. He sags momentarily but advances, arms outstretched. The nails fall to the ground. He grabs my neck, pushes me against the stone wall. I can't breathe. I struggle, gasping for air. I push at his arms, but they only tighten. He inches closer. I'm suffocating. Black hedges my vision.

My right hand pushes against his chest. I start to pray and prepare myself for the afterlife. Suddenly, a severe burning radiates from my shoulder down through my fingertips. Glancing down, my arm glows red-hot. My scorching palm burns through his chest. A hot steel tip for wielding.

His hands drop. I open my eyes. His face flashes again. Ripped and torn. Haunting eyes.

Then—*poof*—a burst of fire I cannot feel.

27

I survey the area. He's gone. I sprint to Brooks. He's still unmoving. I check his pulse, just in case, but he has definitely departed.

I walk over to Damien. He's still out cold. I grab the skates and return to Brooks. I can't leave him here. I'm sure Damien's happy helpers will show their unwelcome faces at any moment. Not to mention—what the hell happened to Levi? And my arm?

"I already called Lani," a muffled voice comes from my abandoned bag on the side of the house. "She has a few friends in Onyx who will take him to Turquoise for burial. You just need to put him somewhere safe until they can get here."

A memory shakes loose. The pebbled wall around the garden has an overhang that turns into a tunnel. A small wooden door reveals a passageway that winds underground and opens to the basement. I practically lived in there growing up. I always thought I was Goldilocks in her underground hideout before she investigates the bears' den. I can secure him in there. There's even a lock on the door.

"Okay Seph, I'm going to lay him in the tunnel," I say, searching for some kind of cloth to wrap him in. Nothing.

Ensuring Damien is still out cold, I go into the house. The scent takes me back to a little girl when things were simple and wondrous. Lavender and Vanilla Snuggle fabric softener and 'All' brand laundry detergent lingers in the air. Shane still uses the stuff, as do I.

I need to hurry. I look around. Boy, things changed with my

parents gone. It seems his room has melted into the entire house. Chewing tobacco cans and half-empty Propel water bottles litter the floor. Clothes and athletic equipment drape over the furniture. Nothing is big enough to wrap Brooks in.

I try the laundry room. To get there, I move down the massive hallway that twists to the east end of the house. I avoid looking at the walls. Framed photos line them. Shane's athletics, my newspaper articles, posed dance photos, family portraits, millions of Shane's action shots—our family memories frozen in time. It was my father's project. He created a photo mosaic of our family.

The large laundry room is crisp white. The scent of detergent and softener is even stronger in here. Again, clothes are draped and strewn about all over the place. I open cupboards searching for a sheet or blanket only to find more random clothing.

"Come on, Shane. You gotta have something to sleep on…" I murmur through the shuffling.

"Ugh." I collapse on a pile of fabrics. The mixture of familiar scents overwhelms me. I feel a tear drop, wetting the material.

Upstairs. The linen cabinet upstairs. I jump up feeling the pressure of time. The house is very large, made larger by the obstacles in attendance.

"Shane, I told you to hire a housecleaner." I make it to the landing and head up the twisty, spiral staircase. Rounding the top, I take a quick right to the master bathroom's linen closet. Scanning up past towels and washcloths, I spot linens at the top. Can't reach.

I peruse the area and spot an armchair in the loft's living room. I push it across the hardwood floor and attempt to climb. It's soft and squishy as if I'm stepping on quicksand. I balance precariously on an arm and reach up. I manage to brush my fingertips on the shelf in question but lose balance and grab nothing.

I try again, this time with a bit more force. I grab the corner of *something*, but my momentum causes me to fly—yes, fly—off the chair which clatters onto its side opposite of me. The shelves follow suit, missing me by inches. I sit up and clear my hair from my face. I find the corner of a flannel sheet pinched between two fingers.

"Yes, this will do." I quickly make my way out to the backyard. Sliding open the glass door, I hear moaning. *Oh yeah. Damien.*

"Arrghh." He growls, wiping his eyes.

I ignore him and head over to Brooks. He hasn't moved. *I'm so tired of death.* I cry silently over his still form—until I black out.

I START COMING to and rub my eyes. I touch the crown of my head where it's throbbing. Warm sticky blood covers my fingers. I see movement to my right where Damien's form is holding an ice skate.

"Whoa, Damien," I say, struggling to stand up. "Let's talk."

"I'm done talking, Lyv. I have to do what Levi says. He wants you knocked out." He raises the skate.

Mentally urging the nails, I say, "I'm not letting you leave with those skates."

"Not your choice," he replies as he swings forward.

"It always is," I reply, sidestepping the strike.

As I round to the left, a nail finds my palm. I swing it at him, but he uses the skate's blade to ricochet the ancient metal. During which time, he swings his other fist and catches me square in the jaw. I flop to the ground abruptly. Unable to lift my head, I stare at Brooks' fallen form. Damien stands above me; two hands hold the skate. I continue to stare at Brooks and hope for a swift ending.

Suddenly an orange, glowing form drops down next to Brooks. The figure is eerily familiar, tall and broad. If I didn't know better, I'd say I spot a fatty tucked in his lip.

Shane?

The Shane-shaped flaming circuitry nods imperceptibly and touches Brooks chest. Damien watches the display with the skate still poised above his head.

Brooks begins to glow from within. A pulsating light. Then a flash of bright white light and the Shane-spirit departs to Heaven. As Brooks begins to sit up, I take the opportunity to roll away from Damien.

A nail finds my palm and I shoot it at Damien's head, knocking him out again. Plus, one more time for retribution. *Come on, my head is in need of serious medical attention here. Fair's fair.*

"How are you?" I ask Brooks once I stumble over to him.

"I'm okay. I really am," he replies, running his hands over his completely intact body. He jumps up, brushes himself off, musses his thick, wavy hair, and says, "Good as new."

"I'm so relieved to hear that," I say, enveloping him in a hug.

"Me too," he responds, returning it. He touches my head and I wince. "Whoa, what happened to you?"

"Damien. He's out cold now." I grab the nails and they return to sandals. Brooks grabs both skates.

"We have to get a first aid kit. Shane's gotta have one inside," Brooks says, walking to the door.

"We gotta find one on the road. We can't stay here. It's not safe. He'll be back. Probably soon," I reply.

"Come on, man," Brooks says, standing in front of me. "We won't take long. We need to patch that up. I'll go in real quick."

"Brooks, there's no 'real quick' with you. I would have to go in there and look through stuff. Trust me, it will take too much time." I start walking around the house.

"With both of us, we can—" he starts.

He doesn't finish because I lose my balance and fall to the ground. He comes over and helps me up.

"See, Lyv. We can do it fast."

"Okay," I acquiesce.

Once inside, Brooks begins throwing things everywhere.

"Hey, this isn't a ransack, okay? Go upstairs and try the bathrooms, under the counters. I'm gonna try the bathrooms down here and the kitchen."

We manage to scrounge up a couple very old kits. Brooks cleans the gash, which is no longer bleeding and not as serious as it looks, doesn't even need a bandage. It seems to be healing very quickly. The headache is nearly gone. We walk back outside and sense something amiss.

"Where's Damien?" Brooks asks.

"Maybe he just left?" I say, hopeful.

"Meh."

"I don't think so either."

"Damien, where-oh-where are you?" I sing-song.

"Oh shit," Brooks says behind a stone wall.

"What?"

"Found him," he replies.

I follow his voice. Coming around the stone barricade, I spot Damien.

He's not alone.

28

*S*hit. *Shit. Shit.*

Damien holds a knife against a young girl's neck.

"Hey, Iris. Whatcha doin out here?" I ask, tentatively approaching.

"I was just—" the girl begins.

"Doesn't matter what she was doing. She won't be around much longer to do anything of any kind if you don't hand over those skates, Brooks," Damien snarls.

Brooks swings the skates upward. The laces straddle his shoulder.

"Yeah... Don't think so, compadre."

"You know, I could keep this one alive, Bryce has been looking for someone to play with," he says, placing the knife flat against her clavicle. He uses his other hand to touch her hair.

That's it. I've known Iris since she was a little girl. *No one, I mean, no one is going to touch her.*

"Don't think I won't do it though." Damien slides the knife back into slicing position against her smooth, white skin.

"Damien, maybe we can work together," I say, stepping forward. *Need to buy some time.*

"Stay where you are," Damien replies. He moves the knife to reveal a drop of crimson below the blade.

Another step forward.

"Damien, you're not getting the skates. You're not taking Iris. If you let her go, I'll let you live."

"Not happening," he shifts the blade, now revealing a small stream of red.

"Damien—" I start.

What I'm unable to see is Iris unclasp a tiny gold bracelet from her wrist. When she does, it grows in size to a long, thick chain. Stealthily, she swings the chain upward. As if a mind of its own, it wraps around Damien's neck. The knife drops to the ground. Iris runs toward us and takes her place behind me and Brooks.

The chain squeezes tightly against Damien's neck. He claws at its links. A futile effort. He passes out. Iris lifts her arm and the chain breaks free of Damien, shrinks, and swings back to its home. Now secure on her wrist.

I decide to leave Damien alive. Call it weakness. I decide to call it not wanting to waste another life.

I throw the skates in my bag surprised to see they not only fit snugly, but their weight adds little to the purse. The three of us round the house quickly. We don't know how long he'll be out.

"Follow me," Iris says.

We do.

THROUGH THE DARKNESS, she takes us to the tunnel where I had been planning to stow Brooks' body. I know exactly where she's headed. The dark tunnel is long and narrow. Rocky cobblestone lines the path. We pass the basement entrance.

We hear it first. Bubbling, rushing water. The tunnel opens to a clearing. A small creek crops up; it's the one that leads to the lake behind the house. She takes us over the bridge. The trees open to another clearing. A small cottage rests in the middle of the forest, nearly invisible. I've been here before. It's been far too long.

Iris scoops a key out of her pocket and slips it into the keyhole. We burst through the threshold. The house is lit up inside. The windows make it appear to be daytime outside, opposite of the windows in Crystal. My eyes have to adjust to the light.

Once they do, I see Iris has kept the cottage much the same from when we would meet here years ago. She's quite a bit younger than me. Our families have been neighbors long before we even came along. I babysat her as a child. As she grew, I became kind of a mentor. Not sure if I was a good one; nonetheless, we also became friends.

When I was a little girl, my grandmother first took me to this cottage. It belongs to my family. I was the only one who ever used it. It actually got left to me with the house when my parents died. I had told Iris long ago that it was hers to use as she wanted—a free rental. I knew she needed to get away from home to work on her various activities free from distractions.

"You living here now, Iris?" I ask, looking around. The cottage definitely appears lived in. I see clothes strewn about. She has designated one corner to her art. An easel is set up. Finished sketches and drawings litter the area. From what I can see, they look amazing. Many eyes peer out from the paper, all different colors and expressions. There's posed figures sketched in black and white. Colorful abstract paintings settle along the wall. She's got a lacrosse stick slung over a coat hook. Schoolbooks take over the coffee table. Her bass leans against the opposite wall with several other instruments.

"Yeah, too many interruptions at my house. I need my own space. Started coming here more often than staying at home. Decided to move in," she says, opening a cupboard in the kitchenette. She takes out first aid supplies and cleans up the tiny cut on her neck. She finishes with a small bandage. It looks as if it may have a vintage cartoon character embossed on it. "Hope that's okay."

"Of course, it is," I reply. "Glad it's of use."

Iris clears off the couches. We settle in the living room to debrief.

"So, tell me about that bracelet," Brooks says, nodding at the thin gold chain now in its resting place while he settles into the oversized memory-foam couch.

"Oh yeah," she says, looking down at it.

I see the delicate chain is adorned with sharp hooks. They look painful.

"I found this here in the cabin," she says, shooting me a guilty look. "I tried it on. The hooks bit into my skin the first time I put it on. It was painful. There was blood, a lot of it. I went to get it off, but the blood disappeared. The pain vanished. I haven't taken it off since. Seems to be something to it. Then when that guy had me, I thought at the very least I could maybe swing it onto his wrist for a quick distraction. Maybe it'd make him bleed and he'd drop the knife. I had no idea it would do *that*."

"Lemme see it," I say, reaching across Brooks.

She slides the bracelet off and hands it to me. I put it on and sure enough, a blinding pain radiates from my wrist. Beads of blood appear where hooks seem to latch in. It begins to stream down my arm. I close my eyes, waiting for the pain to ebb away. It does. When I open my eyes, the blood is gone.

"Must be another relic," I say, removing the bracelet.

"*Another* relic?" Iris asks, eyebrows perked up in question.

"Oh yeah, she's got all sorts of things up her sleeves," Brooks adds.

"You're one to talk," I reply, looking pointedly at his pocket where a certain fishhook resides.

"Do you think he can find us here?" Iris asks with concern. "I'm sure he was out cold, but he could've regained consciousness by now."

"We took the twisty way here," I reply. "Even if he regained consciousness, this is well hidden, and I know he's not used to darkness like we are in Onyx. I doubt he's leaving anytime soon, though. Not without those skates," I add, with a quick glance to my bag. "However, I do think he'll call for reinforcements here shortly."

"Why does he want Shane's skates?" Iris asks.

"I'm not sure. What I do know is that I need them for what comes next."

"What comes next?" Brooks asks.

"I've got someplace to be, and I need both of you to help get me there," I reply.

"Um, hello. Don't forget about me," a muffled voice sounds from my bag. I pull out my Slab and Persephone materializes in front of us.

"Hey, Seph, I can never forget about you," I say.

"Hey, Brooksey," Persephone drawls. She's wearing pigtails with lime green bows. "Been too long. And you must be Iris."

"Yes," Iris responds cautiously.

"Oh, Lyvia has told me much about you. That bracelet, wow, you found a good one," Persephone says. She splays her arms out and a plethora of bangles don each one. "It's a relic, you know."

"We gathered that much," I respond. "What do you know about it, Seph?"

She looks at the thin chain and puts her hand to her chin thoughtfully. Her bracelets jangle like a wind chime disturbed by a sudden gust.

"It was St. Catherine of Siena's. It drew blood each time she moved. She slept on a board, shaved her head, and did pretty much everything she could do to join the Sisterhood. It wasn't until she grew very ill that her parents relented."

"How do you know this?" Brooks asks.

"It's been in the family for centuries," she replies mysteriously.

"Okay, we can come back to that later," I say. "More importantly, I gotta jet, right, Seph?"

"Oh yes, you do."

She sidles over to Brooks and sits on the coffee table in front of him. She pulls out a pixie stick and sprinkles some of the powdered candy onto her tongue.

"She's gonna need both of you," she glances over at Iris. "Let's assume Levi knows where you're headed."

I nod because, of course, he does.

"He's going to have his little army staked out along the way. She's going to need you, Brooks, for protection and distraction."

Brooks nods solemnly.

"Now you," she turns her attention to Iris, while chewing on the end of the pixie stick. "You know the way."

"What? Know the way where? I have no idea where you're trying to go and what you're trying to do," she exclaims exasperated. "I haven't even seen Lyvia in Onyx in a year. I only heard commotion on my way to the cabin and went to check it out. I haven't even seen Shane in forever."

I realize I have yet to share the news of Shane's death. *Sucks. Every. Single. Time.* Turns out, I don't have to. My eyes say it all.

"Oh no. I'm so sorry," she says, silent tears run down her cheeks.

"Me too," Brooks adds, reaching to grasp my hand.

"Don't be. I'm gonna get him back." I look resolutely at Brooks.

"She needs you, Iris, to do it," Persephone cries with a cheerleading clap.

"Say what now?" Iris asks.

"Okay, if anyone knows the way, it's you." Persephone materializes on the ottoman resting in front of Iris. "You know exactly where she needs to be. I know you've been there before," she finishes with a wink.

"She's been to the tomb?" I ask incredulously.

"Oh sure, she has, right, Iris?"

Iris looks at her hands. "I didn't know it was a tomb," she responds quietly.

"What were you doing there?" I ask.

"The first time, I was in Crystal for training. I was assigned to study the landscape. I wanted to figure out what lies beyond the waterfalls. Sure, we know they empty to the ocean, but I have a feeling there's something way below its surface. So, I followed a path around the falls. It wound around cliffs high above the water. I noticed a large rock wedged into the mountain behind me. Then I saw *it*."

"Whaddya see?" Brooks pipes in.

Iris squeezes her eyes shut as if to conjure the image. When they open, the trauma revealed tells me I'm pretty sure I know exactly what she saw.

"It looked like Levi, you know, the Leader of Gold. But, uh, his head was huge, and—"

"There were seven of them," Brooks finishes.

"You've seen him like that?" she asks.

"No, not personally, but a friend of ours had a vision."

"I don't think it was a vision," she replies.

"What did he say?" Persephone asks.

"Keep in mind, this was a few months ago. I've been back there several times since then. I'm not scared. I know he won't come back. He told me so."

"What else did he tell you?" I ask.

"It was more of a threat. He said you would need my help, but I'm not to help you. I'll go to Hell if I do, blah, blah, blah. Dude, is he really the Devil?"

"He sure is," Persephone responds, donning a headband adorned with pointy red curved horns. She turns around, and I notice a red pointed tail and pitchfork have also materialized.

"I can't allow you to do this, Iris. Levi cannot be underestimated," I say with authority.

"It's a little complicated, Lyv," she replies. "You see, I very recently had a dream. I didn't know who visited me at the time, but I have a feeling I know now. It was a male energy. I couldn't see anybody, but a voice spoke. He told me to help you and not to worry about Levi's threats. He said to trust him and keep a look out for you. So, that's kind of what I've been doing. I didn't realize the commotion I heard tonight was the beginning of D-Day."

"You got anything to drink in here, Iris?" I ask, needing something to do while I process this new information. *This guy is never going to leave me alone.*

"Sure, check the fridge."

I do and am pleased to find a plethora of options. I pour myself a cucumber water. She's kept the glasses in the same place.

"Anyone else?"

"Sure, is there any beer?" Brooks asks.

"Yep," I reply, twisting a cap off a bottle of golden ale.

"Just a glass of cucumber water, thanks, Lyv," Iris says. She seems to be in hushed conversation with Persephone.

"Did Levi talk to you for a long time?" Brooks asks as I hand out the requested beverages.

"No, not at all. He's the only one that spoke. The other creepy heads seemed to be under forced silence. He merely said not to help you under any circumstances. If I do, I'll go to Hell, which I don't believe for a second. Oh, and to make sure you didn't have any hockey skates on you. If you did, I was to snatch them and bring them to him."

"What is with these skates?" I say, taking one out of my bag. Seems like a regular old, well-worn ice hockey skate. The blade is sharp and cool. The laces are frayed at the ends. Nothing out of the ordinary. I shrug and put it back.

"Tell them about the map," Persephone says.

"Oh yeah," Iris replies. "I was rearranging furniture for an art area." She points to the designated corner. "I needed enough space to set up my easel where there's light from the window when I paint."

"Tell her about the floorboard," Seph interjects.

"When I moved a rug in the corner, I noticed the wooden floor slightly lifted. The floorboard was a bit stiff, but eventually I pried it up. I found this ancient paper map."

"It's got this secret shortcut to Crystal. You won't have to go the long way through the forest," Persephone finishes.

I think this may be the subject of whispers a moment ago.

"Levi's smart, he may already have that way guarded. Both of them," I say.

"Impossible," Iris replies. "It's not visible to him. It's holy."

"You see, Levi can't step on blessed ground. He can't even see it. It's invisible to him," Persephone supplies.

"Are *we* invisible to him while on it?" I ask.

"Yes," Seph responds. "Get the map, Iris."

Iris goes to the secret floorboard. It takes some jimmying, but she wrests it open and pulls out a yellowed square of paper. She brings it over and unwraps it on the coffee table. When it's open, I see that it is in fact very old. This results in a lack of detail. Still, I begin to recognize geographic locations.

"We are here," I say, pointing to an area covered in black.

"Yes, and here's Crystal," Iris shows me an opalescent region.

I spot a shimmering path through foliage on the outskirts of Crystal.

"Persephone, can you manipulate this map into a 3D hologram?" I ask.

"Sure, easy peasy." She disappears momentarily. A snap and a pop later, she reappears. She swipes her hand through the air and an old-fashioned movie screen manifests. Its white screen flickers before it displays the map. She's got what looks like a conductor's baton in her hand.

"We are here," she says, pointing to the black area on the enlarged map.

When she does so, the movie screen dissipates. The map zooms in on said area and shifts into a 3D replica. Persephone's hologram display has us at the edge of Onyx. With the Lunar darkness behind us, we are facing bright sunlight fitted with large green fields as far as the eye can see.

"Shit, we've still got to get through Emerald, Ruby, and Granite to hit the mouth of Crystal," I say. "And those lands are *not* holy."

"Yeah, Satan's gonna have every avenue and mode of transportation watched," Brooks interjects.

"Seph, what would be the fastest mode of transport to get to Crystal?" I ask.

"Let's see," she points the end of her conductor's baton thoughtfully to the corner of her mouth. The hologram switches back to the ancient map. Persephone ponders it. She seems to see something. She disappears and materializes in front of the paper map on the table.

"That's interesting," she says. Back in front of her map, she zooms in. Split between Onyx and Emerald there appears a tiny glittering door.

"A door?" I ask.

"Seems there's an underground tunnel leading to Crystal," she replies. The map becomes 3D again. A sweeping zoom shows us a darkened path in Onyx. Twisting and turning it ends at a large, old door. The door opens into the tunnel.

"A tunnel that goes to Crystal?" I ask. "Is it holy ground?"

"It is, in fact," Seph says, pulling up a slideshow. It's black and white and shows numerous men digging into the ground. The images go fast through the process and the tunnel gets completed.

"You see, these men," Seph points with her baton. "They are of the Granite Brotherhood monks. When the shires were constructed so very long ago, they figured they would need a secret way to get from Granite to Crystal and Onyx. They took vows of silence and servitude. They did not condone distractions of any kind. More than that, though, they needed safety. At the time, Gold was persecuting those of faith. I'm sure you know this from your studies, Iris?"

"Uh yes, I do." She goes to a bookshelf and pulls out a hefty volume. "Long after the ancient families had established the shires, Gold became heavily materialistic. They looked down on spirituality. They didn't condone it. Yes, here it is."

She opens the book to a photograph. It's clearly Gold Shire. The shimmering pavement and archways betray the landscape. In the photo, a prior Gold Leader stands next to a man in shackles.

"If you were caught on Gold land displaying any sort of spiritual fortitude, you were persecuted. Many souls were sent to death."

"That's why they constructed the tunnel," Seph finishes with a flourish of the baton. Her hologram shows the length of the tunnel opening to the bright sky and greenery of Crystal.

"Well, that just sounds way too easy," Brooks adds his two cents.

"He's right," I confirm.

"You're both right," Seph says. "Your primary concern is going to be from the tunnel to the opening of the Holy Path. They're not connected. That's going to be a concern. The other thing is the door to the tunnel needs a key."

"Where's the key?" Brooks asks.

"Iris, grab the map and give it to Lyvia," Seph says. "I'm not sure if this will work, but I have a feeling it will…"

Iris brings it over to me.

"Lyvia, set it on the ground. Take your shoes off."

I spread the map on the ground and remove my sandals.

"Step on it," she directs.

29

I step on the ancient paper with my bare feet. Suddenly, I'm no longer in the room with the gang. I'm on a field. The paper is gone beneath my feet, replaced with soft green, luscious grass. It's warm. There's a quiet breeze caressing my skin. It seems like a familiar place, but I'm not sure where I am. What I do know, is it's not Earth. When I look down at my toes in the grass, I spot a bronze skeleton key snug in the green between my feet. I want to check this place out before I grab that key, which I assume swings me back to Earth, but there's not time.

I stoop down and grab the key. Grass is replaced by aged paper. I'm back standing on the map in the cottage room. A key secure in my hand. I stick it in my shoulder bag.

"Where'd you go?" Iris asks.

"Not quite sure," I reply. "Some field. Looked familiar. Spirit Plane, I think."

"It seems like we've got two points of weakness," Brooks says, pointing at Persephone's hologram. "From here to the tunnel, then from the tunnel to the Holy Path."

"That's where Iris comes in," I say, the dawn of realization setting in.

Iris is sixteen-years-old. She wears her thick brunette hair in pixie-style haircut that accentuates her almond-shaped, aquamarine eyes. She's got a small, athletic stature. Not afraid of adventure, her tomboy spirited side reveals itself often.

Her sense of style is not one to be reckoned with. In fact, she has helped me coordinate outfits for years. She favors vintage attire, and today she is wearing an antiquated bow-necked white top with small black polka-dots and a ruffled collar paired with high-waisted, straight-legged jeans circa late-1990s and a black grommet belt.

I always called Iris a little earthen nymph. Her love of nature and geography has her exploring nonstop. I've often found her in these very woods investigating the area. It's going to be Iris who gets us to that door.

"Iris, is it hard to locate?" I ask.

"Nope," she replies easily.

"She won't have any trouble getting you there," Seph interjects, with a flip of a ponytail.

"We just need to—" I get cut off by a sound outside.

"Shh, everyone be quiet," Brooks whispers.

The shuffling continues. Not right up near the house. Seems to be some distance away.

"Shit, it's his minions," I say, peering out the window through a corner of the curtain.

"He might see the light—" Brooks interjects, pulling my hand from the fabric.

"No, we're invisible, Brooks," I say, turning toward him. "The whole cottage is blessed. Unless they walk directly into it, they cannot see or hear us. Invisible force field."

"What'd you see?" he asks.

"I saw three figures, but there could be more. One is very large."

"Bryce," Seph supplies. She pulls up a hologram picture of him. It's animated. His serious face pulls into a grim, sickening smile.

"Most likely," I respond.

"Who's Bryce?" Iris asks.

"An ogre," I say. "Works for Levi."

"Oh no," she replies.

"Between the three of us and our relics, this'll be easy," Brooks says.

"We need to hear what they're saying," I tell him.

"Yeah, can't get ahead of ourselves. They're sure to have weapons of their own," Brooks replies.

"Send me," says Seph. "Put the Slab near the door, I can absorb the sound invisibly."

"Great idea, Seph," I respond, setting the moonstone Slab by the door.

Persephone dissipates into thin air.

"Now we wait," I say, exhaling as I settle into the sofa.

Poof. Persephone appears in the cottage. She's got sight-enhancing binoculars on her head. "I can confirm there are three of them."

"Which ones?" I ask.

"Two that will give you trouble—Bryce and Chad. The third, however, may be your ticket to the door."

"Who is it?" I ask.

"Xane," she replies.

"Oh, wow. That is grrr-eat news," I say.

"Who's Xane?" Iris asks.

"An ally," Seph answers.

"There's more," Persephone goes on. "They have weaponry—some serious weaponry. Although, we trust Xane, he could've been converted by now. Otherwise, he's putting on quite a show."

"Well, that does sound like Xane," I reply.

"I know," she says. "I have it on good authority he most certainly is play-acting."

"Who's authority?" Brooks asks, languidly. He leans back into the couch and links his fingers behind his head. If I didn't know better, I'd say he was about five minutes from going into a turkey-coma following Thanksgiving dinner. *This guy.*

"Well, mine of course," she laughs. "I know Xane. He's a great actor, but I can see his true intentions."

"Okay, well, we can't just run out there and start yelling Xane's name, regardless of whether he's on our side or not. There's two others out there," Iris pipes in from the recliner. She's leaning forward, her head steepled between her hands.

"She's right," Seph says. "I've got a plan."

"Before we start with logistics, I think the most pertinent thing we need to know is what weapons they've got. Seph?" I ask.

"It's an artifact," she replies. "An evil one."

"Like?" I ask.

"Okay, another quick lesson," Persephone says, bringing up her movie screen. "Everyone familiar with ancient Greek mythology?"

We all nod.

"Well, obviously, the mythology was completely constructed by humans. And it's not correct. Not quite, anyway. Humans needed to personify things—emotions, love, evil, wisdom, good, hope—these things were given idols. Names, really—Aphrodite, Hades, Athena, Zeus, the Graces, etc. Just to understand and compartmentalize *life*. Of course, this was before the Bible came along and straightened some things out. Like—there aren't multiple gods; only the Father. Still, it was a way for humans to comprehend concepts beyond concrete understanding. Most concepts are abstract; although, there are some that have a bit of truth to them."

"Like?" I ask again.

"A certain box," Iris says, looking up from a book that appears to have materialized out of thin air, probably one of Persephone's holograms.

"Pandora's Box?" Brooks asks.

"Yes, Pandora's box, but it's not what you picture," she answers. "You see, the story goes, when Prometheus stole fire from Heaven, Zeus, King of the gods, wanted revenge. He presented Pandora, the first human woman created by the gods, to Prometheus' brother, Epimetheus. She, by the way, was created with deceitful feminine qualities and an evil flair."

"Misogynists," I remark.

"Yeah, they were," Seph replies. "Anyway, so Pandora comes with this box, which isn't exactly an accurate translation. It's not a box; it's more like a *jar*. Pandora is gifted to Epimetheus. He accepts Zeus' endowment despite warnings from his brother. Once in his presence, Pandora opens the box. Evil and sickness pour out into the world. The only one not to escape from the jar was 'Hope.'"

"Deceptive expectation," Iris adds from behind the hologram hardcover.

"Yes, that has been a more accurate translation, depending on levels of optimism," Seph says.

"So that's all that's left in the jar now?" Brooks asks.

"No, that would be nice though. See, the story of the chalice is not accurate. There was in fact a jar, but it was not handed down by

Greek gods. It was always in the possession of Hades, also known as
—" Seph pauses.

"Lucifer," I finish.

"It was he who unleashed the evils, as we know. The reason 'hope' is better translated as deceptive expectation is because that's kind of the Devil's thing, deception. 'Hope' as we know it, wasn't left in the jar. Once evil and sickness were unleashed, Satan kept the jar. In it, he harnessed fear. He designed the jar to absorb the greatest fears of those within the vicinity."

"How does it work?" Brooks asks.

"When the bearer lifts the lid, any and all in the vicinity enter their deepest personal fears. As long as the holder is touching the jar, he enters no such fear. It's the same when holding the lid."

"We should assume all three will open the jar and continue touching either the lid or the jar, keeping them safe," Brooks deduces.

"What do we do?" Iris asks.

"Well, Brooks is right. I heard Bryce say he would be holding the jar. All three would hang on while he opened it. Then Chad and Xane would hold onto the lid. The plan is to entomb you three in fear, while they tie you up and bring you to Levi. Although, they didn't say where that would be," Seph replies.

"So, they plan to tie us up one-handed while hanging on to the artifacts?" Brooks asks. "Seems stupid."

"Well, Bryce was never one to personify the epitome of intelligence," I say.

"Right," Seph agrees. "That's how you need to circumvent these guys."

"We need to intercept the jar before they even open it," Brooks interjects.

"That would be ideal," I say.

"Ideal, but very difficult," Seph replies. "Bryce has the thing practically glued to him."

"Okay, so there are three of them," I say.

"And three of us," Iris finishes.

"Ah-em," Seph clears her throat.

"Okay, four, and Seph you've helped a great deal thus far," I say with a wink.

She nods spiritedly, her pigtails bouncing. A cheerleader's call for the human pyramid.

"I'll take Bryce," Brooks offers.

"Okay, and Iris, you've got Chad. I believe you can handle him, especially after Damien. Do you have your bracelet?"

"Yep," she says, displaying the glittery gold chain.

"Good, you may need it," I tell her. "I'll take Xane. I'm going to make sure he hasn't switched lanes and get him to help us with the other two."

"Where are they exactly, Seph?" Brooks asks.

"About thirty yards from the cottage. They don't know where the door is located; although, they happen to be on the exact trajectory that leads there."

"So, we follow Iris to the path, then split up to cover our appointed targets as we near them," I relay.

"Sounds like a plan," Iris says.

"We should do some sort of group handshake," Persephone says, bouncing with excitement.

"Seph, we don't really have time—" I start.

"Hands in everybody," she exclaims, ignoring my hesitation.

Iris, Brooks, and I congregate around Seph. Everyone puts his or her hands layering each on top of the other. Persephone places her hologram hand on the very top.

"Repeat after me," she says.

We look at her expectantly.

"Earth, Fire, Wind, Water, Heart—unite!"

Nobody says a word.

"Seph, did you just quote *Captain Planet*?" I ask. It's an ancient cartoon revolving around a protagonist set on saving the world from pollution.

"Umm... Maybe," she replies, eyes wide and innocent.

"Okay, how about: Let's do this, on three," I try.

"Well, it's kind of lame, but I guess..." Persephone utters, dejectedly.

"Seph, count us down," I say, knowing she's dying to lead the countdown at the very least.

She starts—"One, two, three, let's do this!"

We finish the last three words together.

30

I stow my Slab in my bag along with the skates and my other things.

The plan is for me to take the lead. Distract the minions until Brooks and Iris are in place. Persephone showed us a map of the exterior and outlined where the others are located, about thirty yards into the woods.

We filter through the door as stealth-like silent ninjas and peer into the woods. Sure enough, about thirty yards in, we can hear muffled voices. I point Brooks and Iris to a large rock between us and the conversation. They nod silently and split off.

I continue toward the voices inaudibly. The closer I get the better I can make out some words.

"Over … by the way … don't … Fine—"

"No, that's not where … see ... We … find ... She'll …"

I make a few more quick and quiet steps forward and settle behind a huge tree trunk. The conversation becomes clear.

"Come on you guys, look harder. This place is supposed to be right around here, why can't we see it?" A gruff voice. Bryce.

"Because it's blessed," Xane answers, adding under his breath, "You dipshit."

"What was that?" Bryce growls.

"Nuthin' man, let's just keep looking for it," he replies easily.

I peer around thick, dark bark. They're about fifteen feet in front of me, give or take. Bryce's large back faces me, hugging what I suspect is Pandora's keepsake. The other two are ahead of him facing the same way, arms outstretched, feeling the air for a hidden cottage. *Ha.*

Knowing that Bryce won't open the jar without guarantee that Brooks, Iris, and I are in the vicinity, I stand and begin to whistle.

"Why hello, Bryce, Chad. Is that you, Xane? Long time no see."

I can tell they don't know which direction my voice is coming from as they each spin a circle respectively.

"Where are you?" Bryce bellows.

"Oh Bryce, don't worry. I'm coming."

I peer around the trunk. I can see all three figures in the bright moonlight. Still facing away from my tree.

"Where's Brooks and the girl?" he asks. "Damien said they were with you."

"Oh, did he? And where is Damien? Recouping from a headache?" I ask.

"Nah, he's up—" Xane starts.

"Shut up, idiot—" Bryce cuts him off. "Doesn't matter, Lyvia. Where the hell is the rest of your gang?"

"They're 'round here somewhere," I reply.

He turns around finally facing my concealment tree. His giant mitts are wrapped around Pandora's chalice with a death grip.

"What do you have there, Bryce?" I emerge from the shadows into the silvery moonlight.

"Lyvia, there you are," he drawls my name out with menace. The sentence floats through the air like fog on an eerie Halloween evening. His features are ghoulish in the moonlight. His smile stretches grotesquely. Pennywise. *God, I hate clowns.*

"I'm gonna need you fellows to disperse. Find your way to your vehicle and go back to your master. You're not needed here."

"Lyvia, please don't make this hard," Bryce says. "We've got orders, and I want to get back to my hobbies."

"Oh, wow. Sorry to rain on your parade, but that's just not happening, Bryce. And, as much as I'd like to hear about those 'hobbies,' I've got somewhere to be."

"Hey, we're not trying to stop you," he says. "We just need the skates."

"Yeah, we've got orders not to hurt you," Chad adds.

Bryce rolls his eyes. "I'd really love to hurt her, though," he growls.

"Dude, you heard the man. We can't touch her," Chad replies. "But remember, he said you could have fun with the friends."

"That's true," Bryce replies with a sick smile. "Plus, we got a little weapon here." He pats the jar creepily.

"Now, don't make me open this, Lyvia," he snarls. "You'll regret it."

"Why haven't you opened it already?" I ask.

"Because we need your friends."

I sense movement to my right and left and realize Iris and Brooks are now in position. The problem is, so does Bryce.

"Looks like the gang's all here," he calls jocularly. His smile stretches to an obscener cackle than before. He fingers the lid. "Get over here, Chad and Xane."

Then, a couple things happen at once.

Xane and Chad move toward Bryce with panic. In doing so, the jar is nearly knocked out of Bryce's hands. He clutches the piece as tight as he can.

Still, the lid flies off.

I see Brooks race toward it before I'm plummeted into darkness.

It feels as though I've been sucked into a vacuum of blackness. It's so thick I can almost slice my arm right through it. As it envelops me, I continue to free fall. The thick air gives me nothing to hold on to. Still, I claw aimlessly through black thickness.

Then, I land heavily on a floor.

I stand and spin around. No use, total darkness. I touch my eyelids to make sure they're open. They are.

As I try to get some bearing, I see a twinkling light across the way. Seems promising. That is until the creepiest ice cream truck song in the world begins to play. Its slow notes start quiet but build. I begin to move away from the twinkling light. I know it's not an innocent ice cream truck; no bubblegum screwballs for me this day.

The light grows and I realize it is an ice cream truck, though distorted, impossibly so. It would not be able to function in real life. The wheels are way too small for the burgeoning truck that sits atop. It seems to be filled with something. Knowing what is causing this vision—*Oh God, I hope it's just a vision*. I keep telling myself it's not real.

The truck pulls to a stop in front of me. The door is held shut—barely—by a small hook. I can see movement through the cracks. I take a deep breath.

Suddenly, a folded plastic flower pops open between the crack. *A clown's flower.*

The plastic stem reaches up and unhooks the bulging door. It parts open slowly. A giant clown head peeks out. I realize it's a mask. *Ugh, masks are even worse.* I should've expected that. A large body follows the mask and creeps toward me. It wobbles its big belly on matchstick legs. A giant sickening smile leers at me.

Then, a second one steps out. The hollowed eyes are even scarier on this guise. Blood frames the face. I realize at this point—with a sickening jolt—they are not wearing masks. They're donning cut-off human faces stretched in gruesomeness and covered in makeup.

I'm paralyzed with fear.

Still, more clowns file out. Too many to fit in the truck. A familiar trick. However, the clowns that normally spill out of VW Buggies aren't usually holding butcher knives. They edge closer and closer to me. The garish faces seem to be zooming in like a "Pop Goes the Weasel" toy.

I'm not sure if Pandora's box allows these figments to actually touch—or hurt—me. *They're not real. This is fake. Not reality. It's all just pretend. You'll wake up soon.*

That is, until a blade swipes my upper arm. I look down to see crimson blood begin to stream from the slash. It's accompanied by real physical pain. There is now a jagged gash on my bicep. Blood continues to seep through the opening steadily. It's a deep cut.

That's enough of that. I reach to my feet and untie my sandals. One in each hand, I stand. They don't change form. The clowns continue to creep around me, heads cocked to the side. It looks as if they're deciding which part of me to devour first. I feel cold steel against my thigh. Looking down, I spot a short clown about to press the steel into my soft, white skin.

I swing the sandals and they make contact with a thunk. The clown cowers and retreats. They all seem to back away, yet still more come from the truck. The music, which has faded, grows louder again. The door reveals the most terrifying of them all.

A memory shakes loose. I've seen this before. A television show. Yes, *American Horror Story*. It's an archaic show that Shane and I watched together; we'd talk to each other through our shared bedroom wall's vent until we fell asleep afterward. This particular season was filled with clowns and that very ice cream truck. I don't think I slept a wink when we binge-watched that one. These clowns are even more terrifying.

Way scarier when it's real.

The newest clown is abnormally large. Its mask seems to be made up of several painted human faces. At least three pairs of lips are sewn together revealing an overextended and distorted maw. It's filled with pointy teeth. Wait. Those aren't teeth. Metal nails reach beneath the lips, a sharp, grey accordion. The eyes are black hollowed out holes. Skin flaps are sewn together to make them large enough.

At first, I think the nose is a classic innocent, albeit large, red spongy clown nose. It isn't. He creeps closer. I see that it is in fact a human organ. It's bloody and shaped as a squishy half-moon—a human stomach.

With the sandal laces in my hand, I begin to swing the shoes. I'm interrupted, however, when an invisible object finds my left hand.

The clowns start to back away as if someone hit rewind. Blackness sinks back in. I close my eyes as darkness holds its own place in my list of fears. A whoosh of wind blows around me.

Suddenly, it stops. I open my eyes to find myself back in the forest. My shoes still dangle from one hand and in the other, Pandora's lid.

A quick search of the area—I find Iris, Brooks, and Xane touching the jar. No sign of Bryce and Chad.

"Whoa, that was insane." I breathe heavily and lean against a tree.

"Let's close 'er up," Brooks says. He motions for me to join them with the lid.

I do, and we close the jar, sealing up Pandora and her terrifying fears. I replace my shoes and confirm that my bag hasn't left my shoulder and the skates still rest inside undisturbed.

"What happened?" I ask.

"Oh man, this guy—Brooks, right?" Xane asks. Brooks nods. "He caught the lid. Then he stabbed the guy with this big spear and stole the jar. Bryce disappeared. Brooks tossed the jar to me. After that, he had me get Iris, right?"

Iris nods. Clearly, Xane hasn't switched teams.

"Then, I took care of Chad. Sent those two back to wherever they came from," Brooks finishes.

"What's with the skates they keep talking about, Lyvia?" Xane asks.

"Honestly, Xane, I have no idea. They were Shane's." I pull one out from the bag. "It's just a pair of very old, worn-out hockey skates. Why Levi is set on having them in his possession, well, your guess is as good as mine." I replace the skate securely and turn toward the group.

"It'll take them a while to make it back here. Iris, you get us to the door. Xane, you can tag along. We'll get you back to Gold on the way, hopefully. If not, you can take the SkyChariot from Crystal. Iris, you sure you can get us to the door and get back safely to the cottage?"

"Oh yeah," she replies with ease. "I know these woods better than anyone. Plus, I got my bracelet."

"Right. Okay, let's follow the leader," I say, nodding at Iris.

Iris takes the lead deeper into the woods. The trees become dense. She follows a twisty invisible path around the giant trunks. It's farther than I expected. I'm about to ask if she thinks she can retrace her steps when she halts.

"It's here," she says.

We're enveloped by trees. I see no door. She fits between two trunks and kneels down. She brushes dirt and leaves away, revealing an old door fitted flat in the earth.

"Cool," Xane says. "Where does it go?"

"Crystal," I reply. I rummage one-handed in my bag until I unearth the ancient key.

"I think Iris should hold on to the jar," I say. "Keep it safe in the cottage."

"Okay," she responds.

"You got the map?" I ask.

"Sure do," she pulls it from her pocket. "I don't need it though."

"And your bracelet?"

"Yes, Mom." She rolls her eyes.

I return the eye roll and motion for a hug. She comes in for a quick squeeze.

"Be safe," I whisper. "Send Seph a message letting us know you made it, okay?"

"Done." She takes the jar, waves to Brooks and Xane, and disappears into the foliage.

"Well, everyone ready?" I ask, kneeling down to the door.

"I don't even know what the heck for, but damn it, I am," Xane exclaims.

I stifle a chuckle at Xane's enthusiasm toward the dangerous unknown.

"I'm always ready," Brooks replies with a shrug, thumbs hooked in belt loops.

31

I bend down, unlock the door, and return the key to my bag. The door is very stiff from age. Brooks and Xane help me open it upward. We are greeted with darkness. The moonlight illuminates a cobblestone ramp that leads downward. The door shuts behind us. The cobblestone reflection provides some illumination.

"Well, into the rabbit hole we go, Alice," Brooks says with a wink.

I take a deep breath and lead the way down the ramp. Brooks follows, and Xane brings up the rear. The slope descends steadily, then dips into nothingness.

"Whooo are you?" Brooks drawls into the grey-lit tunnel.

"'Well, I-I-I hardly know, I've changed so many times since this morning, you see, Mr. Caterpillar,'" I respond, knowing full well he is channeling *Alice In Wonderland*, the ancient book, one of my favorites. I sit on the edge of the cobblestone. My feet touch something. I lean forward and feel a slick, slippery slide.

"Wow, you're not kidding, Brooks. Sure looks like the infamous white rabbit's hole, if I do say so myself," Xane adds.

I stretch my arms above my head and say, "Here goes nothing."

Before I chicken out, I dip down the slippery path. The other two follow. We fly through darkness. I see doors on each side of the path as we travel downward. The doors are all different, some old, some modern. Some plain, some the many colors of the rainbow. We're going too fast to make out much. Just a whir of exits. Or entrances, I suppose.

Finally, the slide peters out into flat, even ground. I don't know how far we have traveled and realize we need to drop Xane off somewhere, so he can get back to Willow. Where to start with that task seems insurmountable. There's got to be thousands of doors.

I stand up and brush myself off. I look and see the boys doing the same. The tunnel has become lit by lanterns placed between doors. The lanterns seem to be magic. Some eternal flame or something, there's no fuel.

"Welp, here we are," Xane says with finality.

"Where's 'here'?" Brooks asks, arms splayed out.

"Who knows," I answer. "Let's try a door."

There are no doors where we are currently standing. I motion for us to creep forward. About fifty feet down the tunnel I spot a red one. This one is ancient. Looks to open with a skeleton key—much like the one I currently have in my possession.

"What do you think, guys? Try the key?" I ask.

"Sure," Brooks replies, nonchalantly.

"Okay, I guess I'll try it."

I put the key into the antique gold lock. It fits. The door is as stiff as the other. It takes all three of us to jimmy it ajar. Inside, we find a closet. Yeah, a really big closet. It's impossibly long and disappears around a curve. It contains coats, so many coats, all different sizes and myriad of colors. I look at the boys. They shrug.

"Okay, let's see what's next."

The next door we come to is on the right. It's yellow and very old. The key works. Again, it takes all three of us to jimmy it open. We are greeted with bright morning light. The door is situated to the ground as was the first. We poke our heads out. The ground is constructed of shimmering—*wait, are those gold cobblestones?* I push the guys down and quickly shut the door.

"Gold?" Brooks asks.

"That makes no sense," I say. "We're going in the opposite direction."

"You think this 'Holy Tunnel' couldn't have a few secrets of its own?" Brooks asks.

"He's right," I say, turning to Xane. "Well, I guess this is your stop."

"Looks like it," he replies. "You sure you guys won't need any help with Levi or his helpers?"

"No," I respond. "You need to be with Willow in Gold. Act like business as usual. Pretend you're still on their side. Chad and Bryce will be looking for you. They're demons, Xane. They didn't die, just went back to Hell for a minute. That's why they disappeared."

His eyes grow wide. "Demons?"

"Yup, bff's with the Devil, himself," I answer. "Now go back and act natural. If Chad and Bryce ask what happened, tell them you were sucked into fear from Pandora's box. When you came to, everyone was gone. You have no idea what happened, okay, Xane?"

"What happened?" Xane asks.

"Oh my gosh, Xane, we were in the woods—"

"No clue what you are referring to, Lyvia," he says with a dramatic wink.

"Okay, good," I reply, returning said wink.

"Bye Xane," Persephone cries from my bag.

"Goodbye, guys." They shake hands. I give Xane a quick hug and he sets off through the magic door.

"And then there were two," Brooks says, pulling the door shut.

"Ah-em." A muffled voice.

"Okay, Persephone, and then there were three," he corrects himself.

"Onward we march," Seph cries, still in the bag.

We continue our trek down the Holy Tunnel—me leading the way. Confidently, I might add. It's as if I know where I'm going. And what I'm doing. *Oy vey.*

Out of sheer curiosity I stop at a door, five down. This one is different. It's a medieval double-door, wooden and shaped as though it belongs to a castle.

"Let's check it out," Brooks says, joining me up ahead.

It takes all our strength, but we succeed in getting it ajar. It opens to sky and sounds of a bustling town. What we find when we pop our heads out is quite confusing. The rough rock formations allow me to distinguish at once that we are looking at primitive Granite, the city.

I detect no technology upon closer examination. Clothes are very outdated, and not in the modern, bring-it-back, 'cool' kind of way. More so, we just stepped back into the past, kind of way. It seems we are invisible to the passers-by as they bustle around the town in horse-drawn carriages, I might add. I start to wonder if this is even the new world. Or perhaps we're getting a glimpse into the very deep past, pre-Noah's Rain, Old Testament. We duck down allowing the door to close snugly behind us.

"Great Scott!" Brooks exclaims when the door clicks shut. I laugh at his *Back to the Future* reference.

"Okay, Doc, what do you think that was about?" I ask.

"Who knows? You're the one trekking us through a secret tunnel," Brooks replies.

"I know nothin' bout nothin'."

"You seem to be doing good with that," Brooks replies. "So far, so good, anyway. How much further we got, you think?"

"I don't know, but it looks like we're coming up to another slide," I say, spotting the cobblestone that seems to just drop off in front of us.

"Cool," he says. "We can make up some time."

I walk to the edge of the walkway and sit down. I swing my legs over the ledge and feel a slick surface beneath my feet.

"You ready?" I ask Brooks.

He kneels behind me.

"Whenever you are."

I push myself forward and slide into black oblivion. I hear Brooks do the same behind me. We slide through the tunnel. It curves and twists reminiscent of a water slide in an old-fashioned water park. Only thing missing is H2O. We go for what seems like hours. In fact, I'm starting to feel nauseous when the slide suddenly gives out and we are airborne.

We land on a soft surface, sinking into what feels like down pillows. It's not. There's nothing there. I try to get footing on unseen fluffiness, when it changes to a hard, smooth floor. Brooks gathers himself behind me.

"That was fun," he says. The statement loosens a memory. *Skateboard. Sun-glistening streets. Nearby waves. Turquoise.* His skateboard was Brooks' preferred mode of transportation. He always mounted impossible hills with his tricks. I always thought the ones where he caught air were his favorite.

I look around to find the mounted lanterns are back. There's only one door left, however. I'm assuming it's the one we're looking for. It's a double door, similar to Merlin's medieval castle door. This one is made of glittering crystals. Even the doorknob and lock are prisms spreading rainbows from the lanterns.

"Looks promising," I say, fitting the key into the lock.

"I'd say," Brooks replies, touching the craftsmanship.

32

The lock releases its hold with a click. This door swings open easily. Assuming it would stick, our force makes a loud thunk against its hinges. We peek out. Lush greenery surrounds us. We are deep in a wooded forest. It's getting dark now. I think it's dusk. The trees are dense. Yet, we can hear water. Perhaps a Crystal waterfall; it doesn't seem far away.

"After you," Brooks says with a gentlemanly wave.

"Thank you, kind sir," I respond.

He kneels on one knee and helps me prop myself up on the other. He hefts me through the entrance. I tumble on the uneven forest floor. Brooks swings his body up and out with ease, an acrobat in a circus. The door swings shut behind us with a soft click. I do a spin and find only more trees in every direction, no glowing Holy Path in sight.

"I don't know if it glows. Doubtful. That would make this way too easy," I reckon.

"Ask Persephone," Brooks says with a nod to my bag.

"Great idea, Brooks," a muffled Perseph responds.

I pull her out and she materializes. Looks as if she's fully prepared for our expedition. She's got on an old-fashioned safari exploration outfit. Khaki stir-ups, tall lace-up hiking boots, and a breezy cream blouse. She's wearing round magnified coke-bottle eyeglasses and a beekeeper's hat, complete with netting. She's Jane surveying the woods before she discovers Tarzan.

"What do you have for us, Seph?" I ask her.

She waves her hand and a scroll appears. She unfurls it to reveal another map. This one is much more detailed than Iris's. *Oh yeah, Iris.*

"Seph, did you get a message from Iris?" I ask.

"Oh yes. She made it back with no problems. She's got Pandora's box locked up safe. All is well in Dark Shire." I breathe a sigh of relief. *Good.*

"Okay, show us the map," I say.

Seph spreads the map out on the ground. Brooks and I kneel down next to it. It looks 3D. It depicts our exact location with a flashing light. Into the tiny trees adorned on the paper I see a gold glowing path.

"Seph, will it glow for us?" I ask.

"No," she replies. A tiny pinprick in my hopeful pink balloon. *Pop.* "Ugh."

"It's going to be okay, though. You've got one better," she tells me. "The nails will gravitate toward the path. You won't see it, but your shoes will get you there. And you will know when you've reached it."

"That's cool," Brooks says.

"Yeah, I'm pretty attached to these things," I say with a glance at my sandals, which choose this moment to morph into tall stylish hiking boots for the terrain. They're similar to Persephone's although still made of what appears to be flexible hammered metal.

"Back to the map," Persephone tells us.

Brooks and I head in her direction and look at the mini-forest splayed out in front of us.

"Doesn't look far," Brooks says, pointing to where we currently reside and the opening of the Blessed Path.

"Doesn't matter. We have to assume Damien has made his way up here. And, who knows? The others as well," I answer.

"True," he says.

"Do you see them, Seph?" I ask.

Her radius is pretty extensive. We haven't tested her exact boundaries, but she should be able to supply us with immediate surroundings. She vanishes into thin air but reappears moments later.

"Nothing of note yet," she replies. "Empty woods. I do think I may know where they would come from." She points to the map. "You see, the path from Crystal Proper empties into the forest here..." Her finger touches a clearing to the right.

It's smack-dab in the middle between our current place and the clearing to the Blessed Path. *Naturally.*

"I'm gonna get you to that path, Vee. I'll distract or hurt whoever shows up," Brooks says. "Persephone, they can't see her once she's standing on the Holy Ground, right?"

"Right," Persephone confirms, adjusting her googly eyeglasses. She nods her head and the beekeeper netting falls down. She replaces it.

"Are there any markings to lead the way?" I ask.

"No, but you've got your watch, right?" she asks.

I blindly feel through my bag until my hand lands on an ancient gold pocket watch. It was a family heirloom, many great-grandfathers ago.

"It has a compass," she says. "Open it up." I flick open the tiny round golden door that protects the watch. I had never noticed that the inside of the door contained a compass.

"I'll give you a list of the number of steps between each direction change. Count and then adjust, count and then adjust," she says. "It'll get you there." I pull out a notebook and jot down our instructions.

"'Nothin' left to it, but do it,'" I say. The saying attempts to wiggle a memory free. *Who told me that?* The figure is there and definitely male, but features are indistinguishable. It'll come back. Can't concern myself with the originator of that adage at the moment.

"Should we do our handshake?" Seph asks, barely containing her excitement.

"Sure, Seph, count us down."

She does and on three: "Let's do it." We all chime in.

Persephone disappears and I put my Slab away. Brooks leads the way with the map and compass. I do not feel a pull in my hiking boots, yet. We follow the steps and shift direction according to my quickly jotted notes. We seem to be making good time, which is great because we are rapidly losing sunlight. We continue on.

"What comes after this?" Brooks asks. Seems as if he's been holding on to that question for a while. He's a quiet one, he is.

"That's kind of a mystery, Brooks. Once I get to the tomb, I have no idea what awaits me." Brooks stops and turns to face me.

"You've got to be careful, Vee," he says in the moonlight. Nightfall is official.

He tenderly moves a lock of hair from my face. "I can't lose you."

He leans down and our lips meet, or I should say, reacquaint. The memory from the beach comes rushing back. It's muscle memory, but somehow this kiss is even better. After a while, probably too long, yet not long enough, we part lips.

I look up into his eyes. Our gaze says more than words.

"I will. I promise," I say, finally breaking the silence.

He leans down and kisses me again.

33

We are interrupted by a twig snap. It's not in the direct vicinity. We both look around and see nothing. A disembodied voice comes through.

"Oh, Levi's gonna love this. Just like he did the last one." *Damien.*

I swiftly shove the map and compass into my purse.

"Damien, you should just start minding your own business," I say to the darkness. "Maybe, oh I don't know, become your own man. Leave Levi and his evil business aside. You're more than this."

I remember a time when I would call Damien a friend. Sure, it was before I knew who Levi was, but Damien was a confidante. Long, lonely nights when Levi commanded the stage, Damien made sure I had privacy and someone to talk to. No, it was never romantic.

"Lyvs, come on," he replies. "You know I have a vow."

"A vow," I laugh, sadistically. "To Satan. Wow."

He emerges from the shadows. He has a slim metal pole fitted with an impossibly sharp point in his right hand. It has a leather cord wrapped around it. A javelin.

"What? Run track in high school, Damien?" Brooks asks.

"No, Brooks," Damien laughs, facetiously. "This javelin belonged to an old friend of Levi. You might know of him. He was a big guy. Name was Goliath."

Oh great. As in, David and Goliath. One good thing: pretty sure in the Biblical entry, the underdog, David, won. On the flip side, that particular javelin slaughtered many a foe before David came along.

"Uh, didn't he lose?" Brooks asks, voicing my thoughts.

Damien launches the javelin without a word.

Brooks expertly ducks the metal point with ease. He pulls something from his pocket. I think I know what it is. It's at this point I notice the leather cord on Damien's weapon is attached to his wrist. He pulls back and the javelin soars back to his hand, a giant magical yoyo trick.

"You know what I'm here for, Lyv," Damien states. "Some footwear."

"Yeah, I know all about what you minions have been sent to retrieve, and it's not going to happen. Not in my lifetime anyway," I reply.

I look back over my shoulder at Brooks and see his fishhook transform into the spear. I swiftly kick off my boots and the nails find their place home. One in each hand, I swing them toward Damien. He bats them away easily with the javelin.

"Gotta do better than that, Lyvs," Damien snarls before releasing the javelin in my direction.

I use the nails that have made their way back to my palms to dodge the javelin with a handspring on metal points. It sticks straight up from the ground three inches from where I land, then swings back to Damien.

"This is really getting old," I say to Damien with a deep sigh. "I've got somewhere to be."

A nail shoots toward him. It drives through his shoulder and attaches to a massive tree trunk behind him. He cries out in pain. The javelin drops to the ground. I saunter toward him and shoot the other nail in his untouched shoulder. He's completely pinned to the tree. His cries of pain almost make me smile. *Almost. Hey—I'm not Levi.*

About three inches from his face, I point underneath his chin and tell him: "When you get back to Hell, please let your master know he's *never* getting these skates."

Brooks has appeared behind me with his spear.

"I'm leaving now, Damien." I tell him. "Like I said, I have a prior engagement."

"You're not going to make it. You really think I'm the last obstacle?" he asks through gritted teeth. "Levi will get those skates, and *you*—one way or another, bitch."

I look at Brooks.

"Will you do the honors, Brooksey?" I ask.

"My pleasure, Vee," he responds before swiftly stabbing his spear through Damien's heart.

He disappears from the tree. Back to Hell. That's my guess, anyway. The nails are back to boots. I slide them on and pull out the map and pocket watch.

"Let's find that yellow brick road, shall we, Dorothy?" Brooks asks, linking his arm through mine.

"Lions and tigers and bears, oh my," I cry.

We start off when a muffled voice begins singing: "We're off to see the wizard, the Wonderful Wizard of Oz…"

Brooks and I share a smile as we head deeper into the woods in search of the Holy Path—and eventually—the tomb. We're almost there. I can taste it. The trek through the trees begins to get steeper and the compass starts to fail, its tiny dial spinning in rapid circles.

"What now?" I ask my bag.

Seph replies: "Now you rely on your shoes-ies."

As the last word seeps through the fabric of my purse, my shoes begin to pull. It turns into a very strong tug. Forceful. I struggle to keep up with their momentum. Brooks follows closely behind. It's almost comical. My feet seem to be yards in front of my body. I struggle to remain upright. Brooks has no trouble keeping up. We travel through trees thick and thin; the forest floor grows steeper and the sound of water grows louder.

"I think we're almost there," I call through the rushing sounds surrounding us. "Shoes are slowing down."

Just as the last word escapes my lips, the shoes halt. Sure enough, there is a path in these dense woods. No, it's not glowing as the yellow brick road seems to. The moonlight, however, does cast a grey sheen on the forest floor. The path snakes up the steep incline toward the Crystal cliffs, and more importantly, the tomb. *Shane.*

We hike the trail side-by-side. It's twisty and becomes more and more vertical. We struggle up the winding trajectory for quite a while. Suddenly, the incline gives way to a flat clearing, behind which stands a giant red rock wall. The cliffs.

From what I see, there is no way continuing upward besides

climbing the rock. We move to the mountainside. It goes straight up. So high, you can't make out the summit. The dark doesn't help.

"Shit," I say. "How am I gonna do that?"

"Got any clips or rope?" Brooks asks.

"I've got the nails, and I have used them to climb before. It's going to be time consuming," I reply, peering up past the rock to the night sky. The stars shimmer back at me. As I contemplate the ascent above, one of the stars shoots across the sky.

"Did you see that, Brooks? A shooting star," I call.

"No—I must've missed it," he replies, looking upward.

"That wasn't a star," Persephone's voice says. "Look closer."

I do and see that the white glittery star hasn't disappeared. In fact, it moves along the skyline growing in size as it descends.

"She's right, that's no star," I tell Brooks.

"Well, what is it? A bomb?" he asks with concern.

"Nope, it's my ride," I reply.

The "star" begins to resemble a glittery flying white horse. Charley has arrived. She settles down between us. I rub her massive head.

"Oh, how I've missed you, girl," I punctuate with a soft kiss.

Brooks looks on aghast.

"I always knew they were real," he says in awe, while patting her torso.

"Well, you were right. This one's a friend of mine. We go way back, don't we, Charley?" I reply, turning my head to make sure she's still in good health. She nuzzles her head on my shoulder while I look her over. No boo-boos to be seen. The vet would give her an A+. I look up at the mountain again and realize it's time.

"Brooks, I can never repay you for everything you have done for me," I tell him.

"I'm going with you. She can fit us both."

"I'm sure she can, Brooksey. But, to be brutally honest, I must do this myself. I need you to go back to Turquoise where it's safe, until I come find you. Because, wherever I'm going, I will make it back to you."

"Lyvia, I just want you to know—"

"No," I cut him off. "This isn't goodbye. This is 'see ya later.'"

I step onto my tippy-toes and give him a long, languid kiss. We pull apart, and I jump on Charley's back before he can try to say goodbye again. We turn to the sky and lift off.

Through the wind, I hear his faint voice: "I love you, Vee."

"I love you too, Brooksey," I cry, hoping he can hear those four final words before I enter the unknown.

If anything does happen to me, I need him to know that.

34

The journey upward is smooth. Charley's large muscled body flies through the air as if she was made of silk. We fly higher and higher. The anticipation is killing me. I have no idea what waits for me at the tomb. I spot waterfalls to my left and right. The red rock seems to end shortly. Charley breaches the precipice and sets us down on flat rock. I look to my right and see the boulder. The very boulder I secured so long ago. Seems a lifetime ago.

I made it.

I kiss Charley goodbye. She nuzzles me before lifting off to do unicorn things, I assume. I look out over the water. The ocean is mean today. The giant waves fight each other like bickering siblings. The black sky has begun to lighten, dreary grey now. I realize daybreak is around the corner.

I turn around and make my way to the boulder that guards my brother's body. Once I reach the rock, I take off a shoe. It spins to reveal a Holy Nail. I'm about to drive it in the crack between the boulder and the mountain, when I hear flapping. I spin around only to be greeted with the terrorizing vision my friends have described. Six massive, ghoulish faces surround Levi's head. I know for a fact, this time—*he's real.*

"Missed you, Lyvs," the head that resembles Levi says.

"We all have," a blob fish-looking head adds.

"Shut up," Levi sneers. "I told you all to zip it and let Lyvs and I speak in private."

The mouths are replaced with crude zippers at this command. Not a peep comes from any of them.

"Wow, Levi, had I known your true form, I would've married you years ago," I say sarcastically, while attempting to keep the rising bile in my stomach down.

"Lyvs, let's not get nasty. I hear you slipped my goons."

"Yeah, some goons you got there," I laugh cruelly.

"Well, they're not the most intelligent, I'll give you that, but they are loyal," he replies.

"Well, they didn't get the skates, and neither are you," I say, indignantly crossing my arms over my chest. A nail still resides in my right hand. I stand with one bare foot and one boot.

"You're right about that." He returns my cruel laugh. "Couldn't touch those if my existence depended on it, but I think you've already figured that out."

I remember my parent's house and how he forced Brooks to get them. Then had Damien on the task. *What's going on with these skates?*

"So what do you want, Levi? You're not going to stop me from getting into that tomb."

"I know that, Lyvs. Why would I want to stop you? You're about to be in *my* house. It's all I ever wanted in the first place."

With that, I hear a snap and see that Levi has disappeared into thin air.

Okay, back to the tomb. I walk toward it, nail at the ready. I drive it into the space. It vibrates wildly and pushes with an unseen force. It continues drilling when I lift my hand off.

My other boot swishes into the other nail and drives itself into the bottom crevice as before. The boulder sneaks out, an inch at a time. When the opening is large enough, I peer inside.

I notice with a huge sigh of relief; Shane's body has not moved. He is still draped in the cloth and resting on the driftwood. I'm overwhelmed with emotions. I can barely think but notice deep swells of tears streaming down my face. I don't even realize I've been crying.

The nails fall to the ground, their job complete. I grab them and move into the tomb. The boulder rolls shut automatically behind me *Indiana Jones* style. It's silent inside. No more rushing water or wind to fill my ears. I walk over to Shane and kneel beside him. The tears continue and are soon joined with deep, mournful sobs.

"I miss you so much, Shane," I cry.

Then I pray: "Please God, take care of my brother, please make sure—"

I'm cut off by a loud whooshing, wind-like sound. The sound is soon accompanied by actual wind. It blows around the small enclosure. My hair flies around my head in the tornado-like gusts. Shane remains untouched, his fabric barely affected in this wind tunnel.

Then, the windstorm is replaced with the sound of circuitry. It zips and zaps—a motherboard's hardwires trying to connect. Then, a flash of light. A figure soars down into the tomb with me. It's Shane's form but not of any earthly element. It glows orange as fire but circuited like electricity. Bigger, too—radiating light. The spirit form drops down, sits on the side of the driftwood. Then, it lies down melding into his body.

Suddenly, Shane sits up. Looking just as himself, but not completely. He's see-through. In fact, the entire tomb is now see-through. I'm looking at a sunset landscape somewhere. A lake just ahead of me; although, I can still see the tomb's outline—nearly transparent.

"What the hell was that?" I ask, stunned.

"Good to see you too, Lyv," he stands up, laughing as though that was the funniest line ever written for TV. We hug. He feels solid but still semi-transparent. He's a spirit.

"Where've you been?" I ask him.

He explains to me that he is in Spirit World, which is kind of similar to Purgatory. The planes overlap in this tomb. I realize I'm glimpsing the Spirit World from earthbound eyes.

"So this is a—"

"Vortex," he finishes.

"Were you in Heaven?"

"Not quite," he replies. "There is Heaven, but we're all waiting for it, no matter which dimension. See, there's levels in the Spirit World, Lyv. You work your way up. You don't have the physical needs like you do on Earth, and ego is gone, but pain and want... Those remain." He looks off into the sunset. "As does love, magnified. Everything's amplified here, Lyv. It's like the subwoofer in the Mustang, but with feelings too. We do have senses. They're different though. Better. It's definitely better than Earth, but it's not 'Heaven.'

Colors are brighter, and selfish worries turn into concern for loved ones, as we have to watch and bear with them their crosses. But—we can help.

And, time's different here. A year to you is like an hour to us. Except we don't observe time. It simply doesn't exist. We are only aware of it through watching you.

There's still a feeling of waiting. Knowing there's something even better than all this, Lyv. Somewhere with *no* pain or want. And figuring out what to do to get there." He punctuates the last word with a fist against stone.

"If there even is anything," he finishes, spinning away from the wall. He kicks a small pebble. "I don't know, Lyv. Way I see it, we just gotta keep helping each other. And if that means I have to do it from here, then that's what we gotta do."

"I wholeheartedly disagree, Shane," I say, dramatically uncrossing my arms and splaying them outward. I shake my head. "Don't you realize that will just make it easier for Levi to keep trying? We need you, here. *In human form.* Okay, I need you here."

"I know you do, Lyvie, but Levi's been doing his thing since the very beginning. We both know that. God decides when it will end. So if it happens, it happens. Roll with it."

"Roll with it?" I stare at him—completely incredulous. "Roll with it? Are you kidding me, Shane?"

"Dude. You know it's all gonna be gravy."

"Oh my gosh, bro. Now is so not the time. Let's recap: You are a spirit. If your earthbound body gets destroyed by Lucifer, himself, who just so happens to be, walking around like Jim Jones out there getting people to drink the purple Kool-Aid, I don't ever get you back."

"Not in this body," he says, referring to his human state, not the ethereal vision I saw him drop in with.

"Okay, so, 'Spirit Shane' is our back-up. What's the plan to get you back to 'Earthbound Shane'?"

He turns back to the wall. "You gotta get me my hammer, Lyv," he says.

"Levi's got it," I reply.

"Yep. And, he's waiting for you in—"

"Hell," I finish for him.

"Yes."

"You brought the skates?" he asks.

"Of course, but what—"

He cuts me off: "You'll know when you need them."

"Lots of hockey going on down there, Shane? Didn't think they'd be able to make ice with all the fire going on."

He laughs: "No, Lyvs. It'll all make sense."

"Okay, well, how do I get there?"

"You brought the staff, right?"

I take the necklace off and hold it in my hand.

"Is there a phrase? Prayer?" I ask.

"Not sure," Shane replies, shrugging casually. Thumbs hooked in pockets. *Just another day.*

I look at the underside of the snake and spot carved writing. "The Lord said, 'Throw it to the ground,'" I read aloud.

"So..." He makes a gesture with his hand that says, 'Anytime now.'

I picture him not too long ago making the same gesture when I couldn't choose which ice cream flavor I wanted. I savored every sample in the parlor before making a choice.

"Okay, Shane," I say with trepidation. I don't know what these relics are capable of.

Still, I throw down the necklace. For an instant nothing happens. We look at each other and shrug.

Then—*movement at our feet.* The snake grows rapidly while becoming life-like; actually, maybe alive. Big. Larger than any natural snake I've ever seen, and I've seen documentation of some pretty massive serpents. I fling myself against the wall. It slithers curiously around the cavern. I freeze. A petrified statue. Paralyzed.

I look at Shane doing the exact same thing. *Great.*

"What should we do?" I ask as it slinks toward me.

"No clue," he replies, looking around the room as if an ancient cave painting may appear with the answer.

Flick. Flick. Flick—against my toe. In contradiction of everything I stand for, I lower my eyes. *Yep. A huge snake's tongue is darting against my baby toe.*

"Oh my gosh, Shane," I manage, panic rising.

"Settle down," he says, still scanning the wall.

"What is it?" I ask, too terrified to move. A scaly body is now creeping over my feet as it makes its way toward Shane.

"There's writing above your head. Trying to make it out," he replies, squinting his eyes. The cold reptile flesh finishes its tortuous slinking path. Onward toward Shane.

"'Reach out your hand and take it by the tail.'"

"That's all you, broseph," I say, still glued in place.

"Trust me, sis. I got that already." He's used to this process of elimination.

The snake navigates around his ankles but doesn't touch them. *Lucky.* Then I think of his next part in the plan. *Not really.*

"Okay. Okay. I'm doing this," he says, rubbing his palms together and then on his thighs.

"You got this."

"Okay. Okay. I'm doing this." He continues to rub his pants.

"You got this," I say again, staring at the slithering monstrosity.

"Okay. Okay. I'm doing this." Rubbing hands together again.

"Shane." *Like brother, like sister.*

"Okay. Okay, I—"

"Just grab him!"

The snake's tail comes within reach. Shane extends a large hand that barely wraps around a quarter of the body. The snake jerks hard. Fast. Shane holds the tail with two hands. The muscular body whips back-and-forth. It flings its head fiercely.

Then—it freezes. Shrinks. Hardens. A tall staff now occupies Shane's hand. It's wooden and curved. Knotty. Ancient.

Again—*movement at our feet*. We both look down.

The ground vanishes before our eyes. It appears as if we stand on glass; the only thing separating us from the ocean. Beneath us—a deep blue abyss.

"Whoa," Shane says, spinning in a circle. I follow suit.

"Look—there's a shark."

Sure enough, a Great White swirls menacingly beneath us. Also, a stingray and a group of rainbow fish. Mesmerizing.

"Whoa, a killer whale," I say in awe. A giant black and white Shamu now passes below us.

"What's next?" He asks, squatting down to study the ocean life.

"Here, let me see it." He passes me the staff distractedly.

"There's an octopus... jellyfish—look, Lyv." I immediately rush over. I love jellyfish. All floating around as baby ballerina tutus complete with glowing ribbons. A school of them pirouette beneath his outstretched finger.

I go back to inspecting the staff and am pleased to find it too has an engraving. "It says something, Shane."

"Whoa, that thing's scary."

"What?"

He points.

It's too far down to see clearly, but terrifying nonetheless. It has two long spindly arms with hands and fingers similar to human. It is ghost white with a fish-like tail, although longer, resembling an eel. The head features no eyes. A giant mark slices where the mouth should be.

"What the hell?" A quiver runs up my spine. Flash to the Leviathan sketch. Not the one with seven heads. Thank God. This one isn't as detailed as the picture. Not quite formed—an earlier stage of evolution.

"What is it?" he asks.

"It looks like a primordial Leviathan."

"Levi."

"Yep, must be a newbie."

"Rookie demon."

"Exactly."

"Okay, what does it say?" he asks, standing up to join me.

"'And the Lord said to Moses, 'But lift up your staff and stretch out your hand over the sea to divide the water.'"

He looks over my shoulder at the crude indentation and then the sea below us.

"Let's say a prayer like we did that one time with the car," he says.

He's referring to the time we snuck the Mustang out to our cottage in Turquoise. When it was time to jet, the car wouldn't start. We had to beat the wardens home in time for a 'family meeting.' There we were—hands clasped over the battery—a prayer to Heaven. It was answered; we figure now it's mandatory.

We clutch each other's hands over the staff, bow our heads, and say a Hail Mary.

"You ready for this, Lyv?"

I look at the terrifying depths below.

"No," I say uncertain. Then resolve. Purpose. "But I want you back, Shane. *For real.*" With that—I lift the staff and stretch my hand over the waters churning below. An unseen force grabs the rod and pounds it into the floor. The glass shatters.

"I love you, Lyv." I hear Shane's voice go faint as the waters rise around me separated by an invisible barrier.

"Love you," I yell, praying he heard me.

Then, I get sucked down through white rapids. I'm in the center of a massive waterfall, although flowing in the wrong direction. As the water rushes past me, I have a fleeting thought involving that white rabbit's hole and his stoned caterpillar.

I FIND myself landing softly on a mountain of sandy ground. The whooshing water has ceased.

So, this is what the bottom of the ocean looks like. I look through the 'glass-water' walls. It really is just mountains upon mountains of packed sand as far as the eye can see. The glass surrounds me, a circular aquarium. The sea life goes about as business as usual. I see coral reefs, a variety of colors. Mounds of sand in every direction. A shark. A massive squid—frighteningly massive.

I walk closer to the glass toward an area that is kind of murky and very dark. The glass tunnel seems to glow for a few feet but utter blackness after that. A school of fish disrupt the sand in my eyesight, and it clouds in front of me.

Suddenly—a spindly hand slams against the glass. I shriek and jump back. The horrifying blur of a face follows. The hands scratch at the glass fruitlessly. Child-like. Then it turns around and its eel tail waves away—a shrinking alarm.

Not sure what to do next, I check my bag and make sure all items are in attendance and did not get lost in the journey. Everything is accounted for.

I spin in a circle looking for clues. I look upward. "What do I do now?" I ask Shane.

"Well, get me out of here already so I can help," Persephone answers.

35

I pull out my Slab. Her expedition outfit has been replaced with a ruffled bathing suit top, an old-fashioned swimming cap adorned with colorful flowers, thick goggles, and, for the love of God—

"Is that a mermaid tail?" I ask, pointing to the long glittery fin fitted to where her legs should be.

"I've always wanted to be a mermaid," she replies, wistfully.

I want to ask more about that fin, including where I can get one, but we have business to attend to.

"This is supposed to be Hell, right, Seph?" I ask, looking around.

"Not technically," she responds. "Hell is in the middle of Earth—where lava comes from. Fire is definitely an accurate description."

I flop down on the sand. "Well, how do I get there? Dig?" I ask, with a weak laugh. I squeeze my hands in the sand and let it fall through my fingers. Sands in an hourglass.

Persephone's hologram swims through the air in languid circles. "Nope," she says spiritedly. "All you gotta do is sleep."

"Sleep? Go to sleep? Okay, even if I could, how does that get me anywhere besides this sandy ocean floor?"

"Okay, you remember that Hell overlaps Earth, right? Even if it's technically in the planet, the plane overlaps life here on Earth, especially when you sleep. Both Heaven and Hell intersect during shut-eye. Glorious dreams, and..."

"Terrifying nightmares," I finish. "Hell."

"Yep," she says with a somersault above my head.

"So, just go to sleep?" I ask, knowing full well that's impossible.

"Yes, I'll play your sleepy-time music."

I lie down on the sand with my head cradled in my arm and listen to the familiar cords of my favorite sleepy melodies. I have a hard time believing I will fall asleep on the ocean floor, surrounded by water, held by an imaginary barrier with creatures of all kinds floating around me, but somehow, I do.

WHEN I OPEN MY EYES, I'm enveloped in complete blackness. I don't have the best night vision, so I rub my eyes once again to make sure they're open. As they adjust, I begin to make out my immediate surroundings in the moonlight.

The water wall and accompanying sea life has disappeared. I hear an angry ocean beckoning below the rocky cliff I occupy. I look around. I'm in a vast, expansive area. As landmarks begin to take shape in the moon's beam, I see dark puddles spattered along a natural rock enclave. An enclave that I recall is sometimes repurposed as an arena.

I see the platform where Levi's original Great Reveal was planned. With horror, I gather that the dark puddles are not caused from natural dips in the mountainous landscape. No, they're not depressions too deep for moonlight to reach. Instead, pools of blood. It's then that I realize I'm not in present day.

And that, yes, I'm in Hell.

I know what I'm going to find on the 'stage.' Somehow this area of rock has been etched and smoothed by the wind for years creating a half-dome with a perfectly flat-raised area. The stage. The alcove.

"Well, Levi, where are you? Such a sick sense of humor you have. I had no idea," I call to the sky. "So, what? I just re-live this day? Then you show yourself?"

I drop down on the ground. I can't do this. There's no way. I got his body to the tomb somehow that day; I can't do it again. I pull Persephone out; maybe she can help. Nothing. There's no signal in Hell, I guess. *Ha.*

But you have to. A voice sounds in my head—Shane's.

Determined to get to Levi and seeing no other recourse besides reenacting the harrowing events that lie ahead of me, I start off toward Shane with resolution. Quicker I go through it, the quicker I escape the clutches of Hell. At least, that's what I figure.

I'm not immune to the grievous feelings that consume and choke me as I approach Shane's fallen form. I perform all the actions I did that day. Find the driftwood, cover him with the cloth, secure him to the wood. Then I begin the trek.

I drop Shane's heavy form as soon as I try to lift him. Several attempts occur before I comprehend the fact that an unseen force will not be helping me with the task this time around. The shoes won't turn into nails either—most likely due to the fact that they hadn't turned at this point the first go-round. I move inch-by-inch as the minutes tick by. My muscles become sore and heavy. They start to atrophy. It gets dark, then light again. This time, I don't sleep. I just need to get him to the tomb, I reckon.

As the next day begins, I have made little progress. I stop to rest and fall asleep.

I JOLT awake from a nightmare involving a particularly horrific day, before I realize where I am, which is *not* where I ended up last night.

It's dark and as my eyes adjust, I realize I'm living a sick and sadistic version of *Groundhog's Day*.

With renewed vigor, I attack the task before me, yet again. Same routine. I gain a few feet of extra distance this time before falling asleep.

With each repeat, I gain a little more ground. Still, the tomb is way too far away to make the distance.

Day-after-day, I scratch tally marks on the arena's wall. They remain stationary throughout each refresh.

After 10,000 days, I still haven't aged.

Some days, I don't move from the ground.

Some days, I spend the entire time crying over my brother's body.

Some days, I pace the area round-and-round again, having entire conversations with myself. I know I'm starting to break.

Some days, I get destructive. I pick up random rocks and hurl them at the walls and ground until I have absolutely no strength left to give.

Some days, I get self-destructive. I kick and punch said rock walls, until my hands and feet are merely bloody, broken appendages. I find sharp dagger-like rocks and spend the time slicing my skin, careful not to go too deep, mesmerized by the streaming crimson blood until I pass out.

Some days, I imagine killing myself. Get it over with already. I do not do this for fear it will trap me in this Hell forever.

Some days, I simply try to get my brother to the tomb again.

I never make it.

———

ON DAY 14,609:

There's a rewind.

36

I wake up in my usual position. Something's different. It's still dark, but I hear voices. I rub my eyes to confirm I'm awake. Then I creep toward the arena, where I find several figures moving around in the moonlight. I sneak closer to better distinguish words.

"I need you guys to set up right here." Levi stands in the middle of the stage pointing to an area I cannot see. He has his guitar slung over his shoulder. It rests behind him.

"This—*This* is where our Great Reveal will take place."

He spreads his arms dramatically.

I duck around a boulder for a better vantage point and find one. Levi is circling an object. It takes me a moment before I recognize it; Dark Shire's red telephone booth.

"This will be remembered for eternity," he cries and throws his arms up toward the cosmos.

The realization sets in: I'm witnessing the moments before Shane's death.

I don't know if I exist in this hellish scene. However, I'm pretty sure I'd rather not be seen at this point. I'm concealed me from their eyesight behind the boulder; although, I can see the landscape without obstruction.

"I know I've kept you boys at arms-length with my plans," Levi says, circling the booth like a shark to prey. I can't say for sure, but I'd wager he's licking his lips right now. "First of all, my blue elixir is making tremendous progress; we've got lots of new users, and I don't see any upcoming supply shortages. Still tinkering with its effects, as Bryce can attest to."

"I love the stuff," Bryce says as he adjusts his crotch. I force down some vomit. "It could be stronger, though."

"That's the plan, Bryce, that's the plan," Levi drawls as he rubs his hands together thoughtfully, gazing downward. "We'll have everyone on it soon enough."

I realize Levi has been behind blue elixir this entire time. *A drug created by the Devil, himself. Wonderful. There can't possibly be anything wrong with that; an even worse version of Walter White.*

"Now onto New Heaven. You each know a slice of information, nobody has it all. I know you have to be wondering. Any guesses?"

"You're doing a phone booth charity concert?"

Levi shakes his head slowly. "No, you imbecile," he says. "Why is he the one talking right now?"

"Yeah, Bryce, it's gotta be bigger than that," Chad chimes in.

"Yes, so much bigger." He closes his eyes. "I'm going to rule Earth, boys. Just think of it—Hell on Earth, for eternity." He splays his arms wide as if he can see the title in Broadway lights.

"Notice anything about different about this telephone booth?" he asks. "Damien?" He calls him out knowing he is his best chance at an intelligent response.

Damien pauses. Tastes the air as if checking for a coming rain. "It's a vortex gateway," he answers.

"Ding, ding, ding... And circle gets the square," Levi responds with the flair of a game show host. "You see, a vortex is merely a communication device between transcendental planes—that's it. You can't gain entry into other dimensions. What we've created with our Framework is a vortex *gateway*, which is an avenue leading directly to Hell."

"Like a highway?" Bryce asks.

Levi shifts his eyes to an imaginary cameraman, a deadpan stare —'Do you see what I deal with.'

"Okay, I'm going to dumb it down for the Kindygarden class, here," Levi says, walking up to Bryce. He stops three feet in front of him. "Yes, *like* a highway, Brycie Bear." He mimics cars with verbal sound effects. Total patronization. I get a ping of satisfaction at Bryce's humiliation.

"I'm making an honest-to-God, or Dad, I should say," he remarks mockingly, pointing to the sky. It occurs to me that he is just a scorned child, mad at Daddy. Still, his ongoing since-the-beginning-of-time tantrum is inexcusable.

"An honest-to-God highway to Hell, boys. We are opening the floodgates and giving humans a one-way ticket. Soon, our dimension will be the *only* dimension. Free will won't exist. It's a joke, anyway. Humans can't be trusted to make the right decisions. *My* way is the only way. This world will belong to me; dad will take a backseat. Let his son run things for a change, he needs to retire anyway."

Suddenly, a new voice emerges from the shadows. An unmistakably familiar voice.

"Hey, Levi." Shane materializes from darkness. "I happen to have it on good authority that this 'reveal' isn't such a 'great' idea." He laughs at his own pun.

So witty, Shaner, I laugh to myself.

"Ahh, Shane, I've been expecting you," he drawls. "Word has it, you got a pretty cool new toy."

"I sure did. Maybe, you'll catch a glimpse of it before it ends you," he replies.

"You underestimate me, bro," Levi says as he flips his guitar around in front of him. "First I brought a great storm to earth, and now all I have to do is finish the job."

"That's where you're mistaken, Levi." Shane whips his large arm out and a giant, ancient hammer appears.

"*I* am the storm," Shane speaks evenly.

I want to say the hammer looks the same as Thor's—*I've been hoping it would, if I'm honest*—but instead it resembles one from long ago, since Jesus' time. The head is a huge sharp triangular shaped rock, held to a thick ivory handle by leather cords. The thick leather cords wrap down the length of the ivory handle coming to a loop at the bottom. The handle seems made of carved bone, too big to be human. The ancient tool is massive.

Simultaneously, Levi's guitar transforms into his deathly sword. Lucifer's sword.

I watch the fight unfold, powerless.

Shane appears to swing the hammer at Levi, but instead makes contact with the phone booth. It explodes into billions of tiny pieces. A loud ringing fills my ears. I duck behind the rock and cover my eyes. I squeeze them open slowly when the dust settles and sound returns; I resume my standpoint.

Shane and Levi circle each other around the blackened ground littered with shrapnel.

Levi looks murderous.

"Do you realize what've you've done?" he screams. "All that work. All that work for nothing."

He charges at Shane, sword out front. Shane swiftly dodges the motion, knocking Levi's sword to the ground with his hammer. It vanishes upon landing, materializing back in Levi's grip seconds later.

"Did you really think God was going to let you design a highway to Hell?" Shane laughs without humor. "He told me all about this plan."

Shane charges now, swinging the hammer high above his head. Right before Levi disappears, the hammer makes contact with his shoulder. His arm is ripped from his body, spraying blood wildly, before smoldering, and vanishing from the ground.

A second later he materializes behind Shane, completely intact.

"No, Shane—NO!" I scream, running toward him. I go completely unnoticed. I rush at him, jumping up but sailing through him, as Levi's sword slices easily through his back. Shane falls heavily to the ground. Blood pools around his frame. An animal-like howl emits low from my chest, but nobody hears me. I'm merely an invisible audience member here.

"Damien, grab the hammer," Levi says.

Damien does as requested.

"Back home, boys," Levi calls before they each vanish into thin air, only a cloud of black smoke remains.

Levi is the last man standing, and I swear to God, he winks at me before he too, disappears.

I'm left hovering over my brother's body, yet again.

I guess I fall asleep.

37

W hen I wake, I know instantly I no longer reside in the nightmare. Things come into focus. Gold-speckled tiles, a floor made of New Year's confetti. Clean, woodsy spice fills my nose. A familiar smooth and sexy voice. My favorite room in Gold Shire—Levi's penthouse.

"Hey, Lyv. It's good to see you."

"Don't call me that, Lucifer," I spit, fully entering the room.

A sexy laugh. He walks toward me slowly. "Uh-huh, Lyvia. That was my 'given' name," he rolls his eyes at 'given.' Inching closer.

Levi. Levi in all his gloriousness. I swear he has a backlight follow him around everywhere he goes. He shines.

"I gotta say Lyvia, somehow you just get more gorgeous by the day. Even when you've been through Hell."

We stand a foot apart. His familiar form beckons me. His scent grows stronger. *Bumpy car rides. Flashing landscapes. Playing music for me in his loft. Dancing at his parties before sneaking out for secret moonlit strolls, hand-in-hand. Dark windy trails. Warmth in his oversized leather jacket.*

"I miss you, Lyvia. You know, when I get this place all to myself, we'll have a lot of fun. Every king needs a queen, right?" He pulls a strand of hair from my face.

I look into his aquamarine eyes. I loved those eyes. I got lost in those eyes. Two Arctic glaciers slice through icy cool depths.

He's the Devil, Lyv. I mentally slap myself. *Shane.*

"I need the hammer, Levi."

"I don't think so, Lyvs. What you need is to get on board."

"On board the crazy train?" I ask incredulously. "I don't think so, Levi. I am *not* going to be your evil queen, and you are *not* going to rule the world."

"Oh, I am Lyvia."

I urge the nails. They find my palms. I swing them toward Levi. He stops them with his own palms again.

"You think any of that will work on me, Lyvs?" He laughs cruelly. "You're in *my* house." He stalks the room menacingly, hands clasped behind him.

"Lyvia, I'm going to leave you here for a while. You need time to think. You'll come to my conclusion. You'll see our glorious future together. I know it." With an audible *pop*, he disappears from the room.

I run to the door. It's sealed shut. Almost it seems, hermetically. I scream and pound the door and walls a stretch before turning toward the room.

I search every nook and cranny in this fake Gold Coliseum penthouse. Empty every drawer, overturn every cushion, and tear apart the mattress. I rip through each pillow sending a snowstorm of down feathers onto every surface. I plop down in a mound of fluffy white when a voice sounds from my bag. I head over to the bag that has miraculously survived the journey. I pull out my Slab.

Persephone appears. She's in a doctor's coat and scrubs. A stethoscope is loped around her neck. Rimless eyeglasses adorn her face. She embodies a med student. She has an old book open in front of her.

"How are you operable?" I ask. "I tried you in Hell—aren't we still in Hell?"

"Yes," she replies. "I'm actually not sure why I can function in this location. I've been wondering that myself, unless it's a vortex."

"It probably is," I say, looking around.

"How do we break out? Got any ideas?" I ask.

"What good would I be if I didn't?" she replies with a light laugh. She flips through the book. "While you were turning it upside-down in here, I pulled out your medical records."

"What? Why?"

"Because, Lyv, you need the Holy Relics to get out of here."

"The nails?"

"Yes, all three of them. There are three, you know."

"Right, Jesus was crucified with one nail through each hand and the third through both feet."

"Correct," she says while adjusting her glasses.

"What does that have to do with my medical history?"

"Well, Lyv, you already have all three."

"What?"

Persephone materializes next to my right arm and points with a pencil to my scar.

"What." I say again, eyes wide as saucers.

"The metal holding your shoulder together is the third nail. You have to get it out."

"You've got to be kidding," I say, rubbing the raised vertical line.

"Nope, see right here," she points to indentations in the door. Sure enough, there are three.

"Okay," I say with growing frustration. "Let's get this over with. How do I do it?"

"Use one of the other nails," she tells me from the book.

I look at the giant crude metal nail that rests in my hand. *This cannot be sanitary.* I shake my head and pull on my shoulder bag's long leather strap. I secure it between my teeth.

"Here goes nothing," I manage to garble through thick brown leather.

I touch the point of the nail to the bottom of my scar. The pain is blinding. It burns through the first layer of dermis as a branding poker. I think I'm going to pass out, but somehow, I remain conscious.

I drag the point upward. It tears through flesh. The intense pain quickly subsides into numbness. I watch my skin split wide open with detached fascination. I can see grey metal nestled in bone between folds of flesh and tissue.

"Now, pull it out," Seph says, as if she's telling me to take the Christmas pie out of the oven to cool.

I set the giant nail on the floor and brace myself for this next action. I pry two fingers between spongy pink muscle and grasp the metal inside. Still, I can't feel any of this.

"ENHHH," Persephone makes a loud buzzing noise akin to the Operation board game. Scares the shit out of me.

"Not the time, Seph," I manage through the leather while attempting to keep my hand steady.

"Sorry, couldn't help myself," she smiles. "You got this Lyv."

With a strong pull, the metal breaks free of my arm. The bloody iron grows in size in my hand. My arm begins to heal itself, quickly and painlessly. I'm grateful.

When the skin finishes sealing itself shut, I check the appendage. The arm is fully functional, as if it had never been injured in the first place. I'm satisfied to see my scar is still intact. Our scars are our battle wounds. Evidence of life.

"What happens when I put them in?" I ask, surveying the door.

"Not sure, but it gets you outta here," she replies brightly.

"Okay, Persephone, I'm gonna put you away for now," I say, sticking her in my bag.

"Good luck," she calls before I zip it shut.

I stick the nails in one-at-a-time. Once all three are secure, the door clicks open softly.

As it swings ajar, two of the nails return to sandals on my feet, and I keep the third in my hand. I walk into a dark tunnel. At least that's what I think. I can't make out anything for a moment.

Then, the walls gleam a little—floor too. It is a tunnel.

I continue walking toward a door at the end. When I reach it, I try the handle. It's hot. So hot, you would run in the other direction because a five-alarm fire roars behind it.

The metal sears my skin, but then turns.

I swing the door open to reveal a bright glowing room. The walls seem to be on fire. No, that's not accurate. They're smoldering well-tended coals. Ghoulish, framed paintings line the walls. There's tasteful furniture leading to a giant fiery desk.

Levi sits behind it.

38

"**D**idn't expect you so soon, Lyvs," he says, amused. "You make your decision?"

"Yeah, it's tempting," I reply with a sly smile. "But, not my scene."

"When I heard about your stolen kisses, Lyv, that was it. I was going to rescind my offer, but I must have had a moment of weakness. Forgiveness," he says with a pained face. "Wanted to give you a second chance. Now, I realize that was stupid. As indignant as you are, it's your family I would never be able to get along with."

It's at this point, I notice the massive hammer resting atop his desk.

"Even if you do get him back, Lyvs, I've taken precautions."

"What does that mean, Levi?"

"Well, if you ever get a chance to see him again, maybe you should ask how Claire is doing."

"Claire?" I ask filled with confusion.

The name rings a bell. *That woman with the dogs.* The one who felt familiar. I start to put puzzle pieces together. Shane had mentioned someone special to him. I just hadn't had the chance to meet her yet.

"She's mine now," he sneers. "It's my consolation prize. She can be my new queen. That is, if you're sure you don't want the honor?"

"I don't."

"Okay, she'll be just fine for the role," he replies. "And, Shane's spirit form won't be able to do a thing about it, especially since he can't come back to Earth now."

With this, he spreads his arms over the hammer, and it rises from the surface. He throws them up and the hammer explodes. Tiny bits of shrapnel occupy the air. A cloud of white smoke fills the room.

While it clears, I scream, "NO—"

I throw the nails out and they find purchase. Two of them drive through Levi's hands, pinning him to the wall. The third secures his feet.

"Now, you've done it, Levi," I snarl. I feel every bit of good seep from my body. The only thing left is pain. And evil intention.

A voice sounds in my head: *Now's the time.*

I walk to the bag and pull out Shane's hockey skates.

Holding them by the blades, the laces dangle, brushing the ground. I touch the sharp metal edges together. Suddenly, they spin wildly in my hands. The blades meld to each other to create one long, giant sword. The laces morph into leather cords that dangle from the handle. I notice an inscription.

'Michael.' As in, *St. Michael the Archangel.*

For the first time ever, Levi looks scared. I'm pleased.

"You killed him for good, and now I'm going to do the same to you. You will never be able to walk Earth again," I seethe, walking around his massive desk.

Way I figure it, this is how he was banished to Hell in the first place. His very own brother's sword. I also figure it will stop him from ever roaming the world again.

"I'm going to enjoy this, Levi," I say, steadying the sword. "And, you can enjoy your lifetime stay."

I pierce the sword through where I imagine his heart would be, but he disappears before it even makes contact. The nails clatter to the floor.

"What?" I scream, searching the room. "How? Where?"

The frustration is too much to bear. I run around the room in circles hoping he will reappear. Finally, I fall to the ground in resignation.

SUDDENLY, a large invisible hand grabs my arm. I soar through the air. The room spins away from me. I whirl through a tornado before roughly rolling onto uneven ground.

I stand and survey the area. Brooks stands at-the-ready with a spear held tightly in his hand.

"How?" I ask joining him, relieved to see Michael's sword and the nails have also made the journey upward.

He shrugs.

I laugh, shaking my head. I'm relieved to be free of Hell, but I know we are not out of danger. I pick up the sword.

"Had some help," he says.

Before I can investigate further, I spot movement near the edge of a cliff. I recognize the area. We're at my brother's tomb.

Flapping accompanies the movement. Levi—the Leviathan—appears over the lip of the cliff.

"I'm not playing anymore, Lyvs. If you're not going to come willingly, I will take you by force. You cause me too much trouble. Period. If you won't be my queen, you'll be my captive."

"I'm never going back there," I reply.

Brooks throws his spear up in the air. I'm pleased to see it make contact. It pierces the beast, causing howls of agony. All seven heads that is. It's deafening. The body heaves to the ground rolling toward us. I sprint around the screaming heads to its body.

I rush forward plunging the giant blade deep into the beast's chest. The heaving monster sets fire. Its body bursts into flames. The heads cry sickening whines of pain. The fire grows before bursting into black smoke. When it clears, the monstrosity is gone.

I run over to Brooks and throw my arms around him. We kiss deeply. When I pull away, I notice tears are streaming uncontrollably down my face.

The hammer. Pulverized.

He can't come back now. It's over. I have to live with his loss forever. It's real now. Levi said if the hammer is destroyed, Shane will be unable to return to life.

I pick up the nails and the sword and walk over to the boulder. I need to make sure his body is still in there, undisturbed. I drive the relics into the crack. The boulder rolls open slowly. I'm not in a rush. He's not coming back. I have to make myself comprehend that.

I'll never see my one and only partner-in-crime again. I'll never hear his laugh and see his face. Hug his strong frame. Ruffle his silky thick hair.

But when my view is unobstructed, the scene before me is baffling.

Because—

There he is.

His warrior 6'3" form sits on the edge of the driftwood. He's wearing his blue Ford Mustang t-shirt and ripped jeans. Michael Jordan slides don his feet. His huge intricately tattooed arms rest, elbows bent on his knees. A little past shoulder-length, his wavy hair resembles the color of a dark brown bear's fur, yet laced with lighter hues from our teak childhood rocking horse. *Trigger.* He turns his head of ash brown hair, and his beautiful, honey-green eyes meet mine. Eyebrows raised, he's got his crooked, side-smile on, the one that says, 'What? You lookin' for me?' His perfect, white teeth glimmer in the moonlight. He's got a bit of barely noticeable chewing tobacco tucked in his bottom lip. His face sports a short dark beard. In between his hands, rests a large, archaic hammer.

How? The hammer got destroyed. Then I realize Levi is the one who provided that information.

And—He's the Devil. That's what he does. Lies.

ACKNOWLEDGMENTS

First and foremost—God. For bestowing upon me the gift to create my masterpiece, one that has given me emotional catharsis and personal growth throughout the most trying time of my life.

Shane—my soul. My whole peach pie. My heavenly guide and spiritual protector. My movie-quote loving, secret-language speaking, Jedi-mind-trick master, partner-in-crime. You have always been my baby and grew into the man I measure every other man up to. You are my brother. You are my best friend. You are my person.

Mom and Pops—Peach and Spud. For putting up with us kids. For making us who we are. For showing us what unconditional love feels like. For being the giant butterfly net that always catches us when we fall. For our unstoppable sense of humor and excellent music taste. Couldn't live without our Ray Pruitt tunes and Airwolf Hovercraft, right, Shane? Right?

Claire—Shane's soulmate and 'other' partner-in-crime. For giving him the special kind of love on this Earth, the kind that not everyone gets to have. For being my midnight baking accomplice. For coming along on our shenanigans, being the voice of reason, and—of course —the comic relief.

Shevawn—for being my real-life Persephone, I cannot do life without you. You've been with me before I was even born. We've gone from producing and starring in VHS masterpieces to publishing written works of art. I can't imagine starring in music videos, costumed in discarded bridesmaids' dresses and Superman ice cream-dyed lips, with anyone other than my 'sister.' I would be lost without you.

Katie—for being the baby 'sister' I always wanted. For sharing your artistic gift with the world. And, Tom, for sharing your deep wealth of knowledge and many talents. For making up a large part of our DreamTeam.

Meggie—for being my pearl-donning, improv-performing, twinning lifetime co-conspirator. Through losses to streaming tears of laughter, pies and 'hazel' eyes. From the sunlit bus station to the shimmying waitress line, you always have my back.

Porsche—for getting me through many tough times. For our wolfpack. For being my rock in the white water rapids we call life. You have made me a part of your family, and I am forever grateful. Mom, 'Vitamin' (Adrien) and lil' Alex, I love you all so much. Still need to get our fangirl on at BSB live.

Shevy P—for your life-changing words and bottomless fountain of wisdom. Thank you for being my Turquoise Queen.

Grandma Shevawn—for your fierce convictions and nonstop support. For passing your talent down through generations. For believing in my abilities ever since I was floating through your beauty parlor donned in your gorgeous scarves, singing "Zip-A-Dee-Doo-Dah."

Gintare—my very first fan. Best college roommate a girl could ask for. Your ceaseless encouragement for new chapters will never be forgotten. LU and MU.

Jean—my mentor. For sharing your wisdom and unwavering confidence in my gift throughout this arduous journey. For always being there and knowing exactly what to say.

Junkyard Dog Publishing—for taking a chance on me! For allowing my creative vision and development to remain steadfast throughout this entire endeavor. And, for our unstoppable DreamTeam.

Chloe—for being my emotional support dog, writing partner, and forever pitty-bull. I couldn't have done this without my four-legged bébé.

They say it takes an army. I've been lucky enough to have quite a few soldiers in my corner since day one. You know who you are.

ABOUT THE AUTHOR

Trisha Lynn Halaas was a born writer and as a child, dubbed the family reporter. She would go on to write for her college newspaper, *The Madonna Herald*, and eventually a local newspaper in her home state of Michigan, *The Suburban Lifestyles*. Having a strong background in Broadcast Journalism, she managed to keep a diary through it all. Diligently journaling since 1990, she knew that her passion lied in more than reporting.

A true writer, she has always been in love with the story. While in college, she would fantasize and take note of all the stories that she would someday pen after finishing grueling term papers. She is also an avid reader. 'Silent reading time' was her favorite subject in grade school as she continues to devour books daily.

Forever a dreamer, an idea for her first fantasy fiction trilogy set in a dystopian post-apocalyptic future formed in her mind and the words incessantly begged to be put to paper.

So she did, and she went a step further.

After losing her beloved brother, Shane, to the ravages of addiction, she wanted to draw attention to the subject. She meshed her love of the story with her love for her brother, creating their own unique presentation of addiction awareness. Her debut novel explores timely themes, addiction, and grief in a new and unique way.

It can be said that Trisha was handed the bitterest limes life has to offer. From which, she's concocted the most delicious mint mojito in a sugar-rimmed martini glass topped with a tiny pink polka dot umbrella. She is a Michigan native who currently resides in Arizona with her dog, Chloe.

If you would like to order signed books or join her mailing list, visit her website at:

trishalynnhalaas.com

facebook.com/authortrishalynnhalaas
instagram.com/trishalynnhalaas